Domus

The Tempus Crystal

Elizabeth Manzanares Wenig

Isabella Castile Publishing

Website: www.lizzysfeatherpen.com

Dover design by Elizabeth Manzanares Wenig

Printed in the United States of America

10 9 8 7 6 5 4 3 2 1

Dedication

Fantasy isn't for everyone. But, for those who love visiting another world, there are few things better than a recliner, an uninterrupted Saturday afternoon, and an illusory realm populated with implausible, improbable beings. And, it's even better if you have someone to relive the thrilling moments, remember the life or death crises, and swoon over the hero's love gained. For me, one of those comrade-in-arms is Autumn Langley. She shares that love of reading requisite for a good heart-to-heart about imagined domains and faraway places. Autumn is among those whose thirst for and love of books matches my own. It is my great pleasure to dedicate my first Domus book to an idealistic yet practical, quixotic yet grounded, connoisseur of the imagination, and dear, sweet friend, Autumn Langley. Love you, girl.

Contents

Acknowledgements

One of the most critical things this author needs is support. And, I have that in spades. Thank you to my husband, Gary, for allowing me to be me. For giving me space to think, to dream, and to write. Thank you to my children, their children, and their children, who are there for me in ways in which they are unaware.

My daughter, Cyndi, has had a book in her hand since she was able to hold one. She did her share of editing for me and I will always be grateful for her insights, suggestions, and keen literary savvy.

A dear friend of mine has loved Domus for almost as long as I have. We did farmers markets together and she makes heavenly jelly. She was one of my first beta readers and never failed to ask me how the book was coming. Thank you, Karen Whedon, for your unfailing interest and support.

Some of my other beta readers were part of the Barnes and Noble Writers Group back in the day. Thank you, not only for Domus's critiques but for weekly encouragement and collaboration.

And, thank you to my Father in Heaven for His guidance, inspiration, and Son, our Lord Jesus Christ.

Chapter One

Prologue

Hornets. Kenny woke up the morning of his eighth birthday with excitement buzzing in his chest like hornets. Not angry saw-blade buzzing like when you hit the nest with a bat, but smooth, happy buzzing as if they were waiting for the sun to rise so they could go flying. Best friend Brent had spent the night so the boys would be ready to zoom into activity.

Kenny thought this would be the best day of his life. His mother, Beetrum, was taking them to Whiteman Air Force Base where they would get to sit in real cockpits, fly in mock-up jets, and shoot down enemy planes. They would even get to wear aviator jackets and Kenny was sure they would both get "wings".

Kenny sleepily stumbled into the kitchen, poured a glass of milk, and took it into the library, almost as if he were being summoned. He plopped down, his stomach churning and sloshing like the milk in his glass spilling onto the rug. He stared at the logs half burnt in the fireplace, apprehension clinging to him as the cold grey ash clung to the charred wood.

The clock on the mantle seemed to coax Kenny, beckoning him. His throat tightened as he smelled the dead fire, the ghosts of the flames dried his tongue, coating it with the taste of cinder. His hand shook spilling more milk; it soaked into his new fighter jet pajamas, a cold fist clenched around his chest. Kenny was afraid to look at the clock, yet he seemed unable to stop himself. Slowly he raised his eyes and stared into the center of the lavender crystal.

He thought he saw movement, but that would have been impossible. It must be a trick of the moonlight shining through the glass doors that led into the garden. He hadn't wanted to look at the clock, but now he did not want to look away. It locked and held him in an embrace as if it had hands. But it didn't. No hands. No numbers. Strange for a clock.

The clock began to glow. Yes, he was sure of it. He could both see and feel purple vibrations coming from the heart of the clock. He hadn't realized that it had a heart, but there it was beating out pulses that were all the colors of the lilacs growing just outside.

White traveled from the clock through the color spectrum, picking up ever-increasing darkness until it arrived at the blackest of purples. It spread outward and enveloped Kenny, cradled, and soothed him as gently as a purring mother cat protected her kitten. Anxiety disappeared as the scent of his favorite apple cob pie surrounded him. A smile crept silently to his lips. He felt warm and cozy as he closed his eyes and nestled into the comfort of the purple hues embracing him.

His mother was wrong, the clock wasn't dangerous, it was wonderful. Kenny opened his eyes and realized he knew the precise date and time. 3 April 0430 hours. Light within the crystals of the clock began to swirl making Kenny dizzy. Purple beams of varying hues burst from the crystals and spun round and round him, stirring giddiness like chocolate into milk.

The room filled with a sweet spicy cinnamon aroma and Kenny threw up his arms with pure joy; his glass flew into the air in slow motion, and the milk spilled out like a frozen white waterfall, suspended.

Magic! It had to be magic. This was the best day of his life. His laughter broke the spell and toppled the milk and glass to the floor. Kenny whooped and hooted as happiness erupted from someplace deep inside that he hadn't even known was there. He felt as light as the pillow feathers he had thrown from the top of the walnut tree last week. He felt as if he could fly.

A flare of light came from the clock blinding Kenny like the aftermath of a strobe. Frightening charges of tiny lightning crackled and sizzled; smoke hung in the air like the Fourth of July. Kenny stood spellbound. What was happening?

There on the mantle lay a smoldering envelope. Amethyst tendrils surged from the clock through the smoke and wove themselves around Kenny giving him a bolt of courage. He dragged the footstool over to the mantle and scrambled up to inspect the envelope at eye level.

As Kenny picked it up, tiny embers burst into flame like miniature Viking funeral ships floating around the mantle. He squealed, blew it out, dropped the envelope to the floor, jumped off the stool, and stomped it with bare feet. Sparks danced around his toes and died in the marshy wetness of spilled milk. Despite the burnt edges, he read the word written in fancy letters across the envelope.

"Lichen".

It was for him. No one ever called him by his given name.

His legs gave way and he sat down hard on the footstool. Kenny picked up the envelope and stared at his name. He'd always hated his name having been teased and tormented by not-so-friendly kids. Now, looking at it on this paper, all scorched and smoking, it didn't seem so bad. In fact, it seemed different, in a cool way.

Kenny turned it over. The paper had been folded and held shut by a dark green glob of wax, now cracked and broken. Arched across the top of the seal in capital letters was the word DOMUS. In the center a single letter was legible.

"Q". Kenny tore it open.

"Lichen, happy 8th birthday. I love you. Grandfather Q."

Kenny devoured the words. He read them again and again. Happy birthday. I love you. I love you. He had a grandfather. His grandfather loved him. Grandfather remembered him. Grandfather Q.

The library grew cold and dark, like an approaching storm; black, and purple clouds gathered in the ceiling. A bright flash of lightning zipped open the churning violet clouds, tore the envelope from Kenny's hand, sent it speeding into the air, through the little doorway in the clouds, and zapped it closed with a loud clap of thunder.

Kenny heard a scream and turned empty-handed toward the door. Beetrum stood, gripping her robe, fists clenched white. Beside her, Brent was frozen, a look of terror masked his face.

Kenny was immobilized, but only for a moment. Then he detonated. Never in his life had he felt like this. Something bubbled up through him, its effervescence spreading happiness like fizz from a soda. Anything seemed possible. Anything was possible. He jumped onto the sofa; his eyes alight with the certainty of that other world he had always suspected existed.

Domus.

And the sheer happiness of knowing his grandfather remembered him. Loved him. He jumped up and down not caring that his mother watched in horror. What was a sofa compared to a letter from Q? What were mere cushions compared to the possibilities of Domus?

"Wow," Kenny shouted as he bounced into the air. "Wow. Did you see that? Was that the coolest thing ever?"

Brent looked at him, color slowly returning to his face.

"Wicked," he whispered.

"Yes, wasn't it?" Kenny said, his grin easily reaching from ear to ear.

"No! No, not cool wicked. Bad wicked," Brent said as he started to back out of the room.

"No," Kenny said. He jumped off the sofa and started toward Brent. "No, it's ok. It's magic. It was my grandpa."

"Stay away from me," Brent shouted, his voice quivering like a bowstring drawn tight and taut ready to snap. He looked at the clock, his eyes round and black like great caves of loathing.

"Brent..." Kenny said.

"Shut up," Brent screamed, "shut up," as he turned and ran out of the house.

Kenny's mood fell like a teeter-totter when your best bud jumps off and lets you plummet to the ground. Tears spilled down his cheeks as Beetrum ran over and gathered him in her arms. She stroked his head and rocked him, her own tears falling on his hair. They sat cradled together until the sun came up puddling and cocooning them in a little circle of warmth.

"Kenny," Beetrum said.

She held him close and sighed so deeply it must have come from all the way from Domus. "I guess it's time to tell you about your grandfather." Her eyes were sad, and her voice sounded like she would rather have done anything else in the world.

After that day, Beetrum never spoke of Domus or Q again. Kenny sometimes thought he had dreamed the entire scene. Except, of course, Brent had become his enemy.

And, once a year Kenny was reminded about the world of magic. Although the clock never made another sound, thunder never boomed, and lightning never struck.

Once a year without fail, Kenny knew with certainty he had not imagined that his grandfather lived in an ancient kingdom called Domus. Beetrum kept the library locked now, but each birthday Kenny found it open and promptly crept into the forbidden library on 3 April 0430 hours and waited.

Q sent his short, smoking birthday greetings, but unlike his eighth birthday, they arrived with only a muffled pop and small trails of smoke. That would have been magical in anyone else's world, and Kenny felt guilty for being disappointed. It was a far cry from the grandiose display of pyrotechnics he had experienced that first faerie-tale time. However, each year the room filled with that wonderful sweet spicy apple cob pie smell bringing inexplicable comfort.

Kenny loved his annual missives, but Beetrum hated them. She never mentioned them and carried on his birthday celebrations like normal people. But Kenny knew in his heart he wasn't normal.

The birthday notes never had descriptions of wings or tales of magical creatures. No wondrous stories of the Fey. Only "Happy 9th Birthday, 10th birthday, 11th birthday.... Kenny. I love you. Grandfather Q," written in elegant script. Every birthday was the same as if Q was counting down the years.

After that first glorious revelation, on each birthday whenever he looked at the clock, Kenny always knew the date and time. He loved the clock's aura of magic. It was the antithesis of what the rest of his life would be as an Air Force pilot. Structured. Programmed. Regimented.

Chapter Two

The Clock

Kenny started down the stairs shrugging his backpack into a more comfortable position. The full bright moon reflected the apples on the handle of his cane. Apples. What kind of man uses an apple cane? But then, what kind of man was he? When this trip was over he was getting a new cane. Family antique or not.

A cold draft sifted through the leaded window; the old wooden steps creaked under his weight as if in protest. Kenny's leg throbbed but he determined not to dwell on it today.

"Is that you?" Beetrum said looking up as she stuck her head into the hall.

Delta, she was already awake. Kenny had been struggling to clean up his language. He'd tried using substitutes such as the NATO phonetic alphabet. He wasn't sure it was working.

"Yeah, mom, be there in a sec," Kenny answered.

"We don't have much time," she said.

"Yes, I know Mother. Just give me a minute." Frustration edged his reply. This was her bright idea for the love of heaven, and now she was trying to rush him.

"Oh. OK. Yes," she said as she saw Kenny looking toward the library. Her eyes dropped to the floor; her body tensed. Kenny had no time to coddle his mother. She knew what waited in the library and she'd just have to deal with it.

Beetrum never discussed the fact that she only opened the library one day a year, yet by her very silence, she lent it importance. She had the only key and every birthday morning on 3 April 0430 hours Kenny found the door unlocked. Once a year he was reminded that the dream was real; that his grandfather lived in...some other place.

For years after the grandiose display on his eighth birthday, he was filled with excitement and wonder as he received his annual good wishes from Grandfather Q. But, as the years went by disappointment transformed into frustration, then disbelief, then anger.

When he entered the Air Force Academy in Colorado Springs, he vowed never to step foot in that library again, but each year when his birthday rolled around, he was standing in front of that blasted clock.

In the back of his mind, he hoped for more but more never happened. Just the same smokey letter, with the same trite sentiment. Why he continued to come evaded him. But each year he felt powerless to resist the magnetic pull of the clock presiding over the library.

This year Kenny had made up his mind. He was not going through with this annual fool's errand. Beetrum hated the library, hated the clock, and as far as he could tell, hated her father, Q.

When Kenny told his mother of his new resolution, she paled and then exploded into reasons why he had to keep the annual appointment.

"This is the final year," she had said. "After this, there will be no more letters. As soon as you get your birthday message we will leave for a meeting with Q."

Kenny looked at his mother in disbelief. "This is the end? There won't be any more foolishness?"

"It's the end of the letters", she repeated with a cryptic tone. "Pack a few things and be ready to go as soon as you receive the greeting."

Regardless of Kenny's questioning, Beetrum would say no more about it. She retreated to her determined silence about Domus.

Kenny felt relieved and simultaneously disappointed that it all would be over soon. He guessed in some masochistic way he hated giving up the annual early morning meetings with the clock. But the thought of meeting Q overshadowed any misgivings. Since Kenny's accident, he had spent recuperation leave time helping his mother manage Q's estate and his business holdings.

At last, he would be able to speak with Q about them face to face. And discover the deceptive means whereby smoking letters and trick clocks had enticed and fooled a young boy, had frustrated and frightened an adolescent, and infuriated an Air Force pilot. Kenny was going to get some answers.

The respectable old house with its creaky floorboards announced his progress down the windowless hall. Moonlight from the windows in the stairway behind him faded into the darkness of the hallway as if it was going to sleep. Kenny tripped. The blasted cane did come in handy at times.

"Are you all right?" Beetrum called from her bedroom sanctuary down the opposite end of the hall.

"Yes, I'm fine," Kenny raised his voice. Beetrum knew he must pay his annual visit to the room before their departure; why was she so frustrated and anxious? He'd just pop in, wait for the birthday greeting and they could be on their way. The car would be here any moment.

He should have come down earlier but for some unfathomable reason, he chose last night to sleep soundly. Hadn't slept in six months now all of a sudden he sleeps. Go figure.

As he remembered, the unused library would be musty, and full of cold dark corners and imagined shadows. No use lending it more importance than it deserves. No doubt most of Kenny's dreams about that first encounter, when he was eight years old, were exaggerated with childish illusory enthusiasm.

This year, his twenty-fifth birthday, was different. Beetrum had given him the library key yesterday. No words of counsel, no explanations. She had wordlessly pressed the key into his hand, closed his fingers around it, embraced him with an unusual motherly expression, and then turned and went to her room. The passing of the torch.

The lion-head knob on the old library door accepted the key easily. Kenny had expected it to stick; old locks usually did. Especially unused old locks. He stepped through the door into a net of cobwebs. The moon satiated with light filtered through the frosted glass in the French doors casting a fuzzy spotlight on the old-fashioned floral carpet as if in preparation for a show.

The room looked exactly as it had last year and every year prior: stately bookcases reaching to the ceiling as if they stood on tiptoe lining the walls with their knowledge and secrets. A massive desk took center stage. Commanding. Intimidating even now just as it had been when he was growing up.

Chills rose on Kenny's tanned muscled arms like little sand dunes, his breathing shallow, his heart shooting blood through distended veins in his hands. The neighbor's dog yipped and barked and wailed mournful ancestral howls across the apple hedges; it seemed otherworldly in the cold morning fog that covered the garden. Nonsense. Kenny was letting his imagination run away with him. Nothing creepy about a barking dog. Especially that skinny Bonebag.

Kenny tightened the grip on his cane and willed his gaze to the fireplace mantle. There it sat. How many years had he looked upon that big crystal clock? Why it wasn't even a real clock; it had no hands, no numbers. He guessed it was beautiful, in a geo-spelunking-dark-cave kind of way. It had been crazed superstition to keep this room locked, some figment of his mother's unreasonable fear. There was a logical explanation for those birthday missives appearing out of nowhere. Some trick his grandfather had perfected.

Kenny didn't know *where* his grandfather was, but he was pretty sure it was on this plane of existence. All that nonsense about another world, a *faery* world was not only ridiculous, but it also insulted his intellect.

As a boy, he had believed it, and look what it had gotten him. The loss of his best friend, the discord between him and his mother, and ill-advised expectations about his grandfather. As an adolescent, he studied the world's mythologies, trying to make sense of what had happened to him. As a young adult, he turned to science and the art of piloting fighter jets trying to plant his feet firmly in reality.

Kenny depended on sound judgment, on the cool analytical workings of his pilot's mind. He had no time for this idiocy. His world consisted of thrust dynamics and tactical role-plays. Aerial accidents that maimed the operator and destroyed a $138 million F-22 Raptor would have ended most military careers, but not his. In today's computerized world, Kenny's skills landed him squarely amid the nation's best military strategists teaching at CGSC in Ft. Leavenworth Kansas.

His superiors had granted him leave to heal; he had earned it. And, it wasn't every day one met a grandfather for the first time.

Kenny chided himself for his irrationality. Whatever he had *thought* happened in this room hadn't. It had been a childish nightmare. He should never have bothered to come in here. After his accident, he had already determined to stop this annual lunacy and begin his life anew. He should have let old ghosts lie but Beetrum had insisted. She repeated that this would be the last time.

She fidgeted and drew up her mouth like purse strings informing him that they could not leave until he visited the library. Well, here he was. A grimy room full of old books, memories he was determined to discard, and a worthless clock.

The desk was magnificent, however. He may take it as his own when they return. In fact, now that he looked it over he rather liked this room with its private garden entry and cozy fireplace. Yes. It was much larger than the cramped spare bedroom he used as his office.

Lichen and Beetrum were co-administrators of his grandfather's affairs. No small task as his vast holdings took a considerable amount of time and expertise. Their visit to wherever the heck his grandfather had chosen to live would be the first in-person accounting of the estate and business. Lichen looked forward to it. And it would finally put a stop to this ridiculous annual legerdemain.

A warm relaxed satisfaction settled in, and his crooked winning smile flashed. How foolish he had been all these years. And Beetrum. She should have known better than to cater to a child's fearful imaginings. Yes, this would make an ideal office. He would ask his mother to have it cleaned and ready for occupancy before they returned.

Kenny started back toward the hall door when something caught his eye. A small light flickered in the center of the clock. A tiny glimmer of lavender flame grew slowly, spreading throughout the crystals. Kenny's cane clattered to the floor and rolled out of reach as he stared.

It was 3 April 0430 hours. The date and time were stamped on his mind as though done with the precision and clarity of a postal clerk. It was his twenty-fifth birthday. His annual pilgrimage into this room on 3 April 0430 hours popped into his head with stark clarity.

The clock began to pulse and quiver. The air sizzled with brilliant white vibrations that he could both see and feel. They spread throughout the room traveling through the color spectrum arriving at midnight purple as deep and dark as an amethyst cave surrounding Kenny.

The room disappeared as electrical charges flew around him. G forces swirled, compressing his chest, preventing breath. This, *this* was his recurring nightmare these many years. The thing that held and squeezed him with vice-like strength causing a dichotomy of repugnance and admiration then disappeared from memory at dawn like mist rising before the sun.

At eight years old he had panicked at this invisible power and screamed in exultant terror not knowing whether to laugh or cry. But not now. Now he embraced it. He saw it not as restricting but as empowering. Strengthening. Kenny closed his eyes and yelled.

"BOOYAH."

A battle cry. A warrior forging forward into the unknown, realizing there was nothing to fear, finding himself not in a whirlwind of horror but in a vortex of reality. Another world. Another dimension. An unseen world that he had suppressed and stuffed into forgetfulness.

Kenny relaxed into the experience and caught the scent of something spicy. It smelled like comfort, like home, and seemed as familiar as his favorite pair of jeans. For the second time in his life, joy bubbled within. Artesian happiness. It fizzed throughout him like effervescence run amuck. Anything seemed possible. Anything was possible. A single word flashed across his mind.

Demons with chains. Equine shrieks blew ravines through the mist. Valleys to the otherworld.

Kenny stared open-mouthed at the horses; excitement gilded with fear popped from his eyes. Somewhere in the fog, the feverish barking of Bonebag added a dose of reality to this surreal scene.

"Come quickly," Beetrum said. Her strained voice sounded unnatural but at least she had regained her wits. Kenny stowed the little box into his flight jacket pocket, snatched his bag, and followed his mother into the garden.

The driver jumped from the coach, his face void of expression. An eerie frigid presence sculpted his body with icy fire.

"The carriage will remain sealed until our destination is reached," he said, clipping his words and bowing indifferently toward the open door of the coach.

"Hello Chimera," Beetrum said, her neck and shoulders stiff, her icy tone matching his.

"Ma'am," he said with a slight tilt of his head his eyes burning with the same cold blue fire as the stallions. Soulless. Chimera was perfectly and exquisitely formed. Cold as marble. Chiseled from an unknown source in an unknown place. Michelangelo's David in fine clothing. Red hair? Bright red hair caught in a queue at the nape of his neck blazed like the gates of hell, a stark contrast to his arctic bearing.

Kenny appraised him, their eyes locked and level. Kenny wouldn't look away. Or couldn't.

Beetrum grimaced at the male gridlock. "Oh, for heaven's sake, get on with it."

Kenny helped his mother into the coach noticing the fine wood from which it was made. The carriage was small, compact, and magnificently crafted.

"Rowan," Beetrum said.

"What?" Kenny answered.

"The coach is hewn of rowan wood. They consider it sacred. They have groves of the stuff." Kenny stared at his mother. From the look in her eye, Kenny knew she was finally ready to talk.

"Rowan wood. Ogham lettering."

"Oh," Kenny said. The strange carvings of Ogham letters interspersed with berries and leaves curved seductively around the doors as if beckoning. Kenny helped his mother into the coach. Beetrum squealed as the carriage lurched forward. Kenny jumped in and fell back into the seat; his bag caught in the door wedging it open.

"What the...?" he shouted. The unrestrained momentum of the stallions sliced his words; the forward thrust pinned Kenny against the plush blood-red cushions. He stared through the door in disbelief; the ground sped by in a blur. They were off. No turning back now.

The conjured coachman paid no heed to his passengers. Chimera stood reins in hand like a phantasm chariot driver. His whip split the air.

"Onward you black-hearted beasts or I'll have you for dinner," he bellowed. His laugh, deep and throaty rode the air like spider silk. Twenty-four hooves hammered the ground. Frenetic harness bells clamored. Kenny gave his bag a frantic pull; the door slammed shut as a maleficent maelstrom sucked the carriage into mystery.

"He won't actually eat them, you know," Beetrum said. "Chimera says that every time. He's quite fond of those...horses."

Behind them, the garden lay in silent shambles. Flower petals and leaves spiraled back to earth in sacrificial finality. In the library, the crystal clock on the fireplace mantel vibrated, glowing with satisfaction. It chimed one solitary tone as if sending a message. Sentience hovered about it. Knowing.

Before his imagination carried him away he said, "I'm not worried about my clothes." He didn't feel like discussing wardrobe with his mother. Jeans, tees, Nike's, toothbrush, skivvies, he was good to go.

Kenny didn't care about what to take or not take. He didn't care what they wore, or ate or how they belched. He just wanted to get there.

"So, this Domus...My Grandfather lives there? Your father I presume? And why have you kept all this a secret? Why didn't you tell me about him? About Domus?" Kenny thought about the library, the clock, the letters. "Or rather, why didn't you remind me about them?"

"I...I couldn't," Beetrum replied.

"Couldn't or wouldn't?"

"Kenny, please. Just promise me you will keep your wits about you. Don't be taken in. Q can be quite charming. And Domus...well, Domus has a way about it."

The coach lurched. "It's rough," Beetrum said. "The carriage ride is very rough until we get to the Bridge. Then there will be a kind of..." She looked at a loss for words.

"Well, I guess it's kind of like a sonic boom. We'll...I mean *I'll* be disoriented for a while; you're probably quite used to it. From flying I mean. The rest of the ride is easy," Beetrum raised one perfectly plucked eyebrow, "since we'll be asleep." Her mouth made a small red pucker of disapproval.

The coach jerked again and threw Kenny toward the side. He looked at the sealed doors. No handles. No windows, but plenty of soft light and fresh air.

"The carriage will remain sealed until our destination is reached," the carriage driver had said.

Kenny's nerves twitched like downed power lines. Unrestrained. He wiped the sweat from his forehead with the back of his sleeve, his gut tightened with anticipation. He felt similar to the day he had taken his first flight and ironically, he also felt the same on his last. An eager expectancy. The first day had ended by fueling his passion, the last by smothering it.

The coach seats were soft and padded with exotic crimson fabrics. Like a coffin. A blood-red coffin. The analogy made him uncomfortable. A soft breeze wafted by his face as if it had blown through an open window. He thought it smelled like apple cobbler.

Kenny had loved and been calmed by the smell of apple pie since he was eight. On humid summer nights, the scent of hot cinnamon and bubbling apples blew through his bedroom windows and carried him into sleep like an airborne sedative. Yes, he definitely smelled his favorite apple cob pie.

The uneasiness of feeling like he was in a casket disappeared. He settled into the cushions like a puppy against its mother. No room for his usual hands-behind-the-head-feet-out stance, but a fleeting dimple and the small twitch at the corner of his mouth conveyed his change of mood.

"So, yesterday you were all about not going. Now you look like you have a room booked in Oahu", Beetrum said. Disapproval muddied her eyes.

"Yesterday I didn't know where I was going and you were all jumpy and mean. Today I'm being whisked off to Oz to meet the Wizard by Mr. Personality and his six demon steeds. Sounds like an adventure to me. Besides, I'm curious about my grandfather."

Beetrum stiffened. Kenny knew that look. He could forget getting any intel from her. Might as well sit back and enjoy the ride.

"Golf," he said sticking to his new profanity format, "I'm traveling at least the speed of sound and I don't even have to pilot." Kenny smiled and shoved his hands into his jacket pockets.

"Don't get so cocky," Beetrum said frowning at his use of non-swear words. "You have a lot to learn," she finished while yawning.

Kenny's hand closed around the box. He didn't want to open it in front of Beetrum. Didn't know why. It just felt personal.

Maybe she already knew what was inside. How long had she had it? Why did the old gramps want him to bring it?

Kenny could see his mother trying to stay awake. She tried to muster her usual cool reserve and placed her hands quietly in her lap. Her white fingers covered her engagement ring; was she shielding it or herself from the past she was racing toward?

Kenny wondered what her motive was for coming on this trip. She obviously hated Domus. What of Kenny's father? Kenny thought him dead and buried in Ireland but since revelations seemed to be springing from the woodwork, maybe everything he knew about his family was a lie.

Beetrum fingered her ring. It was a mute reminder of love gained, and perhaps of love lost...his father. Her emotionless eyes were open and blank. Her usual feline alertness dimed; her control lost somewhere in this in-between world they traveled through.

"Chimera hasn't changed one bit," Beetrum roused and looked where the window should have been. "You'd think they'd alter the spell to smooth out the ride and make him a bit more civil."

Kenny startled. He wasn't used to his mother being candid.

"Spell?" he countered.

"Well for the lack of a better description," she said.

"How far is it to the Bridge?" he asked. His mind trying to calculate time and distance.

"I have no idea," Beetrum answered. Kenny scowled.

"Well, the details are secret," she said in defense. "They love to keep humans in the dark, you know." She snickered. "It's been a long time, but it's still the same. The carriage shows up. I hop in. We race off to God knows where. Next thing I know, I'm there. Nice and quiet. Tidy and neat. Except for the garden, of course. No one sees me leave. No one sees me return. Just the way Q likes it."

Kenny studied his mother. After years of silence, Beetrum was finally breaking free; her words revealing something of her past. But it was like trying to disentangle parachute chords...after jumping. He rubbed his leg from habit as if to soothe away the ache, and realized it wasn't hurting. And, he had left the cane behind in the library. No loss there.

Kenny felt an unaccustomed empathy for his mother. She'd never been happy. She seemed to carry a boatload of clutter from her past. He hoped this trip would help her lay it to rest and as an extra perk help their relationship. She seemed to be making a good start by talking about Domus.

Beetrum removed a small envelope from her purse. Some of the scorched edges crumbled onto her fingers. She looked sheepishly at Kenny as she handed it to him. "I received this a month ago." Beetrum rubbed her hands together as if cleaning away her yesterdays.

Kenny's muscles worked under the square plane of his jaw; it was the only tell of his emotion. "You receive letters from Domus and they don't self-destruct?" he blurted. "You have a bucket-load of secrets, don't you? Is it from your father?"

"Yes," Beetrum said without apology. "I correspond with him once a month. I send him your financial reports of the holdings."

Kenny couldn't wrap his mind around it. During his recuperation, he had used the boring half of his double degree to do the company's books. Kenny had not realized the reports went anywhere but to the

CPA. "You are kidding me. You have regular communications with your father? And he *owns* our company?"

"Yes. And yes. Well, he doesn't own all of it. I have a good-sized share....as do you. We'll discuss that later. As for now, I want to chat with you about this." She handed him the envelope.

Kenny stared at her a moment before taking the letter. He opened it slowly. The parchment crackled as if to call attention to its importance.

"In all these years," Beetrum said, "I've never received a BelMoon invitation. Not any invitation, actually. It's a summons, really, not an invitation. I could hardly refuse."

"BelMoon?" Kenny said.

"Yes. It's quite a spectacle, heathen as it is. A grand celebration of spring and all that rubbish. People...well, if you can call them... people...People come from all over Domus to The Manor...that's Q's home. Q "officiates" or whatever they call it."

Kenny's pulse began to race. "Oh, my golf," he said. "You..."

"Oh, Kenny, grow up," Beetrum snapped. "I had my reasons for confidentiality. You're finding out now, aren't you? And I see you are still doing that ridiculous swearing thing. Or rather that ridiculous non-swearing thing. If you're doing it for her, well, she's gone isn't she?"

Kenny's jaw tightened. He sat up straighter and calmly replied, "Yes, I still employ behavior modification techniques." And, he thought silently, I don't need you to tell me anything about *her.*

As if on cue, Beetrum glanced at her wrist. "I'm never quite sure of the time in this blasted coach. I don't know why I even bother to bring my watch it always stops the moment I get in. And, I haven't a clue how far it is."

"Have you ever actually seen it? The Bridge I mean," Kenny asked.

"Oh, heavens, no," Beetrum replied. "Only three people...." She flinched at the word people, "...know the location of the bridge. Even the coachman is blinded before he reaches it."

Kenny looked at the wall between them and the coachman.

Breakneck speed. Blind driver. Interesting.

Beetrum's fists balled into tiny white stones veined in blue. "The King, the Keeper and Q." Her mouth grew hard. Her lips exaggerated his name; animosity crusted her words.

'Q knows the arcane location of the Bridge," Beetrum mocked. "The portal hidden between the worlds of Fey and human. It's part of his official responsibility. Quindaro B. LeVard. Ambassador to Domus, the Ancient Kingdom. Q is the only human ever to know the location of the Bridge."

Kenny stared at his mother; the parchment crackled in his hand as he handed it back to her. *Fey? Ancient Kingdom? What the he...? Uhh, I mean, what the hotel?* She seemed unaware that she spouted unbelievable claims. Implausible. Impossible. Weren't they?

A subtle change in the carriage turned Beetrum a very light shade of green.

Like cabin pressure increasing.

Beetrum's eyes widened, hands grasping the seat cushion. "Here it comes," she gasped. Her ruby nails disappeared in the crimson folds of the seat. An earsplitting boom reverberated into the carriage, vibrating, shaking. The sound wave punched Beetrum collapsing her onto the seat.

Mach 2. Holy sierra. Kenny barely had the thought before the swell hit him. Pain stabbed his ears, his body compressed, breath suspended.

Will this coach hold together?

Kenny's vision darkened; memories revolved around his mind in great swirls. His parachute failing, his fall through space. The hospital. Eddies of cinema played out before him. Nausea rose in his throat. Bitter. Kenny doubled over on the seat as the pressure wave broke over him. He waited for the second boom. The instant he heard it, the compression released and he could breathe. He wondered if a white vapor cloud surrounded the coach. How could Mr. Personality and his demon equines survive out there?

Kenny opened his eyes and saw Beetrum lying flat on the seat. Limp. A marionette with severed strings. She sighed deeply, color flooding into her usually pale cheeks, a small smile playing at the corners of her mouth. What was getting into him?...he wanted to hold her like a sleeping child. If he could only move.

Kenny felt as if he had been in a freefall. He wasn't sure he could get up even if he tried. The smell of sweet apple cobbler drifted through the carriage. Kenny closed his eyes and slept.

Chapter Four

New Joy

The carriage door opened. Soft mellow moonlight filled the coach like bubbly champagne sliding into a glass. The night air golden, green, and fresh felt cool against Kenny's face. His skin tingled. Kenny realized he was entering a new world, his new world. It was a defining moment.

Kenny stepped out onto the pavers and froze. He felt light. Like zero gravity. A little giddy but grounded. Connected.

Flat rocks wound their way around the circular driveway and meandered up to the Manor. Pungent green moss growing between the rocks outlined each stone like a fragrant green puzzle. Soft gray-green and plum-pit-blue lichen sculpted each flat slab with velvet making it soft beneath Kenny's shoes. The moment his foot landed on the lichen he felt the charge. An awakening.

Kenny's mind came alive with Domus as awareness flooded him with warmth like the rising sun. Mental images floated and swirled: a man singing to a wilderness, a smiling young woman with child, a leering, chilling black malignant presence. Voices. Some overlaid with laughter; others with grief. At one moment the air smelled pungent, musky like ancient tombs, and the next, sweet as a newborn day. The sights and sounds of the vision made Kenny dizzy. Domus encapsulated. Kenny felt Domus bonding him, claiming him. Domus, a living breathing entity. Domus: home. Lichen was home.

Sweet Juliett, what just happened?

"Kenny," Beetrum snapped. She blatantly refused Chimera's extended hand; he looked amused. Beetrum offered her hand for Kenny to take. "For heaven's sake. Get a grip."

"It's Lichen," he said into his mother's glare as he helped her from the coach.

"What?" Beetrum asked annoyance hardening her expression, accentuating her word.

"My name is Lichen."

Beetrum's face wilted like a flower past its bloom.

Lichen couldn't wipe the crooked smile off his face. His pulse as audible as bleeps on a radar screen sent invisible fingers of exhilaration up and down his spine as if practicing the scales. He'd never seen anything as beautiful as the sweeping ground rolling in every direction.

Deep-ocean-green ivy with tiny burgundy blooms grew in waves around the fountains, hugging the stone manor up the sides and onto the roof then back down, trailing over eaves as if peeking in the windows. Large, variegated vines with purple umbels clung to tree bark, climbing high and swinging from branches like children playing. Subtle greens and soft grays surrounded the Manor and the grounds. A panoramic motherly embrace.

Moss and lichen crept in concert down the slope and around the stables. Plants grew in all directions, their personality uncoiling staggering beauty. He had never used his real name. But now, here, in this place, this time, he embraced it as something wonderful and mysterious. It connected him to this land in a way he hadn't known existed. He was Lichen.

Water, the elixir of life, bubbled gently from Mother Earth and sprayed luminescence at every turn. Murmuring fountains. Redirected streams. Waterfalls cascading down bluffs. Esthetic beauty. Refined and graceful.

Everything twinkled. Effervescent fireflies sated the grounds blinking their bodies like tiny stars in tune with haunting melodies from the virtuoso night creatures. Lichen inhaled the night air, pure, crisp, and clean. He would have been incapable of speech even if he had been inclined to interrupt the moment.

The moon, full and ripe, reflected the grandeur of the Manor. It had the feeling of a cottage, yet the length and breadth of the Manor ran on like the vines covering it. The walls appeared to pulsate and Lichen felt the heart of the Manor beat a circadian rhythm throughout the gardens and grounds. Slow. Steady. Thump. Thump. His heart took up the cadence and pumped primordial passion through his veins in time with the earth. He and the Manor were one. Magic was in the air.

Home. He had come home.

"Don't be seduced," Beetrum said under her breath, a touch of panic in the tone. Lichen ignored her.

Lichen watched Chimera unload the luggage with unusual precision. He wondered where the driver and his herd of specters were before they were fabricated. In some mysterious limbo? Or did they simply materialize, molecules rearranging themselves stimulated by someone's thoughts? Quantum conjured. Was every summoned being cold, remote, and chillingly soulless like the coachman? Or hellishly hot and filled with brimstone like the stallions? What he wouldn't give to hop on one of them.

Can they fly?

Kenny noted Chimera's mechanical movements and impersonal attention. He had had a captain like that once.

"You're very ... efficient," Lichen said.

The driver glowered at Lichen with ball-bearing eyes, not gray, but a strange unworldly blue. Cold and dead. He did not respond. The full moon gleamed off his vermillion queue pulled tightly at the nape of his neck, binding red hair with strands of black cord as if trying to cut off the bleeding.

"For heaven's sake, Ken...Lichen, come on," Beetrum said, as she tugged on Lichen's flight jacket. She started up the path issuing guttural sounds toward her son.

Lichen's glare at Chimera did not waver; his jaw muscle flexed. The coachman had stone-cold attitude. Lichen had hard steel resolve.

A butler, of sorts, appeared at the Manor door. He walked toward them. He looked wise, kind, and ancient, yet his eyes sparkled, his gait strong and sure, his tanned skin smooth and handsome. Ageless.

"Good evening," he said, his voice like a deep melody. His bearing was reassuring. Comforting, but unmistakably commanding. He was impeccably dressed...for the nineteenth century. His collarless shirt was the color of dawn. Starched, ironed. His trousers broke stylishly over the patina of his shiny black shoes. He nodded politely with a ghost of a smile.

"Welcome," Agaso said. "Miss Beetrum, good to see you again." His lips curved in a slight polite smile. Lichen felt a bubble of warmth surround them. Agaso's eyes twinkled as if remembering the young girl he had watched grow up.

He turned to Lichen. "Master Lichen, my name is Agaso," he said inclining his head slightly. "Master Q has been detained. He will see you at breakfast. Please follow me. Chimera will bring your bags."

Beetrum and Lichen followed Agaso as he turned toward the Manor. Lichen stopped abruptly. Chimera collided into Lichen's back, dropped the two bags, and swore. Lichen stood unmoving, staring straight ahead, his mouth agape.

There, on the butler's back, just beneath his shoulders, folded and neat as becoming his station, lay a stately pair of long and tapered, shimmering silver wings. They were the color of a moon-path on a January snow. His matching long hair plaited down his back merged into his *feathers*. The light played sedately around each soft quill, gleaming up and down, turning and twisting along plumed edges, blending from side to side, radiating haloes of splendor.

Well, I'll be delta. Wings. Lichen's hand went to the miniature set of wings pinned on his jacket. *He can fly. Interesting.*

Agaso took them through the foyer toward the stairs. The house seemed comfortable, almost as if the Manor welcomed Lichen personally. The sense of knowing he felt when he had stepped on the lichen-covered stones outside lingered, floating within him as he walked through the Manor. He felt a sense of belonging.

"Stop dawdling," Beetrum snapped, her quick footsteps echoed off the gleaming wood floor. Clearly agitated she marched behind Agaso up the stairs.

Vines climbed the foyer walls, twirling and spiraling upwards as if they were climbing to the moon shining through the open rafters in the roof. Every surface bathed in cool liquid-silver light looked opalescent. As Lichen placed his hand on the balustrade, an ivy creeper moved to touch his fingers.

"Shi...," he said jerking away, "I mean sierra."

Agaso laughed as he looked down from the walkway overhead. "She won't bite," he said. "I think she likes you."

"Looks like poison ivy," Lichen said remembering an embarrassing itching episode.

"Oh, don't worry. She only poisons intruders. You might say she's our security system."

Beetrum's venomous stare jolted down the banister toward Lichen. Several ivy streamers reared up as cobras, leaf-points flared toward her. "Hostile as ever," Beetrum murmured as she turned and marched down the hall.

The ivy didn't stir as Lichen moved his hand cautiously toward the railing. The vine relaxed its rigid pose and rubbed softly against his hand. He almost expected it to purr.

Beetrum and Agaso were inside the suite by the time Lichen reached the walkway. He went into the room still marveling at the engineering of the rafters open to the sky.

A maid stood discreetly just inside the door. Lichen scanned her profile for wings.

Flat. Back... and front.

"This was my mother's suite," Beetrum said. "I'm glad he didn't put me in my old room."

Agaso nodded. The room spoke of taste and refinement. Fine laces and embroideries woven with invisible stitches looked perfectly at home among the ivy vines and flowers. Curved furniture bordered with graceful gold leaf swirls mirrored its living counterpart growing across the backs of chairs and up the tops of pictures. Ivory, greens, and blues of sage and lichen painted the room swathing it with cool beauty. Clear crystal candle-holders hung in tasteful clusters from the ceiling, sat on the mantle and tables, and perched on the walls casting their rainbow hues about the room. Delicate crystal teardrops suspended from window casings twirled of their own accord. All the crystals seemed to be humming, no, singing in unison. The vibrations were palpable.

Lichen's mind reeled. His eyes scanned the room. They repeatedly, magnetically returned to those wings. Agaso's scintillating wings.

"Lichen, your suite is right next door," Agaso said. "I trust it will be to your liking." Agaso's mouth curved with a secret smile. "Master Q will see you at breakfast. I know you must be exhausted from your trip. Please address any needs to Brota. She has brought refreshments. I will see you in the morning; have a good night's rest." The words did not reach Lichen. He was lost in the wings. Mindful only of the wings. He watched as they left the room perched delicately beneath the butler's shoulders.

The reality of Domus settled on Lichen like a cloak. Warm and soothing yet piercing with its new reality. It was a pivotal moment. Like learning about sex. One's perspective changed forever.

Lichen's will to stand abandoned him; it had been a long day. He sank into a downy sofa in front of the fireplace. Flickering shadows swathed the room, their movement hypnotic. He felt drained. Lichen stared blindly at the portrait above the fireplace. It seemed familiar.

"That's my mother, Syringa," Beetrum said. "Wasn't she beautiful?"

Lichen had never heard Beetrum speak of her mother. The mysterious eyes in the painting drilled into him.

"It was painted in the library at home, in Weston. She...died soon after." With an abrupt stiffness, Beetrum turned and examined the clothing left for them.

"Ah, yes. Gowns. Gowns for morning. For dining." She flung them one by one on the bed, fine fabrics puffing out and then landing in a heap. They resembled hot air balloons, deflated and strewn across a meadow. Puddles of color.

"Gowns for riding. Ballroom gowns. Lounging gowns. Walking gowns. Gowns. Gowns. Gowns." Beetrum's voice grew brittle. She looked down at the smart trousers she was wearing. Lichen didn't know whether she would laugh or cry.

Lichen stared at his grandmother's portrait and recognized the library back in Weston. Just behind Syringa's shoulder sat the clock, glowing; shedding a soft lavender hue around his grandmother. Suddenly, Lichen felt a strong kinship to her. A familial bond he had never felt with anyone. Ethereal connection. He had never seen any photographs of his grandparents and after careful study, he saw no resemblance to his mother. Unlike the cool presence of Beetrum, Syringa was aflame with energy and passion. Her vitality burned through the dimension of the portrait into Lichen. The fire of life. Prometheus' fire.

Stolen or given freely?

"Well, I see his majesty dusted off the red carpet for our arrival," Beetrum said. Sarcasm couched disappointment as she spoke of Q. "He couldn't be bothered to welcome us in person," Beetrum said as she dismissed the flat little maid with a vicious wave of her hand. Lichen had known Q hadn't planned on seeing them until tomorrow. Perhaps he should have told Beetrum what had been in his birthday note.

Q's BelMoon invitation to Beetrum had surprised her. Beetrum had not seen her father for over twenty-five years so Lichen figured Q's unexpected summons to Domus had given her a glimmer of hope to which she would never admit. A tiny sliver of optimism that a relationship may yet be forged.

Evidently, the feeling was not mutual. She corresponded with Q about his business interests in the small community of Weston, Missouri. That Lichen had not been privy to these exchanges still stung a little. Had he not improved the bottom line? Suggested updates and factory changes that increased production? Lichens engineering skills and business acuity had broadened the profit margin considerably. Why had the real owner—Q—not acknowledged that in some way? Surely his mother had given Lichen the credit for the improvements.

Still, his feelings aside, Lichen had hoped their stay in Domus would improve Beetrum's relationship with her father. That they would reconcile past grievances. But Q's absence tonight and Beetrum's reaction to it did not bode well for that expectation.

Lichen knew better than to respond to Beetrum's cynicism. Her bitterness was like a lesion. Because she refused to let it heal, it would spew, foul and insidious, at the least provocation.

"Well, I'm going to bed," Lichen said. "We'll see him soon enough." He was quite anxious to open the box in his pocket. And to meet his grandfather, the man responsible for all of this. And, see to Domus. And more wings.

Chapter Five

Memories

Beetrum sat staring into the fire, her emotions crackling and popping in sync with the flames. So. He couldn't take time out of his precious schedule to greet them. After all these years apart, he didn't even meet them. One small, short hello. Would that have been so bad? One tiny scrap of courtesy. She should have known. Once again she had let persistent untrustworthy hope work its way into her mind. Weaseling and worming its way in when her defenses were weak. What was she doing here? What a fool. She should never have expected reconciliation with Q.

Beetrum's nerves pinpricked her skin, and she stood and paced the room. A tiny tap sounded at the door.

"Lichen?" Beetrum asked as she opened the door.

"No, miss. It's Cecelia. I brought ye a bit of nepeta tea. I thought ye might be a bit worked up."

"Cecelia," Beetrum said, "how thoughtful." Cold bitter shards spiked her words. She turned and walked to the fireplace, her stiff back to Cecelia. So, Cecilia was still the ManorMother.

"Well, noo, I'll just leave it 'ere. Ye may be changin' ye'r mind," Cecelia said as she set the tray on a side table. "I thought ye may be more comfortable 'ere, than in ye'r auld room. But I can move ye, if ye'd rather."

"No," Beetrum said quickly. "This will do."

"Mistress, I just want to say, we're all so verra glad to see ye. And the boy. I knoo it must be 'ard for ye to come back. Ye've 'ad so much 'eartache. If there's anythin' I can do..." Cecelia's words were kind, her manner warm. They effectively undid Beetrum's icy resolve and much to her vexation, she burst into tears.

"Achhh, now" Cecelia said. "Come, sit 'ere and drink ye'r tea. Ye'll feel much better." She put her arm around Beetrum and led her to the sofa.

"It's just that being here brings it all back you know," Beetrum sniffed looking up at her mother's portrait. "I still miss her."

"Achhh, well, it's 'ard to lose ye'r mam, now. Yes, i' tis. And ye being just a wee lass of eight. Tchh. Tchh." Cecelia remembered it well. "All of Domus loved Syringa, yes, they did noo. And Domus mourned 'er loss, too. And Master Q..." Cecelia shook her head. "Well, that's a different-all-together. "'e nearly lost 'is mind, 'e did. Yes, 'e took 'is grief and 'oled up in 'is own private 'aven that only 'e could enter leavin' ye behind, Beetrum. We were all sorry for that." Tears puddled in Cecelia's eyes.

"Yes," Beetrum said. "And I retreated into my private hell. I refused your overtures of kindness. I'm sorry for that." Beetrum blew her nose and sipped the tea. "I was mad at my mother for leaving me behind with monsters and creatures with wings. Anything non-human terrified me. Even Agaso whom I'd known my entire life."

"Achhh, well," Cecelia said. "Agaso understood, yes 'e did. And Master Q, too. But, by the time 'is grief 'ealed and 'e was ready to be a proper father again, ye had closed yerself to 'im and everyone else in Domus."

"Yes, my temper tantrums were famous." Beetrum gave a nervous giggle. "I alienated everyone. Everyone until ... Linum." Beetrum had not said his name for years. Had not even dared to think it. Her hand trembled. "Coming here for BelMoon...it's hard for me."

"Achhh, yes, I'm sure i' tis," Cecelia said.

"If you'll excuse me now," Beetrum said. "I'm very tired." Beetrum wasn't ready to talk about Linum. Not with Cecilia. Not with Q's house servant. She stood, her aloofness returning, walked to her bedchamber, and closed the door.

"Poor lass," Cecelia said. She left the room with a soft click of the door. As she stepped into the hallway a muffled sound of hilarity drifted up through the rafters. She smiled and headed for the scullery.

Beetrum felt the numbness return. After all these years his name still sent her spiraling. Linum. She loved the sound of it as it wound its way through her stirring up dusty emotions.

Linum.

Beetrum jerked the bedspread back knocking a small envelope to the floor that embellished the initial "Q". Unaware, she collapsed onto the bed, her mind sinking into her past. A taboo of her own making. She stood safely outside as though looking through glass, protected, and watched the story of her lost love play out in her mind. A faerie tale gone awry.

Linum Ipse came to New Ivy from King Dens Colere. Q orchestrated a grand new building project and went to his old friend in Regnum, the Royal City, for help. The Royal apartment was beautifully and tastefully appointed, but not extravagant. King Colere's austerity and common sense governed the purse strings despite the abundance of the royal treasury. Q leaned back in his comfortable chair and looked the King square in the face.

"I'm going to build a new bridge," he said.

"A new bridge?" His Majesty laughed. A garnet dove with bright purple eyes lighted on the balcony where they sat. She picked unafraid at the crumbs Q had thrown onto the ledge. "What's wrong with the bridge you have?" the King asked, his eyes crinkled with amusement.

"Nothing. Nothing is wrong with it," Q said. "But New Ivy needs another one. A bridge that opens to the east." His gaze rose to the east and his mind's eye filled with his vision.

"To the east?" the King said. "But the Great River Potens is wide there. And extremely deep. Besides, going east puts you nowhere. There's nothing to the east except the Wasteland. And the Vetare Silva, The Forbidden Forest. Why would you want to go east, my friend?"

"Because it *is* a wasteland. Because it's been inhospitable since the Banishment, tens of thousands of years ago. Because, Dens, I want to build a collegium." Q only used the King's given name when they were quite alone. And, when he was quite serious. Dens—fang. The amiable easygoing Regent could be quite formidable when he chose to be.

The King stood up, stretched his wings, marbled with veins of chocolate gold, and stared at Q.

Q continued. "Craftsmen and artisans coming from all over Domus to teach not only from the intellect but from the heart. Apprentices filled with spirit hone their crafts with affection instead of systematic rote repetition; students learn not just academics but every conceivable art, music, poetry, storytelling, and the intricacies and beauty of nature. If these things are taught from the soul and are learned by the soul it changes a person. It changes a kingdom.

"Domus was founded and depends upon the Sacred Songs. The people are losing the very essence of Domus. Divus gave us The Songs to expand our spirit, to extend our love to one another, and to be co-creators. Yet we have devolved into a prideful people who think only of ourselves.

"This new way of teaching would open the hearts and expand the souls of the old, the young, the rich and poor of every species. It would return us to the gentle, kind, and loving people we were born to be and infuse our very being..." Q's voice rose in intensity, his hands emphasizing his emotion... "indeed our very culture, with light, joy, and happiness. These principles would flourish and flow with expertise and love throughout the entire Kingdom giving opportunities to everyone.

"Children's hearts and minds will open to the world of Divus and allow them to pursue the interests planted in their hearts by the Creator instead of being imperiously bound to the craft of their family. Their souls will not be limited and caged; they will be set free to be the sons and daughters of Divus that they truly are.

"A village will grow around the teaching campus filled with light and truth. It will cultivate a budding gentleness that translates into a society that cares for the widow and the downtrodden. New trade routes will open to the other kingdoms not only for the sharing of goods but the sharing of light. Domus could be the nucleus of a great power emanating from our very souls.

"Think of the possibilities, Dens. Envision it. Can you see it?" Fire burned his words, heating and boiling over his passion; it filled the room like hot lava.

"Well," Dens said. "That's quite the plan. However, it sounds as if you are taking over the role of Ecclesia—all spirit and soul and love. Princeps Sapien may not think too kindly of it."

"Oh, no," Q answered. Teaching from the heart doesn't supplant religion, it enriches it. After all, it originates from the divine Center of Divus. We must get back to nature, to the Mother. We must let her reteach us the Sacred Songs."

The King paced as the idea marched back and forth in his head; his eyes glazed as he imagined Q's new teaching metropolis and methods. At last, he said, "Well, if anyone can do it, you can. After all, look what you have done in New Ivy." The garnet dove cooed her agreement strutting her feathers as though the idea were hers.

"A collegium. In Domus. I like it," the King said, "but not everyone will."

Ignoring the gargantuan task of actually getting the academy up and running, Dens tackled the more immediate question. "And how do you propose to span the River? It must be a full league across on the east side." King Dens Colere looked expectant, knowing Q would have the answer.

"With ropes." The garnet dove jumped with a squawk, her plume jiggling; her purple eyes flashed as if the concept quite astounded her.

"Ropes?" she cooed.

"Ropes?" The King echoed.

"Yes, I'm going to build a swinging bridge. I am going to discover and use the secret of Glipneir."

The shocking idea of recreating Glipneir hit King Colere in the face causing him to reel backwards. Glipneir, the magical rope that employed not only great strength but the grace and beauty of butterfly wings. It had not been seen in Domus for millennia. He looked at his feathered companion. "I have no idea how Q will do it but do it he will. There is no doubt. Quindaro B. LeVard, Ambassador, can do a great number of things."

Q left with the King's assent and a jaunt in his step, whistling the tune the garnet dove had been singing.

So, Linum Ipse, the King's Cordage, came to New Ivy. He and all his fathers before him were masters of rope-making. Linum's family had made every rope in Domus. Linum had helped his father make all the ropes in New Ivy. But, this bridge, this colossal project, required more than Linum's experience had taught him. Since losing his father, his mentor, Linum was unsure of his ability.

He had a dreadful trait of going full-on, then losing impetus just before completion. Q assured him he was up to the task and that Linum's knowledge was all obtained from doing. Linum just had to tap into his mental and spiritual resources. He could do it.

Linum wasn't sure *how* to do it, but Q had said, "Just begin, boy. Just begin."

So he did. Linum labored far into each night with his plans. They poured like water through a crack in the dam. Slowly at first, then picking up speed until nothing could hold them back. Torrential inspiration.

But once his ideas were committed to paper, he was gripped with misgivings. Linum's past mistakes plagued him, masking his accomplishments.

Apprehension gnawed at him endlessly. It ate away at his esteem leaving monstrous gaping holes that Linum did not know how to fill. He could not make the decision that would move the project forward; he could not show his plans to Q. Villainous qualms bound him securely in a quagmire of doubt and halted any further productive endeavor. Linum Ipse was forestalled.

Early mornings found him looking across the great expanse of water to the east side of River Potens. Each day Beetrum watched him go to the River and brood. One morning Beetrum gathered her courage and followed Linum down the path to the water's edge.

"You can do it," she said softly walking up behind him.

Linum turned abruptly. "What? Oh, hello Beetrum." His ears turned red. "What did you say?"

"I said you can do it. You can make the ropes to build this bridge."

Linum stood dumbfounded. A secret light of affection burned in Linum's breast for Beetrum. He kept it covered securely by day so its glow would not be detected. But, at night, his soul simmered, and his feverish thoughts reached out for Beetrum.

Linum said nothing. Beetrum rendered him quite speechless.

"I've seen your work. I mean... your plans. Why haven't you shown them to Father? He waits impatiently to proceed."

"I, uh, I'm not finished with them," Linum said. It did not occur to him to question how Beetrum could have seen the plans. His cheeks now joined his ears in glowing brightly.

"Well, then finish them," Beetrum said.

Beetrum's simple words pierced the hidden chamber of light in Linum's heart. It burst forth in brilliant scorching rays spreading heat and joy throughout his mind, his heart. He acknowledged it. He accepted it. At that moment, Linum knew he was in love.

"Well, all right. All right, I'll finish it." Linum beamed. Confidence surged through him. He could do anything. Nothing was beyond his grasp. He would make the ropes to build Q's bridge. A swinging bridge that all of Domus would admire. People would come from everywhere to cross his bridge and say Linum Ipse has done the impossible. No one else could have built such a magnificent bridge. He would be the greatest cordage in all the land. The greatest cordage ever to be born. Joy billowed in great waves sweeping Linum's despair and uncertainty aside.

Beetrum smiled. A similar light coursed through her. Tenderness engulfed her. Feelings sprouted in empty barren places. Frozen years of solitude and loneliness began to melt, dripping like spring thaw on the mountains. She, too, felt love.

By BelMoon, Linum and Beetrum were more than ready to dance the BelPole and the Adoleo. Q performed the Copulo, the Ceremony of Joining, and thought perhaps Linum would be his daughter's salvation. Her safe passage out of self-imposed hell. Since the death of Syringa her mother, Q had not been able to reach through Beetrum's wall of isolation, but perhaps Linum could.

Q recognized brilliance when he saw it. Linum's new method for weaving would triple the rope's strength. Linum took the rendering of Q's bridge and incorporated unprecedented techniques. He used intricate methods of plaiting and entwining. He developed a highly specialized merging of web strands from the giant spiders that lived in river caves. His ropes were formidable.

Extremus Venatio. The Last Hunt. Horses, hounds, and hunters gathered at Q's stables for the last hunt of the season. The Ambassador spared no effort to ensure his guests had the best accommodations for themselves, their horses, and their dogs. King and Queen Colere and Valeo Nox, the newly appointed Keeper, were in attendance riding the potent steeds from the Royal Stable.

Q and Linum rode the latest acquisitions of the Manor and Beetrum rode her trusty mare, Salix. Flexible as a willow, understated, and dependable to a fault. By contrast, Linum's stallion reared and pawed the air. His shrieks filled the dawn as if to force the new day upon them.

"Linum, wouldn't you rather ride Molten?" Beetrum asked, her voice suddenly tight. She felt as if a cloud had floated across the sun. A chill slithered through her body.

Linum laughed. Since he had realized his love for Beetrum that day on the River's edge, she had inspired and filled him with confidence. He felt indomitable.

Beetrum helped him find his inner calling. A living vitality energized him. He could accomplish anything. Anything at all. He would make a difference. Linum's workroom in the stable was filled daily with new, invincible ropes. Come spring, a magnificent swinging bridge would span the eastern expanse of the Great River Potens. Q's bridge. Linum's bridge.

"Molten needs a break today. Yesterday we rode the winds like gods," Linum shouted. His face exultant, his bearing royal. "Do not fret dear wife, this beast will carry me well. We will be the first to reach our prey and I will lay it humbly at your feet."

The trumpets sounded. Not waiting to be cued, Linen's stallion bolted. He was off with Q amidst baying hounds their noses pressed to scents of fear, the thunder of hooves, and shouts of blood-lusty hunters. The hunt drew forth the latent warriors.

Beetrum followed at a contented pace. She squelched her silly misgivings and glowed with the secret knowledge of new life within her. A secret had been made at BelMoon. Tonight, as they lay wrapped in one another's arms, as the fire danced in the hearth tickling memories of Adoleo, she would share that secret with Linum.

The room was abuzz with voices, low and hushed. Beetrum lay on a couch in the parlor. Her eyes began to flutter, then open. She tried to sit up. Q was beside her instantly.

"Beetrum, lie still. Just be still," he said gently. Beetrum closed her eyes, fighting to the surface of her fog. Something was wrong, but what was it? She couldn't remember. The acrid smell of wet ashes filled the room. She thrashed her head from side to side trying to think.

The memory came suddenly and Beetrum began to scream. Deep pain shrieked from a dark and empty place. A space that just this morning had hummed with light; now a silent cavern, desolate and black.

Linum was dead. They found him lying in autumn's leaves, his neck broken. The prey lay crumpled in a bloody heap beside him. The hounds sat quietly around them, keeping watch over death. Linum's horse had disappeared. He had indeed been the first one there.

As the other hunters arrived, and the news reached Beetrum's ears, she fainted dead away. Q had two bodies to take home. The shocked and saddened group traveled slowly. Even the hounds, subdued, followed close at their master's heels. Queen Vintas herself attended to Beetrum on her makeshift travois.

As they neared the Manor on the final slope, Q smelled smoke. He raced his horse to the top of the ridge.

"What...?" Fire. The stable was afire. Smoke billowed into the darkening sky; flames reached after it. Q thought fleetingly of the one rope he had brought into the manor. The one rope saved from destruction.

The men from the village were already passing buckets of water along brigades to the flames. Q's ingenuity and foresight saved the day with ample water supplies piped from the River. The stable was saved, not a single horse was lost.

But the ropes. The ropes were gone. Burned. A sacrificial pyre. Tribute to genius. Linum and his opus destroyed.

The grief of that long-ago day seized and strangled Beetrum as she tossed and turned on her bed, tears soaking her pillow. She didn't know if she was awake or asleep. She only knew Linum was lost to her. Forever.

Chapter Six

Portent

Lichen hesitated. The box felt heavy. Not just in his hand but in his soul, like the weight of responsibility. He flipped open the lid and removed a white silk-like bag with a black drawstring closure. Lichen opened the bag and removed a folded white cloth. As he peeled back the fabric of the cloth he heard and felt a faint vibration that sounded like a perfectly balanced soft melodious note. Middle C. Words began appearing on the cloth where it had been blank moments before. A curious amulet dropped into his hand.

As Lichen began to read; tiny words appeared just ahead of his line of sight. His pulse pounded in his ears; he felt magic around him like the thick heaviness of water when you walk on the bottom of a pool. The words seemed to connect with him, draw him in. Lichen felt tingly from head to toe.

THE PORTENT

Harm is the goal from things unseen

He seeks complete destruction.

From the darkest places, vile unclean
He plans to give instruction.
He lays in wait, the cold dark fiend
His game one of seduction.
A Warrior's Heart that's purely seen
He'll turn without compunction.
He seeks the Charm the ancients told
Had powers of protection.
It keeps one safely in the fold
If held without detection.
Wear Earth and Stars both night and day
Your steps will reach completion.
On tangled paths, a Warrior's way
You'll make the right selection.
Power, his quest; his reason fled,
He has no inhibition.
He will not rest, not find his bed
'Till plans come to fruition.
Beware! Keep watch! You hold the key
To burdens of affliction,
Finding your Soul will set you free,
And halt his domination.

What did this mean? Lichen looked closer at the amulet. It appeared to be gold with engravings of three intertwined circles and a tree. Tiny crystals adorned the branches and the sky.

Lichen's stomach rumbled again. He put the amulet around his neck, stuffed the cloth into the bag, and jammed it into his pocket. He would figure it out later. Right now, he was starving.

Chapter Seven

Raman

His stomach growled in answer. He could use some food, but Brota's sandwiches sat in Beetrum's room. Lichen stepped into the hallway and tried his mother's door. Locked. Perhaps there were more sandwiches downstairs in the kitchen. He had no idea what time it was, where was that blasted clock when you needed it? He had a feeling it was quite late.

Well, here he was in Domus. In Domus and hungry. None of the lamps were lit, but the moon still shined heartily through the ingenious open ceiling. The rafter roof followed the halls filling them with lunar light and night-bird song.

Lichen started down the stairs, the vines on the banister rustled gently just ahead of him. As he drew even with the moving leaves, they stopped and the ones a foot ahead began stirring. Lichen reached the foyer and stopped; there were several ways to go.

"Hmmm," he said aloud wondering which hallway to take. The vining leaves to the right began to quiver. Lichen chuckled. Looking around to be sure he was alone, he ventured ,"Um, I'm looking for the kitchen." The leaves continued their pattern of moving just ahead. So, it was not only a security system, it was a GPS.

Lichen walked the moonlit hall following the movement of the leaves, meandering through the Manor until he found himself just outside the kitchen. He could smell it.

"Uh, thanks," he said to the vines.

I'm talking to plants now?

The closed buds on the ivy opened into wide pale yellow blossoms that looked all the world like smiles. Lichen smiled back, slid open the pocket door, and went into the kitchen.

Lichen stopped in his tracks, and for the second time tonight he was speechless. In the center of the kitchen stood a huge circular stone oven with a blazing fire. Flames flicked like smoky tongues tasting the air. The aroma, which could only have been bread, teased another growl from Lichen's stomach. The baker glanced up.

"Hungry?" he asked.

He looked human, almost. Paul Bunyan arms, thick Sequoia neck, and lumberjack hands dwarfed the kitchen accouterments. His skin was summer bronze stretched over high cheekbones. His jaw, right-angle square. Nose, long, straight, and Roman. Keen intelligence sparked from eyes that slanted up and back, lashless lids stretched tight as drum skin. Small ears perfectly formed. At the hairline, instead of hair, horns grew. Starting above the forehead they curved gracefully, beautifully back, up just a little, then spiraled like a snail shell around his skull. No hair, just horn. He cocked his head and raised an eyebrow. At least it would have been a brow if he had any hair. His eyes were primordial green. Deep. Dark. Swirling with intensity. Infinite patience.

"You must be the grandson. Are you hungry?"

"Uh, yes. Yes," Lichen stammered. "Yes, I am the grandson. And, yes, I am hungry. Lichen Ipse." Lichen walked into the kitchen and extended his hand.

"Raman. Raman of the Mountain Mist Clan. You can call me Ram."

Lichen's half-smile graced his cheek with amusement as he cocked his head and looked at Ram's horns. "Ram? Pleasure to meet you...Ram."

Lichen and Ram sat at the well-worn table eating and drinking as if they had been lifelong friends.

This is delicious," Lichen mumbled through a mouthful of bread and butter. He devoured another large piece. "Have you been the baker here long?"

Ram's gust of laughter filled the kitchen. "Oh, I'm not the baker. But" Ram took a bite of his large piece of bread, a full third of the loaf, "I do love to bake bread." His long, thick, black tongue licked the butter off his chin. "And eat it."

Lichen laughed with him. He felt giddy, happy. "You're not the baker?"

"Nope." Ram doubled over, his laughter coming in great guffaws.

Lichen held his sides, trying to catch his breath. Somewhere in the back of his mind, he wondered what was so funny. Ram pounded the table with his giant fist. The plates and knives hopped up and clattered

Lichen felt at home sitting around the table with his new acquaintances. This feeling of camaraderie was not one he had encountered in his life back home. After *the incident* on his eighth birthday, Brent had expunged their friendship and made sure the other kids steered clear, too. Lichen had not replaced Brent's best-friend position and to this day he privately thought of him as Best-Friend Brent.

Sitting at this table, in this kitchen, in this house, felt good. Right. Once again, Lichen felt at home, relaxed. Comfortable with Ram and Cecelia. Comfortable enough to ask questions. "Well, I do have questions," Lichen said.

"Such as what," Ram said raising his non-brow.

"Everything," Lichen said, the light in his eyes eager. Ram and Cecelia looked at one another.

"Well, now, Lichen," Cecelia said. "I'm sure ye grandfather will want ta teach ye."

Not about to let this opportunity slip away, Lichen said, "OK, then, just tell me about this magnificent house. Did my grandfather build it? How old is it? And I know it's magical.

Lichen could see the ivy peeking over the door. "Tell me about that. And," Lichen looked at Ram. "If you are not the baker, who the hotel are you?"

Chapter Eight

The Manor

Ram sighed and began. "Your grandfather, Quindaro B. LeVard, received The Manor as a gift from King Dens Colere. Of course, he wasn't the King then.

"Q came to Domus as a young man. Ah, he was fresh from your world, from Advena, with a zest for life, unlike anything we had ever seen. He was something. He ignited everyone around him with his motivation and drive. It was like he traveled in a circle of light with Personal power emanating from him with potent force. It opened our minds and we saw possibilities that never occurred to us before. It was impossible not to be infected with his enthusiasm when you were with him. Most of us had never seen a human before and were impressed." Ram nodded his head, remembering.

"Where did he learn about the Bridge?" Lichen asked.

"*The* Bridge?" Cecelia took up the telling. "Q never told anyone the answer to that. But he did share the location of the Bridge with two others. Prince Colere—that was before he became King—and the new Keeper."

"The Keeper?" Lichen asked.

"Yes," Ram said scowling. "Valeo Nox. The Keeper. He's a scoundrel for sure and if you ask me..."

"Well, we aren't askin' ye," Cecelia said cutting in. "The Keeper is in charge of the King's hunting grounds. All the Preserves. The grounds are important for the food supply of Domus. T'is 'is job to keep everythin' balanced. 'e sets the rules for the takin' o' game and reports directly to the King. The Keeper is an inherited position and does'na need approval from the likes of us." Cecelia glared at Ram.

"Keeper Valeo Nox," Ram snorted, his low opinion of the man evident. "He received his appointment just before Q came."

"Prince Colere was quite taken wi' Q from the beginnin'." Cecelia said. "They became close friends and when Q 'atched the idea of New Ivy, the Prince invited Keeper to the meetin' see'ns as 'ow every quad 'as a Preserve an' all.'"

"Q," Ram continued, "came to the meeting with his customary bold enthusiasm. His calm assurance of success when he presented his plan prickled the Keeper. Q wanted the new quad to be an experiment in Fey and human relations."

This "Ram" was very articulate. Lichen could see him getting into the telling of the story.

' "Dens, just think of it," Q said. "A community of humans right here in Domus. It will be the beginning of a new era. You will be at the forefront, forging a great alliance."

"Q," Prince Colere laughed as he gave his great royal wings a flap. "You believe humans can live among the Fey? You think they can live with magic? And the Fey..." the Prince shook his head. "Most of the Fey hate humans. They oppose them living *anywhere* much less in

Domus. It can't be done. Integration has failed before. What makes you think you can build this model city, this paragon quad where our races can live in harmony?"

"He can't," Valeo said, the tiny dark feathers on the back of his neck bristled. "It's insane to try. It will bring disaster. Humans are not meant to live in Domus. We...err...the Fey do not want them here." Valeo gave Q a pointed look. "Don't misunderstand me. I, myself, take great pleasure in your company." Valeo bowed slightly toward Q. "But, most humans are not like you," Valeo continued smoothly, "and most Fey are not like me." '

"Isn't that the truth?" Ram interrupted his own narrative with his caustic remark toward the Keeper, then continued.

' "Do not underestimate humans or Fey," Q said as he stood and paced. "I know I can help bring them together. Just think of it, a society of mutual learning and understanding. An exchange of ideas and culture. It will be an international village blended with progressive thought and ancient customs. Isn't it exciting? Give it a chance, Dens", Ram finished with emphasis, "You won't be sorry." '

Ram took a breath and continued. "So in return for the whereabouts of the Bridge, Prince Colere gave Q a land grant. Four thousand hectares of wild feral ground, crawling, creeping, and vining with poison ivy and other inhospitable flora, and a sprawling derelict cottage. To the Fey, it looked hopeless. But to Q. Ahh, to Q it looked like a gift from Divus, the Divine. The Creator. He fell in love with the land. The Earth Mother.

"Yes, everywhere I traveled," Ram said, "the Domus citizenry shook their heads and laughed at this foolish human. They said the Mother would never accept this enterprise. You see, since the ancient of days whenever the Fey built a new village, The Earth Mother sent the Great River Potens to flow around and through the village dividing it into quad-cities. She nourished, loved, and supported it. And, if they were lucky, a spring erupted from the land complete with a guardian, a Spirit of the Spring. A sure sign of good fortune. The people of Domus felt sure The Great River Potens would never mold the new quad. They knew this human folly would fail."

"Achhh," Cecelia said, "but, they didn't know this 'uman. You see, 'e was a different all-together."

"Q learned the Copia" Ram said, "and stunned all of Domus."

"The what?" Lichen said.

"The Copia, the ancient Song of Abundance," Ram said with a dreamy look in his eye. "He doggedly sang it to his land every sunrise and sunset. No matter that he was plagued with illness and fatigue. The sun blistered him with scorching days, the sky pelted him with freezing hail at night, and still, he sang.

Ivy poisoned him with painful rashes, sores, and fever. Still, he sang. Q held his vision of the new quad in his mind as an offering to Divus. He continued to sing the Copia to his land twice a day from the very depths of his heart. The people watched and began to soften toward him. They had to admit, that this human was committed.

"One morning as a sliver of sun sliced across the darkness, as Q's last perfect note of the Copia, middle C, floated over the parched cracks and villainous ivy, a tiny trickle of water rose out of a fissure in the ground; The Earth Mother was giving her blessing.

Most people had moderate success with the Song of Abundance. Q triumphed. Q's ingenuity, perseverance, and sacrifice transformed the barren hostile wasteland into captivating estates and gardens. Q laid out the quad in graceful curves and circles—a symmetrical dance with the Great River Potens that flowed around the embryo village, encircling each of the quads in the new human-city experiment of Domus. New Ivy."

Cecelia sniffed. "Achhh, Ram, I do love to 'ear ye tell this story."

Ram leaned back into his chair, crossed his sizable ankles, and settled into his storytelling mode.

"When a spring bubbled up in the center of the Manor Prince Colere and Keeper Nox were astonished. Never, in the history of Domus had a Spirit of the Spring allowed herself to be enclosed, and certainly never for a human. She not only became the principal water source for the Manor, but she also infused the old cottage with life. She teamed with Q and blessed his creative engineering to make the Manor a living entity."

Ram paused in his story and looked across the room. Lichen followed his gaze. The room adjoining the kitchen burst with plants and vines. He couldn't see it, but he heard the soft gurgle of water.

"Yes," Raman said. "The spring room." Ram stood and began to pace. "Q built up and around, but instead of a hodge-podge dwelling, a magnificent home took shape. Each day brought more citizens of Domus to New Ivy to wonder and marvel at this human and his creations. They began to think if the Mother accepted this stranger into their land, perhaps they should as well.

"Q engineered the Manor with his usual meticulous forethought. Pragmatism with heart. Functionality with spirituality. It grew to be quite large yet retained an endearing cottage spirit. Q planted a backdrop of willows around the Manor. Willow. The Fey's tree of enchantment. Sacred tree to the Goddess of the Moon. Spiritual rebirth. The willows responded to the Copia by spreading their branches across the roof and down the walls. They were newly planted, yet their leaves caressed the Manor with faint friendly whispers of ancient secrets."

Lichen listened in awe. He could see why Cecelia liked to hear Ram tell the story. He was mesmerizing.

"Each day," Ram said, "The Song of Abundance rode the morning mists and sighed with the setting sun. Its melody of growth empowered sleeping seeds to burst and climb for the sky. Forgetting her poisonous mandate, Ivy scrambled up the Manor's latticed walls, onto the rafters, around the belvedere, into the house, and through the hallways. She opened her vibrant deep-throated flowers, released her exotic scent, and called for winged lovers."

"That sounds more like a love story," Lichen said.

"I' tis," Cecelia sighed. "Between a man and the land." They all sat quietly, thinking about Q and New Ivy.

"Well now," Cecelia said shaking off her stupor. "I'm thinkin' ye best be gettin' to bed me young lad.

Ye'll 'ave a big day tomorrow wi' ye grandfather."

Lichen went to his suite in a dreamy daze. Someone had left him a bottle of liniment for his leg. Since he had stepped into that otherworldly coach, he had felt no pain. Lichen didn't know if it was really gone or if this strange trip had triggered a placebo effect. He applied the liniment for good measure, sighed and lay down on the bed, stretched out his legs, and locked his hands behind his head, his favorite stance. Good thinking posture.

He felt exhausted but exhilarated. He never did find out who Ram *really* was. Maybe he was the Bard. Was there such a thing here in Domus? The moon shined directly on Lichen's face. He dosed and dreamed of wings and fire. Of grotesque shapes overlaid with shadows.

Lichen jerked and was on his feet before he was fully awake. A military response. Where was he? The moon shined through the window illuminating the hillside leading down to the stables. Ah, yes. Domus. He saw a slight movement. Was it Chimera, that snob of a demon? Did he sleep in the stables? And those six wonderfully wicked stallions. Where were they? Lichen wondered if the magical coachman and his horses needed to sleep at all. Or eat.

His mind drifted to the butler, Agaso. And his wings. Lichen was obsessed with those wings. Nothing he had ever envisioned came close to the reality of Faerie wings. Captivating feathered wings. Real wings. Just imagine it.

Voices penetrated his thoughts.

"It's about time you showed up. What took you so long? What have you been doing?" a voice said from the darkness.

"What's the matter, doesn't he trust me?" said the coachman. Conjured, cool, condescending.

Chimera, that frozen fiend. What was he doing?

Lichen's rational mind realized he should not be able to hear the men at the stables as they were some distance away yet he clearly heard and understood every word.

The figure in the shadows forced a laugh. He tried to lower his voice, deep and liquid, slow and dangerous. Like lava. Instead, he failed miserably, and his words cracked and fizzled with impotence. Ashes. He stepped into the moonlight, his back toward Lichen.

Wings. More wings. Highlighted silver by the moon they looked remarkable. It occurred to Lichen that not everyone here in Domus had wings.

"He trusts no one," the Faerie boasted, emphasizing his relationship with the absent mystery leader.

Lichen watched, transfixed, his hands gripped the windowsill. The Faerie was big, not tall, but bulky with huge shoulders. Support for those wings. Intrepid.

His diminutive height increased as he raised his wings high above his head. They flared brown and speckled in the moonlight like a vulture claiming his find. Threatening.

Lichen recognized the male move of dominance. Intimidation. The coachman appeared unaffected.

"I dare not come again," the Faerie said puffed up with self-importance. His voice was like a small dog growling. "Is everything...secure? Have you taken all the precautions?"

"I do not need a babysitter," Chimera said. "Nor do I require instruction."

"Tau'stercus," the Faerie said. "We only have one chance to succeed, don't botch it. I rather like my head attached."

Tau'stercus? Lichen puzzled.

The coachman's dead cobalt luminous eyes bore into the Faerie. He sounded quite adept at verbal dueling. Probably all dueling. His crimson hair burned and crackled with malice, his pale blue lips accentuating his words. "You little peacock, I never fail."

The Faerie flapped his wings. Stable dust swirled around them pirouetting in the moonlight. Straw ballerinas. "See that you don't." He lifted ever so slightly off the ground and backed into the shadows.

Lichen stood rooted at the window. Transfixed.

What was that about?

Chimera had something cooking. He and that little braggart. Lichen almost laughed. It was like a sparrow trying to best an eagle.

But, those wings. Magnificent.

Chapter Nine

A lark to the core, Lichen sprang up and out of the Manor before dawn. There was nothing quite like a good sunrise to collect one's thoughts.

Lichen walked behind the Manor through the willows and sat down on a moss-covered boulder overlooking the river surprised at the missing pain in his leg. Was it the liniment or Domus?

The moon was down, the stars still visible, but faint. The sky twinkled and blinked with tiny white lights making the horizon look like an expanse of black velvet embedded with sugar crystals.

At first Lichen wasn't sure he heard it, a melody drifting over the inky water. Not the music of night birds and insects he had heard the evening before, this was a song. A rich tenor voice singing one perfect note after the other as if coaxing the sun from its slumber rang through the air with simple clarity.

The sky blushed soft pink like a shy lover drawing the sun closer. The notes came faster. The sky grew brighter. The sun moved completely above the horizon as the song burst into fullness. The song evoked exquisite sweetness and love. Lichen could not understand the words, but he felt them. A harmony within him coalesced into a celebration of life. A rekindling of the soul at the lighting of the earth. The sun's rays caressed Lichen's face; the music pierced his heart. He felt liberated. Strengthened. Renewed. When the song tapered to an end, Lichen wished it had gone on forever.

The enchantment he felt last night matured. He no longer felt like a visitor. The beauty and serenity of Domus embraced Lichen and he accepted it. "Enchanting," he breathed.

"I couldn't agree more." A man ducked his head as he stepped from the Willow Grove. Lichen turned and met him. His own blue-green eyes looked back at him swimming with sharp intelligence and crinkled with good humor.

The lines that bracketed his mouth only served to remind one of the many times he had smiled an infectious grin or bellowed a laugh from the bottom of his toes. Strength flowed around him, rugged and capable; Q seemed the sort of man who made you think he was able to accomplish absolutely anything he set his mind to and would make you believe you could as well. The amulet pulsed warm beneath Lichen's shirt.

"It's called the Prima Lux."

Lichen looked puzzled.

"The song. It's the Prima Lux. I sing the sun up each morning."

Lichen stared at him. Who sings the sun up? Who sends letters that combust and a coach driven by the conjured powered by six black demon horses? Who gives mysterious amulets and speaks with a gentleman's soft Scottish brogue?

"Grandfather."

Q smiled. "Lichen." They stood, caught in a moment of processing, evaluating.

Q stepped forward and embraced Lichen with a seasoned grip haunted by lost years. Q's black muslin shirt flowed loosely over muscles well-toned and used to physical labor. Black pants hugged his calves and disappeared into spotless black boots making the striking silhouette of a man in his prime.

Silver shot through his long dark hair as a vein in a mine, but unlike Chimera or Agaso, Q's hair was unbound and untamed. Rather like the man.

"My boy. My boy." Both men unashamed of emotion, Q stepped back and looked his grandson up and down.

"Can you ride?"

The exceptional breeding of the horses crackled in the air around them like something tangible: strength, stamina, bearing. Equine perfection. Lichen's glance swept the stables, but he saw no sign of the six black devils that brought him from Weston. From Advena.

Lichen's steed, a misnomer at which Q laughed heartily, was a dappled, well-tempered mare named Futura.

"Ahh, Lichen, do not rush to judgment. She may lack panache," instructed Q, patting Futura affectionately, "but, she's the mother of my bloodline. She's earned her keep and more. She'll be easy with ya." He winked and swatted Futura's rump.

Q's ride, by contrast, was Mars, The God of War, a magnificent specimen at the zenith of his pedigree. Pride of the Manor. He stood at the ready; commanded by his master. By Q. Traitorous energy rippled and skipped along lean muscles urging Mars into action. He glistened blue-black as his polished hooves pawed the ground. Lichen would not have been surprised if flame had shot from his nostrils. Mars was obviously impatient to be off and running. He was born for it. That, and covering the mares.

Mars reared. Q, an expert horseman, stayed firmly seated, together they cut an enviable figure, not unlike Zorro racing off to save his people. Q's unrestrained laugh vibrated with excitement and pride. The stallion trumpeted a loud and commanding objection at the delay.

Futura was not impressed. She stood languidly watching Mars deportment. Lichen, however, thrilled at the primal force of the animal. Mars reared once more and galloped full speed out the gate.

Futura exploded in her own maternal way. Lichen, even with his inexperience, had no trouble remaining seated.

Mars and Q dashed ahead, Q pointing and talking about the land, his face shining. They rode for an hour around the estate. Animals in abundance, long-haired sheep with quizzical vertical eyes, a pair of dromedaries with bovine faces, herds of dark red deer with zebra stripes. Q drew up Mars and put his finger to his mouth. He whistled loud and clear, trilling. They sat for a moment, Lichen expectant, Q waiting patiently. Lichen heard a rush of wind; a gust of dirt blew into his face.

Q raised his arm as sharp black talons gripped and landed. Wings, a yard across, feathered in shades of gold spread wide, flapping to gain purchase.

"There now beauty," Q said. "Settle." The bird folded its wings and rubbed her head against Q's shoulder.

"This is Sator. What do you have today, my sweet?"

Q smoothed his finger down her breast finding a large lump. He tickled Sator's chin and she crooned, somewhat like a dove or a hen singing quietly to her chicks. Sator quickly reached her bill into the pocket on her breast and pulled out a sheaf of twigs laden with seed. The seeds moved in small jerks like jumping beans.

"What is it?" Lichen said.

"This my boy, is the answer to my rodent problem. Blasted scrimpets are getting into the horse feed. Never had issues before this spring. But this will take care of it. You'll see. Sator has been searching for leaenas for weeks."

"Leaenas?" Lichen said.

"Let's just say I now have cats to take care of the rats," Q laughed.

He pulled a dried piece of meat from his pocket. "Here ya go, Sator. You are my pretty." Sator gulped the meat and launched off Q's arm.

"Cats? From seeds?" Lichen asked.

"Ah, Lichen, I know you have a thousand questions. And, you will have your answers. But, not all today, my boy," Q laughed. "Not all today."

Mars reared and jumped a dozen feet into the air, traveled another twenty before landing in the field and dashing toward the Manor. Lichen sat dumbfounded on Futura.

Q turned and yelled, "Don't just sit there, my boy. I'm hungry."

Lichen clicked softly to Futura and gave her a nudge with his knees. She shot forward with unnatural and unexpected speed. Lichen thrilled at Futura's burst of energy. He leaned forward and raised himself slightly above the saddle.

The ground blurred. Wind hit him in the face, drying his eyes. In what seemed like moments, Futura landed with a solid thump, dust, dried grass and leaves whirled about them. A stable dervish.

Lichen caught his breath, looked around, and saw the barn. They were back at the stables. No sign of Mars. Lichen laughed and whooped.

"Futura! You're a sleeper! Wow, what *was* that?" Lichen was certain Futura's feet had not touched the ground on their wild ride home. He galloped her a couple of turns around the paddock, standing in the stirrups, arms above his head yelling with exhilaration. "Woo ha, what a ride."

At breakfast Q was friendly, but formal toward his daughter.

"Beetrum, so good of you to come." He gave his daughter a quick hug. I trust your accommodations are suitable?"

Lichen saw disappointment on Beetrum's face. "Yes, thank you."

"Good, then. Like I stated in my note, I had business at Spes."

"Note?" Beetrum said. But Q looked at Lichen with whom he was obviously enthralled.

"This boy has become quite a young man," Q said appraising Lichen with admiration.

"Indeed," Beetrum responded, a light going out in her eyes like a door closing on a room that would never be entered again.

Q and Lichen became accustomed to riding out each morning on Mars and Futura. Q beamed as he squired Lichen around the New Ivy Quad.

"There's a lot to see, my boy," Q said. "First, we'll explore the Manor and its grounds. That will take a few days. Then we'll catch, the Village and Preserve."

"Aren't there four?" Lichen asked. "Four *quads?*"

"Yes," Q answered. "The fourth is... the Darks."

"The Darks?" Lichen said.

"We'll get to it." Q held Lichen with a steady gaze. "Eventually."

By the time they reached the Village the news of the Ambassador's heir had spread like pollen on the sweet spring breezes. Q introduced Lichen to his crofters; most had been in New Ivy since the beginning: the tradesmen, the farmers, the craftsmen. Most were human, but to Lichen's unabashed joy, a few were Fey. Not faeries with handsome wings like Agaso, but various non-human species that sent Lichen's mind to whirring.

"Faber," Q said as he dismounted Mars. "This is my grandson, Lichen." Futura whinnied a greeting as Faber walked toward them.

"Lichen, this is New Ivy's blacksmith, Faber." The bellows sat deflated on the large stone table; the fire roared with internal energy as if to confirm that this was indeed the blacksmith shop.

Various tools of the trade hung neatly on the walls or lined up efficiently on the table. The tools were huge. As Faber walked closer his size grew more apparent. Lichen froze in the saddle, unable to get a pleasantry past the surprise in his throat. Faber reached Futura, took hold of her reins, and standing flat-footed he met Lichen eye to eye.

Faber said nothing, just stroked Futura's neck with a hand larger than the horse's hoof and glared at Lichen. Lichen couldn't pull his gaze free; his mouth went dry and no amount of will could force a mannerly greeting.

Faber's bare body gleamed pitch black to the waist. Whether natural skin color or soot and grime from the forge Lichen couldn't tell. Black-slitted pupils slashed vertically through yellow eyes. Faber's large bald head seemed directly attached to bulky, thick shoulders.

"Hi," Lichen finally squeaked out, unnerved by the sheer size and presence of Faber.

Q, over six feet himself, barely came to Faber's chest. Faber squinted at Lichen and clenched his jaw, hard and square as an anvil. His muscles bulged, great, knotted swellings under the ebony skin like river rock just beneath the water's surface.

Faber extended his wings, great raven feathers stretched and flexed, enormous shadows blocking the sun at least five feet above Lichen's head. Faber threw his head back and roared, deep and prolonged, not unlike a call to battle in the rocky crags of Viking Scotland. He reached for Lichen, his breath gusting out as from his own bellows. Lichen opened his mouth to yell as Faber's large hands closed around him.

"Welcome," Faber said, his voice rich and smooth as hot oil. He lifted Lichen out of the saddle and sat him gently on the ground. A grin split his face like lightning across a midnight sky.

Q burst into laughter and Faber's hoot tingled in the soles of Lichen's feet. They both laughed, holding their guts like schoolboys until they were out of breath.

"Very pleased to meet you," Lichen said dryly.

Lichen nestled into New Ivy society like a baby bird in the soft down of its mother. He loved the feel of it, the smell of it. It was comfortable and inviting. Everything was as it should be here in a faerie tale land. The baker's wife was round and plump, all smiles and teeth; the milkmaid's skin gleamed like porcelain, her dimples flirting.

The villagers flocked to greet them as they rode in and pressed all manner of gifts upon them; Lichens and Q's saddlebags filled each day. Children and small animals ran with them as they paraded through the crofts, the children singing songs, laughing, and trying to outdo one another.

Lichen fell in love with the ambassador's pride, Spes – the orphanage. Human and Fey, Q's dream.

They walked into the open courtyard in the center of the complex. The building curved gracefully in a circle around a small but striking lawn. Different grasses patched the ground making various patterns with their colors. Tables and chairs scattered in twos and threes invited onlookers to stop and enjoy the garden. As was the case in all of New Ivy, flowers and ivies grew riotously scenting the courtyard with their gentle fragrance.

"It took years to persuade them to bring their unwanted infants here," Q said as he took a seat at one of the small tables and motioned Lichen to sit.

"Where did they take them before?" Lichen said.

Q looked solemn. "To Diaboli Jugulum," he answered, his eyes hard, his mouth set. "The Devil's Throat."

Lichen paled; his breath caught in his chest and his eyes sought comfort in Q's. Lichen's mind flashed an image of babies flailing frantically, their screams begging for their mothers. He didn't know what the Diaboli Jugulum was like and he wasn't sure he wanted to know. Finally, he choked out his words. "Well, I'm glad you have given them an option."

Q understood the look on Lichen's face. "Many in Domus opposed the orphanage, and most still do. But" Q said, " bye the bye. They will come 'round. I have the patience of a rock."

A small girl ran up to Q and threw her arms around his legs. "Q, you're late," she said with a tiny fake pout. Q reached down and without standing hurled her high into the air, laughing. She squealed in a high-pitched, but musical way. Lichen gasped as the tiny girl began her fall downward. Just as she reached eye level, she extended two transparent wings, giggled, and flew around them. "I've been waiting all morning."

"And, good morning to you, too, Miss Manners," Q said, raising his eyebrows.

"Oh," she said, "good morning, Q." She fluttered around them with a soft whirring sound. And, good morning, sir, you are...?"

"Lichen," Q said, "may I introduce Palus, our resident pixie. Palus, this is my grandson, Lichen."

"Hmm, pleased to meet you, finally," Palus said, raising her eyebrow at Q. She buzzed Lichen's head like a large blonde mosquito.

"Palus is our unofficial proctor here at Spes. She keeps an eye on the other children."

"*Other* children?" she said.

"Excuse me," Q said, "but you are *technically* still a child." He looked at Lichen. "What she lacks in size, she makes up for in tenacity." Palus sniffed. "Run along, Palus, and gather everyone in the commons so I can present Lichen in a civilized manner."

Q cleared his throat and whispered to Lichen. "Palus was found in Harrow Bog when she was only a few hours old. Left to die. Probably because she has no toes. Completely unadoptable. Created quite a stir when we took her in."

Lichen listened as the full impact of Q's orphanage struck him. No wonder most of Domus didn't like it. The orphanage flew in the face of tradition. "What do the villagers of New Ivy think of Spes?"

"They're split. But they know the orphanage is here to stay, so they live with it."

"Ambassador." A tall thin man approached Q, his chin extended as if leading the way.

"Mentum," Q said standing up. "My grandson, Lichen. Mentum is the overseer at Spes. Been with me since we opened our doors."

"Assembled," Mentum said, his Adam's-apple bobbing.

"Thank you," Q said. "Mentum is a man of few words, Lichen." As they entered the commons, a group of motley faces stared back in total silence. Expectant. Smiling. Lichen looked from one to another; they were beautiful. They reminded him of colors on a palette just waiting to become part of a painting. From light to dark, shining to dull, each in their way adding to the whole. Lichen felt their childhood innocence, their spirit of light, their hope capturing his heart.

Q bellowed his famous infectious laugh. "Marvelous, aren't they?"

Chapter Ten

Choice

Q continued to squire Lichen around: their days active, their evenings relaxed. They talked, planned, laughed and bonded. Beetrum watched. And smoldered.

Lichen thought he had met every last one of the Villagers and inspected every inch of the Manor. Q promised the Presereve would be next on the tour, but, there was one quad Q failed to mention.

"Why haven't we gone to the Darks? And why do you call it that? Lichen asked.

Q reined in Mars and turned to face Lichen. The sad look in his eyes shadowed the light tone of his voice.

"All in good time, my boy. All in good time."

Lichen could feel his days in Domus slipping quickly by. Like he was in white water headed for the falls. Lichen wanted to see everything before his month was up; it was hard to squelch his impatience. The proverbial clock was ticking.

"What about the rest of Domus, outside New Ivy Quad?" Lichen said. "After all, most of the populace of New Ivy are human. I want to meet some other Fey before I go."

Q bellowed his infectious laugh. "Well, Lichen, this is a human village, after all. Don't worry, my boy, you'll get your fill of Fey at BelMoon." Lichen was not appeased. The famous BelMoon would be here in a few days then he and Beetrum would return to Weston. There were so many things he had not seen, so much of Domus left unexperienced. Why wouldn't Q take him outside New Ivy? And why hadn't they gone to The Darks?

A storm was brewing so Q canceled the morning ride. They had spent a lot of time riding the estate quad and canvassing the village quad, but Lichen still found time to explore the Manor itself. Just when he thought he had seen it all, he discovered a new hallway, a different room, an obscure wing. Lichen decided the Manor was much larger than it appeared. When Q extended an invitation to his library, Q's inner sanctum, Lichen anxiously responded. He stepped through the door and felt like he had fallen down the rabbit hole.

Except for the lighting, it duplicated the library at home in Weston. The ornate furniture, the magnificent desk, the bulging bookshelves, the oversized fireplace. *The clock.* Identical. Cold prickles dominoed down Lichen's spine. As always, the crystal clock drew him toward it. No hands. No numbers. Lichen knew it was nine A.M. 29 April.

Q chuckled. "Extraordinary isn't it?"

"Spooky, actually," Lichen replied. He turned to question his grandfather. Q raised his hand.

"All in goo..,"

"I know. All in good time," Lichen said. Q gave him a good-natured chuckle.

The soft beeswax light in the library illuminated the pages strewn about. Lichen surprisingly adjusted to life without electricity. Q and Lichen bent over a large mahogany library table, the Manor's books and papers spread out before them.

Beetrum's job after leaving Domus was keeping the books on Q's Weston holdings—those holdings being substantial. She sent monthly statements to Domus via a strange little courier. During Lichen's convalescence, he took an interest in his grandfather's business. In contrast to his classes in Ancient Folklore at MU, Lichen had a head for making money. His Air Force experience sharpened his intellect and honed his natural prowess. Lichen's innovative ideas, perceptive strategies, and keen insight substantially increased Q's portfolio.

Beetrum, having never liked her task of minding the store, made full disclosure to Q about who had been the wizard behind the screen. Lichen inherited Q's talent for business. Beetrum had not. Q had vast interests in real estate, manufacturing, and shipping in Missouri. They all burgeoned under Lichen's management. And, since his accident, Lichen spent a substantial amount of time on Q's financial interests.

Lichen's obvious intelligence and business acumen thrilled Q. As he received the monthly P & L reports, he began to hope. And plan.

Q watched Lichen intently and leaned back in his chair. It creaked softly. There was a considerable amount of information to digest.

Lichen studied the rows of leather-bound books. The Weston statements forwarded by Beetrum then Lichen were bound in handsome brown leather. No need to spend time on those. But the other rows of books were new to Lichen and of infinite interest to him. Each set of books was a different color. The four quads were different colors, but trimmed in black: The Manor and Estate: bound in soft taupe calf; The Village: pale green leather—*wonder what animal that is?* The Preserve: dark green; The Darks: brown. The other books were Q's various interests and enterprises like Spes: a soft burgundy; Ambassador: bright blue; Royal Correspondence: purple; Genealogy: black; East Bridge project: yellow.

Lichen read. Studied. Thought. Asked questions. Several hours ticked by and he had only perused a fraction of the library. Cecelia kept them supplied with tea and sandwiches.

"Grandfather, why are you showing me all this?" Lichen asked, his eyes deciphering an accounting of the brick factory in The Village.

The familiar squeak of Q's old chair drew Lichen's attention. Q leaned forward; his eyes fastened on Lichen's.

"Lichen, I want you to stay. I want you to help me with...things."

"Stay? Here in Domus?"

"You are my heir. I need you. New Ivy needs you. And, yes, even Domus needs you. You love the Manor and New Ivy. I want you to love Domus. You were born for Domus." Q paused. "Your mother... well... Even before your father was killed, she wasn't happy here. She wanted to return to Weston. Your grandmother and Beetrum spent summers in Weston. Perhaps I should not have allowed it, but her mother thought it would be good for her. Give her balance and experience she said. I could never say no to Syringa."

Buried memories stirred in Q. He stared at the fire. His body slumped. His face cracked and lined like a riverbed long devoid of water. His hands shook and his eyes glazed and went vacant as a dead bird. Q sighed. A shroud of grief and betrayal lay upon him like mold on a melon. Q never came to terms with Syringa's death and his daughter's hatred of Domus.

He looks old.

Lichen had become accustomed to Q's vitality, but now the very essence seeped out of Q like the fading of day into night.

Just how old is he?

Lichen stood and began to pace. The mantle clock looked on with a disinterested face. "I could go back and forth. Between Domus and home, I mean." Lichen said without heart. He remembered the Bridge. The percussion. The disorientation.

"You could," Q said. "But there are limitations. That's why your stay here had to be at least a month. Holy Grove, your mother would have been out of here the moment she arrived if she could have. It's dangerous to go across more often. Even a monthly trip is not completely safe. Two or three times a year is more advisable.

"I need you here full-time. Can you give it up, my boy? Can you give up your friends, your life in Missouri?"

Lichen listened. Thought. And paced. Life in Missouri. In Weston.

For all these years Lichen had successfully buried any questions about the eighth birthday episode, but a hint of the family secret had driven his curiosity. His medical leave from the Air Force had given him the opportunity to finish his graduate studies at MU: mythology.

This field of study was diametrically opposed to his chosen career path in the Force and an embarrassment to Beetrum. She had been unwilling to discuss the existence of Domus with Lichen and he had been unable to discuss it with anyone else. But Beetrum's reticence was now irrelevant. And, she had recently become engaged to be married so she would hardly miss him if he did not return to Weston with her.

As for friends, well Brent had burnt that bridge. And now Holly and Brent. Their names spontaneously combusted burning Lichen from the inside out. Holly had been his companion, his confidante, his counterpart. Lichen had planned to ask her to marry him. The night of graduation, barely after the cum lauds, they disappeared. Best friend, Brent. Best girl, Holly.

The day after Brent and Holly eloped Beetrum and Lichen received the invitation to BelMoon celebration at the Manor in New Ivy. In Domus. What life back home? The timing couldn't be more perfect.

"Yes." Lichen turned to face Q. "Yes, I can give it up."

Q's spirit sparked back to life. He rose, his face beaming. He gripped Lichen's shoulder. "My boy."

Q's words were cut short as lightning ripped the sky. White light seared the library and a piercing crack of thunder shook the Manor. Q looked out the beveled windows. "We've never had a spring like this," he said, his voice a mixture of unbelief and concern. The clouds boiled as sheets of water slapped the Manor in fury.

A glass-breaking crash came from somewhere in the house.

Chapter Eleven

Cecelia

Lichen sat in the kitchen hovering over steamy hot chocolate. Ummmm, some things were the same regardless of which world you were in.

The nighttime storm had blown itself out like a naughty child throwing a tantrum. But not before the limb of an enormous willow crashed through the belvedere sending water and shards of glass raining down on plants and pots, benches and fountains. Q orchestrated the clean up to which Lichen gladly lent a hand.

When Q enlisted two neighboring trolls, Lichen jumped at the chance to see them; Fey having been in short supply since his arrival.

He wanted the experience of them. Beetrum, on the other hand, went to her room.

The trolls were a fearsome sight. Physically powerful, tall bulky frames with thick, rough skin covered in pockmarks. Sewer breath. One of them had an ear missing, evidence of altercations, brutal and often. "Just clean up all this wreckage and glass and take it to Faber," Q said.

"Umphh," One Ear grunted; his eyes on the floor. Trolls were not prone to conversation.

"When Faber has new window panes forged and built, I'll have you return to install them," Q said. One Ear nodded and began the clean-up. The trolls worked picking up debris shooting covert looks at Lichen between loads. Q and Lichen stepped to the other side of the solarium.

"What's their problem?" Lichen asked realizing the troll's formidable appearance did not cloak a good nature as Faber's did.

"Why don't you get a bite to eat?" Q asked.

"Good idea," Lichen said. "You coming?"

"No, I'd better keep an eye on things," Q answered as he looked at the trolls. Lichen started for the scullery and as he went through the door he glanced over his shoulder. One Ear was staring at him, his troll eyes narrowing slightly, a small curve appearing at the corner of his mouth. A parody of a smile. Threatening.

Lichen sipped another mug of cocoa and munched a sandwich while Cecelia drank her hot nepeta tea. "This is awesome," Lichen said chewing, "what is it?"

Cecelia chattered endlessly reminding him of a bottle of Domus wine that had set too long in the sun. Once uncorked, it took on a life of its own and nothing stopped the flow. Effervescent.

Since Lichen's encounter with Cecelia on his first night here, he had formed the habit of stopping in the scullery each morning before his daily ride with Q. Cecelia answered many questions. Questions a lifetime in the making. She was an amiable soul and an infinite source of information. Cecelia, and Raman when he was here, filled in the gaps about Domus.

"Lacerta," Cecelia answered.

"Oh," Lichen said as he continued eating. "Like, I said, what is it?"

"Water lizard," Cecelia said, watching.

Lichen stopped chewing for a few seconds, digested the information, then continued eating. "Tastes like chicken," he said as he swallowed.

Cecelia was round in stature and face; her soft brown eyes twinkled with kindness. Lichen didn't think he had ever seen anyone's eyes actually twinkle before. Cecelia reminded him of a Raphael cherub. Her tiny white lace-patched cap set askew gray curls springing out in all directions. Cecelia's gentle manner often gave way to her boisterous laugh. Her laugh, as she would say, was a different all-together. It came from a deep reservoir of goodness making the kitchen come alive.

A loud banging noise came from the solarium. "Those trolls are a nasty business," Cecelia said. "If it was up to me they wouldna set foot in New Ivy. But Master Q, well 'e sees good in every soul. If they even 'ave a soul. No' that there aren't good trolls, mind ye. It's just these two are no' among them. Wha' wi' their shifty eyes and the 'ard set of their mouths. Ye can tell a lot from a person's mouth, ye know. Take Brota, now. She's a mild, sweet thing..." Cecelia prattled on about the Manor staff, the trolls forgotten.

"What about you, Cecelia? How long have you been here?" Lichen asked.

"Achhh, yes. I was birthed in Domus. Agaso and me came to work for Master Q straight away when New Ivy wasna more than a whisper. Took to 'im, right off, we did. Yes, sir, Master Q is a different all-together, 'e is. And 'e's mighty glad to ha'e ye 'ere, 'e is." Cecelia's voice grew soft when she spoke of Q. Her devotion was obvious.

Lichen thought of Agaso. And, of the stranger he'd seen speaking with Chimera on his first night in Domus.

"Agaso is Faerie, right? I thought faeries were, you know, small." Lichen held up his thumb and finger with an inch gap.

"Achhh, well," Cecelia said. "Yes, Agaso is Faerie, now. The fact is, my lad, Faeries *are* small." Lichen stared at her. She had the knowing look of one in possession of uncommon knowledge. She squinted one eye and smiled. "An', so are ye."

Lichen creased his brow, uncomprehending.

"When ye cross over the Bridge, 'umans fall under a charm that makes everyone the same size, proportionately speaking. Ye see, that way, 'umans dinna 'ave a size advantage. It makes everyone a little more comfortable wi' one another. And we can all live together, 'appily ever after." At that, she let out a hoot. No one could hoot like Cecelia.

Lichen was speechless. Cecelia eyed him and continued kneading thyme into the bread. BelMoon celebration was only two days off. "Achhh, now, it dinna 'urt much, did it? When ye came across."

Lichen remembered the Bridge. No. It hadn't hurt. Much.

"It's not the same for everyone. Some, like ye, 'ardly feel anythin'. Others, well..." She shook her head.

"Now," she continued. "For the Fey, it's a different all-together. When they cross over to Advena—the human side—they stay small. Unless o' course, they 'ave a charm for it. I dinna knoo of any charms. But, they say there is one. I dinna care to knoo for that matter."

"So, if a Faerie crossed over into...Advena, they would stay faerie-size unless they had a specific charm to make them human-size?" Lichen asked.

Cecelia's hands rolled the dough. Roll and push. Roll and push. Three maids scurried back and forth to the outside oven casting surreptitious glances at Lichen. "Aye," she answered.

"And, you don't know that charm?"

Cecelia's eyes lost their humor. She shook her head, put her hand on her hip, and pursed her lips. She glanced around the room. "Noo and ye dinna need to be learnin' charms either, mister," she said.

"So, do you know any charms, Cecelia?"

"Never ye mind. Ye'r grandfather would serve me up on a platter if 'e thought I be teachin' ye Faerie ways afore ye were ready."

"You mean before *he* was ready," Lichen retorted. "He always puts me off. Like my first night here I saw a Faerie talking to Chimera. They were up to no good, I know it."

"A Faerie? What did 'e look like?" Cecelia asked.

"It was dark..." Lichen described the scene at the stables.

"And ye told ye'r grandfather?"

"Yes, but he acted as if it was nothing. I know they were plotting something. What could it be? And who was that Faerie? Does he sound familiar to you?"

"As long as Q knoos about it, 'e'll take care of it," Cecelia said confidently. "Achhh, I knoo ye're anxious to knoo all about Domus, Lichen. But now that ye are staying 'ere, ye'll 'ave plenty o' time to learn. Master Q wants to wait until ye're mother goes back to Weston.

'e loves her, ye knoo. In spite o' what she thinks. 'e dinna want to rub 'er face in it, so to speak. After BelMoon, now, that's a different all-together. Ye'r education will begin in earnest. Ye will learn every-thin' there is to knoo aboot the Fey. And probably some things ye'd rather not knoo."

Cecelia's mood lightened. She teased Lichen about monsters that ate humans for breakfast. Especially one as good-looking as he was. Or at least he thought she was teasing.

Chapter Twelve

Squamata

Mars plowed through the swamp at full speed. Powerful muscles crushed small trees as they tore through hanging vines. Water sprayed and rooted birds and tiny swamp animals rudely from their sleep.

"Godspeed, my boy," Q shouted. He kept an expert seat, riding being second nature to Q. "They come out of the water at daybreak. We must be in place before the Preserve comes alive."

Lichen galloped behind on Futura. Persistent. Steadfast. She might not be the first one to arrive, but sooner or later she trotted on the scene. No fanfare since that first day. Lichen suspected Q had somehow put the kibosh on Futura's flying.

The moonlight cast its diamonds on the mirrored surface of the water. The swamp temperature remained cool; Futura's breath blew in great puffs surrounding Lichen in fog.

Q reined in. They stood on a small dry rise overlooking Lacertilia Lake. "Quiet, now," he said. "We'll leave the steeds here."

Q walked ahead; Lichen about six feet behind; they made small ripples as they waded into the lake. The lunar diamonds scattered with the ebb and flow of walking. Q stopped behind a clump of bamboo-like lake grass. Fistfuls of skinny green fingers grew from the rocky bottom, white rings circling the joints. Q silently pointed to his eyes and then to the water. Lichen nodded.

Lichen gripped the lance; his fingers growing numb. The longer they stood in the pre-dawn water, the colder it got. He should have had one more cup of Cecilia's breakfast grog. Hot. Spicy. Hearty. Pure magic. Beetrum ruined the morning by demanding Lichen not go into the swamp.

"We must go after the scaly devil," Q had said. "He's killing the stock. We can use the meat and the hide. Besides I hear Lichen likes lacerta sandwiches," he said with a mischievous grin.

Q turned to his daughter, his mood darkening.

"Why can't you ever give an inch?" he said. "Holy Grove, we are just going hunting." Beetrum left the kitchen in a huff, her back ramrod straight.

Lichen's leg had not given him any trouble since his arrival even in the cold water of the swamp. He didn't know what was in Cecelia's liniment, but it would be worth a fortune in Missouri. Lichen had no reason for the absence of pain prior to the application of the liniment except for his high endorphin output.

plated armor along the muscles of his back, then trailed muddy brown down his tail.

He towered over Lichen and stared down with hungry viper eyes. Only his wings were small and ineffectual. The carnivore. Lichen took a lame look at his spear. Yes. He should have taken the blue one.

"Remember the spot," Q shouted. His voice laced with exhilaration. He relished this encounter. "The spot. You know, the spot."

The spot. Yes. The spot.

Lichen took a firm grip on his lance. The lizard advanced, unafraid. Lichen stood his ground, undaunted. The lizard roared again and lunged at Lichen. Lichen ducked and tried to step aside but his feet moved slowly in the water. The lizard caught him in the ribs, tearing away his shirt as Lichen squirmed loose.

The pain in Lichen's chest awakened a primal instinct. He gripped the spear with both hands and thrust it at the scaled face. The lizard turned slightly causing Lichen's weapon to glance off. The spear jerked from Lichen's hands and landed harmlessly in the water. Impotent. A giant claw swiped at Lichen pushing him beneath the water. Lichen struggled but the creature held him firm against the rocks. Lichen reached for the knife strapped to his belt. The lizard squeezed the last remaining air from Lichen's lungs.

Lichen slashed his knife across the lizard's foot as it raised him up out of the water in its mighty grip. Lichen saw the mouth, open and waiting for breakfast. His carnivorous breakfast. As the claw clenched Lichen and moved him toward the teeth, Lichen stabbed the knife driving the point home. Into the spot. The only vulnerable spot in the 20-foot lizard body. The ear.

Lichen's legs were in the mouth, the teeth just beginning to pierce. The creature stopped, stood still, then slowly collapsed into the water.

The claw relaxed. The jaw relaxed. Lichen pulled himself away and stared at his knife buried to the hilt sticking out of the lizard's head.

"I think I'll be having a sandwich," Lichen panted as he planted his foot on the creature's leg partially submerged in the lake. "Plus boots *and* a coat.

"Well done, my boy," Q shouted. "Well done."

A rider tore through the underbrush, heedless of the overhanging branches. His monstrous warhorse thundered, sending sprays of water flying in sheer waves across the ferns. The giant stallion bellowed as he half flew, half galloped across the swamp, his mighty green-black wings reverberating, keeping sync with the wings of the rider. They rode in tandem, as one.

Mars's head came up snorting; responding with a roar of his own. Loud and fierce.

Searing pain shot through Lichen's head. A ruthless hunter. Searching. Probing. A cruel penetrating lance of blackness. Lichen felt as if his head would burst wide open and spill his brain onto the lifeless Squamata at his feet. In seconds the pain was gone leaving Lichen dazed. Q looked at him curiously.

"Greetings," the rider called as he reined his horse to an abrupt stop in front of Q. His clothing shimmered green and earthy as the forest. His wings were great black-green shadows held high above his head, parallel to his horse's outstretched wings. The blade of his sword reflected jade light into Q's eyes.

"Valeo," Q said in a low cautious voice, his eyes slightly squinting. "Patrolling The Preserve, I see."

"Doing a bit of *hunting*?" Valeo raised an eyebrow. "The Preserves are Kings Grounds. Lake Lacertilia belongs to the *King*." His words were like a finger exploring an old scar.

"Indeed," Q said. "And we have the right to hunt a stock killer." Q jerked his head toward the lizard, iridescent blood floating, swirling on the water. Valeo sat imperiously on his mount and flicked water droplets off his cape as he would vermin. His stallion reared his head, eyes wild and feral. His long mane waved across a wide face as he screamed into the mist. He stomped his massive hoof and sent water splashing into Q's face.

"Yes," Valeo said with half a smirk. He adjusted his seat on Gravis and glanced at the dead lizard. Anger smoldered in his eyes. "The stock killer," his lips curling tightly around the words.

Q took note of the weapons hanging from Valeo's saddle. "Looks like you are doing a little hunting yourself."

"Just doing my duty," Valeo replied slowly his eyes scanning Lichen. "And you are?"

"Forgive my manners," Q said. "Valeo, may I present my grandson, Lichen Ipse. Lichen, this is Keeper Valeo Nox. He is the overseer of the King's Preserves."

Valeo looked into Lichen's eyes. "So this is the long-lost grandson." A villainous query slinked into Lichen's mind. This time Lichen instinctively slammed the gate and stopped the pain.

"Ah, yes. He is your grandson," Valeo said as he felt the mental barrier. "We shall meet again." He nodded his head ever so slightly towards Q, flapped his wings like a strutting rooster, turned his horse, and sped away. Gravis's whinny echoed through the forest. Mars answered. Challenging.

"The Keeper? Lichen said remembering Ram's tale.

The Kings Keeper. Only three know the location of the Bridge. The King, the Keeper, and Q.

"He... violated my mind."

"I thought so," Q said. "I have known him many years. He is not to be trusted. Be on your guard." Q whistled for the horses. "Let's get this beast home."

Lichen felt the black probe in his mind. Laughing.

Chapter Thirteen

Amicus

The Manor was never still. Something or someone was always about. Not that it was distracting or annoying; you could usually find a niche to sit and relax; lose yourself in a private world of your own making.

Lichen walked down a hallway one afternoon, just for curiosity's sake, exploring yet more of the Manor he had missed on other excursions. He heard a most ribald and cacophonous racket coming from a wing he had not known existed. He looked around and over the balustrade for someone, anyone, to inquire as to the nature of the riotous carryings-on. The ivy rubbed against his hand affectionately.

"Hello, anyone there?" Lichen looked down the hallway with slight trepidation. Curiosity overcame reticence. He walked three doors down the corridor and immediately determined that whatever was making the noise was coming from this room. Lichen stood transfixed, listening to the snarls and growls, yips and woofs overlaid with a high-pitched crooning tone. The hair on his neck rose appreciably. He knocked and there was mmediate silence from within.

"Who is it? Who's there," inquired a voice graveled with irritation.

"It's Lichen." Nothing. No response or sound whatsoever. Why was it so silent now when it had been so loud just moments before? Lichen knocked once more.

"Oh. Ah .... Lichen, one moment, please."

"Grandfather?"

"Um, yes. Well, do come in my boy."

Lichen opened the heavy door cautiously. Anxious yet wary. Midway over the threshold, he froze, his mouth a cavern of silence.

"Well, don't just stand there gaping. Since you found me, come in, my boy. Come in and close the door. You're getting quite adept at negotiating these hallways. I was going to introduce you after BelMoon, but never mind. This is as good a time as any, I suppose."

Lichen took one step into the cold room, closed the door, and stood transfixed. There before him were Q and three ... three... Well, for lack of a better description, he would have to say small dragons.

"Close your mouth, my boy, before you drool. Aren't they beauts?"

Lichen's heart stopped and raced concurrently.

"Yes, yes. They are... beauts. But what are they? They look like, umm, little dragons."

The dragons in question were sitting lined up like firedogs in front of the hearth quietly watching Lichen. No sign of the boisterous behavior heard moments before. Their eyes were dark, deep pools of jet. Bright. Intelligent. Their ears long pointed and laid back close to their heads. They were approximately all the same size. Q stood beside them; their heads coming to his waist.

They had definite dragon characteristics. Horns on top of the head and a small horn on the nose. Long pointy eyebrows. Chin whiskers. Scales of the most striking, vibrant, dizzying colors.

One was varying shades of iridescent blue, soft meadow greens, and primrose yellows. Another, jet exhaust red, scorching orange, and burning sun amber. The third vibrated with deep rusts, earthy chocolate browns, and burnished copper. Tiny spikes ran down their vertebrae. Lichen wanted to run his finger over them like a keyboard.

Claws, clipped short and neat. A long tapered tail capped on the end with a small arrow. Like little devils. And the most wondrous of all... wings. Wings folded angelically as they sat in perfect stillness. Watching Lichen.

"Well, yes and no," said Q with hesitancy. "They are not quite dragons. They're drogs."

Lichen tore his eyes from the magnificent animals and looked at Q. "Drogs?"

"Yes, drogs." Q walked to the window; his hands clasped behind his back. "They are the only ones of their kind." Q turned and looked at the perfectly behaved trio with affection. "They were born and bred right here at the Manor."

Lichen stood as though he had grown roots. The shock of seeing the small dragons in the Manor began to dissipate. Excitement welled within him as he studied the creatures. They were marvelous beyond belief.

"What do you think?" Q asked. He watched Lichen closely, squinted his eyes, and waited.

"Well, I..." Lichen took one step forward. The drogs simultaneously stood up, raised their scaly hackles, and emitted low menacing growls. Their ears stood upright; their mouths open slightly.

"Stop!" Q ordered.

Lichen obeyed. Three sets of black eyes bore into him; he felt a cold chain slithering around his legs and chest. He couldn't breathe.

"Not you, my boy. I was speaking to them. You see, they are trained to protect. They perceived you as a threat."

Q commanded the drogs to sit. When they relaxed, Lichen's legs regained movement as the invisible chains slipped away and the death grip released his lungs. He gasped for air.

"Yes, well, sorry about that, Lichen. They are not used to anyone else being here. Continue to walk into the room, slowly, my boy, slowly. Just walk toward me."

Lichen carefully walked towards Q. His eyes on the drogs; their eyes on him.

"Well, what *do* you think?" Q's admiration of the animals apparent.

"Awesome," Lichen said softly. "Epic."

Q broke into an infectious grin. "Aren't they?" he beamed proudly. "They're not babies, they're two years old. I've been training them since they were hatched."

Lichen looked at Q. "Unbelievable. Marvelous. Magnificent."

"Sit down, my boy, and I'll tell you the tale." Q stopped short of rubbing his hands together and chuckling, but it was obvious he was bursting to tell the drogs' story. Two worn leather chairs faced the fireplace as if expecting a show. Q took one and Lichen sat in the other. Q flipped his hand and the drogs dropped to the floor beside him. Q smiled knowingly at Lichen.

"What?" Lichen said. Q looked toward the corner of the room. There in the shadows sat number four. A head taller than his littermates, the last drog sat watching, waiting.

His sleek magnificent head remained perfectly still, his eyes never leaving Q. Q moved his fingers ever so slightly. The drog leapt up, came forward, and sat directly in front of Lichen, staring up at him. The drog looked over at Q as if in inquiry.

Q's eyebrows furrowed; his head tilted. "So. You've chosen," Q said to the drog. "Hmm, a bit unexpected, but all right." With surprising resignation, he looked at Lichen. "I hope you're ready for this, my boy." With a barely perceptible flick of his fingers and nod of his head to the drog, Q acquiesced.

The sleek black creature turned his gaze back upon Lichen. Lichen looked into those inky depths and lost his mental footing. His head began to swim. Together they swirled, Lichen and drog. Through time. Through space. Alone, together. Blackness surrounded them; their eyes locked. Around and round at a dizzying pace.

Suddenly a flashing black light combusted, and they were bound. The drog and Lichen. Lichen could feel the drog within. And the drog felt Lichen. Separate, yet not. Fused. Hearts beating in sync, blood flowing in tandem, thoughts pulsing in concert. Lichen could see through the drog's eyes, the drog through his. One.

The black light expired as quickly as it had ignited. They were back in the room, but the drog's presence remained a part of Lichen.

Q stood up. Shocked. His face was white, his hands trembled. "Oh my. This is remarkable."

Lichen tore his eyes from the drog and looked up at Q. He felt... transformed.

"I never expected that to happen so soon," Q said. He walked over to the black drog. "So, that's the way of it, eh?" The drog stared at Q.

"Amicus," Lichen said. "His name is Amicus." At the sound of his name, Amicus looked back at Lichen. Lichen smiled. "Yes, that's the way of it."

Chapter Fourteen

Lorelei

"I know what that feels like, trapped and cold," the voice said.

Lorelei had dosed or feinted. She didn't know or care, which. Her body encased, immovable. Undines were cold-blooded, but Lorelei knew this was different. This sucked her life force like some great frigid, yet fiery vacuum that left her weak and senseless. Lorelei wavered in and out of consciousness and had long since lost any will to struggle.

At first, she had used her undine instincts. She tried to *be* water. To flow out of this bitter, steamy muck that entrapped her. But, even as water, she didn't go anywhere. She couldn't move. She was trapped. In her panic, Lorelei thrashed about; regardless, the acid bog held her firm. Unrelenting. Unyielding.

Did she really hear a voice? Was it in her mind?

"Yes, you did hear a voice," it said. Mocking humor resonated in the words. "Yes, it is in your mind."

Lorelei's attention jerked. "Who's there?" she asked.

The voice laughed. "Does it matter, my little fish? The point is I am here. And I am going to get you out. That is, if you want out."

"Yes," Lorelei shouted. If one can shout in their mind. And, if it could be called shouting in her weakened condition. "Yes, get me out of here. I'm dying."

"Not so fast. Who put you here in my wasteland, in this stinking bog? Is someone punishing you? Have you been banished?" the stranger said.

"No, no," Lorelei thought. "It was an accident. It was just an accident."

"And, will you repay me for my kindness, water baby?" he said.

Lorelei felt darkness swirling around her once more. She knew she was blacking out again. "Please, please help me. Yes, I'll repay you. Somehow, please...." Her conscious mind slid over the ravine into silence.

Lorelei felt swirling and dizzy, and her stomach heaved. She rose off the bed and gagged into a pan that sat on the floor. Nothing came up. Just painful spasms, over and over, as if her insides were ripping apart. Her head split with pain. Red, fiery blotches and streams ran up and down her skin covering her entire body; angry welts burned and throbbed. Lorelei fell back onto the bed exhausted.

"Achhh, I see ye are awake." A stout woman waddled toward Lorelei. Violets and blues pulsed in the air with each step, ebbing and flowing as she walked. Her hair curled out around her head golden yet pink like a kinky burnished sunset over a river.

"Poor little dear. That's good noo. My name is Lemna and I'm 'ere to take care of ye. I knoo ye dinna feel verra good, but ye will. In time, now, girlie. Just rest. Ye'll be fine noo."

Lorelei tried to speak, but her parched throat closed around the words.

"Dinna talk now, girlie. Just rest." Lemna patted Lorelei's face with a damp cloth that smelled of grass. Lorelei thought she looked like a diminutive frizzy sun goddess. Maybe she was. Lemna refreshed the poultices that covered Lorelei's entire body.

"Ye're goin' to be just fine. I promise. Close ye're eyes now me little bairn. Rest noo."

"Where am I," Lorelei croaked. She tried to concentrate, but the cool soothing herbs on her skin lulled her into half dreams.

Lemna looked at the poor lassie on the bed and shook her head as she stirred the pan of herbs with her fingers. Exchanging energy.

"What does that madman want wi' this poor wee nymph?"

A harsh painful stab shot through Lemna's head. The herb water splashed onto the stone floor.

"I told you to call me the instant she awoke," the voice shouted in her mind. "Fools, I am surrounded by fools," he said.

Lemna felt her head being squeezed as between two rocks during an earth tremor. Grinding pain. He didn't want or expect an answer, so she gave none.

"Must I do everything myself?" he enunciated clearly, precisely, as he appeared in the doorway.

The black hat pulled forward and down allowed the wide brim to cover half his face and throw the rest in silhouette. The swirling cape floated around his knees, more shadow than substance. “Get out. Get out now,” he sneered.

“She needs these ‘erbs,” Lemna said firmly. “’er condition is serious; she could still die.”

Lemna planted her feet and stood stubbornly beside Lorelei’s bed. The black-clad man struck Lemna across the face with the back of his gloved hand. She fell across Lorelei’s feet, her substantial girth compressing her breath in a huff; her violet glow faded like a dying ember.

“You healers. Always think you’re better than everyone else. Lot of good it’s done you down here, *teacher.*” He spat the words at her like darts, poisoned tipped. “Well, don’t worry,” he laughed. “You’ll have your star pupil before too long.”

Lemna paled. Her mind barriers clinked into place as his vile thoughts assailed her.

His expression hardened. “Get out,” he shouted. “Get out, witch-pig. And take your stinking potions with you.” He picked up the fallen pan of herbs and threw them out the door. Flying bits of remedies.

“Wake up, little fish. Wake up, now,” he crooned as he took hold of her shoulder. Lorelei, shrouded in poultices, pulled away from the painful touch and groaned.

“I know you can hear me. Open your eyes. Open them this instant.”

Lorelei tried to force her eyes open, they felt weighted, and the effort lasted only a moment. The figure above her bed looked distorted and twisted. She tried to speak a thank you, but she could not form the words.

“You’re welcome,” he said. His voice smarmy and counterfeit. “Do not try to talk, I can hear your thoughts. I want to see your eyes.”

Once again Lorelei struggled to open her eyes. She saw him, dark and blurry standing above her like she was lying on the bottom of a riverbed looking up through the flowing water. Her savior.

"Thank you," she thought. "Thank you for saving me. Who are you?"

He looked into her eyes, all aquamarine and deep. He saw eternity forward and backward spiraling around and around. Time as far as you could imagine swirling like an eddy in the river. He smiled.

"So, you *are* an undine, just as I thought." He bent over Lorelei, holding her gaze, not wanting to lose his connection. "Teach me," he said to Lorelei's mind. "Teach me the Song of the Undines."

An overpowering stench assailed her and once again she retched. His link with infinity snapped. She reached for the pan, but as before, nothing came up; she closed her eyes and collapsed back onto the bed. Lorelei felt him retreat from her and knew he was angry.

"I'm sorry," she thought. Thinking took much less effort than speaking. "I've been doing that a lot."

"No matter," he said. "You will grow accustomed to me. The odor is a symptom of my affliction. And I can mask it to a certain degree just as I can alter my appearance so as not to pain my acquaintances' sensibilities. But I prefer my natural state. It keeps me in touch with who I am and reminds me of my goal. Part of my goal is to learn the Songs. All of them. You will teach me yours when you are better."

"And who are you?" Lorelei asked again.

He paused before answering as if deliberating. At length, he spoke out loud instead of in her mind.

"You may call me Latere," he said simply. "I, too am of the water. We will talk more later after you have regained your strength."

"How can I repay you?" Lorelei thought. She struggled to open her eyes. "You have saved my life. I am indebted to you."

Latere looked into those blue-green eyes, felt the soothing coldness of the water, comforting waves, the hypnotic motion of the river grass.

"Yes, yes you are," he said and turned and left the room.

Chapter Fifteen

Betrayal

Q and Beetrum used their mutual affection for Lichen to navigate their relationship. She interpreted Q's cool attitude toward her and responded in kind. Beetrum camouflaged her disappointment. She couldn't wait to return to Weston. And Ronald. She felt the engagement ring, loose on her finger. She'd lost weight. After BelMoon. Yes, after BelMoon she and Lichen would leave this heathen place. She would return to Ronald.

Beetrum turned the diamond to the top of her finger. She loved the ring; it was her ticket to normalcy; her safeguard to a world where people walked instead of flying and plants were just plants. She certainly wasn't madly in love with Ronald.

Not like Linum, Lichen's father, whom she tried not to think about. But she did care deeply for Ronald. And he loved her. Ronald said he would take care of her. She would never have to think about Domus ever again.

Of course, Ronald didn't know about Domus or faeries or notorious weird rivers that changed course on a whim. He thought her father was in Europe. Not in some heathen godforsaken land where you talked to the trees and sang the sun up each morning. If Beetrum had any compunction regarding Ronald and the truth, she buried it. Deep.

Q had requested a meeting with his daughter in the library.

Lichen reached for the lion's-head knob on the library door. His hand stopped mid-air. The door stood ajar, conversation filtering through the crack. He knew he should not be listening, but the words trapped him. He felt like a hare mesmerized by Q's enormous hounds. He knew he should run, but couldn't move.

His grandfather's voice was controlled and steady. His hallmark. Anger punctuated his words.

"I said, I've asked Lichen to stay in Domus."

Lichen stood rooted outside the library door unable to move. He had not told his mother about Q's offer. Or about his response.

"You what?" Beetrum said, her tone incredulous. "You can't be serious. I'm not leaving my son here."

"He's my grandson," Q replied. He stood tall and unmoving. His morning coat impeccably tailored; his demeanor likewise. "When do you plan on telling your son the truth?"

The truth? Lichen puzzled standing motionless outside the door.

"You're out of your mind." Beetrum said ignoring his question. "You are out of your mind," she repeated somewhat louder emphasizing each word with maternal sharpness. "You can't just take over his life. He's human and he's going to live in the human world."

Q looked at his daughter. His resolve hardened. "I'm human," he replied icily. "New Ivy is a human village. Practically everyone here is human, or partly so."

Beetrum laughed. It was a hollow sound echoing from an empty place.

"Here?" she said with sarcasm. "You call these people *human*? They've lost any resemblance to humans."

Lichen looked through the slit of the open library door. The lion's-head knob grew damp beneath his palm. Beetrum walked briskly to a chair by the window overlooking the grounds and sat down to compose herself. He'd seen her do it many times. Her hands rested in her lap, her breathing slow and steady. She told him this had been her favorite chair as a child. The gardens stretched leisurely across the estate, beautiful and soothing. They calmed her. The gardens had a similar effect on Lichen.

"Tell me, *father*, why do you prefer Domus to your home in Weston? This *inhuman world* of faeries and other despicable creatures. You could have come back. But you chose to remain here. Here in this, this pagan place."

"That's enough." Q said. "I know quite well what you think of Domus. The time is past for you to understand this people, this land. Me. But the time is just beginning for Lichen. His place is here. His future is here. With me."

Lichen saw his mother's face blanch. The last visage of her hope melted.

"Your invitation for me to come here was a ruse," Beetrum said. "You don't want me, you never did. You want Lichen. Well, you can't have him. We're leaving." Beetrum stood and moved toward the door.

Q stood his ground. He stepped between his daughter and the door.

"Beetrum, be reasonable. I can show Lichen another world. Another way of life. Domus is unique. Lichen can have experiences he never imagined. Do not deprive him of this. It's his heritage. For once in your life, think of others. Don't let your bitterness destroy Lichen's chance."

"Chance? Chance for what? Disappointment? Death? He doesn't need that," Beetrum said. "I'm taking him home." She reached for the door.

"He's already agreed to stay"

Beetrum stopped. "I don't believe you."

Lichen opened the door. Beetrum looked at him and stood like a bird, frozen mid-air.

"Lichen?"

"Mother, I've been trying to find you." He glanced at Q.

"Oh, no. It's true." Blood drained from Beetrum's face.

"Mother, please. It won't be forever. I'll visit. You'll visit."

Beetrum raised her head. She stood plumb-line straight. Lichen thought she looked like a little soldier. She walked past him and up the stairs; the clicking of her heels emphasizing her stony silence.

It was well past midnight, but the stables were a beehive of activity. A BelMoon invitation to the Manor was coveted, only 500 were issued. Three times that many would have come. Q had been sorting the marriage requests for months. It was a privilege to be married at the Ambassador's Manor. BelMoon was a fire celebration of life and fertility. For people. For crops. It was a sacred time for nuptials. Earth moved. Branches felt the caress of tree sap, stirring. Seeds felt their young within, struggling. Young lovers felt fire, burning. Life was beginning. Again.

Beetrum went to the stables and found her way to the coachman's bunk, she'd been there before. He was cleaning the harnesses, applying the oil with a tenderness he never showed humans.

"We'll be leaving tomorrow after the celebration," Beetrum said. He paused in his ministrations to the leather. Beetrum thought there was something off about him, but then there was something off about all the damned.

"*We?*" he said not looking up, continuing his task.

"Y...Yes," Beetrum said. She must not lose her nerve. This creature was a servant, nothing more. She must be firm and confident. "Lichen and I."

"That's not what I hear."

Curse Chimera. Why is he always so difficult?

"Well, that's why I'm here. I need a... favor if you will. A discreet favor."

The coachman smiled. A chilling smile. His favors were expensive.

"Anything for you. Ma'am," Chimera purred.

Chapter Sixteen

Reception

Lichen looked in the mirror. *Who is this man*? Tan. Muscular. Smiling. Shirtsleeves loose and flowing. No zipper in the pants. Who would of thought he could get used to that? And his leg, apparently healed. No sign of that nightmare fall from the sky.

In the month since his arrival, his hair had grown and he queued it back with a ribbon—very unairforce-like. Lichen put his foot on a stool and ran his fingers around his boot. Squamata leather. What a fight that rascal had put up. Big one, too. A twenty-foot lizard is big regardless of what Q said. Lichen threw back his head and laughed. Long and deep.

Holy Grove, as they say in Domus, I'm happy.

Then he heard them coming across the bridge. Noise. Lichen looked out the window and saw hordes of small children. Laughing. Crying. Wings flapping about like excited finches. Barking dogs running to and fro like deranged yo-yos. A mélange of unidentifiable creatures veiled in a swirl of dust.

Horses, mules, and other mysterious beasts of burden neighed, brayed, and nickered their way up the road dumping steaming deposits as they came. Scoopers followed in their wake yelling crude jokes. Wagons of rosy-cheeked peasants with arms and wings thrust about one another in jovial abandon. Carriages of festooned ladies and elegant gents. Sentient creatures of every conceivable size and color. Beautiful. Grotesque. Two wings, four wings. No wings.

Trolls by the score. Drab gray-green skin freshly scrubbed for the occasion but somehow still grimy. Pushing. Scowling. Quarreling. The entire lot looked as if they could descend into a sensational melee at any moment. A large dour fellow led the troop. Lichen looked closer, squinting to focus his vision.

One-Ear. The ragged troll grimaced as if he could see or feel Lichen and continued on his way. That troll made Lichen's skin crawl. He didn't like him or trust him. Why does Q even let him on the grounds? Lichen would have a word with his grandfather about it.

In the next moment, the troll and his foul disposition receded. Faeries. The top of the mythological chain as far as Lichen was concerned. An ethereal procession of light coming into New Ivy. Just across the River the faeries in flight landed and walked over the bridge in accordance with the village ordinance. The Domus equivalent to the no-fly zone. The human population of New Ivy could be persnickety.

The faerie gentry came in magnificent coaches embellished with flowers; live butterflies swirling above them. Sedate ladies sat across from their husbands, hands and wings folded demurely. Drivers flicked their whips with an elegant tap on their horses' rumps.

Behind them rolled humble buggies rigged with streamers and bells pulled by draft animals painted with swirls and circles. The faerie men sang in rich baritone, their voices mingling with the general confusion of the procession. The women reprimanded children in a good-natured way, swatting their behinds lightly.

Two perfectly matched Pegasus with golden bridles emerged from the covered bridge. Their white luminescent skin shimmered in the sunlight. Powerful wings held aloft as they clipped along in flawless unison. They pulled a magnificent cabriolet that emitted soft sensations. Of color? Of music? Of scent? Perhaps all.

Flowers covered every inch of the carriage as if they had grown from the wood in full bloom. A gentle indigo blush wafted behind them suffusing the air with lavender hues and faint floral aromas.

The driver dressed in white and gold stood holding the reins, chariot-like. His white wings extended; he was a perfect match for his Pegasus. A distinguished couple sat lower in the coach, two young women across from them.

Lichen leaned toward them, straining to see the maidens more clearly. One dark and one light.

"Beautiful sight, isn't it?" Q said. "Your door stood ajar," he said by way of apology for intruding.

"Breathtaking," Lichen said not taking his eyes from the girl with the jet-black hair. "I've never seen anything so beautiful." As the carriage drew nearer Lichen could see that it was *she* who emanated the indigo vibrations. They floated up and into the window surrounding him. Confusing him. Suddenly he felt very hot. She looked magnificent. The breeze was caressing her hair. That black, black hair.

Q followed Lichen's gaze and cleared his throat.

"Yes. Yes, she's beautiful, too. That's Isabella Fae Duco, daughter of Princeps Sapien. He is the Princeps of Ecclesia the State religion of Domus and the head of the Animus Consillium the governing body of Ecclesia. He's our spiritual leader if you will. He is second only to the King in authority."

Spiritual general of the faerie.

Lichen was glad those Latin courses came in handy in Domus. He'd have to ask Q why the Domus language was filled with Latin.

"So, if the Princeps is second only to the King, why doesn't he know the location of the Bridge instead of the Keeper?

Q's eyes narrowed; his brow drew together in concentration. He sighed as if a heavy weight lay upon his soul. "That is another story for another time," he said and changed the subject.

"Isabella is a caduceus, that is, she will be. That's why she is surrounded by lilac hues. It's a sign of a healer."

Lichen suddenly remembered the lilacs that grew outside his bedroom window in Weston. "I love lilacs," Lichen said. "And I've always been teased unmercifully for it. There is a great stand of it growing outside my bedroom window in Weston. It's always relaxed me."

"I know," Q said.

Changing the subject, he continued. "They come from all points in Domus. I always host one of two BelMoon celebrations and the King hosts the other. All species are invited, of course. But I am especially interested in the faerie-human relations." He studied Lichen.

"The orphanage, you know, it helps to unite the cultures. I hope to live long enough to see the two worlds living in trust and peace."

A diplomat to the core.

"Yes, trust and peace," Lichen said absently. Isabella's carriage was nearly out of sight.

"You must stand in the receiving line with me today, Lichen. Come, our guests await."

Q and Lichen walked across the thyme lawn to head the line. Lichen looked down the hill to the stables. Chimera was standing apart from the throng, looking back. There's another one that made Lichen uneasy. All that cold, frosty attitude. The bloodless conjured.

Beetrum walked up behind them.

"You look fabulous, Mother." Her simple damask dress became her. Light. It moved gracefully with the breeze. Her hair was down, flowing across her shoulders like a dark river. She looked relaxed. Perhaps she had come to terms with him staying in Domus.

"Thank you, my noble son," Beetrum said. She smiled and gave Lichen a most royal curtsy. "See, I haven't forgotten how things are done in Domus."

Lichen was surprised but glad to see his mother in good spirits for once. Probably because she planned to leave soon, then she'd be with Ronald. The reason didn't matter; to see her calm and smiling did his heart good. He loved her even though her perpetual cold demeanor had kept him at arm's length his entire life. Perhaps that was why he couldn't wait to get to Domus. To Q. To find warmth. Love.

The receiving line for guests wound under a beautiful grove of willows. Lichen could see the large majestic BelPole in the garden. A giant Silver Fir tree represented the birth of a Divine Child. It was sheared of its branches and stood resplendent against the sky. It dominated the horizon. Flowers abundantly woven around two circles near the top filled the air with heavenly scents. Multi-colored ribbons wound tightly around the tree and tied in a bow at the bottom, like a dazzling gift. One tug at the ribbon's end released the mystery of the dance.

Lichen flushed slightly. In his dissertation for his masters, he had termed the BelPole dance as old-fashioned and provincial. A meaningless ritual that empowered the rich and lured the poor into hopeless dreams of somehow changing their status. His paper's explanation was a far cry from this elaborate celebration.

However, Cecilia had schooled him in the way of proper BelPole dancing. Lichen thought he knew the history, but Cecilia knew the traditions, the old ways, not the book ways.

"Achhh, ye may think ye know aboot the BelPole," Cecilia had said. "But the actual dance is a different all-together. It's like courtin'. In the beginnin' ye're shy and flirtatious. Ye build a relationship. Ye explore. Ye venture into the unknown. Ye'r overtures grow bolder. She will either accept ye or reject ye. If she submits, then later that night, ye dance again at the Adoleo."

Lichen listened intently. This wasn't in any of the textbooks.

Cecilia continued. "The Adoleo will be lighted at dusk. Now, that my sweet is when true love, if i'tis there a'tall, will be ignited. If the BelPole dance is like courtin', the Adoleo dance is like reachin' into ye'r soul and discoverin' ye'r eternal mate."

"Lichen," Q said again. Louder. Mildly irritated at Lichen's inattention. They stood in the reception line greeting guests.

Startled out of his reverie, Lichen looked at Q.

Q cleared his throat. "*I said*, I'd like you to meet Princeps Sapien Duco and his wife Coxi. They hale from Vinca Village."

Lichen clasped the extended hand. Sapien's modest blue robe did not properly illustrate his great authority. Only the King wielded more power. The Princeps governed the vast number of congregants of

Ecclesia and ruled over the powerful Animus Consillium. Yet this unassuming man was warm and friendly. Understated dominance.

"Lichen, it is indeed a pleasure. Your grandfather has told us so much about you. I understand you studied us at your University." Sapien's eyes twinkled. He wore good humor easily.

"Sir, the pleasure is all mine. Welcome to the Manor. I look forward to our discussions. I'm sure there's more to The Fey than myths written in great tomes can tell," Lichen said.

The two young women Lichen had seen in the Pegasus coach accompanied Sapien and Coxi. Yin and yang of The Fey. One was light and luminous. The other dark, powerful, and mysterious.

"May I introduce my daughter, Isabella Fae Duco, and my niece, Skye Pudor. They will be graduating at Iter. Top of their class," Sapien said as he stepped aside.

Lichen felt ambushed by beauty. Isabella stepped forward, her hair black as the bottom of a well in which he plummeted, down, down... She extended her hand and curtsied ever so slightly. Lichen took her hand and lightly touched it to his lips. Protocol. Her skin was soft and smelled of lilacs. And violets. And lavender. Hades, he didn't know. He was thunderstruck.

"Isabella Fae," Lichen murmured. "Delighted."

That hair.

Isabella's slight build uncharacteristically emanated strength and sirenic mischief. Her cambric shift flowed and swayed as if alive. Fine white linen embossed with a hint of purple hues caressed her every move, and her scent, her fresh, clean scent drifted around them. Alluring. Her hair, the color of lost conscientiousness was wild and primeval. It escaped its bonds with long black tendrils reaching for freedom; Lichen wanted to capture and tame them.

Sapien nodded and smiled at Q. He was quite used to Isabella's effect on men. Skye smiled as Lichen gave her a perfunctory welcome. She was quite used to Isabella's influence on men as well; she didn't like it, but she was used to it. As the Ducos walked on, Isabella glanced back at Lichen. A flame ignited. A BelMoon fire.

Curious. None of them had wings. Lichen would ask Q about it later.

Lichen greeted a long line of guests, but it never grew tedious as his desire to see wings was abundantly granted. Full feathered and robust; downy soft and airy. Unornamented. Membraned and austere. Embellished and teeming with ornamental ephemera. Lichen saw every kind of wing conceivable, and some that weren't. Daily jaunts with Q around New Ivy were great but only served to tantalize Lichen's curiosity. The few Fey he had encountered had been exciting, sharpening his desire to experience more of Domus. Q had promised longer excursions after Beetrum left for Weston. Lichen's impatience gnawed like a scrimpet. He was anxious to get on with this life. Too much time had already been wasted. Time was flying like he was in a free-fall. That's ok. He had the rest of his life to live. In Domus. To get to know Isabella Fae Duco.

That hair.

The receiving line grew short. Representatives of the Royal Court were always last. In Domus, the end of the line symbolized the last word in authority.

"Lichen," Q said, "it is my honor to introduce Her Royal Highness Princess Phyta Colere from Regnum, our Royal City and you remember her escort, Keeper Valeo Nox."

Lichen formally greeted the Princess. Her royal presence was overshadowed by the haunting melody of Isabella, playing repeatedly throughout his mind and body.

The Princess was older than Lichen expected. Her pale hair swept up with a tiara that seemed to overwhelm her delicate features. Her soft yellow wings held close to her body like a timid songbird's. Cloudy blue eyes veiled sadness as she smiled and extended her hand to Lichen. He took it lightly, kissing the air above it. She trembled.

"Your Highness," Lichen said. "It is my great pleasure to meet you." She had an underlying fragile quality. Lichen felt protective of her. Loyal. Her reticent graciousness stood in stark disparity with her escort. Valeo Nox, The Keeper.

Being the younger, Lichen waited for Valeo to extend his hand, as custom dictated. Valeo was clothed in his traditional dark green of the ancient forests. Forests dense with trees a thousand years old and a canopy impermeable to light. His small cape draped melodramatically over one shoulder with the Keeper's Royal Seal prominently displayed. Raven-green wings held high above his head in a conspicuous display of virility.

Exhibitionist.

Valeo gripped Lichen's hand, hard. "Nice boots," he said.

Lichen grinned, squeezing Valeos hand. "Just a little something I picked up in the swamp."

Foreign strands of villainy groped and searched Lichen's mind. Once again a serious breach of etiquette. Lichen's defenses in place, the probes withered.

Valeo's expression hardened. "I hope your stay in Domus has been...memorable. I wish you a safe journey home tomorrow. You must visit us again sometime."

"Yes. Memorable," Lichen said. "In fact, so memorable I won't be leaving."

Valeo's smile froze.

"Yes," quipped Lichen, "I've decided to make Domus my home." Valeo dropped Lichen's hand.

Beside him, Lichen's mother stiffened. Valeo shifted his gaze.

"Beetrum," he nodded curtly toward Lichen's mother.

Beetrum offered her hand. "Keeper," she said. Their eyes met briefly. Lichen watched as unshielded hatred flared from them both.

What was that about? Of course, his mother knew Valeo, she had lived here before.

Valeo bowed over her hand but did not touch it.

He turned to Q. "Q, old friend. We will talk later."

Chapter Seventeen

BelPole

Isabella Fae went in search of a drink. She felt very warm despite the cool spring breeze, dampness clinging to the back of her neck, tiny rivers running down her spine as if they were quite anxious to be on their way.

She was slightly out of sorts and wasn't quite sure why. It had nothing to do with the intense way the grandson had looked at her. What did she care about him, she didn't even know him and didn't particularly want to. She was just thirsty. And, curious about the spring.

Her spirits had been high this morning as she and Skye dressed for the BelMoon celebration. This year they would be going to the Ambassador's Manor and both girls were quite affected. Usually they attended the King's BelMoon soiree, but Isabella's father had declared they would be going to New Ivy in honor of the Ambassador's grandson; even the Princess would be in attendance.

Isabella wasn't interested in Q's newly arrived relative one way or the other, she didn't care about, nor did she have time for men, but she was delighted to finally get to see the Manor. It was famous. Ambassador Q was famous.

Isabella's father came to New Ivy quite often in his official capacity of Princeps and he and Q had become quite close over the years. But Isabella wasn't concerned about any visitations that did not relate to her herbal studies so she had never come along. She found trips whose sole purpose was to exchange pleasantries quite tedious and great time wasters; there were so many other things that had to be done, so much botanical information to study and memorize, countless medical theories to think about and apply. Tertius, her graduation, was not far off and she had much yet to learn.

Skye always chided her for not going when she had the chance. She did not understand why Isabella would pass up an opportunity to see the beautiful New Ivy and meet the famous Ambassador. But then, Skye was a social being who loved being around people and seemed to gain even more vitality just by immersing herself in their midst.

The Manor was known for a great many things one of them being its astonishing spring. The water ran clear, cold and nurturing, but there was one element that continued to elicit the attention of the populace and cause any number of riffs among them during an evening at the local pub. The spring was *enclosed.* This was unheard of in Domus. Even when the Earth Mother blessed a new quad with water from the Great River Potens and occasionally gave the village a spring, it shocked the entire land when a spring allowed walls to be built around her, enclosing her.

Some say the Manor is blessed, others swear it is cursed and that they have seen evil specters circling the New Ivy quad during full moon. Isabella's mentor, Lemna, had taught her of the unusual spring and affirmed that the spring was indeed a blessing. She told stories of its healing properties, of its ability for soothing even the most excited of patients and of reviving those who slip into unconsciousness.

Lemna said the Spring's Song of The Deep could envelope one with the most sensational feelings of well-being and allow recall of any memory regardless how long past. Of course, it was up to the Spring, she could bless or not according to her pervading mood; merely sipping the water did not preclude automatic bliss.

The sweet and heady concoctions on the buffet did not appeal to Isabella, not today anyway. Mountains of rich food piled high and wide along the tables almost made her swoon just looking at it. She had sampled the many fresh greens of urtica, nasturtiums, alliums and enjoyed the sambucus and lonicera gelatos all from the Manor gardens and admitted they were exceptional.

And, the roasted burbirds did smell delicious, and on another day she may have been tempted, but, her stomach churned and food was just annoying her further; her mission was to find the spring. Water. She really did just need a drink of water.

She was not seeking out the spring because, well because she was curious. She was not trying to get a glimpse of, what was his name, oh yes, Lichen. Where had he got to anyway? She entered the scullery where Cecelia eyed her with a slight proprietary air.

"Well, 'ello there. Lost are ye?"

"Oh, hello," said Isabella. I'm sorry to intrude. I'm looking for a drink of water. I know you're busy, but I didn't see any outside and I'm quite warm." Her skin flushed a most becoming shade of rose. She waved her hand back and forth in front of her face, the indigo aura fluttering in silky waves.

Cecelia took in Isabella's presence and muttered to herself.

"'ere, please sit doon," she said, eyeing the girl carefully. "I'll get ye the sweetest water in Domus. I'm Cecelia, the ManorMother."

"Oh, please forgive me. My name is Isabella Fae Duco. My father is Princeps."

"Yes, weell, that explains it," Cecelia said her voice losing its edge. "Nice to meet ye. Ye'r father visits the Manor occasionally, but I 'aven't seen ye 'ere." Cecelia took up a pitcher; condensation beading the surface like a little jacket and poured a drink. Isabella squelched disappointment at the water having been already drawn from the spring.

She drained the glass. "Oh, this *is* good. It lives up to its reputation. Thank you so very much. It's nice and cold."

Cecelia refilled it. "Yes," she smiled. "The spring gives us cold water in the summer and warm in the winter." Cecelia stood watching Isabella, the indigo hues swirling and dancing around her like vapors off the river; she nodded ever so slightly. "Ye look a might piqued, lassie. Are ye feelin' alright?"

Isabella felt a little light-headed; what in holy grove was the matter with her. "I'm just a little warm," she said putting her hand across her forehead.

Cecelia thought a moment, then looking as if she had made up her mind she said, "Feel free to rest in 'ere awhile." She motioned to a cot in the Spring room. "I assume ye've been through the reception line already?"

"Yes, I have."

Did Isabella just blush? "Achhh," Cecelia nodded with understanding. "So ye've met the grandson," she continued with a knowing look.

Isabella knew Cecelia noticed her discomfort; Cecelia seemed the sort to never miss a thing. Lichen's impression on Isabella had taken her by surprise. She was not interested in men. Not even charming grandsons with crooked smiles and piercing blue eyes that made you feel as if you were looking beyond the heavens. She had plans. She had goals.

"Are ye quickenin' this year?" Cecelia interrupted Isabella's thoughts of Lichen.

"Yes, I am finishing Tertius and will graduate at Iter. I've studied to be a caduceus."

Cecelia nodded her head knowingly, her gaze fixed on Isabella. Isabella squirmed under her scrutiny. "Weell, that's a different all-together," Cecelia said. "Achhh, yes indeed, that's wonderful. We need more 'ealers in Domus, yes we doo." Her voice grew anxious. "Terrible times when even our 'ealers are no' safe."

"Yes," Isabella said. "My own tutor, Lemna, disappeared two years ago." Isabella looked at Cecelia, anger and grief shining in her eyes. "She mentored me all my life," Isabella said. "She inspired me, and most of the time pushed me beyond the pale. Lemna believed in me. She was more than a teacher." Isabella's throat thickened, but her gaze on Cecelia remained strong.

Cecelia nodded her head again. "Yes, Lemna. An extraordinary caduceus, a good woman," she said very slowly, staring at Isabella. Cecelia's expression heightened as if a secret had snaked its way into her thoughts. The silence grew uncomfortable.

"Achhh, weell," Cecelia continued. "New Ivy's caduceus was the first to be killed five years agoo by the Pavors. Then they went village by village, quad to quad seekin' out 'ealers and curas, torturin', slaughterin' until at last, they found the Solis." Cecelia sat down as if the weight of the memory was too much to bear. "Worse than the plague i'was. Terrible, terrible time."

"My Uncle Ira was elected Kilotax of Vinca Village right after that first caduceus murder," Isabella said. "He tells about joining all the village Crioсts together to hunt and capture Pavors. It was a great tragedy for all of Domus when the Solis was murdered. Lemna was heartbroken, yet she refused to go into hiding."

"Achhh, yes, I remember when she disappeared," Cecelia said sadness tugging down the corners of her mouth like a child on a willow branch. "They caught many o' the vermin but 'oo knoos 'ow many escaped. And, the leader was ne'er caught, the black devil. 'is gang o' murderers ne'er gave 'im up. Though, I'm no' soo sure they even knew 'is true identity.

"Soo, anyway, it's BelMoon, a new beginnin'. And Iter 'tis no' that far away. The people are always glad to 'ave new young blood come into the practice of 'ealin'. I can see the 'ealers mark a floatin' around ye like the Great River Herself."

"Yes, it's all I've ever wanted to do," Isabella said. "Of course, I'm looking forward to getting my Crystal and Totus Vita at Tertius. I'll admit to being a little nervous. I mean, I've always feared that my Vita has something in it that would guide me to a different vocation. Being a caduceus is all I've ever wanted. Even when the Pavors were hunting them down." Isabella stopped talking. She couldn't believe she was yammering on to Cecelia. She hardly knew her.

"Achhh, yes. Weell. Ye're a natural-born 'ealer, ye are. I kin feel it. Your kind is few and fewer. Those that seek out the 'ealing profession for other reasons, weell, that's a different all-together. But, ye, lassie, ye have the mark aboot ye, now. I wouldna worry none about what's in the Vita. Divus, the Creator knows ye're a 'ealer, lassie, after all, He made ye what ye are."

Isabella felt comfortable with Cecelia, relaxed, and perfectly at ease. She'd nearly forgotten her original goal, to see the spring.

"Now, ye just come on in 'ere and rest a spell," said Cecelia. She waved toward a small room at the back of the kitchen. Isabella stood in the doorway enthralled with the blue-green energy floating around the room. It was beautiful.

"The spring will get ye right as rain before ye knoo it," Cecelia smiled and went back into the kitchen.

Isabella walked over to the cot looking all inviting and comfortable. It nestled near tall, plump rosemary bushes covered with tiny blue flowers in a little nook. It smelled heavenly and reminded Isabella of Lemna's cottage. This was indeed a magical room. Her father's account had not begun to describe it.

The stone spring room extended from the kitchen and encircled the mouth of the spring with ancient arms of rock stacked waist high. The top half of the walls was translucent; light streamed in from every direction as if bringing the best of news.

All manner of herbs grew around the spring: Baneberry with its red, black, and white clusters of berries, calendula in full yellow bloom with a green border and orange stamen, tiny peppermint with red veins, purple parsley, and bronze fennel.

The heady smell reminded Isabella of her own herb garden she had inherited from Lemna. Perhaps Cecelia would exchange starts.

Ivy, the unofficial mascot of New Ivy, grew along the top of the walls. Isabella had heard tales of the Manor's ivy and wondered if it was an exaggerated story perpetuated by the bards. The spring water's constant temperature kept the kitchen cool from Windluna to Harvestluna and warm from Bloodluna to Stormluna.

The spring flowed out of its main pool, through the cress, and down a little waterfall, then along a tidy rock bed veined with thyme that led under the wall and outside. The design was quite ingenious. Q was known for his genius.

The spring not only supplied the Ambassador's household with all the fresh water they needed but apparently, there were additional blessings. Rumors had it that Ambassador Q knew the name of the spring and had learned The Song of the Deep. If he did, he could petition for anything he wanted. Isabella doubted if this were true. It seemed a little extreme even for the Q.

Isabella nestled down in the soft cushions; the gentle gurgling lulled her into that place that was neither asleep nor awake. It felt so cool. She was so tired. They'd left Vinca Village before dawn to come to New Ivy. She'd spent most of the night studying. There were only a few exams left before Floraluna break. It would be nice to be finished with that part of her courses.

During the remaining time before Tertius Isabella would study outside the classroom; she had been looking forward to this for lunas. She would travel all over Domus collecting specimens and preparing medicines.

Sapien built Isabella her own dispensary on the grounds just beside their Willow Grove. She used to play there as a girl and pretended to be a great healer giving Skye any number of foul concoctions. Skye was not always a willing patient.

Isabella had used Lemna's herb room and gardens for two years, but now it was time for her own. Sapien had planned a spectacular herb garden surrounding the dispensary with any number of swirls and twists. Ian, the Princeps own personal troll and gatekeeper, had been busy planting all spring. By the time Tertius came and Iter was over, the herbs would be flourishing and her dispensary would be all hers. She would be a caduceus.

Isabella drifted further into that hazy, relaxed place. That defenseless place where reality shifts and the unreal becomes real. She saw Lichen. He smiled, radiating that sensual warmth she felt in the reception line. It cocooned around them holding them close, intimate.

A sinister presence rose and hovered over them. Dark. Cold. It descended with razor claws and rapier beak, screaming. Lichen held her close, shielding her and she felt his heart hammering against her breast as if signaling safety. Isabella tried to call out, but her throat closed.

"Isabella." Cecelia shook her shoulder. "Are ye all right little lassie? Ye was thrashin' aboot mightily."

Isabella sat up. Her head throbbed. What nightmare had she seen? She couldn't quite remember. "Yes, yes, I'm fine. But, I think I'll have another drink of water."

Isabella looked toward the bubbling spring. Cress and lilies floated on the surface and ivy vines grew down the rock and trailed into the water. She had the strangest sensation that someone had been watching her or watching over her, she wasn't sure which. Isabella shivered. The spring flowed gently on, unconcerned.

Lichen walked the entire grounds. Unsuccessfully. He was not looking for Isabella Fae; he was being a good host. It was his duty to mingle and speak with the guests, to meet the citizens of Domus, to learn about the Fey.

He did not encounter Valeo and was relieved. He wasn't sure if he was avoiding Valeo, or if Valeo was avoiding him. Keeper or not, the man was sinister, and Lichen didn't like him. He got under your skin worse than glider worms. Lichen wasn't sure what glider worms were, but according to Faber, they were to be avoided at all costs.

The afternoon wore on, the sun traveled across the sky marking time. People were beginning to pair off, some first-timers to the BelPole were shy and hesitant, other veterans knowing who and what they were after, primal instincts already stirring them to action.

Lichen nodded to Skye standing across the yard looking at him. Where the devil was Isabella? He intended to dance the BelPole with that woman and was quite sure he wouldn't be the only suitor.

"Aren't you going to dance?" Q walked up beside Lichen. "It's a tradition, you know. Someone must represent us. The Manor. For good crops and all." He gave Lichen a gentle shove toward the BelPole circle. Lichen smiled a half grin and started down the slope.

The flutes began first, calling, luring the dancers. A slow, haunting melody struck a chord of memory. Had he heard that tune before? Q gave a short soliloquy that only slightly touched on the eternal nature of the dance and let loose the ribbons.

They fluttered through the air like seductive feathers of a great bird, each ribbon a spectrum of color, from light to dark. Two of every hue, companions, printed with spiraling Ogham letters. A violet ribbon floated by Lichen, wrapping itself around him, choosing him. Lichen caught it and looked around for its mate. Skye started toward him, but he looked up and saw Isabella on the far side of the circle, laughing, her arms in the air, the ribbons breezing by as if flirting. She looked radiant. Lichen couldn't take his eyes off her. A violet ribbon, identical to Lichens, brushed across her cheek and as she took hold of it she turned her head and saw him. They were paired. Skye turned away.

Cymbals joined the flutes, beating a pulse measured and steady. Lichen bowed his head slightly toward Isabella, his eyes not leaving her face. She walked like a goddess and stood beside him. The dance began. Slowly, Lichen moved in tune, the beats of the drum pulsing. His entire body began to flow with ethereal currents. She danced beside him, close but not touching. Very close. Excruciatingly close. Unbearably close. Their eyes remained locked, their feet moving in sync while lava coursed through him burning its way. He was wordlessly asking. Silently courting. It seemed like they were alone in the circle, the other pairs having danced into their own private realm.

They wove their ribbons to the music braiding their passion tightly, one around the other. In and out. The drums beat; the flutes sang. Under and through. Around and around. Sweetly pitched the music rose to pursue a love not of this world. The braid was almost complete. They were almost there. Lichen must have Isabella or he would perish.

Then the dance reversed and all was lost. The ribbons unwound as their steps took them in opposite directions, a great and ugly gulf opening up between them. Lichen felt as if his very life ebbed away; as if she was his breath, his blood. She danced farther and farther away, their strands of violet color fraying from one another.

Panic surged through Lichen as the gulf between them grew ever wider. Beads of sweat trailed across his body, the breeze felt cold and foreign, his breath stopped and tiny dark dots pricked beneath his eyes. The music became his enemy as the tempo carried Isabella across the circle away from him as if she were a float bobbing in the ocean.

All grew still as if caught in a painting. The dancers stood mid-step, halted as still-life captured perfectly by the artist. The trills from the flute and beats of the drum hung in the air like little black notes resting between measures.

Lichen held Isabella with his eyes, drank her as if she was sweet wine, tasting her very essence as she became a part of him. He did not need air to flow through his lungs or blood to pump through his heart, he only needed her.

The music became the force of life, composing their movements, orchestrating their steps, creating a sonata for them alone. Lichen came abruptly to the knowledge, slammed into it as one does the wall in running. The dancers came to life moving to the music as if nothing extraordinary had happened. Shocking comprehension shot through him as the revelation took hold, impossible as it was. He loved her. And, he would love her forever.

The pace quickened and the others intruded on their sanctum. The music played gently at first, starting slowly. Wooing once more, bringing them closer, winding their ribbons ever tighter. The music played faster, its frantic pace propelling the dancers, their hearts pounding until they stood breathless before one another, ribbons now plaited to the end.

Lichen's chest heaved as he caught his breath causing his amulet to rise and fall as if it moved of its own accord. Its golden beam transfixed Isabella like a beacon to a ship on the shoals. He held his ribbon tightly, the back of his hand touching Isabella's. Desire had given way to exhilaration and a grin spread across his face.

Isabella looked up at Lichen her eyes shining, her breath quick and shallow. She handed him her ribbon, the two ribbons now twined as one; she turned and sprinted across the yard.

Lichen stood holding the ribbons looking after her. This was, without a doubt, the most extraordinary thing he had ever experienced.

He looked forward to the Adoleo later that night.

Chapter Eighteen

BelMoon

The song of the flutes filtered in the window as Beetrum watched the BelPole dance. Filthy and heathen. It was disgusting that's what it was. Look at them. No shame. No sense of decency. Her father was beyond hope. She knew that now. How many years wasted, waiting on Q to come home? Waiting on him to be the father she wanted. The father she needed.

Beetrum clutched the heavy brocade curtain, crumpling it in her fist. She saw Lichen and Isabella dancing. Look how that little tramp lusts after my son. I know what she's after. And her father a priest of some sort to a heathen god. The filthy witch. Well, she wasn't going to get him.

Lichen leaned his head toward Isabella, caught in the spell. Beetrum recognized that move. Just as the ribbons were entwined. Just as two became one. She remembered. Beetrum's heart raced when she saw Lichen's expression when he looked at Isabella; she had seen that look in his father's eyes.

Panic congealed in Beetrum's throat. She couldn't breathe. Isabella was Fey. Lichen could not fall in love with a Fey, Beetrum simply would not allow it. Her resolve strengthened like cement changing into a hard unyielding substance. Domus would not claim him. Q would not claim him. Beetrum would stay the course and follow through with her plan.

Lichen may hate her, but she knew he would come round in time. She was more than willing to take the risk. Beetrum packed her bag and went to the stable, changed her clothes, and waited.

It was full dusk. Isabella stood on the fringe of the Adoleo fire. It crackled and popped as it searched for fuel. Isabella couldn't believe the feelings that rippled through her, the thoughts that assailed her. What had happened at the BelPole? Her world felt upside down as if Midgard himself were shaking it between his powerful jaws. She wasn't sure, she was conflicted. She felt as if she must dance the Adoleo with Lichen. And feel his arms around her and lose herself in his eyes. But Isabella also knew she must not.

She knew of the special blessings of BelMoon, of course, it was possible to become paired, but not likely. Knowing it had been possible had not prevented its hold upon her. She did not want to fall in love. She had intentions for her life. She was going to be a healer and travel Domus. Not a wife. Not in this life and certainly not forever.

Perhaps she had imagined the BelPole encounter. Perhaps Lichen's effect on her was only a result of the dance, the music. Perhaps she had not slipped into eternity and felt the most exhilarating, exciting moment of her life. Perhaps the grandson had not looked into her eyes and transported her to heaven.

As host, Q gave the annual Adoleo blessing. He was slightly annoyed that Lichen was not with him.

"Tonight we give thanks for all our sustenance from Divus the Divine. All that has been given to us, and all that will be given to us. We ask for blessings on our homes. Our land. The harvest and the hunt. Our children. Our love.

"May you dance with single-mindedness and focus, but also with amare—fire and passion. And those of who you are paired, dance the Adoleo with a love and commitment forged to last throughout the worlds to come in eternity.

"May the Earth Mother yield her bounty. May love yield children. May our barns be full, our larders overflow, our pastures teem with stock. May our hearts beat with compassion. Our minds allay our differences and seek out similarities. Dance for our future. Dance for Domus."

Q gave the signal to begin. The drums beat low and slow. Long-time partners who had joined years before started the dance, followed by the new BelPole pairings. Last were singles. They wanted to dance. They needed to dance. Singles searching for forever love.

Isabella stood at the edge of the circle. Her eyes cast down, her heart racing. She should run. She should turn and race back up the hill as fast as she could go. She had imagined the pairing. Her feelings were only the result of Lichen's eyes holding hers, of his arms encircling her body, his breath upon her cheek.

Surely her commitment to healing, a gift given to her by Divus was her life's purpose. How could that be if she gave in to this powerful force pulling her toward Lichen? Isabella felt as if she was being pulled apart at her very center.

Had he felt the pairing, too? Who was he, really? She didn't know this outsider from Advena. Just because he was the Ambassador's grandson didn't mean he was honorable, just, and true. She had plans and he did not fit into them. She'd only known him a few short hours, it's impossible to have fallen in love with a stranger.

The drums became louder, faster, quickened by passion. The fire grew, the flames fiery ardent fingers reaching, calling to the moon, full and ripe. Isabella walked the perimeter around the happy couples, scanning the grounds for a glimpse of him. Perhaps he would not come at all. Perhaps he had felt nothing at the BelPole.

Isabella spied her parents dancing, lost in one another as if alone in the galaxy. Skye danced solo, flirting and laughing, the steps meaningless, just another social rite to her.

Round the fire they went. Swaying, turning to the music. Most of them committing to one another for time and eternity. Bare feet beseeching the Earth Mother for favors: good crops, plentiful harvests, fruitful stock. Hearts imploring Divus for blessings: children, faithfulness, honor.

Where was Lichen? Had she been mistaken? Perhaps he had not felt the fire within. Perhaps they had not been paired. Perhaps he was being the diplomat, the Ambassador's heir. After all, he was leaving soon. Isabella sat down on the cool grass and closed her eyes. She felt the Earth Mother below her, around her. The Earth responded to the vibration of feet, the pounding of hearts. The Adoleo fire roared, the dancers' hearts soared.

Isabella didn't try to sort out her confusion about Lichen. He didn't show up and that was that. She let herself go, her thoughts floated into the air, swayed with the music. She felt the blazing heat from the fire on her face and arms. At her very center, she felt it, rising becoming intense and scorching. Torrid, passionate. Amare.

It was more than physical, it was transcendent. Unbound by Earth Isabella's spirit rose in response to Divus, the Creator beckoning. She began to weep with the sheer magnificence of it. Never had she felt so much Love, such Tender Caring, and Sublime Compassion. It tingled on her skin, then dived to her very core. Divine Affection surrounded her, upheld her, embraced her then placed her lovingly, gently back on the ground.

As Isabella opened her eyes, she knew. Lichen was hers and she was his. Nothing else mattered. Divus had a plan.

Round and round the dancers moved spiraling fervently around the blistering flames lost in their private Amare. Where was Lichen?

An unearthly roar came from the Manor, fierce, powerful, piercing the revelry of the dancers. Isabella jerked up and looked toward the window. Lichen's window. Somehow she knew it was Lichen's window.

Amicus had been sleeping in Lichen's quarters since his bonding with Lichen. Although old enough to bond, he still required the sleep of a pup and lay snuggled in Lichen's robe at the foot of the bed. As if a lance had pierced him through, Amicus felt the sharp pain of separation. Lichen was gone. A mournful bellow came from deep within his chest. Amicus felt bewildered, hurt, and angry.

An agonizing scream came from the stables and floated up the hill gaining momentum. Isabella turned toward the stables, puzzled. Cecelia ran break-neck up the slope from the stables, her skirts ballooning behind her, cap askew, hair sprung wildly in all directions. She paid no heed.

"'elp me. 'elp. 'e's dead," she sobbed.

Isabella leaped to her feet, falling in step behind Q as they ran down the slope. Cecelia pointed toward the stables and Q kept running not stopping to question Cecelia further. Isabella was a good runner, but she could not keep up with the Ambassador. A black fireball jumped from Lichen's window yelping and howling, half flying, half running streaked past her and loped beside Q.

Isabella reached the stable just as Q knelt beside the body and gently turned him over. Life bubbled out of the slit in his throat making tiny gurgling sounds. His eyes were anxious. Isabella bent over him and laid her hand over the wound, pressing. She feared it would not be enough.

"Old friend, do not speak," Q said. Agaso grasped Q's hand, his grip hard and desperate. As Q put one hand behind Agaso's head, he struggled to speak forcing out one word, harsh and raspy.

"Lichen."

Isabella went cold. Agaso collapsed as something fell from his fingers. A small gold talisman with three circles and a tree, tiny crystals twinkling from the branches. Isabella stared as Q picked it up and put it in his pocket. Lichen's pendant.

Amicus burst into mournful howls as if his little dragon heart would burst.

Q sat in the library, his old leather chair holding him tenderly. Keeping her own grief at bay, Cecelia had prepared him her special brew, but the tea sat cold and forgotten.

Sapien Duco stood in front of the fire searching the flames for answers, they were cold. No answers tonight. Not even for the Princeps. He had sent his family home and Skye with them. Isabella was distraught and close to panic with worry for Lichen and Sapien had ordered her straight to bed with a double dose of valerian. She may be the caduceus, but he was the father. He hoped Coxi would take her daughter in hand and see to it she obeyed his instructions. Isabella had a headstrong temperament and Sapien had seen the BelPole dance; he knew she had paired with Lichen. He knew the depth of her worry.

Q and Sapien sorted their thoughts in silence, a comradery born of years floating between them. People milled around the grounds shocked at the murder. Shocked at the interruption of the Adoleo. This had never in the history of Domus happened before. What did it mean? Would the Mother yield for them this year? Would their crops wither and blacken with blight in the fields, their lambs sicken and die in the womb, their hunters and foragers fail to find meat or nuts or berries? What did it mean?

Women whispered fearfully to one another envisioning a cold hearth, an empty larder, and hungry children. Men shook their heads with ominous foreboding. Who could have done such a thing? Who brought this calamity upon them?

A thorough search failed to find Lichen anywhere on the Manor grounds. It had also failed to find Beetrum ... or the carriage...or Chimera.

Q was furious. He wouldn't admit Lichen had fled. Not yet. Not yet. And who could have killed dear Agaso?

Sapien walked over to Q's desk. "Q, the Criocts will be here shortly. They will need to question all of us."

"Yes, I know. I want this scoundrel found." He thought of Agaso. Dear loyal Agaso. What the devil was he doing up at the stables? He must speak with Cecelia about it.

"Q," Sapien said. "Lichen ... where do you think he went? Is it possible he went back to Advena?"

"I don't know." Q fingered the talisman in his pocket. "Sapien, Lichen did not do this; I know he didn't. I must find the one responsible, and I will."

"I believe you, but the Criocts..."

A loud pounding on the library door interrupted Sapien. Q stood up and saw the lion's head knob turn slowly.

Where the devil was Lichen? And where was his blasted daughter?

Chapter Nineteen

Death

Lichen's head hurt. His head, his neck, his shoulders.

What the ....? He groaned.

"Be still darling," Beetrum said. She held a wet cloth to his bleeding forehead. "Don't move, Lichen, you're hurt."

"Where are we?" Lichen's voice was hoarse. He pushed his mother's hand away jerking off the cloth. Spots moved behind his eyes off and on like a computer cursor. He sat up and blinked to clear his vision. Blood red cushions. Doors with no handles. The gentle sway of a moving carriage. Realization of his location bolted him fully awake.

"Holy grove. Mother? What have you done?" His throat felt raw, his jaw was throbbing, and his head continued to bleed.

"Lichen," Beetrum said, her voice and manner condescending, "lie back now. I needed to get you away from there, don't you understand? They were blinding you. You'll see that when we get back to Weston. Back home where you belong."

"You! You hit me?" he said rubbing his jaw. "You kidnapped me?" He stared at Beetrum, not wanting to believe it.

"Home?" he croaked. "Home?" he croaked louder. He beat the side of the carriage leaving bloody fist marks, stamping the walls with desperation.

"Stop this carriage," he shouted. Lichen pounded faster and harder. "Stop this carriage you bloodless bane."

"Lichen, quit it. You know he won't stop the carriage. Now, just try to relax. Here, put this cloth on your head."

"Mother, how could you?" He slapped the cloth sending it flying into Beetrum's face. "How dare you."

"How dare I?" she said, her voice escalating. "How dare I?"

Golden spears slashed across the green of her iris. Her pupils grew large, gapping, and bottomless. Delirium bubbled like pus from deep and long-festered wounds.

"I dare because they destroyed him. They destroyed him and his beautiful ropes." Beetrum buried her hands in her hair, and tears of grief and anger exploded from her eyes. She started rambling and grabbed Lichen's shirt.

"They killed him, Lichen. They killed him." Madness contorted her features. A stranger's face. "He was good and kind. And good and kind. He was good." Beetrum let go of Lichen's shirt and wiped her tears smearing them across her face.

She has lost her mind.

"But not you. No, they couldn't get you. Because I ran with you. Yes, I did. I took you and I ran. Just like tonight. Yes. I took you and ran."

Beetrum's voice faded as she slipped into silence. Lichen felt blind-sided, ambushed by his own mother. He must get back. He had to get out of this coach.

"I smell brownies," Beetrum said her expression suddenly looking like a girl, her voice child-like. "I smell brownies fresh from the oven. The coach knows. The coach always knows how to calm."

Lichen smelled apples and relaxed against the cushions. How was he going to get out of here? Wait until he got his hands on that driver, he would never turn loose. How had Beetrum ever persuaded Chimera to kidnap him? How had this happened? Isabella Fae. He must get back to Isabella.

"Delta." By force of habit, Lichen used the NATO phonetic Alphabet. But, if any situation warranted swearing, it was now.

"Delta." He just couldn't do it.

The light in the coach dimmed. The carriage began to sway and Beetrum lurched across the aisle, slamming into Lichen's chest.

"What's happening? Lichen said as he caught his mother in his arms. She was quiet, docile. She did not answer him.

The coach lurched again, and the light went out. Beetrum screamed through the darkness like a knife slicing through pitch, the blackness closing quickly after. They began to hurl and heave as if caught in the forces of air or water. There was no light and now there was no air. Lichen felt as if he were suffocating, his chest moving in and out but there was nothing there to breathe. They were tossed to the ceiling and back to the floor. A macabre dance. Lichen felt for the talisman under his shirt. It was gone.

Beetrum rallied. "Go home, Lichen," she gasped, clawing for air as she reached for Lichen. "Home to Weston. You'll be safe."

The carriage split in two as if cleaved with an ax. The horses screamed and launched piteously off the Bridge. Horses and driver disappeared like bubbles popping in the air. The carriage halves toppled over the side of the Bridge tumbling end over end like a pair of dice. Lichen thought of his parachute that hadn't opened, the free-fall to oblivion.

Not again.

The mind is a curious creature with a strange sense of its mission. His leg had just healed, now it would probably be broken again. No thought for his life, no horror of falling to his death; just a single thought about his leg.

A tumbler of fear, the carriage halves splintered into The Great River Potens, lusty and deep with spring rain. The wind whipped the freezing water into a frenzy. The River swallowed the broken coach, cushioning its descent to the bottom like She was putting a sleeping child to bed.

Lichen reached for his mother as they fell, the water dashing her from his grasp and onto the pointed rocks beneath the Bridge.

"Mother," he screamed. "Mother."

The wind and water drowned his words and thrust him ashore. Lichen landed on his stomach in the mud just beyond the rocks. Blood plastered his hair across his face. He looked back at his mother's broken body. The rocks twisted the angle of her head, her eyes glazed with a cold blank stare. The horror of it paralyzed him.

Lichen laid his head on his arm and prayed it was a dream. To whom did he pray? His mother's god or Q's? Were they the same?

He began to shiver, and his teeth knocked together, chattering like an old crow with her dying breath. The mud beneath him felt cold and soft; he let his mind slip away.

Lichen opened his eyes and saw the moon. The full moon. Bel-Moon.

Isabella.

Lichen felt Isabella's breath softly on his neck, her hand in his. The BelPole music flowed around them, joining them, making them one. He lay suspended, Isabella smiling at him sweetly, beautifully.

Isabella.

Lichen awoke as rocks slid down the hill and splashed into the river. Someone was coming down the incline from the bridge. Someone was coming to help him. The driver? Grandfather?

Lichen started to call out, but then he saw them. The horrifying sight chilled him as the cold sucking mud had not. There were three of them. Trolls. Ugly, slimy, huge trolls. They spoke in gibberish, slobbering and drooling on one another. They smelled of sewage and disgusting rotten things with no names. Their eyes bulged, bloodshot, and stupid. Their brute strength was apparent as they tossed aside boulders with ease.

Lichen crawled up the bank to the underside of the bridge. Pain stabbed his side. His ribs. His head. But, oddly, his leg seemed fine. He slowly wedged his mud-greased body between the beams. He squeezed, constricted, and willed his body to conceal itself in the bridge supports. Lichen slowed his breathing.

I am a warrior. I am a warrior.

He prayed his blood did not drip. He hoped they could not hear his heart pounding.

Lichen lay jammed into the timbers, hidden high over the trolls as they continued down the bank. They poked his mother's body and kicked her into the river.

The predators grunted as they searched among the boulders. Searching for something. When they found nothing, they turned to leave. Their gray bulky shoulders drooped; their husky voices disappointed. Lichen stared in disbelief; he knew that troll. It had a missing ear.

They began to walk back up the slope; they were leaving. He had escaped their notice. One Ear tripped, lost his balance, and fell backward onto the rocks bellowing with a deafening roar. His open mouth revealed swollen, rancid gums with sharp black pointed teeth. Lichen thought of the black iron fence in front of the Manor. He felt and smelled the rush of putrid air coming from the depths of the troll.

Lichen gasped, then gagged. He tried too late to control his movement. The troll opened his eyes and stared directly into Lichens.

A lone rider sat atop the crest of the hill; three gigantic hounds milled around his feet; their hackles rose. Stench surrounded him in heavy viscous waves. The rider watched. His disfigured face twisted into a ghost of a smile. The scarred skin pulled against muscle; tugged his lips into grotesque crooked lines. It was painful. He rarely smiled.

"Look there, Mors," he said to the ghostly hound at his feet. "They're dead. The Warrior and his mother are dead. Our time has come."

He spurred his horse. It reared and turned. "Letum. Obitus," he said to the other dogs, "Come."

His long thick cloak billowed in black rolling boils behind him as he galloped away. Large clumps of dirt struck the hounds as they watched the spectacle at the Bridge a moment longer. Their keen yellow eyes were intent and focused as their bodies shimmered in and out of sight. Their noses twitched, searching for the smell of death. Finding it, they turned and raced after their master.

Chapter Twenty

Warrior

Certus walked into the library alone. He had been Kilotax of New Ivy for many years, much longer than the thousand-day term, he had been elected again and again. The people of New Ivy loved and trusted him, and he had Q's unequivocal support.

Certus' good judgment generally kept the peace and when it didn't, well, he had his ways. His mere presence quelled many a miscreant and thwarted the plans of mischief-makers regularly. He didn't look the rough tough sheriff; he was in fact, rather small and rumpled, a shriveled prune with authority.

Q fostered a public library containing books not only from the Kingdom but from Advena as well. Certus loved to read and spent his evening bachelor hours holed up before the fireplace walking Baker Street solving crimes. He insisted on his now famous costume of the Sherlock variety, complete with pipe and walking stick, and, who knows, perhaps it did aid him in his investigations. If nothing else, it garnered attention.

"Q, Sapien." Certus nodded with grim authority to his old friends, his neck and shoulders stiff with seriousness.

"I just finished with Cecelia. She's pretty worked up. She and Agaso were..... pretty close I take it. Tell me your stories," Certus said as he licked his pencil end and applied it to his small tablet. Q and Sapien related the events of the evening as they knew them and even to their ears, Lichen appeared the culprit.

"The Criocts are searching the grounds now. We will need to search the Manor as well, Q. I am sorry, but it needs to be done. Your guests are being interviewed and dismissed; you know we will treat them with the utmost respect."

The wiry hair of his eyebrows, thick and bushy, springing out in all directions, wiggled expressively. Certus was a very animated man. "I understand Chimera and your Rowan carriage are missing?"

Q clasped the amulet in his pocket. He would not reveal it to Certus....yet.

"Yes, yes, but I believe Chimera has taken Beetrum and Lichen back to Weston. Chimera will return to me when they are delivered and I shall have some answers. But that won't be until morning.

"Certus, Lichen did not murder Agaso. He could not. I will stake my life and reputation on it." Q sat down at his desk.

Certus looked apologetic, his wrinkled brow deepened like spring-plowed ground. He adjusted his hat, unaware this mannerism signaled he found this line of questioning distasteful. He liked and respected the Ambassador.

"I know, Q. I know. Meanwhile, we must continue with our investigation. I appreciate your..."

An unearthly bellow came from the grounds and guest conversations halted mid-sentence. Amicus ran through the crowd, fire, and sparks shooting from him. Great flames accompanied his roar that cleared the path as he jumped half-flying in great leaps. Sleek black skin rippled over his lean muscular frame. A formidable package.

"What in the..." Certus started. He walked toward the library window and watched as Amicus' flaming body raced toward the stables.

Q immediately put one hand over his eyes and held the other one up to halt Certus' questions. He focused and centered his mind, calmed, and steadied his body. He garnered strength, gathering it around him as if loading a weapon.

Amicus! Amicus, stop.

Surprise halted Amicus in midair and he fell to the earth with an undignified plop. His fire went out and he looked somewhat like a burned-up match. His young ungainly legs sprawled in all directions; smoke spiraled from his nose like snuffed ashes. Amicus looked toward the Manor like a sad and disciplined puppy.

Get back to the Manor. Now.

Amicus obeyed so quickly, that guests wondered whether they had really seen a little black fiery dragon terrorizing the grounds. He disappeared into the Manor and the crowd began talking in cautious whispers nervously inspecting the charred bushes and scorched path.

Certus stood at the window momentarily speechless. He straightened his jacket, adjusted his hat, and nervously tamped the tobacco in his pipe.

"Well. I won't ask what that was about," he said as he regained his composure and stuffed his pad and pencil into his coat pocket. "And I won't trouble you further tonight," Certus said, fiddling with his hat, "however, under the circumstances, I must issue a Bans for Lichen and Beetrum. We do not know for certain that they have left Domus. I'm sorry, Ambassador, murder is a serious crime. I will forward my report to King Colere.

"Gentlemen, until tomorrow..." Certus gave a stiff nod, put his pipe into his mouth, tapped his cane on the floor, and walked out the door.

A Bans would locate Lichen and Beetrum if they were still in Domus if they were still alive. And, if they had left Domus boundaries, the Bans would prevent re-entry.

Which would suit Beetrum just fine. Q thought.

Sapien paced the library, his long arms clasped behind his back; it helped him clarify his thoughts. He wore the long dark blue coat of his office, the simple seal of the Princeps embroidered on the front, a circular knot.

"I heard your silent commands to *Amicus,"* Sapien said. "Who or what Amicus is, is your business, old friend. I know you have powers, Q. Many powers. It is abnormal for a human to have been granted that much authority over the elements. Although most of the Fey respect you, there are some who do not. Some are jealous of your powers, angry because a human possesses them; they would be happy to see your "little kingdom" of New Ivy come to ruin. Never mind that King Colere considers you his closest confidant in spite of the Keeper. I fear for you." Q started to interrupt; Sapien held up his hand. "I just advise caution, that's all. There will be some who revel in your current trouble; perhaps even have caused it."

"Sapien, you are a trusted friend indeed. I will be careful, but I must find and clear my grandson."

'Q, I do not need to remind you, if you need anything, any help, you can come to me. I do not for one moment think Lichen guilty of murder.

"But, for now, I must get home, Isabella is quite distraught. Having to pronounce Agaso dead has taken its toll. Not a very auspicious way to begin the caduceus." Sapien started for the door.

"I will be back tomorrow. Try and get some rest."

Their gaze locked in a moment of shared trust.

"Good night, until tomorrow." Sapien walked out the door and bumped directly into Valeo. Sapien glanced back at Q with a knowing set to his mouth.

"Keeper," Sapien said.

"Princeps," Valeo answered drawing his wings back and up.

"Come in Keeper," Q said sitting down at his desk. Q felt Valeo's probes, tentative and hesitant on the outskirts of his mind.

Would the fellow ever learn his manners?

"Q," Valeo said. "Q, my dear friend. I am so sorry."

"Thank you, Valeo," Q answered. "Please sit down."

"I have news. Chimera came to QuinVerga."

"Your house?" Q said. "*My* driver came to *your* house?"

"Yes. He says the carriage wrecked at the Bridge, a terrible ordeal. Beetrum and Lichen were both thrown into the river... I'm so sorry Q. They were killed," Valeo blurted.

Q paled, but remained silent. His breath felt like it froze to a solid stream of ice. Heavy. Solid. Impossible to breathe.

Valeo continued. "Your carriage was destroyed. Chimera and the horses transported to QuinVerga because..." he hesitated. "...It was closer, you see."

Q did not respond. He could not.

Valeo blundered on. "In the moment they flew off the bridge, the carriage split and fell toward the shoals. No one could have survived it. I am deeply sorry, old friend. If there is anything I can do..."

Valeo's oily condolences did not reach Q. He sat as stone. Cold. Quiet.

"I do apologize, Q," Valeo said. "It is not my intention to intrude on your tender feelings at the moment. I will depart. I will notify

Certus of all the details and, of course, send word to the King. If you should need me in any way, send immediately and I shall be here." Valeo turned on his heel and marched out the door. Insincerity trailed in his wake.

Q's breath thawed, slowly finding its way through his lungs. Replenishing. Oxygenating. He gasped. The enormity of today's events flooded his mind in a wave of horror. Beetrum and Lichen dead. Agaso dead.

Lichen, my boy.

The library filled with a darkness unrelated to the night. A chill beyond this world. A jealous grief allowed nothing else to enter, nothing else to exist besides itself. Consuming and black. A grief that laid waste to the will to live.

A small knock came at the door, hesitant. Then a louder one, then a pounding. Receiving no answer, the door opened slightly.

"Master Q," Cecelia said. She entered the library and turned up the oil lamp. An ingenious innovation of Q's. She saw him then, sitting at his desk. Staring, sightless out the window.

"Master Q," she said again, terror beginning to strangle her. She knew that look. He was slipping away into a place he'd been before. A private hell of anguish and misery.

"Noo," she said. "Noo," she shouted. "Not again." Cecelia ran to Q and grabbed his shoulders. "Master Q." She shook him. "Master Q." Easy at first. Then harder, Then violently. "Curse that Keeper to inferi," she mumbled. "Comin' 'ere wi' 'is tales of woe. Master Q, look at me."

Q's hands fell from his lap dangling lifelessly at the end of his boneless arms. His face relaxed into ancient lines; muscles slackened like the dead. His hair fell around his face as if to shield him, failing. His head bobbled over to the side carrying his body to the floor.

Chilling howls curdled the air as a blast of flames flew through the library door and landed beside Q.

"'oly Grove to 'eaven," Cecelia said. "Scare the livin' sense outta me why dinna ye. And stop tha' flammin'. Ye'll burn the 'ouse down."

Cecelia was familiar with the drogs. Cecelia was familiar with everything that went on in The Manor. "Can ye 'elp 'im wee lassie?"

The drog's head lay across Q's chest, both of them deathly still; she looked up at Cecelia. With a small whimper accompanied by a tiny puff of smoke, she closed her eyes.

Cecelia watched as waves of light began to glow under every scale. Illuminating. The reds tipped with burning yellow glowed as embers in a blacksmith's fire. Her brilliant orange legs pulsed with energy, sparks arcing from her toes up her spine discharging down her blazing tail completing the circuit around Q. Electrifying. The voltage swirled around the drog and Q. Faster and faster the current twisted, catching Cecelia in a dizzying array of blurred shadows. Oblivion.

"Cecelia," he said, "Cecelia wake up." Cecelia opened her eyes. Q knelt over her; the drog beside him; both peering into her face.

"Master Q, ye're back."

"Something isn't right, Cecelia," Q said. Cecelia poured them both another cup of nepeta and lemon balm tea. Her experience taught her to hold her tongue, to let Q talk it out.

"During the bonding," Q said, "and oh, by the way, this is Torri," he patted the drog affectionately. "When Torri and I...bonded just now...I saw Lichen. Alive. Injured and bound, but alive." His eyes glistened; his voice caught. "I knew it. I knew he could not be dead. Valeo lied."

"I tell you, Cecelia, something's amiss. Chimera should have come home," Q said. "Why didn't he? Conjured coachmen are loyal. Beyond loyal."

Q paced and spoke to order his thoughts, his tea mug balanced in his hand. "Domus has three sets of identical coachmen, Rowan carriages and stallions specifically conjured: Chimera for me, Manes for Valeo, and Lares for King Colere. And now Valeo says Chimera is at his estate? He isn't. I saw him during the bonding. I don't know where he is, but it didn't look anything like QuinVerga. Why would Valeo tell me that?"

Q sipped his tea. Torri, a pensive look on her red-scaled snout as if she were trying to figure it out as well, wagged the arrow tip of her tail and sighed a smoke plume.

Q withdrew the amulet from his pocket. He stared at it as if to glean answers about this night's tragedies. It warmed in his hand; Lichen is alive. And he is innocent.

Lichen is not only the heir to New Ivy but also the future of Domus. He is everything. Domus will not survive without him. Q closed his eyes and knew he should get up and tend to Amicus.

Amicus! That little rascal may know something.

"Come on, Cecelia." Q stormed up to Beetrum's suite, Cecelia and Torri close behind. Beetrum had always been a neat child to the point of exasperation. Q was not prepared for the sight before them. Everything in the room had been destroyed. Every upholstery shredded. Every piece of furniture marred, cut, or broken. Every glass, every mirror shattered. Plants overturned. The only thing unmarred was the portrait of Syringa.

"Achhh, me 'oly grove," Cecelia said. "What 'appened 'ere?"

They walked slowly into the room, the shock ebbing. Q picked his steps through the carnage and went into Beetrum's sleeping chamber. The bed curtains hung in tatters. The pillows and mattress slashed open. Feathers lay in the chandelier, the fireplace, the windowsill as if manic birds sought new and extraordinary places to nest.

Q checked the wardrobe for Beetrum's bag. Gone. Every gown, every garment he had given her lay in shreds. Dresses ripped apart and strewn around; footprints tromped across the fabrics. Q yanked the bureau drawers open. Empty. Every personal item she brought with her from Weston was gone.

Q went into Lichen's suite. Amicus sat on the window seat looking thoroughly chastised and snorted a smoky greeting.

"Hi old boy," Q said. Torri trotted over to Amicus, they touched noses, sparks flew. Everything in Lichen's suite looked in order. A book lay open on the desk. Lichen's riding boots stood on the floor and pants lay neatly across an open chifforobe door. Inside sat Lichen's travel bag.

"Amicus, come here," Q said. Amicus bounded off the seat and stood before Q, his tail slowly moving from side to side.

"Tell me, boy. What do you know? Show me." Q placed his hands on the side of Amicus's head; they both closed their eyes. Q saw Lichen enter the stables and a few moments later pain shot through Amicus and a desolate void covered everything blocking any further revelations. All sensations of Lichen ceased. Amicus whimpered.

"So, he was hurt, then, just disappeared, did he?" Q said. Amicus woofed a small grey poof of smoke. Q knew that once Lichen was in the carriage, Amicus would no longer be able to sense him. If the carriage had been destroyed and Lichen was alive, then where the devil was he? Why couldn't Amicus sense him now? And, what of Beetrum? And Chimera?

"Well Cecelia," said Q, "it looks as if Beetrum intended to leave as planned. And Lichen did not."

Q went back to the desk and opened the drawer. A little white bag with a black ribbon drawstring lay just inside. Q picked it up but he already knew what was inside. He loosened the drawstring, tipped the bag and a small blank piece of fabric fell into his palm. The ancient prophecy. The Portent.

Q reached into his pocket and withdrew the amulet. "Cecelia, Agaso had this in his hand. Do you know anything about it?"

"Aye, I know it wa' crafted many generations ago. In fact, there are two amulets of protection. Some say they're as old as Domus. But ye know this, Ambassador."

"Yes. I know that, Cecelia. I gave this one to Lichen. I know who he is and I believe you know it, too."

"Aye, I know it," she said. Neither of them could say it aloud.

The Warrior.

Q folded The Portent and carefully placed it and the amulet in the bag. "Lichen, where are you, my boy?"

Downstairs the mantle clock in the library groaned and churned with dark blue and purple clouds. It matched everyone's mood. Outside the Adoleo burned, but no one danced.

Chapter Twenty-One

Rock Faeries

Lichen saw nothing but blackness when he opened his eyes. He felt crumpled and wadded; rubbish discarded.

The rank air inside the course woven bag barely found its way to his lungs. He was in pain. White-hot searing pain, inside and out. Where in Hades was he? He fought to remember what had happened; the carriage lurching, breaking apart, his mother's mutilated body sinking below the waves, the trolls.

One Ear.

That traitorous murderer, he would pay for this. His mind rambled. Did Chimera and his infernal horses escape? If he did, he would inform Q of what happened. But, if Chimera had been instrumental in Lichen's kidnapping, he wouldn't return to Q.

How did Beetrum get Chimera to go along with her scheme? What if Q didn't know he had been kidnapped, what if he thought Lichen had returned to Advena of his own accord? Was Q looking for him? And Isabella. Would he ever see her again? She stirred things within him. Powerful things. And why did those pus pockets put him in this insufferable bag?

As if in answer, a sudden kick rammed the bag and sent a searing pain through Lichen's back. His moan brought an affirmative grunt from a troll as if it confirmed that Lichen was alive. Lichen yelled insults and proceeded to punch and kick back, but from his cramped position, his efforts went unrewarded and only served to bring more blows and stomps upon the bag.

They proceeded to drag the bag along a path perforated with sharp rocks, jagged points pierced Lichen's body as he plummeted back into unconsciousness.

Sometime later icy water dipped from the adjacent river penetrated the bag and brought Lichen abruptly awake. Troll laughter roared with a brute force and an underlying mockery of their captive; it reinforced Lichen's resolve to escape his bag prison.

The water, in spite of bringing fits of shivers, refreshed Lichen and cleansed him of urine. He heard the river following them in its bed beside the path, its roar tormenting him. The river seemed alive. Mocking. He tried to block out the memory of the floodwater under the Bridge sucking his mother's body into its depths, but he saw her time and time again sinking, disappearing.

The trolls gave Lichen no food, just frigid ablution. New voices accompanied the latest dowsing of river water; someone else had joined the troll trio. Lichen strained to hear, trying to relax his cramping muscles. Were they bartering for him? They argued for quite some time and in other circumstances, he might be gratified by his apparent worth. Lichen thought fleetingly of the Bachelor Bid. Looking dapper in his dress blues he had made the largest sum for the Air Force charity as local females had bid for his company during dinner. Wonder what they would pay if they could see him now.

An agreement apparently struck, the trolls opened the bag and unceremoniously dumped Lichen onto the ground. He landed in a heap like wilted greens, pain throbbing throughout his body. Lichen tried to open his eyes, but his lids were sealed. How long had he been in that bag, one day? Two?

Lichen rubbed his eyelids with filthy fingers until they opened. Stringy matter clung to his lashes blurring his vision. Eventually, the trolls came into focus. The sight of them sickened him. He hurled in vain, for his stomach was as empty as the bag that lay beside him.

Lichen heaved and gagged and moaned until One Ear shoved him in derision. He howled ugly troll laughs and shouted troll epithets.

Lichen stumbled face-first into a thorny bush covered with pink berries. Somewhere in his mind, Lichen wondered if they would be good to eat.

Black rage usurped any thoughts of food or danger. It began deep within, from a place under the Bridge, and grew as an impending storm, breaking its fury on the gray figure standing behind him.

Lichen turned and launched out of the bush. One Ear bellowed an inhuman wail, a fitting response in this land of non-humans. Lichen's eyes were wild, lit within by a flame fueled by loss. His adrenal rush ignored the pain of broken bones, bruises, and festering wounds. He hit the troll in the chest full force, yelling. A warrior's yell. A yell fueling the charge against the enemy.

Lichen clamped his arms around the beast and hung on. One Ear lost his balance, and fell back into his partner, who also grabbed hold. The three of them, a ball of seething, shrieking anger rolled down the steep rock-spiked river embankment.

Lichen sank his teeth into One Ear's shoulder; the troll screamed in pain and fury. The second troll seized with a fit of terror, hung on for dear life, apparently along for the ride.

The bloody, muddy, screaming triad slammed into the river with dynamic force. The boiling and churning floodwater of the Great River Potens had turned the normally placid river into a fluvial beast. The great screeching tangle of Fey and human sank below the surface of the water; caught in the maelstrom of the river. The force of the water sliced Lichen from the trolls and carried all three of them downstream at a frenzied pace.

The remaining troll and the four traders watched the scene, transfixed. As their captive and two of the trolls bobbed in the current, they raced downriver yelling. Close to the water's edge, the rocks gave way to mud. The mud's suction tripped them, slowing their feet in slippery gaols. The pursuit was slow but persistent.

Lichen was a strong swimmer even with his injuries. The powerful current was a formidable opponent, but Lichen conquered the rapid flow of the river. He reached the shore, spent and panting. The soft muck from the floodwaters was comforting. He knew he should get up, he must escape, but his traitorous body would not obey.

The troll and his four potential buyers were in a wild frenzy when they reached Lichen. They shouted, shook their fists, and kicked Lichen to test for life. The troll rolled him over and peered into his face. Lichen thought if he feigned death, perhaps they would leave him behind in pursuit of livelier game.

But, they had more collective gray matter than Lichen had assumed. After squabbling, spitting, and what appeared to be swearing, they formulated a plan. Three of the newcomers stood guard. Their comrade and the troll followed the riverbank in search of the two missing trolls, One Ear and his cowardly friend.

Lichen peeked out the slits in his eyes. The traders were smaller than the trolls, about Lichen's size. They had long thin hair growing out the top of their heads. Lichen had no idea what they were. Mythology books were ineffectual.

And, if Q had taken Lichen outside New Ivy, maybe, just maybe he would have information about the creatures of Domus that would actually be of some value. As it was, he was down in enemy territory with no map and no reconnaissance. And look at his handsome Lacerta boots. Ruined.

The traders had ugly thin wings protruding from gray bony shoulders. Skinny arms hung low beside equally thin and bloodless legs. Lichen thought of skinny Harold on his swim team. No upper body strength.

Without further thought, Lichen jumped to his feet and dove for the nearest scrawny captor. Lichen's spontaneous ill-conceived escape was quickly thwarted. The skinny fellow calmly raised his skinny arm and swiped Lichen across his throat with a long flat rock. He fell limp at their feet.

Lichen awoke tied to a tree. He raised his throbbing head and saw his captors huddling around a fire. The trolls were gone, apparently having successfully traded him to these skin-and-bone beasties.

They were darker than the trolls, more like the black-gray cliffs on the side of the mountains. They had gray leathery skin and bat-like wings. Their bone structure was more refined than the trolls, more human.

Long and pointed noses dripped, continually and disgustingly. Lichen stared at them. Were they faeries? He thought of Sapien's grand entrance across the bridge into New Ivy with his white Pegasus leading the way and all the beautiful faeries with him. And Isabella. Beautiful Isabella.

These animals could not be faeries. He narrowed his eyes, thinking.

Thank you, Cecelia. He remembered her telling him of a tribe exiled centuries ago. They had broken the Primordial law, the code that governed the village. For generations, they have lived in various settlements in North Domus at the foot of Lode Mountain in some God-forsaken place called the Proscriptio. Lichen reasoned he was a captive of a Rock Faerie tribe.

How long had he been unconscious? From the look of numerous drinking vessels strewn around and the drunken hilarity among his captors, quite a while.

Cecelia said Rock Faeries were infamous for their drinking. They laughed and were apparently telling tales, each trying to one-up the other. No different than humans. Lichen strained against his ties ignoring the pain. Some sort of rope, he was securely bound, but not hopelessly.

Lichen evaluated the faeries' besotted condition; another half hour and they would be beyond caring about him—if he could maintain consciousness that long. Lichen thought he could use a stiff drink of faerie liquor himself.

The Rock Faeries started to slur their words and began their descent into oblivion. When their heads nodded, and their eyes drooped, Lichen stretched his foot toward one of their cups. It looked like a thinly hollowed rock resembling a squat, fat wide-mouthed jar. Crude cruet. Lichen hoped it was breakable.

He maneuvered the jar towards the tree and grabbed it with his bare feet—the trolls had taken his boots, the sadistic thieving dung buckets—and smashed it against the rocky ground.

Lichen froze at the noise and looked at his tormentors around the fire. Two of them were already snoring and the third lay in a stupor, his blank eyes staring.

What was going on in that head? Not much.

The jar broke in half exposing a sharp hard edge.

Yes. Yes.

Lichen maneuvered it up the tree, grasped it with his hand, and cut the ropes. He tumbled to the ground and lay there, his breath short, his heart pulsing pain throughout his weak body.

Triumph.

Lichen looked at the gray faeries passed out cold and scattered around the fire in blissful unawareness. His eyes sought what his nose already knew. Food. There on a spit several roasted carcasses, charcoaled and dripping juices into the dying fire. Culinary seduction.

Boney remains were strewn around the camp, a testament to faerie voraciousness. How long since he had eaten? Lichen's stomach growled. He salivated.

Caution was gone. One thing mattered. One thing only. Food. His eyes riveted on the sizzling meat. Scrimpets? Sator and the cat seeds flashed across his memory, nothing could supplant his hunger for long. The aroma would drive him mad before he reached the spit.

Lichen crawled slowly toward the fire, only his reserves of willpower kept him from breaking into a full run. He took the lance from the flames, stood, and darted toward the trees. The impaled scrimpets were a banner of defiance.

All fear of pursuit lay buried beneath his ravenous intentions. The first bite was in Lichen's mouth long before he reached the protection of the underbrush. He had never tasted anything so good in his life. He was chomping and gnawing like an animal. Lichen afforded himself a grin as he chewed, scrimpet grease running down the corners of his mouth. Faerie etiquette.

Chapter Twenty-Two

Cave

Lichen had been on the move for hours. Uneven earth mined with rocks, shards and tree roots hampered his progress. He drudged on.

He remembered the feel of rock on bone, the sickening sound of it. It had been necessary. The drunken faerie may have awakened while Lichen was stealing his shoes. Lichen looked down at his feet. The shoes fit, sort of. They weren't Nikes, and by perdition, they sure weren't his prize lacerta boots, but at least they protected his feet from these dagger rocks. Vertical switchblades.

Every few steps Lichen looked over his shoulder. No sign of them. He walked and limped and stumbled; he needed rest. The interminable brush and vines caught at his legs. Thorns scraped his arms and strange creatures scurried about, angry or frightened at his intrusion.

Where was the lush countryside, the blooming flowers as far as the eye could see? Soft grass, thyme walkways, ivy that stood guard against danger and the lichen that had connected him to Domus?

He noticed a mountain dead ahead, bearing zero point one; according to the sun, he was traveling north. Did the same parameters apply here in this derelict place?

It was only a little further, he could make it. But shouldn't he be going south? Cecelia said the Proscriptio was in the north. She also said no one could get in or out.

Wrong.

He was pretty sure he was in. He would press on toward the mountain, rest, then make some decisions.

Lichen curled up on the floor of the cave, his arm pillowing his head just as the sun went down. He opened his eyes but could not move, pain raking his body.

Pain from injury. Pain from hunger. Pain from loss. He hallucinated. His mother rose up out of the river, her face a Rock Faerie, her slivers of wings flapping grotesquely. She grinned with the black jagged teeth of the trolls.

"Lichen, I told you so. I told you," she cried. Her skeleton arms reached out for him.

Lichen awoke and knew he had to get up. If he could make his way back to the river and follow it to the Bridge, he would find the road. Then he could find the Manor and Q. And Isabella.

Or he could get back to Weston. His world, his human world.

Lichen's enchantment with Domus was fading, morphing into something cold and hard. Did he want to go home? He wondered if Brent and Holly would believe him now. Brent and Holly. Another world. Advena.

Giggles interrupted his thoughts.

Giggles?

Lichen lay perfectly still. He had concealed himself with branches and leaves before sleeping, but he could see through them.

Rock Faerie children were entering the cave, boys, covered with the same tattered gray skin as the men, chattering among themselves.

Lichen had a good chance of remaining undiscovered. The children grew quiet. Lichen held his breath and closed his swollen eyes. He thought about praying, but then someone kicked him in the back sending shoots of pain throughout his body like arrows tearing through a melon.

The kick sparked a deluge of laughter from the boys bringing three adults on the run. They pulled the branches off Lichen and jerked him to his feet.

Lichen stood unsteadily glaring at them. More Rock Faeries. For a fleeting instant, Lichen thought they might help him. After all, Grandfather Q was the ambassador. Q was well known. Well-liked. Mostly.

"Q," Lichen said. "Q...Q," he shouted. Lichen pointed to himself. "Q...grandfather."

The smallest and ugliest of the creatures leered, raised his arm, and stabbed Lichen through the shoulder with his spear. Lichen screamed, as much with anger as with pain.

Pain. Pain was nothing. Pain was his constant companion. Pain was his friend, his teacher.

Disgust and rage gripped Lichen. His jaw muscle tightened grinding his teeth and producing a wild grimace. Strength born of despair surged through him despite the blood running down his chest.

Those little roasted scrimpets he stole from the campfire had more than sustained him. He felt strong. He felt impervious.

Lichen raised his good arm above his head, yelled "I am a warrior" and charged.

His face contorted, mirroring the ferocity in his heart. He ran toward the skinny adult with the spear. The surprised faerie fell back onto the cave floor with a grunt. A shorter but much, much larger faerie stepped toward Lichen, amusement playing on his face.

Lichen stopped, apprehension gluing his stolen pointy shoes to the cave floor. This faerie was four times Lichen's size. He walked toward Lichen with the attitude of quieting a noisy child.

Lichen stood, mouth agape. The faerie lumbered toward Lichen, one of his giant fists clenched, a satisfied grin puckered the corner of his mouth. Lichen didn't feel the blow.

Lichen awoke, arms and legs tied together behind his back. His head was drawn toward his feet as if preparing to catapult something off his brow.

This is just wrong.

Lichen shivered from fright, cold, both. Or perhaps he was in shock. He heard voices obviously discussing him and opened one eye. The adults and children were huddled around the fire. It was still dark, or was it night again? His legs and arms cramped; pain screamed through his tendons.

Another group came into the cave and began to argue with his jailors. Lichen's eyes opened wide in recognition; it was the drunken bunch that had tied him to the tree. He tried to shift his body to hide his feet and the stolen shoes. Like that was the least of his worries.

A man with no shoes and a sizeable lump on his head stomped furiously over to Lichen. He yelled and waved his arms and jabbed his fingers in the air. One of his comrades laughed and pointed to the shoes Lichen was wearing. This further infuriated the shoeless victim. He aired his grievance to the others still seated around the fire, obviously demanding the return of his goods.

The Short Fat One, satisfied with having conquered Lichen with one solitary punch, acted proprietary toward his new captive. He rose slowly and threateningly from his hollowed-out rock seat. Towering over the shoeless faerie, he glared silently down at the victim. Shoeless faerie quickly indicated a desire to abandon his right of ownership. Short Fat One chuckled, great rolls of stomach jiggled. Gray jello.

The young boys began bragging in excited tones to the newcomers, no doubt telling of their brave exploits in finding the captive. They ran over to Lichen and repeatedly kicked him in the stomach and unprotected groin asserting their neo-virility, laughing in their cracked juvenile voices.

When the adults began to talk among themselves, the boys lost interest in Lichen and turned their attention to a large lizard in the back of the cave which reminded Lichen of his handsome boots. He just couldn't let it go.

He lay on his side and dozed in a numb stupor with his half-closed eyes on the campfire. His shoulder bled, ran down his chest, and pooled into a hollow place in the rock. Thank god he couldn't feel his body. Fettered and numb.

Rest now. Escape later.

A knife-edged rock cut into Lichen's cheek. He could feel it slicing into his face but was powerless to move. He felt like one of the boulders, cold and heavy.

Short Fat One walked over to the fire, his shoulders broad, his back wide. Muscles rippled beneath the tough gray skin along his back. Massive arms, raw strength. Lichen had never seen anyone so big. Not even on WWW. He wondered how the beast would look in bright yellow wrestling boots and a satin cape.

"And in this corner..." Lichen's mind wandered out of control.

Short Fat One squatted in front of the fire, his back still to Lichen, his wings battle-tattered and drooping. Lichen thought of the grace and beauty of Agaso's wings.

Short Fat One said something to the others, they cheered, nodded assent, looking toward Lichen. Lichen's stomach rolled and muscles tensed. He didn't like the feel of this.

Short Fat One stood, turning toward Lichen; his eyes glinted mischievously. He had something in his hand. Lichen stared in disbelief as Short Fat One walked toward him. Drool slobbered from his smile onto his chin. Slimy mucous dripped from his nose; he used his free hand to smear it across his face.

Lichen recalled the legends Ram told in his sing-song tales. Legends because who really knew what happened in the land of the banished. In the Proscriptio. Tales of tribes who captured one another and anyone else to use as slaves. Different tribes, different slaves. Different tribes, different brands.

Short Fat One was almost to Lichen. Lichen knew with a sickening certainty the faerie's intent. He looked at the object clasped in the massive fist. Lichen struggled to stand, but it was hopeless.

Short Fat One came slowly, enjoying his moment. Lichen rolled his back against the cave wall. Fear left. Hatred came. Black, cold, strong.

Short Fat One turned to speak to the onlookers. Lichen spun his body toward Short Fat One, tripping him. Lichen screamed with pain. Shoulders. Back. Legs.

Short Fat One stumbled but did not fall. Instead of angering the giant faerie, Lichen's impetuous and futile act of defiance elicited a surprised admiration.

Regardless, Short Fat One's resolve was unchanged. Two of the others grabbed Lichen, ripped off what was left of his shirt, and turned him over on his stomach jamming the spear wound on his shoulder into the dirt.

They cut the rope, freeing Lichen's hands; hot searing blood rushed into his limbs. The gray faeries splayed his arms and stepped on both his wrists pinning him to the cave floor. Snot strung from their noses as they bent forward.

The brand glowed red in the shadows. A fire-pit demon, descending. Short Fat One held Lichen's shoulder and lowered the brand. The sizzle and smell of his own burned flesh did not affect Lichen. He had fainted.

Chapter Twenty-Three

Liber Vitae

Sapien approached the gate to the Grove absentmindedly. He must visit the gazebo; he must find some answers. He couldn't pinpoint it exactly, but something was wrong. He could feel disharmony in the air around him and in each step he took, the ground vibrated with unease. The troll stepped in front of him with an official air recalling Sapien to the moment.

"Who goes there?" the troll grunted, puffing for breath with each word.

"You startled me, Ian. You know who goes there; now stand aside. I've no time for foolishness today," Sapien said somewhat irritated.

"I do beg your pardon if my thoroughness grates you, Princeps," said Ian patiently without malice, "but I must see to my duty as I have done for thousands of years. State your name." Ian stood resolutely in front of the gate his bulk successfully blocking the entire path.

"Sapien Duco, Princeps of the Animus Consillium and Guardian of the Sacred Crystal Grove. And I beg *your* pardon, Ian, Ancient

"The trolls saw Manes, the driver, and the horses pop out just as the carriage split in two. They saw Mistress Beetrum in the river, dead, sir. They captured Lichen, stuffed him in a Bansbag, and sold him to some Rock Faeries. That's all I know."

Ian, having performed his duty, nodded, gave his perfunctory bow, put on his hat, stepped aside, and disappeared into the gate.

Sapien stood staring blankly after him. He would have liked to have gotten more information from Ian, but he knew Ian had said all he would. Trolls were generally fiercely loyal to one another, but Ian felt a responsibility to Sapien. At least as long as he was Princeps and lived here at Numen.

So, Beetrum was dead, but Lichen was not, just as Q suspected. Why had the Keeper lied about it? What could Ian possibly have meant by incident, not accident? Lichen had been captured by trolls and sold to faeries? The Bansbag would explain why the Bans had not located him, but, surely, they wouldn't keep Lichen in it indefinitely. As soon as they removed him, the Bans would focus on his location and lead them directly to Lichen.

And Manes? Manes, not Chimera? What was that about?

Sapien must dispatch word to Q, Certus, and certainly the King. He would leave Valeo out of the loop for the time being.

But first, he must visit the gazebo. Sapien was disturbed. Something was wrong. Very wrong indeed.

Sapien drew his cloak closer around him as he walked through the gate. The sky rolled with black clouds turning and moaning like a woman in labor. The weather grew worse each day and it reflected the turmoil in his mind. Nothing had been right since BelMoon.

The well-worn path forked. One went to the Grove where Iter would be held and where the Totus Vitas were kept. Sapien took the second path; it ran along the curves of the Great River Potens and went to his private sanctuary, his gazebo. Sapien loved the River, The Earth Mother; She gave him balance. He gave thanks to Divus, the Creator for all his many blessings.

He remembered many years ago when he first walked this path he knew immediately he wanted his gazebo here, beside the Great River. Magic and Divine Love flowed heavily in and around her waters. Sapien had prayed Divus would support and inspire him, guide and influence his decisions, and help him be a wise counselor to his people. He loved this estate and thought it aptly named. Numen: divinity.

Within days after coming to Domus and settling in Numen Sapien had gone out just before sunrise to find a place for his gazebo. He had chosen a flat expanse of rock surrounded by a Rowan Grove; its branches, thick as mystery, whispered among themselves.

He sat in the center of the rock, closed his eyes, and began to sing the Copia. Love. Privacy. Solitude. Inspiration. Wisdom. Empathy. These things he sang into the creation of the gazebo. These things he prayed would become a part of him.

The Rowan Grove vibrated; hummed with sweet gentle music that surrounded and entered Sapien. He had never before felt so loved, so protected, so accepted.

The gazebo grew, infused with power entwined with love. The Rowan branches created an intricate pattern, its leaves sheltering, and private, while allowing gentle light to shine through. It became Sapien's favorite place in the world.

This morning he needed a bit of that balance, that wisdom. Agaso was dead, Lichen missing, Beetrum was dead and Q was distraught and distant.

Isabella....his beautiful daughter. His heartgem. She had not been the same since BelMoon, neither she nor the weather. In fact, the whole country seemed at odds.

Sapien stood before the gazebo and quickly said the prayer. The gazebo opened letting Sapien step inside and closed behind him. It didn't take long to receive his answer.

It began to rain as Sapien left the gazebo. Not much, but it felt like tiny needles when the wind blew it against his skin. Sapien hurried and almost ran as he pulled the hood of his cloak over his head.

He had to get to the Sacred Crystal Grove. Normally, he would not enter until the day before Iter, but he knew he must get there. Now.

Sapien played the scene from the gazebo over in his mind. He didn't understand what he had seen, but he knew he would, soon. Rain came heavily now, driving water spikes into his face, his arms. The sky grew dark; thunder boomed.

He slowed his pace as he approached the gateway. Something was not right. The air around the Grove had been disturbed. Sapien walked through the gateway directly to the Life Room. The sacred room where the Totus Vitas slept.

He stood in the doorway, frozen; disbelief locked his body and mind. Someone had breached the Grove and entered the Life Room.

Impossible.

The Totus Vitas, the life books of all faerie-kind were lying all around the floor. Open. Disrespected.

Sapien stood momentarily immobilized with disbelief. A large ornately carved box that normally stood alone on its pedestal in the center of the room had been knocked to the floor. The box had been violated and lay on its side with the lid strewn carelessly across the room.

The beautiful rendition of the Lex Scriptura lay face down crumpling some of the pages. The Primordial had been torn from the book and savagely ripped and wadded and strewn about the room.

The horror of the scene was not to be believed. Sapien gasped and stood immobilized unable to comprehend the reality before him.

The Liber Vitae was gone. This cannot be. Never in the history of Domus had such a monumental violation of the Grove occurred. This book, this sacred book held the original illuminated manuscripts of the creation and mysteries of Domus, holy words, and divine revelations written by the hand of the Creator himself. No one was allowed to touch these hallowed pages. In fact, no one except Iris and the Princeps could touch the Holy Book without the pain of death.

The impossible had happened. Someone had not only touched it, they had stolen it.

Sapien gradually came to himself. He used his personal crystal to gather vibrations around the room and tucked it inside his cloak. He touched nothing, turned, and faced the pelting rain. Now he understood his vision. He must sing the Consistere.

Chapter Twenty-Four

Grotto

The dampness of the caverns suited her, Lorelei felt like a child again. She dived and swam in the pools, exploring the water tunnels, swirling in the eddies. Joy coursed in her veins, spewed into her heart, and pumped out through arteries like the underground river. It became her; she glowed with health. Luminescent.

But she was never alone. Latere's presence, whether physically or mentally, was constant. It had become part of her. Like breath. In spite of the gratitude she had toward Latere for saving her, she missed her privacy. Undines were solitary creatures.

"Good morning, my little fish." Latere's words flashed through Lorelei's mind.

"Good morning," she replied.

"I see you've had your morning playtime. Lemna has prepared you a marvelous breakfast. I am leaving and when I return this evening you and I will begin your instruction. You do recall your promise?" Latere asked. "It's time."

Lorelei dove to the bottom of the pool. She had made a small bed in the sand, for thinking. Small trinkets lay in a pile. Treasures collected.

"Lorelei? Answer me. You remember your promise?"

"Yes. Yes, I remember," Lorelei responded quickly. Latere didn't like it if she took too long to answer. "I'll be ready. Whatever you ask of me. As I promised."

"Very well. Do whatever you like today. It will be your last in the Grotto."

Lorelei swam as fast as she could toward the falls. If she hurried, she would have time for one more ride before breakfast.

She felt the vibrations of the falling water far before she reached it. As if it was sending her a secret message. The magical underground light shone softly. Lorelei loved the Grotto.

He never came here. It was as if it held too much beauty. As if he couldn't bear the loveliness of it; he preferred to skulk in the depths of the caverns. Pulling his dark thoughts around him, a depraved blanket keeping in and intensifying black feelings lest they should be diluted with light.

Lorelei climbed gingerly up the rocky slope. Tongue-like spikes anchored the foot of the falls with curving stems of pale moon-shaped flowers. They grew up the incline; the absence of the sun no matter. Lorelei felt their freedom, their independence and coveted it. Her bare feet cupped the rocks, her fingers holding sure. Her tiny body practically flew up the indoor mountain.

Lorelei stood for a moment at the summit exhilarated at the anticipation of the jump. The wind from the crashing water caressed her face. Lorelei felt as if the water sent her assurances of its love.

And Lorelei loved the water. The Earth Mother. It was the only thing she had ever loved. Lorelei smiled, took a breath, and dived. The waterfall roared magnificently over the cliff and took her with it.

She soared. The perfect blend of swimming and flying. She heard the river singing its secret song of joy. Of love. They dropped deep into the pool, down, down. Finally, reaching the bottom and swirling round and round like a wondrous water carousel.

Lorelei lay breathless in the sand. Her heart raced. The Mother embraced.

"Lorelei Unda," The Mother whispered. "Lorelei."

"Achhh," said Lemna as Lorelei walked into the cave room. "There ye be. I was beginnin' to think ye decided to swim the river oot o' here."

Lorelei was startled. "I would never leave without permission. I have given my bond," she said solemnly.

"Oh, child," Lemna said, " I know ye wouldna'. I was just foolin' wi' ye. Come now, eat ye'r breakfast. We 'ave a lot to discuss and no' much time."

"A lot to discuss?" Lorelei asked.

"Yes. I think ye will be leavin' this place verra soon. I must tell ye... Well now, there are some things ye should know," Lemna said. "I know ye 'ave given an oath to *'im*. But I feel 't is my duty to..." Lemna stopped abruptly.

Pain seared her mind, blinding red and hot. A lance from the bowels of the devil. Lemna cushioned her head with her arms and lay over on the slab she used as a bed.

"Lemna," Lorelei said. She rushed over and laid a hand on Lemna's forehead, the other one cradled the side, smoothing Lemna's hair. Cool. Gentle.

"Achhh. Yes, I'm fine now. Dinna ye be frettin' over me. Jus' gi' me a minute, now. I'll be right as rain."

Lorelei anguished over Lemna. Lorelei knew *he* was listening, watching, whatever Lemna had to tell her, *he* didn't want it told.

Lemna laid still, eyes closed. Lorelei thought she had slipped into sleep, her body relaxed, her breathing deep and steady.

"Lorelei," Lemna whispered. Lorelei started slightly.

"Shhh, just rest," Lorelei said.

"Noo, Lorelei, listen to me. Listen carefully and remember. I have shielded me mind. 'e canna 'ear me, but 'e knoos the shield is there. I only 'ave strength to keep it up for a short while. So, please. Listen."

"All right," Lorelei said. "But he will punish you for this."

"Noo, 'e will not punish me. 'e will kill me. But 'e's goin' to kill me anyway. This is the only chance I 'ave.

" Listen, I am goin' to teach ye 'ow to shield ye'r mind from 'im. I believe ye will be able to put up the guard without 'im knowing. Undines have a knack for it. Are ye willin'?"

Without hesitation, Lorelei replied. "Yes. Yes, I am willing."

Lorelei's capabilities surprised them both. She not only learned to put up the shield, she conjured numerous camouflage; variety would be the key to hiding the barrier from him.

"Now," Lemna said. "Do ye know about the Warrior and the Charm? The Portent?"

"All of the Fey know the Portent," Lorelei said. "It warns of a great destroyer; the fiend who wants to control Domus. Only the Warrior who wears the Earth and Stars can stop him, but first, he must find his Soul. The Charm is needed for protection."

"Yes," whispered Lemna struggling to control the barrier. Sweat beads bubbled across her face "I believe *'e* is goin' to ask ye to do somethin' regardin' the Warrior. I dinna know what. I 'ear 'im rantin' and plannin'.

"In order to control Domus, he must first 'ave the Tempus Crystal. I dinna think 'e can get it 'imself. 'e will need the Warrior."

Lemna held out her hand and Lorelei took hold. Lemna squeezed, whether, in desperation or emphasis, Lorelei knew not which.

"Achhh, I dinna know 'oo the Warrior might be. But, Lorelei, ye must not allow 'im to get the Crystal. Oath or noo. If 'e gets the Crystal, 'e can control Domus. An', everyone in it, aye."

"But," said Lorelei, "surely he will not lay such an important task on me. I am nothing. I live to swim the waters."

"Achhh, not true my little' darlin'. Ye are everythin' I believe ye 'old the future of Domus. And, because of that, I trust ye with this. I believe that the Charm isna' jewelry. I think it's a person and I think I know their identity."

Lemna gasped. The strain of holding the mental shield lay as a shroud across Lemna's face.

"I am a caduceus. One of my students...accchhh" Lemna fought to speak. "One of my students is truly gifted, a natural healer. She will be a caduceus and I believe she is the Charm foretold in the Portent. That is why *'e* sent the Pavors to destroy all caducei, to be sure and destroy the Charm. You must find 'er and protect 'er."

"But I cannot. I am here. I am bound by pledge."

"'e will let ye go soon and then..." Lemna's words trailed to silence. She wheezed and choked, her breath blocked as if fingers tightened around her throat.

"Lemna!"

"Go. Go to the Grotto. Now." Lemna's words came into Lorelei's mind. Clear. Commanding. "'e is comin'."

Lorelei felt the connection with Lemna break as footsteps echoed in the stone corridor rapidly approaching. A sense of panic rode on the sound. She knew he would be there in a moment. Too late for the Grotto.

"Lorelei," he shouted. "What is going on here? What treachery did this hag confide in you? Speak, my little fish. You can hide nothing from me."

Lorelei flourished the barrier in her mind with pale moon vines and cold rushing water. Mother's bosom. She would keep Lemna's words behind the falls. He shied from Mother's beauty. He would not or could not enter this sanctuary.

Lorelei would stay close to truth when replying to him. The truth is safe. The truth is protected. Falsehoods shouted for his attention and detection. They instigated exposure. He could recognize the tiniest of lies. Lorelei would walk the line carefully. Undine instincts were sharp. Lorelei would use her talents. She was more than a fish.

"She went in her sleep. Lemna. She is dead," Lorelei said as she placed her fingers on Lemna's eyelids. The eyes stared blindly, watching a world only the dead could see. As Lorelei started to close the lids, a soft beam detonated into Lorelei's eyes and then was gone. A swift moment of light. A fleeting image or sound, Lorelei could not distinguish which. But she knew what it said. She knew Lemna gave her one last message.

Save Domus.

Isabella loved the stillroom, it was Lemna's legacy. Lemna had been Isabella's official teacher for two years; she had been Isabella's mentor all her life. But Lemna was gone. Disappeared. Now, Lichen gone as well.

Isabella walked along the rows looking at the clean jars of herbs. Tiny bits of green, crushed and dried, packed into the jars to the top, almost. Legend had it that when humans in Advena made herbal medicine they left enough room at the top for faeries to sleep. She would ask Lichen about that. If she ever saw him again. And, if she ever spoke to him again. Faeries left a little room at the top of the jars for the Mother's blessings. Green blessings.

She walked on. Oils, steeping potent cures from sleeping herbs. Fruits and vegetables, fermenting, bubbling, growing their tiny civilizations of health. Salves. Vessels of healing. High, rough rafters held herbal bouquets hanging like floral bats. The room seemed to expand breathing in the curative fragrance.

This room, Lemna's room, felt safe and familiar, hugging her in its earthy essence. Rain beat against the windows as if it, too, sought to come in and be comforted. It hadn't rained since BelMoon. Nothing felt right since BelMoon. What was happening?

Isabella tried to keep her mind off Lichen. After all, he chose to leave Domus. To leave her. Perhaps she had misread him. Misread the BelPole dance. She wouldn't think about that.

She would put her mind to the task at hand and not spend time daydreaming about someone she would never see again. Someone who obviously didn't want to see her. Besides, she had a lot of studying to do before exams. Deadlines to meet. Goals to achieve.

Isabella sat down at her desk and opened the Phytablia, Lemna's botany book—now Isabella's. The brown leather cover glowed with a well-worn patina reflecting centuries of learning. It felt soft and smooth beneath her fingers. Lemna had added many pages to the original. In a small, neat hand, Lemna wrote her expert herbal knowledge with clarity and illustrated the plants in sharp, loving detail.

Isabella thumbed absently through the pages admiring Lemna's skill and feeling the pain of her absence.

"Where are you Lemna?" Isabella said.

The Phytablia lay open on Isabella's desk, and she folded her arms across the beautifully illustrated pages and laid her head down.

Instantly Isabella felt a cold damp wind blow across her face as if she were falling into a hole. Falling, falling.

Isabella screamed, but it caught in her throat as if the passage was too small for the sound. When she stopped falling, it was not abrupt so as to cut off the breath, but soft and gentle as a bird lighting on the edge of her nest not to disturb her brood.

Isabella looked around. "Hello," she called. "Hello?"

"Isabella." A voice spoke from the darkness. A soft voice with an accented lilt. A voice that had taught her and guided her and loved her.

"Isabella."

"Lemna, is that you? Where are you? Are you all right?" Isabella asked.

"Isabella, you are in danger. Domus is in danger. You must go to your father and..." The voice stopped abruptly as if a barrier cold and dark had sliced off their communique.

"Lemna? What? What did you say?" Isabella said. "Lemna. Lemna come back."

Isabella jerked her head off the Phytablia. Of course, why didn't she think of it sooner? This had been Lemna's book. It could bridge the space to her.

Isabella made several more unsuccessful attempts to reach Lemna, but the obstruction still blocked her. She grabbed her cloak and ran out into the storm.

Chapter Twenty-Five

Sax

Lichen was getting accustomed to waking up in pain. The enclosure around him was made of small trees planted in a circle, their branches and leaves forming the roof. The trees were woven together with grape vines, bearing grape vines.

Lichen realized he was no longer tied up. He was free to move around within the confines of the cage. The grapes, luscious and ripe on the vines, awakened his hunger. He stood and lurched clumsily toward the wall and fell on the grapes with animal lust.

Lichen crammed the large red grapes into his mouth, chewed as fast as he could, swallowed, and gobbled some more. Grape juice stained his hands, his face, his chest. He was sticky with satisfaction. Lichen leaned against the wall of his new prison and closed his eyes. He was full of grapes.

Odd, I'm perfectly content to sit here full of grapes.

The ludicrousness of his situation struck him as funny, and he began to laugh. It started as small silent chuckles, then grew louder until Lichen roared great drunken guffaws.

He was full of grapes, and he was in a grape prison. It seemed hilarious to him and some part of him wondered if the red grapes were related to the ebri butter he and Raman had imbibed in the Manor kitchen a lifetime ago.

He laughed until he couldn't breathe. He hurt with each gulp of air, and the more he hurt, the more he laughed. The more he laughed the more he hurt.

Lichen didn't know whether it was the grapes or not. He was in the firm grip of hysteria and was helpless to stop.

The tribe of Rock Faeries gathered around the grape cage and stared. Men, women, adults, and children stopped what they were doing and came to look at the strange human. Children laughed and pointed, mothers pulled them away from the foreign being, uncertainty in their eyes. Men yelled unfamiliar words and made rude gestures. They all whispered and wondered at this creature on display.

Lichen rolled away from their jeers and prying eyes trying to avoid the brand on his left shoulder, and the spear wound on the right, trying to protect what he knew were broken ribs and not break open the cuts on his leg, but not quite succeeding.

His laughter degenerated into sobs. The pain sent him further into delirium. His wrists and ankles were raw and scabbed from rope burns, his body battered, fractured, and mangled. Lichen lay curled like the crescent moon and drifted once more into unconsciousness.

The days rolled into one another like waves; Lichen could not distinguish one from the other.

What does it matter?

Day by day he became more lucid. His body healed, slowly, surely. Once a day they brought him food. They threw buckets of water into the cage cleaning it of his own filth and filled his water bowl.

He was not alone. A dark and shadowy thing came to relieve his despair, his pain. It comforted him with its black presence. It swirled around and in him and gave him sustenance. It nourished his ravaged soul and gave him a reason to heal. Revenge.

Hatred drove Lichen to movement. The grape cage was six feet in diameter and not much taller than Lichen's six feet.

He squatted. He lunged. He worked his fingers between the ceiling branches and pulled himself up. Over and over. He did pushups raising his body off the floor again and again. The tribe watched. Daily they began to gather at his cage, watching.

They ceased their verbal abuse and started encouraging him. They shouted with each sit-up, counting. A young skinny male began exercising with Lichen copying every move. Lichen grew stronger. He clowned with the children and flirted with the females. He strutted, dazzled, and charmed. And inwardly he hated.

As Lichen's body grew more vigorous, his need for retaliation grew with it. Each day became tougher, harder. Both body and revenge in tandem grew more formidable, more resilient. The malignant blackness consumed Lichen giving in return a resolute purpose. A dark determination to destroy these creatures of the rocks.

Daily Lichen sat in his cage and watched them; the bat faeries with their revolting puke gray skin, their pointed boney faces, and runny noses; their ugly vile wings.

His eye missed nothing. He evaluated their habits, examined their movements, calculated their strength; Lichen plotted their destruction. Retaliation became his goal, his life. His body healed; his soul festered.

Isabella. He could not think of her now. *She is faerie.*

The Rock Faerie encamped next to a large rock outcrop. It suited them well. Tall cliffs for scouting, deep caves for sleeping and storage. Large trees grew within the compound; a river roared nearby. Was it the same river the Bridge crossed? The same river that encompassed New Ivy?

Two faerie hulks jerked Lichen from the grape confinement, holding him between them. Short Fat One glanced at Lichen with indifference then turned and led them through the village toward the edge of the encampment.

Lichen had not seen him since the branding. He acted as if Lichen was just one more prisoner, one more slave, one more branding. Lichen kept his hatred at bay. It was his first foray out of the cage and he was determined to scout the area and analyze the guard situation.

They stumbled clumsily along one of the crooked paths. Lichen's contraband shoes were missing; his feet tender from long confinement. He wondered if they had made it back to the original owner or if someone else had a new pair of shoes.

And where in hades are my boots?

The path like everything else in this village-of-the-damned was spiked with jagged rocks like a vertebrae half buried.

They approached a clearing with a huge boulder in the center, the mountain loomed ominously behind it. All the rocks and cliffs and mountain profiles were serrated and sharp, except this one. As Lichen neared the rock he began to differentiate a round gray shape separate from the round gray granite.

Petroglyph?

No. A woman sat cross-legged on the curved outcrop of rock; she looked as old as the boulder. Part of her hair caught up in a circlet of scrimpet bone on top of her head, the rest streaming in dreary silver spears around her shoulders and down over her dull gray sparsely feathered wings; her dismal skin, weathered and furrowed.

The pallium was the only color in this pathetic achromatic palette of despair. By contrast, it looked like pale red lipstick on an aging gargoyle. The ragged faded scarlet pallium draped over one skeletal shoulder. Her wings protruded like broken clamshells. The woman's mouth puckered as she surveyed Lichen with her veiled gray eyes.

"Supra," Short Fat One said and bowed his head.

Lichen, unsure of what to do, simply stood and stared; Supra stared back. Interminably.

Lichens' guards fidgeted. Lichen knew she wanted him to throw himself prostrate and petition for his release, but he couldn't. He could not, would not beg and bow to a faerie. He continued to glare at her, she at him, her cloudy eyes expressionless.

Lichen stood, resolute.

He felt the power she exuded over the faerie band. Since his arrival in this village, he had begun to have unusual sensations. Unusual knowledge of things. Unusual dreams. He felt her power, he felt his own.

Strange probes strained against his forehead. Little needles pecking to get in. Lichen remembered Valeo's intrusion into his mind during BelMoon. Keeper Valeo Nox had entered; this ovarian barbarian would not.

Lichen fortressed his mind. He felt her probing searching seeking. She looked surprised at his power. Her eyebrow lifted ever so slightly, held Lichen with her eyes, and smiled.

"Greetings, Your Majesty, Queen of the Bat People and Regent of Guano. How do you choose to die?"

The tone of Lichen's words conveyed insolence and insult. Short Fat One stepped up to Lichen and kicked him behind his knees.

Lichen fell to the ground, cutting his face on a piercing rock; blood spurted tiny graffiti in the dirt. One more injury; one more scar, one more twist of kindle on the pyre of hatred.

Supra sat still and inscrutable on her throne of rock and delivered her pronouncement with a voice that belied her wrinkled skin and sagging breasts. Her voice rang strong and clear with authority. The two Hulks jerked Lichen to his feet and started back down the rocky path.

But instead of going back toward the grape cage, they turned toward the river. This path of soft gray mosses was smooth as felt beneath his bleeding feet. Cool and comforting. At least in the beginning.

The Manor had wonderful moss and lichens. *Was Q looking for him?*

After about a half-mile jagged, sharp rocks once again became the norm, the faint sound of rushing water that permeated the camp began to roar. It grew louder as they rounded a bend thick with foliage. The brush under the trees was dense and thorny. Sharp pointy tree shoots grew in abundance and protruded from the ground like cypress.

Lichen realized spring must be giving way to summer; he tried to calculate just how long it had been since the accident at the Bridge. Every thought of the Bridge welded and shaped his loathing into a hideous entity growing more powerful. It dominated Lichen, he felt it, reveled in its black potency, and gave way to it. Revenge.

The path ended by a granite cliff that rose through a cloud of mist and towered into heights unseen. Sheets of water roared down the side of the cliff into a large lake. A crude dam separated the lake from a hot spring. Cold, frigid lake water flowed over the dam into the spring spawning a great cloud of steam. It covered everything with a wet shiny gloss as it floated skyward and returned with lazy drips into the water. Lichen stopped walking as the warm spray hit his face.

The mountainous cliffs towered along the north and west of the lake and ran south along the river. Gray, forbidding, and impossible to scale.

Lichen saw the lake flow toward the west side of the pool and disappear under a ledge worn smooth by the water's exit. Where did this river run? Ferns and wild, thick foliage grew among thorn bushes all around the lake. Few flowers braved an appearance. It had a desolate and forlorn beauty.

So, this was the captive part of the camp. There were twenty-five or thirty people milling around, glancing nervously at Lichen and his Hulks. Mothers pulled their children close; babies suckled; men turned back to their work knowing one more slave would not lessen their appalling existence.

Lichen looked at the vertical mountains imprisoning them and knew there was no need for shackles or grape cages here. He had merely been on display while he healed.

Two faerie captives dipped water out of the lake with crude buckets pouring it into a slough that sloped down toward the outcrop, the central non-slave area of camp. Their shoulders were scarred with white lines in perfect symmetry. Brands. Lichen stared.

SAX?

He rotated his shoulder inflamed with memories and full of pus. SAX. What did it mean?

Lichen saw two men and three buckets. He walked over to the spare bucket, picked it up, and started dipping water out of the lake and into the slough.

Short Fat One stood watching. Lichen flashed him a grin. Short Fat One nodded to Lichen and turned back toward the path, the Hulks followed.

Lichen decided to work, to gain their trust. He needed to continue rebuilding his strength. It took strength to escape. It took strength and health to think of a plan. Was Q looking for him? Did Q think he had run away, left with no word to anyone...to Q...to Isabella?

NO!

He would not think of Isabella. Isabella was faerie. Lichen studied his two companions. They neither spoke nor looked at Lichen but plodded along with their task, bucket after bucket with dead eyes, skinny shoulders supporting skinny wings, and despair clinging to them like rotting flesh. Lichen wondered how long they had been here.

A plan. He must think of a plan.

Chapter Twenty-Six

Revenge

The Hulks guarded Lichen with brutality but were indifferent to other prisoners. Did being human matter? One of the other captives looked human, but the Hulks left him alone.

They cursed and swore and screamed. They took perverse delight in his discomfort and elbowed him sharply in his broken ribs. They tripped and shoved him, spilled his buckets of water, and made double or triple the work.

The brand on his shoulder still festered, so they slapped it and bellowed great guffaws at their cleverness. The Hulks dropped his food in the dirt and peed in his water. Their vocabulary was limited, but their cruelty was not. Lichen knew reprieve only when Short Fat One came into the camp. He curbed the Hulks' juvenile pranks; Short Fat One had a no-nonsense approach to life.

One of the other captives seemed friendly, of sorts, if you could call staring and not kicking Lichen friendly. Day-lingo's easy-going and quiet manner made him a comfortable companion and he became a fixture in Lichen's daily routine.

Lichen tried to persuade Day-lingo to teach him the language, but he wouldn't; or couldn't, maybe he wasn't too bright. He was faerie, but not a Rock Faerie. He seemed more refined, well at least he didn't wipe his nose with the back of his hand. Pale brown patches splattered up and down his lanky frame. Day-lingo's muddy brown skin sat close to the rock faerie gray on the dull scale, and he still had the bat-like quality.

But his face was round instead of sharp. His cheeks hung loose; perhaps they had once been full and healthy. Day-lingo's lips cracked from constant licking. Lichen thought he might be from a city, the Rock Faeries were rude and crude; this fella had a little more class. He blew his nose in the bushes and cleaned his hands on the moss.

It happened at Midsummer. Lichen gathered firewood for the cooking hearth when he overheard some children talking about Iter. They had wandered into the slave camp chasing a dog-like animal with three legs they called Terni.

He stopped dead still holding the tree branches close as if they were the key to understanding the children's conversation. Suddenly a barrier crumpled; he had a paradigm shift. Understanding flooded his mind. It was like 10th grade algebra; all of a sudden it just clicked.

Terni? Terni, Latin for a group of three. The dog had three legs. Was it really that easy? He had been so consumed with anger, so bent on revenge, his emotions so strong he had blocked any understanding of their language. For the first time since the carriage wreck, Lichen smiled.

Slave children had no time for games or idle conversation, these children had to be from the outcrop. He listened to them discuss Iter and what it might be like to go.

Iter, he remembered was Isabella's graduation. It was celebrated during Hycintholuna, a blue moon. The children ran off, giggling and chasing Terni. Something caught Lichen behind his knees; he fell and dropped the firewood on his foot. Hulk One or was it Two? laughed loud and vicious.

Enough!

Lichen picked up a large piece of wood, grasped it with both hands limped over to Hulk, and swung. It hit him in the stomach forcing the laughter out with a rush of air.

Lichen had had enough. They couldn't treat him much worse and Lichen didn't care if they did. These two had goaded and prodded and kicked and beat and berated him *enough*.

Hulk Two watched his comrade try to catch his breath, then threw back his ugly head and laughed, long and loud. He choked on the mucus in his throat, spit, and kept on laughing.

"Well, I told you the human would finally get his fill," Hulk Two said, holding his side from laughing.

"Shut up, just shut up. I'll teach him a lesson," Hulk One said as he crouched bent over, still holding his stomach from pain. He stood up and started for Lichen.

"Quit playing with the human and get back to work," bellowed Short Fat One as he walked down to the slough to investigate.

"I told you two to leave him alone. You have enough to do without tormenting the human all the time. Tau'stercus. You're worse than a pimple-face."

The Hulks unwillingly acquiesced. "OK, Ventas," they said, and under their breath they added, "yes, your righteousness," and giggled like two pimple faces.

Lichen grinned. Ventas was Short Fat One's name. The strange accent must be why he hadn't caught the Latin dialect before, but now it was falling into place. Ventas, hunting. And his little slave comrade wasn't Daylingo, it was Delingo. Delingo, to lick. Delingo always licked his lips. Their names fit their personalities. Terni had three legs. Ventas must be a hunter. Lichen felt like he had when he first stepped into the pilot seat of the Raptor. In control.

Tau'stercus indeed. Bull dung.

Now, he could make a plan. Now he could escape this gehenna—this conflagration of misery.

"And you," Ventas said to Lichen, "get your lazy carcass back to work." He made a gesture with his arm, and Lichen picked up the firewood and turned away.

Escape was closer.

Lichen continued to work; his body as busy as his mind. He must keep fit. He arranged firewood using trees for end supports.

He used gestures and body language to organize the workers into teams; no need for them to know he understood their language. They repaired the slough and cleaned the slaves' campsite.

Utilizing the ubiquitous rocks, Lichen revised cooking methods, built latrines, made smoother pathways, and started makeshift huts for the captives.

Lichen put his Eagle Scout to work, and all the while he gained knowledge of the Rock Faeries. And he listened.

Ventas watched Lichen's industriousness and natural leadership of the slaves. He hated being in charge of the captive camp; he should be scouting or hunting. In days gone past, centuries past, he was a proud hunter, respected by all.

He hated this dung pit. He began to give Lichen more and more responsibility. That slave could give him more time for himself. More time to pursue Fuligo. Yes, he needed more time for her.

Lichen delivered produce and supplies regularly to the supply cave. Ventas had long since given Lichen freedom to go between the slave camp and the outcrop.

Lichen had crafted crude shoes from cast-off scrimpet leather to protect his feet from the jagged rocks on the path between the camps. He carried bundles of herbs and cabbages and pulled baskets of little gray potatoes on a sled.

The supply cave was in the granite slab that backed up to Supra's throne of power. The throne he had refused to bow to on his arrival. The door into the cave was not visible from her seat, but tiny vertical ventilation slats looked out upon her.

Supra was perched high on her holy rock. Long strands of silver hair blew in her face and stuck to trails of mucus slimming from her nose; she wiped them away impatiently.

Supra. High and above.

Lichen had arranged the supplies in the cave in a logical and orderly manner. Perishables, non-perishables. Stacks of dried scrimpet meat; vegetables packed in dried grass; fruit fermenting in hollowed-out rock containers—the Rock Faeries did like their liquor; herbs hung in bundles upside down from the ceiling, their pungent scents improving the dank cave considerably.

Lichen wondered if the bat-like Rock Faeries could hang upside down. He began to put the vegetables in their proper bins when he heard voices through the slats. Two Rock Faerie men Lichen had never seen before spoke quietly with Supra. Lichen leaned closer. They were discussing Iter.

"Supra, you must have your tribe ready by the fourth week of Morningluna. We will join you to begin the trek to Vinca Village."

Vinca Village? They were leaving the Proscriptio; they were going to Vinca Village?

The faerie's voice ruminated from his barrel chest. A ragged cerulean cape was draped about his shoulders. A darker blue cap sat low over one eye; his long gray hair trailed down his back. He held his wings stiff and unbending, he spoke to Supra as an equal. His man stood two steps behind, alert and watchful.

"Do not presume to command me, Alveus," Supra said in her even flat tone.

"We *must* go," Alveus said. "It is Septmillia. We have received the vocatio. You know we must go. It is our last chance. We have endured this dung pit for centuries," he said as his eyes swept over the outcrop. "You may want to die here in this craggy barren litho-hell, but I do not. I am finished here. The noxious vapors of the Miasma Swamp are killing The TOR. Every month we are fewer. We want to take advantage of the vocatio and make our transformation. We want to take the oath. We want to go home. I cannot speak for the rest of the Proscriptio, but we are leaving."

He held up the dispensation from the goddess Iris. "We have the vocatio; we can leave the Proscriptio. I know you have received yours as well. We are going. What say you?"

Supra shifted on her rock. After a moment, she raised her eyes and nodded.

Lichen stood in the cave frozen in place. They were going to leave. They were going home. Lichen did not entertain the thought of going home himself; he only had thoughts of the vengeance that lay festering in the bottom of his soul, black, vile, dark, and suffocating as a coal pit.

"Very well, Supra," Alveus said. "I am going to speak with Tribes GEL and ARI. Whether they join us or not, I will return the fourth week of Morningluna. Be ready. If you are not, be ready to die. We are at the end of our banishment. We must choose life or death.

"You and all of Tribe SAX will die if you stay here. As for Tribe TOR, we choose to live. We are going to Iter. We are going to transform."

Lichen trembled and tingled from ears to ankles. Apparently, Iter was not only for faerie quickening, *Isabella's quickening*, but also a grand celebration and renewal of some sort.

Transformation? Everyone attended, and this year, even the outlaw Rock Faeries were invited? Why hadn't Cecelia or Ram mentioned it?

This was their only opportunity to renew. Transformations could only be done if participants were issued a dispensation from Iris, a *vocatio.* The Rock Faeries had been in the Proscriptio for years, for centuries even, and this is the first time Iris had extended a vocatio.

If they did not accept it, another invitation would not be issued. This was their one and only chance. They *had* to renew, to transform. Their life depended on it. If they didn't, they would die.

Lichen's choice was clear. He must stop them from going to Iter.

The Rock Faeries must die.

Lichen felt his pulse quicken, pumping an idea through his mind. If the renegade faeries couldn't go to Iter, they would die. This is how he would exact revenge. This is how he would kill the Rock Faeries. Prevent them from going or disrupt Iter altogether. But how?

Chapter Twenty-Seven

Mole

Lichen stood tall, panting, and sweaty over his opponent.

"Ha, now what do you think you filthy degenerate pig?" Lichen felt confident to say whatever popped into his mind as he knew the faeries did not understand a word he said.

Wrestling had become a routine competition. With Hulk One standing close guard, Lichen wrestled Hulk Two weekly. And weekly Lichen beated him.

"So, what will your reward be today young warrior, swimming again?" Hulk Two asked, Lichen understanding him perfectly, realizing the irony of the term warrior.

Lichen pointed toward the falls, still pretending not to understand their speech.

The water was cold. Lichen slashed through it, swimming effortlessly to the falls nearly a hundred yards away. Lichen lived for this moment each week; it was the nearest he ever got to solitude.

Diving in this clear water was like soaring above the clouds. Even Delingo didn't trail him here. He climbed onto the ledge and sat in a small, hollowed space behind the falls. The Hulks weren't worried about escape, where would he go? Solid granite mountain. Behind. Above. Below.

Sun shined through the falling pane of water, rainbow colors warmed him. Lichen dosed.

A mournful sound awakened him; he jerked up on his elbow. He drew a thick clear crystal from his stash bag, amazing the stuff he had collected in this lake.

He raised it to his eye for a makeshift telescope and saw a girl across the water. She sat on the sand; knees bent, head on her arms. No one else was about; the Hulks must be picking on someone else.

She was crying, a desolate, miserable moan.

"A new captive," Lichen said to a small crab backing into a hole. "Probably, hmmm, let's say 19 or so." Instinctively he felt like swimming over and consoling the girl. A quick, automatic response.

"No one ever consoled me," Lichen said, his voice hard. The crab wiggled his antennae.

The girl used her meager skirt to wipe her eyes. Her long red hair flowed around her body like a cloak. The wind blew it aside and Lichen could see the fresh SAX brand. He shrugged his shoulder, remembering.

And, Lichen had to have a plan to exact his revenge on them. He hated them, all of them. They were cruel and bitter. And ugly. Their runny noses were disgusting. It would suit him just fine if they all died. And he knew just how to do it. Keep them away from Iter.

How?

"Lichen," a voice whispered. "Lichen, are you awake?"

Lichen sat up abruptly and strained to see into the night. "Who's there?"

"I'm new here. I saw you today in the cooling pool...watching me."

Lichen blushed in the darkness. He didn't know she had seen him. He wondered if she saw him get the jewels. Were they hers? If so, where did she get them? And why did she throw them into the pool?

Lichen opened his makeshift door. Dry twigs and branches laced together with grass scraped along the dirt, sweeping it clean of pebbles each time the door opened.

"What are you doing here? It's the middle of the night. If they catch you here we'll both be publicly thrashed." Lichen spoke from experience. He had been thrashed before...on numerous occasions. Lichen clenched his jaw, remembering. Yes. He wanted revenge.

"I must speak with you. Now," Lorelei said.

"OK, OK. Come in but make it quick. And be quiet." She walked past him into the room. Lichen closed the door and saw muddy footprints in the dirt. Water dripped from her dress, her hair. Had she been swimming? At night? Her SAX brand looked red and painful, even in the scant light.

Lorelei stood watching him. Silent.

"Well," Lichen said. "What is it?"

"I want to help you escape," she said.

"Well, we all want to escape," Lichen said. "Where are you from?"

"I can help you," Lorelei said.

Lichen laughed softly. "Yea, well, why don't you just go on back to your bedroll before you get us both whipped?"

"I can help you," she said again. "You want to escape and destroy the faeries. I can help you."

"Well, you don't have to be a mind reader to know that. What makes you think you can help me? You just got here. If you can escape, why don't you just go? What's your name anyway?"

"I have information. Information you need. You want revenge, I can give it to you."

Lichen mulled over her words. This little half-pint snippet knew where to get jewels. Maybe it wouldn't hurt to just listen.

"OK. Shoot," he said.

"Shoot?" Lorelei asked.

"Talk. Give me your important information." Lichen raised his eyebrows and emphasized his syllables. He just realized her speech was different from the faeries. But he could still understand her. And she him. "And tell me about Iter. About this *transformation*."

"All right," Lorelei said. "Iter is always during Hycintholuna. Transformation requires a true change of heart. Their bodies will be restored and their souls cleansed, but the process is agonizing. If one joined in Iter and was not truly remorseful for his actions, the evil in his heart would destroy him."

"So, they have to be sorry for what they did? Sorry for whatever got them banished in the first place?" Lichen said.

"Yes," Lorelei said. "After the cleansing, renewed faeries must declare a new allegiance to Divus, the Creator, to the Earth Mother, to Domus, and to their fellow beings."

"Hmmm," Lichen mumbled.

"Most banished Fey prefer death to life in the Proscriptio." Lorelei looked around. "It is barren and void of joy here."

"So," Lichen said, ignoring Lorelei's sadness. "How long have they been here? How long have they had to think things over, so to speak?"

"Seven Septmillia," Lorelei said.

"Seven what?"

"49,000 years," Lorelei replied.

"Tau'stercus." Lichen was dumbfounded. " They've been here that long? Her Holiness Supra is 49,000 years old? Good grove, no wonder she's wrinkled."

"Yes, no one dies in banishment, they live on and on in their misery. Not all of the banished are offered a vocatio," Lorelei said. "Some remain here...for eternity."

Lichen found his voice. "Let me see if I have this right; if in a ...Septmillia...*seven* Septmillias...like *that* wouldn't be enough time," he muttered, "...their hearts are not changed," he snorted thinking they did not have hearts, "and they are offered the vocatio but do not accept it, they'll die. But, if they *have* changed, and participate in Iter, Iris will give them a new life."

"Yes."

"Wow," Lichen said, "apparently all the tribes of the Rock Faeries have received a vocatio, which indicates that they will probably all go to Iter."

"Apparently," Lorelei said.

Lichen's hatred boiled; his eyes snapped. "A second chance? They get a second chance?"

Lorelei flinched; Latere coiled in her mind reminding her of her task.

"If you want to kill the Rock Faeries, you must have the Tempus Crystal," Lorelei said.

"The what?"

"The Tempus Crystal. It controls everything in Domus. The time, the weather, everything."

"OK. How will that help me kill these soulless villainous inhuman creatures ?"

Lorelei flinched at the venom in Lichen's words.

"If you have the Crystal, you can control anything. Like Iter. If you control Iter, you can control the Rock Faeries," she said patiently.

Lichen sat down on the bed. Lorelei stood watching him. Dripping.

"So, if I have this crystal, I can manipulate time and weather. If the Rock Faeries cannot go to Iter, they will die. I know that. So, the Crystal can stop Iter from taking place?"

"The Crystal can do anything. It controls Domus," Lorelei said. Latere laughed in her mind, very pleased.

Lichen's mind whirled and pieces began to link together like a well-tooled machine. He had the bribe money: the jewels. He knew the means: the Crystal. Now, he just had to get out of the Proscriptio. Escape.

Chapter Twenty-Eight

Proscriptio

As adults, the GENS brothers were bold in action and stunning to behold. They had boasted a wingspan greater than any in Domus. Their intellect was renowned, respected, almost revered. They were fair in judgment, quick in decision and their people loved them.

Each of the brothers excelled in specific skills they had learned from the Mother and they used that knowledge to govern their villages. They prospered as they taught their tribes to love and respect Divus and the Earth Mother. They established the Primordial, the first tenet of Lex Scriptura: Honor Super Omnia—honor above all.

Supra had learned the GENS' history well. She loved and respected the Brothers for their relationship with the Mother and for their genius in planning the Quad. She was proud that all of Domus followed their example.

Supra excelled in skills necessary for guiding their tribe. Confident. Clever. Charismatic. So, at the death of her father, Supra assumed leadership of the SAX. She relished in it. Her temperate manner had gained her the respect of, not only her own tribe but the other Quad leaders as well.

They looked to her to maintain harmony and foster cooperation within the Quad. The King and The Princeps depended on her to mitigate problems and offset any extreme behavior with her fair and balanced judgments. But, she had failed.

Supra had underestimated the intense unrest of a small group of Torrens led by Narro. Each of the four tribes in the Quad was charged with specific jobs and historic duties handed down through the generations. Tasks designed by the Brothers GENS; responsibilities given by the Earth Mother.

The Torrens' charge and sole duty was the River and all the water. The Great River Potens Herself had taught their forefather and founder, TOR, the Song of the West. The Torrens were responsible for keeping the waterways clear and free of debris; for making sure the springs, fountains, and canals were always clean, pure, and healthy. Life-giving and life-sustaining.

"Why must we always be about this task? Isn't the Great River Potens able to care for herself and for us?" Narro said to his little band of rebels, his emerald ancestral eyes gleaming.

"We are wasting our time; we have many other things to do. We cannot spend our days watching over the River. It is her duty to watch over us. Must we constantly watch over the irrigation? Does not our daily water come from the Mother? Does she not carry away our waste? It is *her* duty to care for us. She is insulted that we feign to watch over her. Come; let us leave her to her duties. Let us be about our own tasks and not waste our time presuming to do hers."

Disrespect and malcontent spread throughout the Torren's tribe infecting minds and poisoning hearts. A virulent seductress.

Narro whispered his distorted vision of The Mother throughout GENS tribes. He planted the pestilence of bribery in the venal and saturated the unprincipled and corruptible with false direction.

The Gelu Tribe's duty was administrating, organizing, and distributing ice to the Quad.

"My brothers," Narro said. "The Mother makes ice and transports it through channels to our central Ice Houses."

Narro stood high on a boulder looking down on the villagers. "Surely the Gelu do not need to watch over the Mother?" Narro said, his palms upraised over hunched shoulders, his expression incredible.

"Unquestionably, the Mother knows best how to care for the ice. The Mother is affronted by your presumptions," he shouted pointing an accusing finger at the crowd.

"Leave this now, he thundered, "and be about more important matters." Gilded trickery settled upon the tribe like an invisible and indiscernible net.

The Gelu listened. The Gelu agreed. Their heritage forgotten amidst their plans of how best to use their leisure.

Narro grew bolder, cocky as overconfidence fed his growing power. Narcotic. He stood tall and beautiful reveling as his supremacy slowly rose over the tribes. His wings, the color of a spring-fed lake, stretched to the sky, the sun highlighting each blue-green feather. He raised his arms and threw back his head; his hair blew behind him, thick and shining with the rich browns and coppers of the earth. Triumph blazed from his face. His pervasive gospel spread.

Narro paid no heed to the tempest brewing; no heed to the unrest and displeasure of the Mother.

Narro reasoned with the Aridus Tribe. "Do you know more than The Mother? Do you presume to do her job? She knows when the crop is ripe.

"The Aridus should not interfere with The Mother's timing. She will drop the fruit and dry it where it lays. Do not insult her by constantly monitoring Her actions. You do not need to haul it to the drying sheds.

"She is our sustenance. She will supply our every need. Does She not give us our water from the sky? Is this not a marvel? Every drop a precious gift." Narro lowered his voice. His tone, persuasive.

"Would you insult this gift by mopping and swabbing Her very presence from your homes and your lives with your filthy rags? If The Mother wants your homes to be dry, She will dry them with her most powerful sun.

"You mock her by gathering dead trees to burn in the winter. She needs no help from such as you. She needs no supervision by the Aridus. The Mother knows her business, leave her to it," Narro said, his words worming their way through tribal consciousness. Dysfunctional logic.

Meetings were held. Heralders sent. Narro was right. The Mother was in charge, and no one should intervene with Her great wisdom. To look over The Mother's shoulder was paramount to blasphemy. It showed a lack of faith. Distrust. And we must trust The Mother; we've always trusted The Mother.

To do The Mother's work for her was slavery. The Mother did not want slaves. Drones. The renegade faeries congratulated themselves; they were the chosen. They alone knew The Mother's will.

"You must honor your responsibilities, Supra charged. "The Mother gives Her gifts and you must work in tandem with Her. Our ancestors, the Four Brothers GENS swore to keep their obligations to the Mother, generations to come." Supra was met with indifference.

"We must keep the vows made by the Brothers. It is what keeps us whole, and living," she said. The GENS laughed. Mocked.

Supra continued, "We must respect The Mother. We must care for The Mother." Futile words. Deaf ears.

Supra traveled throughout the Quad. She spoke to groups, to families, to individuals, to anyone who would listen. She appealed to their good sense. She implored; she invoked the name of the King, the Princeps, and Divus. She pleaded and pressed. But, Narro had prepared the people for her coming.

"They will come. The King. The Princeps. Supra. They will come to dissuade you from your destiny with old precepts and understandings. They will enslave you and charge you to disrespect The Mother. To whom will you listen, The Divine, or the damned?" Narro said. Cunning. Pervasive.

The Saxitilus, Supra's tribe, was the last to succumb to Narro's proselyting. The SAX was charged with the quarries of the Quad. The mines supplied precious stones for trading. And rock for construction. Roads, bridges, fences. Homesteads, mansions, cottages. Sand for glassmaking. Lime and clay for mortar and cement. Narro's pernicious doctrine pandered to the greed of the Sax.

"You work hard mining the gems from The Mother. She wants you to keep them for yourselves. Look at the slothfulness of your brother tribes," Narro said.

"The Mother does not want them to share in Her bounty. Unlike you, they deserve nothing of the riches of The Mother. She has made a special place in which you can store the precious stones. Look to this cave; see how clever The Mother is. Your stones will be safe here."

The Fey listened and believed. They had forgotten the sacred Songs.

Day by day, the villages fell into disrepair. The streets and waterways became clogged with refuse and litter. Slimy vegetation crawled from infested banks choking the food supply. Herbs deteriorated in the ground, their medicine impotent, neutered by neglect. In places, the land was arid, fallow. Once-beautiful trees dripping with repugnant black foam dropped their bounty on hard, cracked, unyielding ground.

In other areas, swampy quagmires of fetid vegetation lay decomposing like the life of the quad slowly ebbing away. Anything edible was ruined left rotting in the dark where the sun had ceased to shine.

Tons of melted ice carried refuse along the streets, stinking, polluted water rose daily in the shops and homes. Pomanders of stench. Insects and vermin infiltrated the hamlets bringing disease and sorrow. The animals died from want of grass; the fields dotted with maggoted carcasses and swarms of blackfly. Pandemic scourge.

"It is them," Narro accused. "It is Supra and the Princeps. They insult The Mother with their admonitions for slavery so She punishes us all."

Craftsmen became slovenly, trading ceased. Children ran truant throughout the villages, unlearned and unclean. Even the laudable, the last holdouts to Narro's dogma, subsided into apathy. The Mother would take care of them. They were her children. Disciples of deceit.

Supra despaired. What happened to the industrious tribes she loved? Where were the bright and beautiful people of the GENS? What dark and villainous worm had eaten its way into the heart and soul of her people?

Nothing she said or did affected them. They became lazy and prideful, quarrelsome and discontent. Raping and plundering. Covetous. Adulterous. Murderous.

The Princeps visited the Quad warning of calamitous consequences. Narro laughed at him and the tribes laughed with him. The Princeps told Supra she would be spared if she came with him to Vinca Village, to Numen, and the Crystal Grove.

"No," she said. Sadness weighed her words; they fell heavy in the air. "No, I will stay. I have failed my people; I will accept their fate."

"Return to your Crystal Grove old man," Narro yelled at the Princeps. "We know what The Mother wants. We will insult her no longer. It is you She despises. It is you who cause Her pain. Leave us now and go back to your futile, ineffective prayers. Be gone from our land. Let The Mother care for us, love us, and make us happy."

They took up stones against him, hurling and shouting their words of hatred. When they thought him dead, they left him bleeding in the sewage, laughing and proud of their deed.

A vagabond troll watched from the shadows until the mob walked away intent on other mischief. He did not know his letters or manners, but he knew this man was Princeps. He picked him up gently and stole him out of the GENS quad and back to Numen.

Supra sick at heart at this last atrocity retired to her chambers. She stood before her mirror, felt the collapse of her people, and looked at the failure she had become.

Her beautiful skin was bloodless, drawn, and pinched, like one of the neglected pears rotting beneath the tree. Her raven wings had lost their turquoise lights and hung lifeless like the branches of the willow outside her window. Her lustrous jet-black hair, stripped of its vibrancy, clung to her head and shoulders and straggled down her back with stringy grease-like fingers. Already she was losing her color.

They had broken the Primordial. Banishment from life as she knew it. From color. Her world would be gray. Her life would be gray. Legend said the Proscriptio was gray. Devoid of vibrancy. Devoid of color.

Supra had never known anyone to return from the Proscriptio. Perhaps they all died there. Perhaps. She did not know where it was. She only knew that it was gray.

It began the next morning. The Great River Potens rose up out of her bed with a ferocity no one had ever witnessed. Leaps of torrential waves engulfed the Quad. She covered the villages and everything in them. The tribes ran screaming, clinging to one another, clinging to their lives.

Supra did not run. She sat in her chambers, waiting; she did not have to wait long. The river did not rise gradually. One minute it wasn't there, the next, Supra was under the water, suspended in the frigid grasp of the Great River Potens.

For a moment she felt as if she were in the arms of The Mother. The Mother was rocking her, soothing her. Supra wanted only to sleep and never wake up. Blissful unawareness.

But she did wake up. The tribes and all their animals, alive and dead, were scattered around her on the riverbank. Despite the injuries and misery, the thing Supra remembered most was that everyone was gray.

Gone were their beautiful colored wings, their radiant complexions. They were all multi shades of gray. Membranes replaced feathers. Leather replaced skin. Her cape, pasted to her shoulders with mud, was the only thing that had retained its color. A red reminder of all that she had lost. Crimson shame.

Supra rose from the gray mud and stood on her feet. Gray oozed through her toes. Her skin looked no different from the muck. She turned toward a mountain that loomed in the distance and began to walk. The sharp rocks cut her flesh, but she continued. Brush and thorns tore at her clothing and pierced her arms and legs. On she walked. A small outcrop jutted from the foot of the mountain. Supra could hear a waterfall in the distance.

She climbed on a boulder, sat down, crossed her legs, and closed her eyes. She lay over on her side and slept, her cold ugly wing covering her. Supra's banishment was complete.

The Great River Potens roared through GENS and back down into The Mother. By daybreak, the water was gone, the earth dry and barren. The wind stirred dust into whirls, large and small, spinning mindlessly. No sweet songs drifted on the breeze, only silence. The Wasteland was born.

When Supra awoke the next morning, the tribes were lying all around her sleeping. She was still on her boulder. Villagers sprawled on the ground as if strewn among the shards and splinters of Inferi. Narro was nowhere to be seen.

Before the banishment, Supra had been the one voice of reason, but no one had listened. Now they asked, what should they do? Where should they go? Supra was still the one voice of reason.

Supra could create synthesis, they thought. She could weave them together again. She could join their fragmented lives and recover that which was lost. They stood before her with vacant eyes and hopeful expressions.

I cannot do this. I have no heart she thought.

"No," she said to the Fey crowding around her boulder. "No. You must leave me. You must find another. I have failed you. Leave me." She turned away from them and put her face in her hands.

"No," came a voice from the back. A very gray, very short, and very fat faerie stepped forward. "No, it is we who have failed you. We would not listen, so we are here. Banished. We do not deserve you, but we need you. Please."

Supra raised her head and looked at him. The minutes ticked by. Silence. The Fey watched. Waited. Supra's eyes, blank and gray.

Finally, she stood. "What is your name?"

"Ventas," he replied. "I am a hunter."

Supra raised her chin slightly. Her bat-like wings rose with it. "Then hunt," she said.

Ventas blinked and stared. After a moment he straightened his shoulders, turned toward a group of men, and barked instructions. He divided the Fey into their former tribes and organized a hunting party. They didn't know what the Proscriptio had to eat, but they were about to find out.

Chapter Twenty-Nine

Murderer

Ira Lungwort. Now there's a name. It seems to fit him. He comes to the Proscriptio every few weeks to trade and he is never in a good mood. Strange for a trader. Today was Lichen's first glimpse of the traveling monger.

How does he get in here?

Lichen instantly disliked Ira the Trader. Well dressed and well spoken, but all air and no substance. Ira expertly ingratiated himself with Supra; he knew which side of the bread his butter was on.

The trader's bulky short stature appeared taller because he kept his mocha wings extended in a strutting sort of way. Narcissistic.

Brown, short-cropped hair tipped in white stuck out all over his head. Raptor-like. It grew down the back of his neck fusing into his feathers.

Lichen thought Ira the worst kind of predator. His mind, calculating. Intense black reptilian eyes that missed nothing. Wings, always threatening and posturing. Ira reminded Lichen of a major he knew:

demanded attention and exuded imitation power like a dud missile. Lichen was repulsed.

But, he knows how to get out of here, and that information is probably for sale.

Ira had a poker face. Lichen was very good at poker.

Lichen watched him arbitrating with Supra. He was shifty. She was shrewd. Ira never quite managed to negotiate the intricate caverns of her mind; she always stayed one step ahead. Supra paid for her contraband with aes, small gray pebbles the faeries used for money.

As Ira left Supra's presence, he put away his premium goods; the rest of the village got trinkets. Like America's indigenous people.

The non-negotiable Supra System, among other tedious rules and regs, forbade the captive slaves to trade, but Lichen's upgraded status allowed him the freedom to wander among the outcrop tribe and watch the goings on.

Ira got his first glimpse of Lichen walking freely among the villagers. On previous visits he had heard of the paragon captive who single-handedly and systematically reorganized the entire camp. According to Ventas, instead of sinking into a quagmire of self-pity and forced labor, this strange slave willingly coordinated not only the other captives but the tribal members as well. He had new ideas.

Ventas drank more than his share of berry liquor and expounded about this extraordinary slave quite freely to Ira. Lichen extended the existing slough that ran from the falls to the outcrop and added another slough to the hot springs. Now, Supra and her tribe had both hot and cold continuous running water. This eliminated the cumbersome and sporadic bucket brigade. With Lichen's ingenious water-plant siphon the new flushable latrines and bathing pits improved the odor and health of the camp. Considerably.

Gardens flourished. Cooking became a pleasure instead of a chore and it showed in the quality of meals. Ventas allowed the slave unprecedented freedom because of the heightened standard of life, as long as he had a bodyguard, of course.

It was almost possible to forget they were in the Proscriptio. Forget they were the outlaw tribes of Domus. But not quite.

Months ago when Ira first listened to stories of Lichen's accomplishments, he wasn't impressed. What was another slave more or less; it was nothing to Ira.

But, on each subsequent visit he could see the tribe's improved living conditions and was puzzled as to where this exemplary faerie had been captured. Today, however, Ira was shocked to see that this model of excellence wasn't faerie at all. He was human. Ira hated humans.

Ira narrowed his eyes as he watched Lichen walk around the camp. Boys mimicked Lichen's confident gait stretching their wings to equal his height; girls cast sidelong glances with twinkling eyes and suppressed giggles; men asked advice on tool making and the physics of removing huge boulders from the outcrop; and women, well Ira knew from experience what their expressions revealed.

"Tau'stercus," Ira said under his breath. "What inferi did he come from?" A shadow slithered from crevice to crack in Ira's devious mind. It slowly followed each possibility. Flicked its tongue in search of a clue to this human's identity. Something...he had heard something. What was it? Other tribes along his trade route? Ira considered each village, in and out of the Proscriptio. No, nothing.

Suddenly the shadow reared its head and caught the memory in venomous fangs.

"Regnum!" Ira said. "Q!"

Ira traveled all of Domus plying his wares. Two weeks after Bel-Moon he went to the large marketplace in Regnum, the home of

Domus' Royal family. The market buzzed with its usual fervor and flurry.

The scandalous news of the day concerned the murder of Agaso, the Ambassador's manservant, the death of the Ambassador's daughter, and the disappearance of the grandson.

Milkmaids gossiped that the handsome lad could not possibly have committed such a heinous crime; wagon makers argued it was very likely, and, for that matter, how did they know he was handsome? And even if he was, what did that have to do with being capable of murder? The maids accused the wagon makers of being jealous and the conversation ended with exchanges of riotous flirtations and swats on plump rumps.

Ira's mouth gapped open. The grandson lives. Q's grandson lives. Those dirty deceitful trolls; he knew it had been a mistake to trust them.

What about Keeper Valeo...What will he do when he finds out Lichen Ipse is in the Proscriptio?

And Latere...tau'stercus. What would Latere do?

Time enough to worry about that later. Ira relaxed. Right now his bags and pockets bulged with aes. Worthless rocks found only in the Proscriptio. But Latere paid him well for them.

Latere. Ira cringed. *Tau'stercus.*

Ira must be sure to make the exchange before he tells Latere about Lichen. Alive.

Supra always allowed Ira to stay the night. He would sit around the cook-fire and flirt with young women, assessing, comparing. His lying lips spewed red berry liquor and stories of artificial heroic adventures.

As long as Arx accompanied Lichen, he could go anywhere within the camp. The perimeter was well guarded. The Great River Potens protected the South perimeter with deep whirlpools and rapids; an impassable granite mountain with roaring falls on the North and sheer cliffs on the West, and most of the East.

Supra's handpicked Gestapo watched the only trail into camp day and night. Lichen's prominence as a Renaissance man did not annul his slave status. He still had Arx. His personal escort.

Tonight Lichen stayed at the outcrop with the tribe so he could have a word with Ira. Arx stayed a reasonable distance, his dull witless eyes watching females. Berry liquor flowed freely, and soon raucous songs and general hilarity gave way to snores and the surreptitious passing of gas as the Rock Faeries succumbed to stupor.

Lichen began to pick his way through sleeping bodies in various states of inebriation toward Ira. Ira stood and whispered quietly to a girl. He put his wing around her and walked his fingers down her face. She leaned against him, shyly nodded, and strode towards Ira's bedroll.

Lichen interrupted Ira's leer. "Trader," Lichen said, "may I have a word with you?" There was something about this faerie, had he seen him before?

"Well, young man," Ira said, "you've made quite an impression here. For a slave," Ira mocked slurring his words.

Lichen towered above Ira with a superior swagger; Ira's dislike of this human showed on his face. Lichen stood erect and proud, oblivious to his captive condition.

"I earn my keep," Lichen replied. He felt his hackles rise, but his face remained impassive.

Ira raised his wings a fraction. "I don't see many humans up here. Where you from?"

"I don't see many traders up here. Where are *you* from?"

Ira's eyes hardened. What to do about this boy. What to do.

"You have a pretty good trading scam going on here. Probably make a little fortune," Lichen grinned. "How much are those gray pebbles worth?" Ira didn't respond.

"I might be able to make that fortune bigger," Lichen said. Crinkles deepened around Lichen's eyes as they caught a subtle shift in Ira. He counted on Ira's greed to get him out of this hole.

Lichen decided to take the plunge. "I'm leaving here, and I want you to help me."

Ira started at Lichen's boldness. What would Supra give him to learn of this escape plan? What would Q give him to have his grandson back? What would Latere give him to know the whereabouts of the grandson? And what would Keeper Valeo do when he learned Lichen lived?

"My name is Lichen Ipse and my grandfather is the Ambassador. He will reward you well."

Ira leaned against the rock wall that housed a privy. He folded his arms across his chest and smiled at Lichen. "I doubt if he would pay a reward for a murderer."

Lichen blanched. "A murderer? What? What did you say?"

"You are wanted for murder. Which do you prefer, imprisonment here or execution in Regnum?"

"What are you talking about? I've never killed anyone," Lichen said, his voice rising.

"Yeah? Well, Agaso's dead and you ran away. So...,"

"Agaso?" Lichen thought of the distinguished old butler and his wonderful wings. He wiped his hand over his face and back up through his hair, his thoughts of escape temporarily eroded.

"Who could have done that? And why?" He sunk to the ground and laid his head down on his arms. *Murder?*

Ira scrutinized Lichen while he tried to calculate his options. His thoughts scurried down one trail, then another worse than a manic scrimpet.

The Crioсts of New Ivy had issued a Bans for Lichen. Just to question him, of course, but he was the only suspect in Agaso's murder.

Ira could tell the Criocts Lichen is in the Proscriptio, but then Ira wasn't supposed to be in the Proscriptio.

And what would that get him? He could go directly to Q. The Ambassador insisted on Lichen's innocence, and he might give Ira a reward.

But I must tell Latere. I have to tell Latere, don't I?

What would happen if he didn't tell Latere? But, if Latere found out Ira knew where Lichen was and hadn't told him...tau'stercus.

What to do?

"Ira, you must get me out of here," Lichen said. He jumped to his feet and grabbed the startled faerie by the shoulders. "You know the way; you must help me escape."

Ira stood staring up at Lichen with distaste.

"Don't be so human. There is no way out of here, and I won't risk my arrangement with Supra to help a *human*."

"My grandfather will pay you."

Ira froze. "I...I don't know." His mind was whirling. Sweat bubbled up through berry-liquor stains on his lip.

"Supra would boil me for dessert if she caught me stealing one of her slaves." His voice escalated. "Not to mention her own precious *icon of industry*."

Arx eyed them suspiciously and started lumbering across the yard. Lichen held an open palm toward Arx and put his other hand in his pocket. Arx settled back into his mindless female watching.

Lichen stooped over and laid something on the ground beside Ira's boot. Ira looked down. There, reflecting, pulsing in the firelight lay a large uncut ruby.

Ira caught his breath and for a moment he couldn't move. The ruby transfixed him. Mesmerized him. Lust surged through his veins; he wiped the perspiration from his lip. Ira looked up to see Lichen grinning at him.

Gottcha, Lichen thought and gave Ira a quick wink.

"Pretty, isn't she?"

Ira stooped over and retrieved the ruby. He held it tenderly like he would a woman. Ira needed time to think of what to do. When manipulation was involved, he reigned supreme; but stressful complicated situations invoked a thick mental fog. It disengaged Ira's reasoning capacity. He needed time.

Ira's mind raced along overgrown paths of confusion. He rambled.

"Well, I don't know. Tau'stercus. I don't know how to get you out. And Supra...." Ira nervously pulled at the spiky feathers on his neck.

Lichen shrugged his shoulders. "Well, alright then," he said as he reached for the ruby. Ira clenched his fist around the stone and stepped back.

"I would normally return at Morningluna. If I come back sooner, Supra will be suspicious. And, I have to consider my other routes. They depend on me you know. I'll need to renew my supply of wares and I was supposed to..."

"Ira!" Lichen commanded. He stepped closer and stooped to look into Ira's eyes. It was like watching a gyroscope off-kilter.

"I don't want to know your laundry list of responsibilities. Now, when can you return?" *Good, holy grove, this creature is annoying.*

Lichen's abrupt irascible behavior cleared Ira's fog. He clutched the ruby, squared his shoulders, and raised his wings.

"OK. OK, I'll do it."

Lichen relaxed. "How?" he said. "Do you know how you will get me out?"

"Of course, I do," Ira snapped.

He had no idea.

Lichen turned toward Arx. "OK, Pus Pocket, time for bed."

How would they ever pull this off?

He had no idea.

Chapter Thirty

Gens

Supra had known this day would come, but she felt no joy. Seven Septmillia ago she had vowed that when this day arrived, she would march the SAX along with the other tribes over the bridge to Vinca Village and into the Grove with pride, showing all of Domus that the Tribes of GENS are resilient. Strong of will and valiant of heart.

But the exile had been too much. Forty-nine thousand years of gray deprivation. Forty-nine thousand years to atone for breaking the Primordial.

The Primordial. The first tenet of the Lex Scriptura. The rules of conduct essential to Fey society. Unbreakable. Unalterable. Unavoidable.

The Primordial: hono super omnia. Honor above all. If anyone disobeyed, destroyed, or dishonored the Mother, they would be banished by Divus the Creator. The Earth Mother had but one rule, the

Primordial; every other law or ordinance depended on that concept like berries on a bush.

The Earth Mother must be protected, loved, and honored. The Fey took care of The Mother; the Mother took care of the Fey. Supra perched on her rock and remembered.

Supra had returned to her quarters, alone. For two days she had been in council with the tribes who shared her Quad: her own tribe, Saxitilus, and the other three, Gelu, Torrens and, Aridus all named after the four founding brothers. They were commonly called the SAX, GEL, TOR, and ARI.

For two days she had heard nothing but contentious, belligerent, combative debates between the tribes. Now, she needed solitude. Time to prepare for the tribunal. Time to accept their inevitable fate. Banishment.

Supra was born here in GENS. GENS was the oldest quad in Domus; the only quad to found tribal villages led by brothers, and the only quad to be directly established by the Mother.

All the quads of Domus modeled themselves after the GENS, before that the Fey were nomadic people wandering aimlessly throughout Domus.

The GENS brothers were grand physical specimens, tall, strong, and beautiful. Saxitilus—SAX—had dark mischievous eyes that sparkled with humor. Full brow, square jaw, thick neck. Bulging hard muscular arms and legs. He wore his long waves of jet hair tied back in a queue. His powerful wings glistened blue-black and carried him on air currents for leagues.

"SAX, " The Mother said. "SAX, come with me and I will teach you the Song of North." The Mother led him to Mt. Vetare in The Vetare Silva, The Forbidden Forest.

"But, Wise Mother," SAX said, "this is a forbidden place, I cannot enter."

"SAX, it is not forbidden to me. It belongs to me and it is mine to share. Come."

SAX circled cautiously, his powerful wings gliding silently. No Fey had ever ventured into this forest or upon this mountain. The Mother called and SAX obeyed.

The mountain looked green and growing from the air and when SAX landed under the living canopy, he saw caves, thousands of caves filled with crystals singing ancient melodies. The precious stones were gleaming and humming; the notes floating through the air like dandelion tuft.

SAX put his hands on his head not believing the beauty of what he saw and heard.

"They sing the Song of the North," The Mother told him. "It is Earth's sacred song. She sings it with joy and intent and so, must you. Learn it, SAX. Learn the Song of North as my gift to you. But remember with knowledge comes responsibility."

SAX listened and learned. Time lost meaning and disappeared in the slit between sunset and mountain. The moon grew dark then full again as time flowed easily on Mt. Vetare. SAX learned the Song of North and sang it in clear sweet tones that resonated within the crystals of the mountain. The melody set the hues of the precious stones. SAX laughed and The Mother laughed with him.

SAX continued to develop his gift and his Song was the sweetest ever heard on Mt. Vetare. When he returned to GENS, he shared some jewels with his tribe but kept the sacred music of the mountain, the Song of the North, and the way of the stones to himself.

Gelu—GEL--was opposite of SAX in color. His hair straight and white, his eyes the white-blue of solid glacial cold. Long legs and slender but muscular arms gave him a graceful beauty. His extended wings could blind you with their brightness like ice reflecting the sun.

As he grew older, he coveted solitude. GEL spent days alone riding invisible paths in the sky, floating on streams across the heavens. He flew to great heights above Domus just to experience the frigid air.

"You love the coldness and see its beauty?" The Mother asked GEL.

"Yes, yes, I do," GEL replied. "I love the crisp freshness. I love the sharp thin edges of cold. I love the way it molds you to its form and holds you there. I love its quiet stillness and powerful silence. I love the cold."

"Then, I shall teach you the Song of the East. It holds the secret of cold and must be honored. Consequences are grave for any who forget this, with knowledge comes responsibility."

GEL rode the icy currents day and night, absorbing the melodies. Harmonies vibrated through his slender muscular frame, swam in his blood, and nourished his soul. The Song of the East was his.

"Well done," said the Mother. "Now, return and sing for your village."

People gathered as GEL began to sing, not able to resist the beauty of it. Domus rumbled, trembling as the sacred song progressed.

The villagers became afraid as the mountain broke apart opening a gaping tunnel like a great hungry mouth.

GEL sang on, the melody unsettling yet comforting and reassuring, a balm on the villagers' unrest. Large white boulders, unlike anything the people had seen, slid through the tunnel crashing onto the ground with smoking vapors and cracking thunder, chilling the air around them as a sudden onset of winter.

Women shivered, held their babes to their breasts, and cried to their men for protection; children hit the white boulders with sticks hiding their fear with a thin veneer of bravery. The tribal men shouted, waving their arms and fists not knowing how to combat this new enemy.

GEL calmed his people by explaining the wonders of ice and the amazing ways it would improve their lives. He taught them to be grateful to the Mother for this great blessing, showed them how to build structures near the tunnel to store the vast blocks of ice, and trained the villagers to love, use, and care for it.

Aridus—ARI—flew with the sun. The hotter the better. When others rested in the heat of mid-time, ARI practiced intricate loops and flips, a garland of maneuvers strung across the horizon.

Wings of gold carried him further and further each day into the fiery heart of Domus. Skin bronzed and stretched tight over powerful arms and chest glistened with effort. ARI's flaxen hair blew free, curls trailing, blending into his feathered back.

Downy feathers covered his neck and shoulders and continued along the backs of his arms to his elbows. He'd been compared most unfavorably to a goose, but ARI took the good-natured ribbing from his brothers in stride.

The Mother rose in the waves of heat, fluid as liquid fire.

"ARI," She whispered on the wind. "ARI."

ARI's chestnut eyes searched the horizon. His powerful wings held him steady in the fiery air. "Who's there? Who is it?"

"ARI, it is I. It is the Mother. You love the Mother, ARI?"

ARI's gaze searched for the voice, but he couldn't get a bearing on it. Where was it? In the earth, in the sky, in his head?

"ARI, do you love the fiery blasts of the Earth? Do you love her blazing trails through the sky, ARI? Do you seek the conflagration of her infernos?"

ARI looped over searching behind him, below, above. He saw nothing but the wildfire blazing in the air. Transparent heat. Scorching. Burning him with life.

"Yes. YES," he shouted. "I love the Mother's fire."

"Then, listen, ARI. Listen and learn the sacred Song of the South. The wildfire teaches you, ARI, and trusts you. You will learn how to use the heat to preserve your food, warm you in winter, and keep you dry. Be true to her. Do not misuse the power she gives you, ARI. Remember, the consequences are great, with knowledge comes responsibility ."

The Mother chose Torrence—TOR—when he was still a child. The brothers seldom noticed their youngest sibling, but TOR followed them everywhere. He emulated their every move and absorbed their words like sunshine. They strutted their wings and boasted of newfound manhood. They practiced flying with clumsy adolescence falling into one another in the air, crashing, diving, laughing.

"A race to the river," SAX challenged his black eyes pools of mischief. The wind was unusually strong, but the brothers were heady with confidence. No one noticed TOR running behind on the ground, trying to keep up with his soaring brothers.

They couldn't agree on a winner, so settled on a three-way tie. They laughed and chided one another and rode the airwaves above the Great River Potens. Gods of their world.

TOR stood on the bank his green eyes watching, admiring. A powerful torrent of wind roared up the valley, threw TOR into the river, and sent his three fledging aviator brothers plummeting into the water.

The older brothers sank under the waves, wrestling with good humor, still trying to best one another. Powerful eddies drove them to the river bottom scraping knees and chins.

As one body, they pushed off the river's rocky bed and surged out of the water into the sky. Their wings flapped throwing water in every direction. Choking and laughing at their adventure, they flew toward home unaware of TOR gasping for breath on the bottom of the Great River Potens.

TOR's body screaming for air went limp. Black and cold pressed him from all sides; his head and chest felt crushed like a garden pea between his molars. A dark curtain lowered around him enfolding him in silence and peace.

TOR stopped struggling and relaxed into sleep, or was it death? Then a mighty rush of breath filled his lungs. But, it wasn't air, it was song. The melody coursed through his body, a consonance of bliss awakening his body, his mind, his soul.

"This is my gift to you, TOR. Use it wisely, my young son, use it wisely," the Mother crooned in his ear.

TOR floated in the River his long auburn hair floating in delicato waves suspended around him like a soft nest. He was aware only of the sacred Song, being the Song, breathing the Song.

Two days later TOR walked into his cottage, his family rushing to embrace him, question him, and finally be in awe of him.

TOR never divulged what transpired between him and the Great River Potens, but all could see the change. TOR was mature beyond his years, wisdom shone from the green depth of his eyes.

Daily he sat for hours beside the River, communing. One day he burst into song having finally mastered the sacred Song of the West.

TOR fastidiously kept the shoreline spotless, every shrub trimmed, every weed gone, any trace of unsightly grime quickly cleaned away. He loved the River and the River loved him; a gift from the Mother.

Chapter Thirty-One

Storm

The old oak, Quercus, had stood in this spot on the bluff overlooking the River for hundreds of years. It was one of Skye's favorite places; she often came here to think. Her golden hair floated out behind her like rays of sunshine as she arced in the swing, regardless of how old she became, she would always love Quercus and her swing.

Skye looked out over the valley at the Great River Potens as she flowed restlessly in her bed. Skye ignored the black clouds rolling and tumbling, a reflection of the river below. Sometimes a girl just needed to get away. She had to think. The swing soared up and back, up and back. A pendulum backlit with lightning.

Everyone was in such a dither since BelMoon. Lichen and his mother disappearing as they did, Isabella was over the moon upset; she could hardly keep her mind on her studies.

Skye did well in school, but she was not obsessed with her lessons like Isabella. It was life or death for Isabella. However, Lichen had upset the gourd wagon with his arrival in Domus, and Isabella, the never-look-twice-at-a-guy-Isabella, had been smitten.

They had been the talk of the BelPole dance with their spectacular pairing. The very air around them had snapped and popped with intensity; Skye's mother said there hadn't been a pairing like that for a gnome's age. Skye could hardly blame Isabella; just look at him, all dark and muscles and so very male. But, Isabella, according to her self-imposed rules, wasn't supposed to be interested in males; Skye was definitely interested. Yes, Lichen was definitely interesting. Now that he was missing, Isabella couldn't seem to get back on track although she made a great show of not caring that Lichen left.

Rain began to hit Skye's face in tiny cold splashes. Miniature drinks of water on her tongue. Up, up to the heavens, is this what it felt like to fly? Skye thought of her wings, still lying dormant under her skin. Most of her friends were developed already, or at least had evidence of buds. Everyone except Skye and Isabella. The two smartest girls in class, yet they had no wings.

It wasn't unheard of, not to have wings; perhaps it ran in the family after all, they were cousins. And, Uncle Sapien and Aunt Coxi didn't have wings either and he was the Princeps. But still, it was frustrating and embarrassing. Skye knew the other girls whispered about it, giggling in a passive malignant way cloaking their taunts with smiles. But Skye knew what they really thought.

Skye's thoughts drifted to her father as she let Quercus swing her back and forth. Nidus, her father, had been gone most of the night in a meeting with Uncle Sapien. She wondered what was going on; they never told her anything.

When Uncle Sapien became Princeps, he appointed Nidus, his brother-in-law as his counselor. Nidus, a quiet, intelligent man, accepted this trusted position with his usual humility. Skye thought he should be a little more assertive. Sapien was in charge of souls; Nidus was in charge of money, and, after all, they couldn't do without money; money was important.

Nidus returned home this morning with a note from Isabella saying she would be over shortly. Skye knew she would, the ever-prompt Isabella. The note said their fathers talked with low voices in Sapien's study all night.

Isabella also said she had something important to tell her about Lemna. Lemna? What could she possibly have to say about Lemna? Lemna had been missing and Vinca Village had been without a caduceus for two whole years.

Thank goodness they had Isabella. She was almost as good as a full-fledged caduceus and she was beginning to gain quite a reputation. Although, thought Skye, her own mother, Ofella, was quite capable with the herbs. Isabella already had her calling and Skye thought it a trifle unfair. She wondered what her own Totus Vita would reveal about her calling. She couldn't wait for Iter.

Up and back. To and fro. Higher, higher the swing arched as the rain grew thicker. Skye thought about the strange meetings and hushed conversations of their fathers of late. And, now Uncle Ira was here as well; Skye raised her brows at the thought of him. Of course, she loved him, he was part of the family, but she didn't like him very much. He always seemed full of himself, puffed up with self-importance like a bloated toad, and lately had been agitated, even more than usual.

As the swing reached its zenith and started backward, Skye saw him. He had not been there a moment before she was sure of it. He was standing just beyond the knoll where Quercus grew. His dark green cloak whipped in the wind. He stood quite still. Watching. His hood was down so the heavy rain pasted his hair flat against his skull.

Sculpturing. His folded raven wings protruded above his shoulders shadowing his face. Then, as if he came to a conclusion and made a sudden decision, he yelled.

"Stop. Stop the swing. Get out. Get out of the swing."

A sudden surge of wind blew Skye's hair into her face and twisted the swing. A loud crack of thunder reverberated along the ropes finding a small chink in the weave not left by the cordage. A fray that weakened the braid, an unraveling that had been started with furtive fingers.

Lightening darted across the sky searing the retina and slamming shut the pupil; Skye screamed in reflex. The rope broke, flaxen fibers reaching, searching for each other in vain, the wind whipping them into snarls. Skye fell from the swing at the apex and arched up in a horrifying trajectory. For one terrible, glorious moment, Skye thought she really was flying.

But then the ascent stopped, and time seemed to stop with it. Skye hung midair. The rain appeared to move excruciatingly slow; the wind barely touching her skin, Quercus branches moving as though they were submerged in thick, gelatinous liquid seemed to reach for her. Stretching. Straining.

Another lightning strike, this one crawling through the gloaming inching across the air toward Quercus. Skye began her descent. Once she started down, time normalized. The lightning hit the tree with incredible speed, splitting Quercus in half.

"No," yelled Skye as she continued to plummet. Quercus's enormous trunk cleaved in two and the centuries-old tree hit the ground with an ancient force.

Skye's dismay subsided into chaos as the wind whipped her upwards; rain slicing her, cutting her with its frozen edges. Up, up she went, tiny ice balls pelting, beating her. Just as her consciousness left, just before the blackness covered her with a warm soft blanket, she thought she saw wings. Green-black wings beating furiously, green cloak gyrating in the wind, strong arms closing around her.

"Skye, Skye," Nidus yelled as he came running from the house, his wings flapping furiously. Gusts of wind lifted him off the ground and flung him back again. Ofella, Skye's mother, trailed behind him. Ira struck dumb by the scene before them watched in impotent horror. Nidus got to his feet and kept his wings tucked close to his body. "Skye, darling." Nidus reached for his daughter lying white and still on the ground. He cradled Skye in his arms and carried her toward the house.

Ofella ran up the hill and opened the door. The wind tore it from her grasp, and slammed it backward against the house shattering the glass. Nidus carried his daughter through the door while Ira nervously looked about wondering what to do.

The stranger stood in the shadows, watching.

"Close that door," Nidus barked to Ira as he took Skye further down the hall.

Ofella ran to the sofa in the antechamber. "Here, put her here," she instructed patting the cushions. "It's a good thing Isabella supplied my herb room. Oh, I wish she were here. That girl's a natural." Nidus laid Skye down and when her mother saw the lacerations striping Skye's face and arms, she gasped.

"Skye, Skye. Oh, Nidus, just look at her. Skye, wake up darling, wake up."

"Now, Ofella," Nidus said giving Skye a cursory examination, "the cuts are shallow. Skye will be fine. Just got the breath knocked out of her I expect."

"Right. All right then," Ofella said. Her tiny foot tapped the floor with abandon. Ofella had a lot of energy, her mind always going into a frenzy like fish after a water bug when it lights on the water's surface.

"I'll get the symphytum and calendula for those bruises and cuts. Yes, yes. Oh, I wish Isabella were here. She's supposed to be coming, but, with this storm, who knows? I'll brew some passionflower tea for when Skye wakes, yes, and I'll fetch more blankets. Don't want her taking a chill. Ira, don't just stand there, stoke up that fire," she said as she marched out of the room. Skye was already stirring.

"Lie still darling," Nidus said. "You've had a nasty fall."

"But, Quercus," Skye said. "Quercus is ruined." The ancient oak had been her touchstone. Her grounding.

Ofella came into the room with a tray. "Here, my little dulci, drink this tea, it will calm you and warm you, Ira, get that wood on the fire," Ofella said. "I'll bring the symphytum." She glared at Ira who grumbled to himself as he started toward the fireplace.

"Skye," Nidus said, soothing her, and holding her hand. "Quercus will survive. He's strong and has weathered many a storm. His roots grow deep; he will survive. You and I will bind him. Rest now, let your mother tend you."

Nidus and Skye looked at Ofella scurrying around gathering her remedies. Nidus smiled, winked, and left Skye in Ofella's determined hands.

Skye rested comfortably with a passionflower-soaked cloth on her head, passionflower tea beside her, a passionflower pillow under her neck, and a small dish of dried passionflowers on the table. Skye smiled at Ofella's ability to take instruction to its grandest height.

Ofella had a propensity to make any task she undertook a benchmark of achievement. If passionflower infusion was good for settling one's nerves, then a passionflower compress would be the bellwether of tranquility. A passionflower pillow would be the model of placidity and dried passionflowers beside the afflicted would be the exemplary zenith of sedation. Symphytum leaves and calendula flowers dotted Skye's face and arms. Patches of mother-love.

Skye, thoroughly relaxed, drifted and dosed and dreamed, of being tumbled around and around, head over heels with sharp white balls clanging into her, cutting her. A man with gentle arms and giant wings cradled her in his warm green cloak and she was safe.

"Father, did you see him?" Skye asked, her voice low and groggy.

"See who, dulci?" Nidus said as he entered the room.

"The man in the green cloak. He saved me. He caught me in midair. He...," she said as she drifted off, her words lost in slumber.

"She's dreaming," Nidus said. He secured the broken door against the storm and went into the study. Ira trailed along, asserting opinions that were as welcome as bird droppings at a banquet.

"This infernal weather," Ira said. "Tau'stercus. What's gotten into it? I've never seen so many storms. We need to do something I tell you. We need to get it under control."

"And what would you suggest?" Nidus asked in his usual mild-mannered tone trying not to let his wife's brother irritate him.

"Well, I don't know. That's for you and *The Princeps* to remedy," Ira blustered. "After all, you two are the Consillium's best and brightest."

Ira never missed an opportunity to exhume past disappointments and display them with wounded pride. He had hoped to be Princeps instead of Sapien, at the very least, a counselor. And what did he get? Nothing. The new *Princeps* marched around Domus with the King and the Ambassador; why Sapien didn't even have wings. It was their fault he got involved with Latere. If he had been appointed Princeps or counselor, he never would have turned to Latere.

Having been elected Kilotax was a consolation, of sorts, even though he knew Latere had brought it to pass by fixing the election.

Latere. Ira paled at the thought of him. He wished he had never gotten involved with the man.

But, then he wouldn't have his Nata. Nata, the love of his life. It was hard to believe he had allowed himself to be indebted to Latere for so many years. A man he didn't even know, had never seen really. A vile and threatening man veiled in secrecy, always keeping to the shadows with that thing wrapped around his head. Ira was done with him. Yes, he would tell him they were finished. Hadn't Ira done everything he'd asked? And look where that had gotten him. Yes, he would tell Latere their partnership was ended. Even if it cost Ira the Proscriptio trade route.

Over the noise of the storm Nidus heard a loud banging on the front door. He ignored Ira's impetuous sarcasm and nasty mood and started down the hall. Ofella beat him there and flung the door wide expecting Isabella. The Consillium Scriba stepped into the hall, dripping sheets of water from his cloak, his wings flattened tight against his body, useless in the wind.

Acta Diurna was a serious young man who took his appointment to Scriba in grave earnest. Fathers trained sons in an unbroken line for generations to keep this most sacred of trusts for each of the Princeps. Acta kept the minutes of Consillium meetings and served as Sapien's personal secretary. Most important of all, the Scriba was responsible for the Totus Vitas—every faerie's Life Book.

"Master Nidus Pudor, Princeps Sapiens has called an emergency meeting of the Consillium," Acta said, "and has asked that you please return with me."

Nidus nodded and turned to make ready. Ira rushed forward.

Emergency? In this weather?"

"It may be precisely because of the weather," Nidus said reaching for his cloak on the pegs beside the door.

"Then I shall come as well," Ira blustered trying to don his cloak with a flourish and failing miserably. "After all, I am the Kilotax, and if Vinca Village has an emergency, then I shall be there. Who knows what we are facing with these malicious winds and depraved deluges. You need me."

The Scriba faltered over his words. Sapien had been clear that only Nidus return with him. "I.. uh...well..." He looked pleadingly at Nidus now standing behind Ira.

Nidus shrugged. "Ira, perhaps you should investigate the stranger in the green cloak Skye said she saw. After all, you are the Kilotax. You should leave no stone unturned. It's your responsibility."

Ira sputtered. "But, it's raining, any traces would have been lost."

Nidus appeared not to have heard. He twirled his cloak gracefully through the air and it landed on his shoulders with all the refinement of a singing bird lighting delicately on a leaf. Without a glance at Ira, he turned and walked out the door.

Acta turned toward Ofella and with great formality said, "Miss Isabella will not be visiting today." That being said, he followed Nidus into the storm closing the door firmly behind them.

Ira stood looking after them. "Tau'stercus".

Chapter Thirty-Two

Consistere

Isabella Fae awoke with such a start that she kicked Papilio off the ornate bed. The caterpillar hit the hardwood floor feet first and squalled a surly meow. Papilio sat staring disapproval at her charge with eyes half-closed and cranky. Papilio had been peacefully and perfectly curled into a round fuzzy ball at the foot of the bed.

"What's the matter, did I interrupt your dreams of flying again?" Isabella teased. Papilio jumped back onto the soft blue coverlet and nosed her way in circles. Isabella stroked Papilio's soft yellow fur, which invoked vigorous purring.

Papilio's purring brought a subdued radiant light – the Arca Lux-encompassing her and Isabella. Papilio turned onto her back, stretched all eight short stubby feet into the air, and prepared to take another snooze. Caterpillars loved their sleep.

Isabella relaxed into her feather bed and tried not to think of Lichen. Her MothersMa had made it for her from molted swan feathers.

Many years ago Mothersma took young Isabella each day to Cygnus Plaza, a swannery near the Great River Potens. They patiently collected swan feathers. Day by day. Handful by handful. Mothersma quietly hummed as Isabella skipped along beside her.

"Mothersma, will we ever have enough feathers to make my bed?" Isabella asked.

Mothersma took Isabella's face into her hands. "Oh, my child. It takes time to make magic. Each feather the swan gives to us is an offering. So, when they share their feathers, they share their love. Love, my child, makes the best magic of all."

"Well, I wish we were finished. I wish my bed was done," Isabella complained. Mothersma smiled. "When your bed is done, you will not be happy. But remember, love shines a magical light."

When at last the day came, when the last handful of swan feathers was stuffed and sewn into the casing, Mothersma died. Isabella was heartbroken and wished the bed wasn't finished. She remembered Mothersma's words about not being happy when the bed was done. She wished she and Mothersma were back at the swannery looking for feathers. She refused to sleep on her bed, she refused to even look at it.

Weeks went by. Nothing Sapien and Coxi did could draw Isabella from her darkness. She did not cry. She simply, quietly, stared into nothing. She slept, but not on her swan feather bed.

One day Isabella walked aimlessly along the Great River Potens stopping to peer into the swannery. Isabella's loneliness for Mothersma became so overwhelming, that she sank to her knees and sobbed into her hands until she fell into an exhausted sleep.

A fat yellow caterpillar curled around Isabella's little body when she awoke. It was soft as swans down. It was purring. A soft light glowed around them, and Isabella felt warm and protected. It was love's magical light, just like MothersMa had said.

Isabella went home, the caterpillar trotted along beside her. That night they both slept on the swan feather bed.

Isabella stroked Papilio and thought about her current dreams, nothing but treachery and betrayal. She had awakened terrified, thrashing about on the swan feather bed kicking poor Papilio awake. Darkness had haunted her dreams ever since BelMoon.

And, Lichen, gone back to his world without one word to anyone. Isabella snorted. How could she have let her guard down with him? The poor Ambassador, what must he be going through, distraught and depressed over losing both Agaso and Lichen.

And Beetrum. What a disaster. The entire country was up in arms over Agaso's murder and the disruption of BelMoon. Who could have done such a thing?

Angry voices in the courtyard violated the peaceful room once more. Papilio turned her whiskered face toward the open window, growling softly. The curtains moved with the breeze and Isabella smelled spring in the air. Isabella had been Papilio's charge for many years now, and she had learned to trust Papilio's instincts. Papilio bounded off the bed and onto the windowsill in one smooth feline-like leap. Isabella followed.

Despite the warm morning, the sight in the courtyard below chilled Isabella. Her father and Uncle Ira were locked in verbal combat.

"What? You did what? You have no right to make that decision," shouted Uncle Ira, his round face reddening. In Isabella's mind, he was puffed with self-importance and could use a little deflating.

Sapien parried Ira's pointed words with his usual calmness. "Now, Ira, you're getting yourself all worked up. I do have the authority and you know it. The deed is done."

Last night at their impromptu meeting Sapien had informed his Consillium that a traitor was at work in Domus. Sapien had evidence of a violation of the sacred Crystal Grove. The Vitas were strewn about and the Lex Scriptura was missing. The horror of it was too much to contemplate.

They discussed when each of them had last been in the Grove to try to arrive at the time of the violation. Sapien looked around at his counselors; each a stalwart of integrity and loyalty to Domus. He could not, would not imagine that one of them was responsible for the theft.

Sapien had told his Consillium he decided to initiate The Consistere. It would close the bridge over the Great River Potens and halt all travel in and out of Vinca Village until they had the opportunity to question the citizens and set wards of protection around the Grove.

Each village and settlement in Domus was surrounded by water. The Great River Potens flowed throughout Domus, winding her venerated waters under mountains, across valleys, and around each hamlet regardless of how large or small.

She gave of herself to quench the thirst of every creature, bring vitality to every plant and tree and sustain, protect and nourish life in Domus. When a settlement started, within days the people would see The Great Potens trickling her way around their camp. As the settlement grew, the River grew and the people were never without water. And when the floods came, The Great Potens deepened her channels to help protect those within her custody.

This morning Sapien had shown Ira the same report he gave the Consillium. Now, Ira stood in the garden and glared at Sapien.

"No," Ira screamed. "Sapien, you go too far. I don't care if you are the Princeps, you cannot do this. As Kilotax, I forbid it." Ira stopped talking abruptly. Even he knew he had overstepped his bounds.

As spiritual leader of Domus, Princeps had supreme decision-making authority second only to the King. The Kilotax was the head of the Criocts, the town council, and every town had one.

Sapien had not progressed to Princeps without cause. His wisdom and generosity were legendary throughout Domus. The respect and reverence afforded him by every citizen was a result of Sapien's extraordinary capacity for compassion coupled with justice. His pronouncements were infused with integrity.

Only the corrupt would call his judgments unfair, his decisions unsound. In the eyes of the people of Domus, one thing kept Sapien from perfection—the lack of wings.

Isabella held her breath. She had never heard anyone speak to her father in that manner. Papilio gave a throaty warning and bristled her fur; she had never liked Uncle Ira.

Sapien stiffened and looked down on his diminutive brother-in-law.

"Why do you fret about the gate being closed? It will only take a few days to sort this out and you can be about your trading. We must determine who breached the Sacred Grove. This is serious, Ira. Otherwise, I would never take this measure. I assure you, you have nothing to worry about."

Ira looked affronted. His eyes narrowed as he said, "You know nothing about my trading and what this delay will cost me. It had better not take longer than a couple of days, or you'll be sorry, I can promise you that." Ira knew he had gone too far but was powerless to stop himself.

Isabella watched as Uncle Ira shook with anger. The blue of her father's eyes turned a cold hard gray. His stance was firm and formidable.

"Are you threatening me, Ira?"

Ira gapped at Sapien. Panic jumbled his words. Ira thought of Lichen in the Proscriptio, he must get back to him; of Keeper Valeo's anger and most of all Latere's cold fury when they found out Lichen was alive. Fury aimed at Ira.

Jumbled thoughts mingled with his frustration at not being able to get out of Vinca Village.

What to do? What to do? Tau'stercus.

Isabella decided it was time for a diversion. She leaned out the window as far as possible; Papilio balanced on the sill. Isabella articulated her most pleasant voice and beamed her irresistible smile.

"Uncle Ira, is that you? Did you go by Skye's house? Is she with you?"

Both men flinched visibly and looked up toward the open window; Isabella knew they didn't want her to have heard their angry words.

Their intense discussion cooled immediately. She caught the look in her father's eye—he knew her well. She had diverted wrath and cooled tempers many times in the past. Sapien always said she could charm berry juice from a river rock.

"Oh, hello Isabella," Uncle Ira said with obvious constraint. "No, uh, yes. I mean ... Yes; I went by their house. No, she is not with me. Ofella said she should remain in bed today. And rest." Ira looked uncomfortable.

Isabella took amused delight in Uncle Ira's awkward attempt to make nice. He was no match for her; she had been besting him at family dinners since she learned the subtle art of verbal parrying. Civil scorn.

Deflecting his boorish comments with grace had become second nature to her. Isabella practiced prudence mostly for the sake of Coxi, her mother, and Aunt Nata. Coxi had been aware of Ira's coarse nature from the beginning and had stopped voicing her opinion only after her sister married Ira. Of course, Nata soon realized her error but determined to sleep in the bed she had made.

Papilio snarled and curled her lip, small but sharp fangs glistened in the morning sun.

"Yes, I heard about Skye's unfortunate fall from the swing. I plan to visit her this morning," Isabella said pumping up the cheerful lilt to her voice.

"I'm sure Aunt Ofella would welcome some moral support. I'll take her some of my new hypericum salve for Skye, I have an entire section of my garden devoted to it."

"Yes, you do that," Ira intoned, disinterest glaring through his transparency.

Sapien looked at his brother-in-law and with resignation said, "Ira, if you leave immediately, I will let you pass. You have until midnight, then I am singing the Consistere."

Without a word, Ira turned and left; his wings stiff and foreboding banged against the gate. He marched on, mumbling to himself, his wings rigid with anger. Those wings transformed instantly from beauty to horrid menacing weapons with ugly points and sharp corners. Most faerie's wings changed with mood, but Ira's had an air of malevolence.

Papilio snarled as Ira strode out of sight. "I know girl, I know." Isabella stroked Papilio's fur all infused with vigilance and standing on guard. She bent to rub her cheek against the downy softness, like smoothing ruffled feathers. Papilio purred; the Arca Lux glowed brightly around them, ever diligent.

As the storm subsided into midnight, Sapien stood on the bridge that leads into Vinca Village and sang the Consistere, the charm that would halt all bridge traffic. No one would be allowed in or out.

Chapter Thirty-Three

Meeting

The street was dark and shiny. Lampposts reflected water conjured from the thick and heavy air. A shabby barely legible sign squeaked to and fro. Mullein's Pub.

The Pub, a downtrodden establishment in the Darks of New Ivy, sat in a nest of squalor; its human patrons living desperate lives. Stuck in a world between human and beast, they hated all non-humans, especially faeries. Their hopeless existence bred violence and seethed with resentment.

Once a beautiful, inviting part of New Ivy, the occupants separated themselves by continuing down the murky path of despair and disobedience. The Great River Potens had no choice but to sever their infection from the body of New Ivy. Already divided physically, the Darks Quad now stood across a spiritual divide. It was unprecedented. One day they were part of Q's opus, the next they were wallowing in their hatred and malcontent. The people of the Darks refused to recognize their dismal path and continued to revel in their black moods and brutal ways. They were blind to their responsibility for this disconnect and could not see the path back home.

Inside the Pub Ira Lungwort waited alone at a table, fidgeting. He hated the Darks and the feeling of doom that permeated its borders. He had left Vinca Village before Sapien sang the Consistere barely making it out in time.

Sapien, always overplaying his hand. So what if someone had gone into the Grove. Sapien, Mr. High and Mighty.

A waitress and the other regulars glanced curiously across the room at him. They could always tell. They could always pick a faerie out of the crowd, wings or no. He knew it. He hated being here. He loathed this malicious human village. The people represented everything Ira abhorred about humans. They were crude and rude, and they smelled.

Ira hated the way they looked at you, the way they dressed, the things they ate. He would banish them all from the Kingdom of Domus if he could.

And Lichen Ipse was no different. Curse the man. He had caused Ira untold difficulties.

Lichen should be dead or at the very least, banished to Advena. Instead, he played the industrialist in the Proscriptio. Lichen had even gained old Supra's respect. Curse the man to inferi and back.

The other diners continued to cast sidelong glances at Ira as they ate their meals. Raucous laughter filtered out of the kitchen. Ira's stomach growled incessantly. He was hungry, but he wasn't hungry enough for human food, besides, he was too nervous to eat.

For years Ira met Latere in these remote misbegotten places in the Darks. It was prudent...neither of them liked it, but they had agreed it was necessary. Their business was...private. Their relationship, confidential.

"Where is he?" Ira grumbled to himself as he glanced at his gold timepiece. The ornate dials representing the sun, moon, and stars said 7:30. Five minutes later than the last time he looked.

Ira was usually the consummate professional during these meetings, but tonight he was sweating and anxious. Ira requested this meeting because he had the unfortunate task of telling Latere about Lichen's captivity in the Proscriptio. What would Latere do when he learned Lichen was alive?

Ira had done everything Latere asked. No way he could blame Ira. Nevertheless, perspiration continued to drip down the center of his back beneath his restricted wings.

He had met with the coachman to arrange Lichen's kidnapping on the very night of Lichen's arrival. He had rather enjoyed spying on them as they disembarked from the carriage. He had been curious to see Q's daughter; she'd aged as humans do living in Advena, but was still a looker, not as beautiful as her mother, but still quite pretty. For a human. Ira had a prurient eye for that sort of thing.

Ira congratulated himself on suggesting to Latere that they switch coachmen to ensure their plan. Send Manes instead of Chimera. No need for Latere to know it was someone else's idea.

Too bad about Agaso. Ira had always admired the old faerie. Ira wondered what had gone wrong. Surely, it was Manes who had killed him.

After arranging the kidnapping with the coachman Manes, Ira met with One Ear. All he had to do was make sure Lichen was dead, wouldn't you think he could do that? Just that one thing. The unpleasant meeting was short, Ira hated trolls. Not as much as humans, but nearly. They were ignorant disgusting creatures.

It wasn't Ira's fault those greedy trolls double-crossed him. They had taken the gold quickly enough. It had been the perfect plan for Ira;

two men paid him to accomplish the same thing: make sure Lichen Ipse was dead. Now that cussed human was alive and well in the Proscriptio.

What to do, what to do? Tau'stercus.

In addition to Lichen, Ira had another matter to discuss with Latere, if he could screw up his courage. Sapien had shown him a classified report of the Consillium. The report was unthinkable, impossible. But, if it were true, Ira needed to know. And he knew who could tell him. Latere. Latere was in on every scam, every deal, every conceivable underhanded scheme in all of Domus.

Ira shrugged his shoulders and grimaced. His black raincoat was tight, too tight. Wings were the only obvious difference between the species human and fairie since Domus law had a perpetual charm that reduced humans to faerie size.

So, here in the Darks, Ira hid his wings. It was dangerous to be faerie in the Darks. His wings and shoulders cramped and started to hurt. He hated hiding his wings; he hated wearing this human coat. But coming to the Darks required sacrifice.

He needed to tell Latere about Lichen. And, he had to tell him about Sapien's report. As much as he hated being here, as much as he hated Latere, he had to meet with him.

Conversations hushed as a dark figure appeared in the doorway. His black hat pulled low on his brow shadowed the half-masked face; the brim dripping rain onto the floor. His cloak swayed arrogantly and added to his commanding presence; his boots echoed on the wooden slats as he walked across the room to Ira's table.

"Good evening, Ira. Nice to see you again." His tone, reserved and sharp, implied quite the contrary.

He pulled out a chair, leaned heavily on his gold-topped cane, and sat down.

"What will we be trading tonight?" Shrewd stormy eyes looked out the holes in the mask. They washed over Ira contemptuously noting the strained fabric, the nervous hands, and the pinched look on Ira's face.

Ira trembled slightly. He had traded many things with Latere, made a lot of money, and had become the Kilotax of Vinca Village because of Latere, but just at this moment, Ira wished he had never laid eyes on him. Not that he *had* laid eyes on him. Latere's face was always in shadows. The top covered with cloth, the bottom horribly scared.

Ira pulled a bag out of his pocket and dumped the aes on the table. First things first.

Latere sighed quietly, reached into his cloak, dropped gold coins, and scooped up the aes.

"Is *this* all you wanted little toad?"

"I need to talk to you," Ira said, his voice breaking, sliding the coins into the bag then into his pocket.

The corner of Latere's mouth moved slightly, and his eyes narrowed.

"Interesting. I need to talk with you as well."

"I have information...two things actually." Ira hesitated. Should he ask Latere for more money?

Latere's expression did not change; his hard eyes fastened on Ira. Ira decided not to push it.

"It's about Lichen Ipse."

Latere's voice clouded. "Yes?"

"Umm...well...you know I trade in the...in the ....Proscriptio," Ira's voice lowered as he glanced around the room.

"I know you do you indolent worm, I arranged your passage."

"Yes, well, and thank you, sir. Thank you for that. But, well, sir, L atere...."Ira stammered. He hated it when he stammered. The humans across the room looked down their noses at him, staring and laughing at his faltering speech.

"Lichen is alive," he blurted. "He is a captive in the SAX camp."

The air grew hot. Uncomfortable. Ira squirmed and felt anger radiating from Latere. Silent. Deadly. "Tell me something I don't know, you bungling weasel. I pay you to get me Lichen and now he's in the Proscriptio."

Ira felt feint. So, he already knew.

"You idiot. You incompetent fool." Latere's voice remained steady, but his eyes flashed.

"That slimy troll has my gold and I have nothing. Speak up you pathetic maggot. What went wrong?"

"I...I don't know. I paid Manes to "pop" just before the Bridge. I paid One Ear to make sure Lichen was dead. The next thing I know, Lichen is in the SAX camp." Fear punctuated Ira's whine with desperation.

Latere stared at his long-time partner in crime. His head began to hurt. Latere hated Lichen Ipse. A scourge and a plague on that boy; he had done nothing but cause problems.

Latere's mind raced through its devious paces. "You must rescue Lichen and deliver him to the edge of the Forbidden Forest," Latere said.

"But I thought you wanted him dead. Isn't he just as good as dead in the Proscriptio?" Ira asked.

"That is not for you to decide, is it? My plans have changed. Now, go get him and take him to Vetare Silva. Do you think you can accomplish that much?"

"The Forbidden Forest?" Ira said. He went pale as the implication coiled in his mind. The sacred Mt. Vetare was in the Forbidden Forest. The Tempus Crystal was in Mt. Vetare.

"Sapien told the Consillium yesterday that someone overcame the wards and broke into the Sacred Grove. Lex Scriptura is missing," Ira watched Latere closely, "the book that describes the workings of the Tempus Crystal."

Could Latere have possibly stolen it? Latere sat stone-faced.

"And," Ira said incredulity giving him a kind of courage, "Sapien also reported that this strange violent weather is not a coincidence. Something disrupted the power grid. Sapien fears the worst."

Ira's voice quivered, realization stabbing him. The facts went round and round in Ira's mind. The Lex Scriptura, missing. That book held all of Domus's mysteries. The mystery of Tempus Crystal, how to control weather, time, everything in Domus.

The Tempus Crystal is in Mt. Vetare. Mt. Vetare is in the Forbidden Forest. Latere wants Lichen delivered to the Forbidden Forest, to Vetare Silva. Fear gripped Ira with a fist of doom.

Latere rose abruptly, his chair falling backward as he grabbed his cane. Water dripped from the brim of his hat as he leaned into Ira. The light haloed around Latere as if revealing a black demon rising from hell.

Ira fidgeted, his eyes bulging. Terror condensed his voice to a mere rasp. "If you tamper with the Tempus Crystal, with time, we will *all* die. The Fey, the humans, everyone in Domus."

Latere's eyes never blinked. They were granite, streaked with jade, cold and hard.

"Yes," he said slowly. "Domus could be destroyed. Or not. My option."

Ira's empty stomach convulsed. Pain shot through his bowels. He drew back from Latere and sat up straight in his chair.

Latere smiled at Ira. "Well, my little crab. You'd better be about our business. Deliver Lichen to the Forbidden Forest. And don't screw it up."

For a moment Ira was speechless. His mouth gaped in disbelief. Rage seethed. Boiled. Spewed toward Latere. Ira felt dizzy.

" You... unspeakable, disgusting...." Ira's voice grew louder with each word.

"How could you do this? No. No, I'm through with you." His glass tipped over as he spoke; the ice tumbled across the table like cast dice.

Latere burst into laughter. The other diners stared at him.

"Why, Ira, have I taught you nothing over the years? *Par para revere*. Like for like. I helped you. You help me. Your wings are clipped my filthy little pigeon. You owe me."

Ira's dry tongue struggled to form words. He looked at the empty glass. He felt the hollowness of it.

"No. No, I won't do this," Ira said.

"You repulsive coward," Latere said with loathing. "I've put up with your sniveling all these years. Let me remind you of a few things, on the chance that you could puff yourself up and try to play the hero. I've known all along what you are. You buy elections from me, scam everyone you know, and pretend to be the all-mighty answer to everyone's prayers. Mr. Important. The Kilotax of Vinca Village. Well, where would you be without me? I've helped you get everything you have and everything you are, including your wife. And now she wants a baby. Isn't that just cozy?"

Latere's words splashed Ira in the face. Cold reality "Leave my wife out of this," Ira said. Nata was his life.

"Leave her out?" Latere said. " Leave her out?" he said louder. "Why, she's right in the middle of this."

His eyes took on a curious, malicious gleam. He smiled. "As I recall, she was my first..." Lightning sizzled the air. Thunder vibrated the windows.

Ira had made a bargain with the devil, but now he was finished. He had helped this rogue achieve his depravity long enough. He had paid many times over for the love of his beautiful Nata.

Sweat beads glistened on Ira's lip. Pellets of fear and anger. He gasped. His hands trembled. His voice was unsteady.

"You go too far, Latere. I've done everything you have ever asked of me. I will rescue Lichen and deliver him to the edge of the Forbidden Forest. But this is it. We're through. I want no part of your traitorous plans."

Latere laughed like good friends sharing a joke. Ira hated this spawn of darkness. Molten emotion surged through him.

"You filthy vermin. You no-good menace to society." Ira stood up, flailing his arms about, gesturing wildly as he spoke. Uncharacteristic courage added emphasis. The burgeoning storm accentuated Ira's manic movements.

"You scurrilous, obscene…. ," he yelled. "I detest you. You reek of your evil deeds and the stench of it makes me puke."

Ira's tight-fitting coat split up the back. His wings, unfettered from their binding, popped out of the coat flapping wildly.

The patrons of the restaurant gasped in shock.

"It's a faerie," they said one by one with various levels of disdain.

"I knew it."

Faeries were rare in the Darks.

Latere watched this spectacle with humor. "You defame me, Ira," his tone warm honey. "And after all we've been through together," he said clicking his tongue.

His demeanor changed; his voice iced over. Latere towered over the humans in the room and completely overshadowed the irate faerie across from him.

"It's just this simple," he whispered in Ira's ear. "Get me Lichen, and you and your little family all live. Don't, and you die."

Latere turned and walked into the storm.

Ira watched Latere leave, then twisted around to see the diners and the staff, staring at him. He drew himself erect, gave his wings a mighty shake, walked toward the door, and left the patrons with their collective mouth agape, eyes fixed and staring.

Chapter Thirty-Four

Heritage

Latere leaped into his coach a block from Mullein Pub seething with anger. That degenerate faerie always managed to dig into his very soul.

He removed his hat, flinging water onto the plush cushion, as his cloak dripped darker patterns among the fleur de leis on the fabric transforming them into twisted grotesque shapes.

"To the Receptus," Latere shouted to the driver. He needed refreshment and refinement. The Receptus was the finest club in New Ivy. He needed to be cleansed of the foulness that was the gutter district. The Darks.

His coach pulled up to a side private entrance. Latere was met with sycophantic cordiality and shown to his private rooms in the pinnacle of the Receptus. Ambassador Quindaro had secured them many years before. Q never used it anymore, so Latere enjoyed it frequently. It had been easy, really, to forge the proper papers. What fools they all were.

"Lorelei," Latere said raising his voice as he entered the suite. He knew she was within earshot. She had a way of always being within earshot.

Lorelei walked calmly into the room, her bare feet making no sound. Her hair lay in shades of auburn waves across her shoulders and down her back. As she walked toward him her pale luminescent skin shone and sparkled like a moon path upon the river. Her eyes, deep aquamarine pools vacant and devoid of emotion stared into his.

"Welcome back, Latere. How may I serve you?" she said evenly.

"Bring me a drink," he answered flatly, kicking off his boots. He fell onto the couch with a sigh. "That blighted bloated excuse for a faerie. That disgusting abominable faerie," he said speaking to himself. Lorelei stood unmoving and looked at him.

"They *know.* They know about the Tempus anomaly. How? How does he know?" Latere stared out the window. The storm still raged.

Lorelei handed him his glass. He gulped it down. "Another," he barked. "That supercilious Sapien. He's the only one with half a brain. I should have known he'd figure it out."

Latere downed his second drink. He thought of Isabella and smiled. Now, there was a faerie. That little charm would soon be his.

"This doesn't change a thing, Lorelei. There's nothing they can do to stop it now. Time marches on," he said and laughed.

He raised his hand in a mock toast. "To its death, time that is. And to Domus, and her new monarch...me." Latere grinned and handed the glass back to Lorelei.

The liquor blazed. Faerie liquor, nothing quite like it. The Receptus had the best. "Fill me up," he said.

Lorelei poured the red fire. Her skin was smooth and wet; Latere's eyes swept her up and down.

"You, my little nymph, have done quite well. Finding my prize in the Proscriptio. I'm proud of you. Come here."

He patted the couch affectionately. Lorelei hesitated. She owed her existence to Latere. Without him she would still be confined to those murky depths, trapped. But, he was Dark, and Lichen was Light.

"I said, come here."

"Latere, please. I must get back to the camp before I am missed it will be light soon."

Latere grabbed her arm and drew her to him. She was quite moist. She was always moist. He loved that. He kissed her shoulder and ran his finger over the brand.

"SAX. I kind of like it. It becomes you. Makes you, oh, I don't know, rugged. Tough. I find it very..." Latere licked the scar, "stimulating."

Lorelei tried to pull away. He had always done whatever he wished with her. But, since she met Lichen, it was different. She was different. Vulnerable somehow. Pain seared through her head. She screamed.

Latere clapped his hand over her mouth. "Quiet, little water baby. We wouldn't want to disturb the other guests now, would we? So, let's see what's going on in that little fish brain."

Lorelei's head seared and throbbed; Latere had become much stronger since the last probe. She felt his dark presence, prodding, searching.

"So, that's the way of it, is it," he said. "You think you're in love with Lichen. The filthy little half-breed got to you."

Lorelei looked stunned.

"Surprised, are you? What, just because he's Q's grandson you assumed he was 100% bona-fide human?"

Latere through his head back and laughed. An ugly, chilling laugh. "When I rule, half-breeds and humans alike will be exterminated. And I'm going to find that bridge to Advena and destroy everything there, too. Domus will once again be pure. That's right. Faeries will take their rightful place. And all of Domus's creatures will be subject to us.

"Now, let's take care of the business at hand. Then, you can be on your way to deliver your little half-human to me at Mt. Vetare."

Latere took Lorelei by the hair. "Do you understand me, squid? Take Lichen to Mt. Vetare. I'm getting that Crystal."

Latere pulled her toward the bedroom. When she fell, he dragged her. Lorelei thrashed and fought, but she knew it wouldn't matter. In the end, he would have his way.

"Oh, yes, the Tempus Crystal. Such power, I can feel it now." Latere kissed her hard on the lips. Power had its effects on a man.

Chapter Thirty-Five

Receptus

As Ira left Mullein Pub, he ducked his head into his shoulder and tried to avoid the driving rain. He hated the Darks. As he slogged along the sidewalk, the storm heightened. He could hardly see or stand. His hand shook as he tried to pull his torn coat around him. His stomach growled.

"Curse these humans," he muttered as if they were the cause of the storm. One meeting down. One to go. Ira looked forward to a hot meal and a warm bed. But, he had to meet with Keeper Valeo at the Receptus dining room in New Ivy Village first.

Ira wanted to go home after seeing Valeo, but that was impossible; Sapien still had the Bridge into Vinca Village closed with the Consistere. Curse this day and everything in it.

Ira had a room rented in Trumpet, a hamlet just across the River from Vinca Village. Nata expected him to be away overnight, so no problem there. If it weren't for this storm, he would attempt to fly to

Trumpet after this meeting with Valeo, New Ivy no-fly law notwithstanding.

The PTP, public transportation port, was well-lit and provided shelter as Ira waited. The coach was due in five minutes according to the posted schedule.

Three pubescent humans ran into the port, laughing, shoving, and swearing. They were bursting with energy much like popcorn kernels just prior to turning inside out.

"Hey, look at the *faerie,"* said the tallest boy, his acnied face breaking into a wicked grin. His long hair was streaked with purple and tied back, slick against his head. The soaked tee shirt and pants revealed the muscular form of a man. A swaggered look to his comrades for confidence revealed the insecurity of a boy.

"Wow", said the round-faced girl. Her blonde hair bushed around her head defying the downpour. Her wet clothing emphasized tiny rolls of baby fat; she wasn't quite the woman she pretended to be.

"I hear they can fly," she said with half a smile, her braces impeding pronunciation.

"Well, now, I don't know since it's against the law to fly in New Ivy," said the self-proclaimed leader. He glanced at his friends and strutted toward Ira.

"What'd ya say *faerie*? You up to a little flight? Or are you a law-abiding citizen?"

"Aw, Jake," said the second boy, "leave him alone. Come on, leave him be." He was shorter than Jake and apparently last in the group's hierarchy. He wore a cap of sorts that did little to protect him from the rain. He struggled to keep his teeth from chattering, gooseflesh pimpled his arms.

"But I'm just trying to be friendly. I want to learn about my fair-feathered cousins. We *are* cousins. Aren't we faerie?" asked Jake.

Ira stared at Jake but didn't answer. He was in no mood to be cajoled by adolescents, especially human adolescents. He was cold, tired, and hungry. And fear gnawed at his guts. Fear for his life, fear for his world. He had to get this meeting with Valeo over and warn Sapien about Latere.

Ira turned away from the trio, trying to control his anger. The last thing he needed was to draw the attention of human authorities. Ira's position on the city council had guaranteed proper traveling permits for all of Domus. Except the Proscriptio. Ira was officially supposed to be miles from New Ivy; it wouldn't do to be noticed.

The coach came around the corner right on time splashing water and street filth in a muddy spume.

"Well, looky here. Guess he can't fly," Jake prodded as Ira walked toward the coach. The storm had subsided somewhat, but there was still a stiff wind punctuated by jagged streaks of light and booming reverberations.

"Here, let me give you a little boost," shouted Jake as he grabbed Ira and threw him into the air. Ira's wings had been folded benignly, but the second he was air-born, they unfurled into huge majestic menacing inhuman appendages. They began to flap instinctively. Ira's wingspan was not large by faerie standards, but it dwarfed the humans.

Ira's face contorted with anger. The diminutive wet and helpless faerie transformed into a grotesque fiend backlit by blinding lightning and peals of thunder discharging into the night.

The terrified girl screamed and clutched the smaller boy. The wind snatched Jake's gutter language. The horses reared; the coach slammed into the port and the ground trembled.

Ira hovered theatrically, wings pounding the air, and pointed his finger at the trio.

"Curse you, despicable humans. May you and your kind vanish from Domus."

As the words flew from his mouth, he realized what he had said. He realized all of Domus might vanish. Ira turned into the storm and was gone.

Ira Lungwort removed his torn coat and stepped onto the plush red carpet of the Receptus Lounge in New Ivy Village.

Decent food, even if it is human.

Bartus, the concierge immediately greeted Ira.

"Good evening, Mr. I. Nice to see you again. Dinner or the bar?" he clipped.

Ira nodded toward the dining room. The impeccable concierge guided Ira toward his usual table in the back of the room. Ira and Bartus both preferred discretion. The Receptus prided itself on its multi-cultural flavor, but a faerie's presence often provoked mischief.

New Ivy's charter was granted to Q by King Colere and bestowed unheard-of autonomy. This caused a great stir among the natives of Domus so most of them stayed away; too many restrictions. Like not being able to fly. Faerie wings always drew stares and comments from the other diners. Ira knew Bartus was nervous. Usually, Ira wore a jacket to conceal his wings, but tonight he was obviously in a mood.

Bartus pulled out the chair for Ira and turned his head discreetly as Ira adjusted his wings. The busboy poured water; the ice tinkled softly against the crystal.

"Thank you," said Ira stiffly. Whispers and curious glances further irritated Ira.

Déjà vu.

He took the menu from Bartus.

Tau'stercus.

Ira's stomach growled. Then again.

"Your waiter will be right with you, sir." Bartus raised one eyebrow and walked away.

Ira felt better now. He was warm, dry, and fed. Should he go back to Trumpet after meeting with Valeo? On occasion, he did stay the night here at the Receptus. He tried to decide whether to go to Trumpet or stay here in his room.

What to do? What to do?

As if in answer, the wind hurled rain against the leaded windowpanes. Ira shuddered. He was too tired and too comfortable to brave this ill-conceived weather again.

Ira felt drained after Latere. At least Latere had not killed him. Who the inferi was Latere anyway? Always shrouded. Always secretive.

And the mighty Keeper Valeo Nox, too. Who did he think he was? Always Mr. Essential. Chief of Magnitude. Third under the King in the famous Domus power triad: Dens The King, Sapien the Princeps, and Valeo the Keeper. And, where did the mighty Q fit in?

Ira was sick of all of them. Where would they be without him? After all, who had found Lichen? Not any of them, that's for sure. He would deliver the news about Lichen to Valeo and go straight to bed. He deserved a good night's sleep.

"Good evening, Ira," Valeo said. Ira jumped, then scowled. "Tell me, what is so urgent in the dead of night....and a night such as this?" The Keeper glanced toward the black window sheeted with rain.

Bartus appeared and took Valeo's dripping cape and hat, stone-faced with a slight impatient nod. Whether Valeo's wings were visible or not, everyone recognized The Keeper.

Ira's stomach clenched. His hard-won calm fled.

"I apologize for the inconvenience," Ira said averting his eyes. Valeo sat silently, staring at Ira. Ira always dreaded this moment. The Keeper's prying mind. Dark, sharp tentacle probes. Ira knew defensive tactics, but tonight he struggled with the shield. He was tired and sick to death of playing games with these two self-proclaimed rogues.

"Careful cockroach", Valeo said into Ira's mind.

"Well, what is it?" Valeo asked aloud. "Why am I here on this dreadful evening? And, it had better be worth my while."

"It's...well, it's about Lichen. He... He's alive."

Valeo's stony expression didn't change. "Excuse me?"

Ira wished this were over. Why had he ever allowed himself to get involved with these two blackhearts? "He's alive. He's in the Proscriptio," Ira said. "I heard it on my trade route," he added sidetracking the whole truth.

Disbelief clouded Valeo's eyes, replaced a moment later by Valeo's legendary temper.

"What? What?" Valeo pounded his fist on the table and struggled to keep his voice down. "You blundering little dung beetle. How did this happen? I paid you to make sure...Manes told me..." Valeo stopped.

"Alright, alright," he said clenching his teeth. "Let me think." Valeo drummed his fingers on the table and screwed up his mouth. "Go get Lichen from the Proscriptio and haul his infuriating coat tail to New Ivy," he spat. "Deliver him personally to Q's doorstep and don't expect one more aes out of me."

"But, how am I supposed to accomplish that?" Ira whined. "Lichen's a *prisoner.* How will I get him out? And," he added, looking down at the table, "how will I get in?"

Ira hoped Valeo was finished searching his mind. It wouldn't do to have Valeo know Ira could enter the Proscriptio.

"I don't care how you do it, just do it," Valeo sneered.

"Uh....I will probably need to bribe my way in and out....." Ira said haltingly. Valeo sat for a moment, holding Ira with his steel trap eyes then he reached into his pocket and withdrew a small pouch.

"Here, then," Valeo said slamming the bag onto the table. "But, that Ipse boy had better be home licking the shoes of his dear old grandpa."

"There's one more thing," Ira said hoping to ingratiate himself. "Sapien says someone broke into the Sacred Grove and stole the Lex Scriptura. Also, something is wrong with the Tempus Crystal.....it could...destroy everything...everyone," Ira stammered.

Valeo paled. "Holy grove...." He looked sharply at Ira, "Who?" he demanded. "Who stole it?"

Ira blushed. "How should I know?" he blustered. Ira's short spiky hair pointed in every direction. He smelled like wet feathers.

Tau'stercus, just let this be over. Tau'stercus.

"Deliver Lichen to Q's Manor within a fortnight," Valeo said as he stood to leave. Ira saw panic beneath the cool exterior.

"OK. OK," Ira blurted. "Valeo, what about the Tempus Crystal? What will happen? What can be done?"

"I don't know. I just don't know," Valeo shouted. Restaurant patrons looked at them. "I must speak with the King. I must speak with ... Q. I expect to see Lichen at the Manor. Do not fail me toad." Keeper Valeo Nox grabbed his cloak, crammed on his hat, and marched out the door.

Ira nodded. He didn't trust his voice.

He straightened, raised his wings, and turned toward the elevator anticipating his soft warm bed.

Ira needed to make a decision. Latere wants Lichen taken to Mt.V etare; Valeo wants him delivered to the Manor.

What was Latere doing with Lichen at Mt. Vetare? It obviously has something to do with the Tempus Crystal.

Ira wanted no part of the Tempus Crystal or tangling with the Mother on Mt. Vetare. He needed Lichen and Q to get a baby from the orphanage for his precious Nata. Nata, the love of his life. The only good thing in his life.

He would go to the Proscriptio, rescue Lichen, *God knows how,* and take him to New Ivy, to Q. Tomorrow.

He wouldn't allow thoughts of Latere to disturb him tonight. Crazy Latere. Dangerous Latere. Ira let himself sink into the soft nothingness of the night.

Ira awoke with a jolt. Thunder still boomed and he wondered if that's what had awakened him. He sat up and swung his legs over the side of the bed. His feet touched the carpet; it was wet. He drew them back into the bed and turned on the light. On the floor lay a stained brown letter with the Receptus seal. He picked up the damp envelope and saw the carpet was soaked with water.

Someone's been in my room.

Ira threw back the covers and jumped out of bed. He stalked to the door and jerked it open. The hallway was empty. He looked in the closet, and the bathroom, then went to the balcony. Nothing. No one. He sat down in the chair and broke the seal. It contained a single document; untidy lettering as if someone had scribbled it in a hurry. Ira's hands began to shake as he read the page. Sweat broke out on his forehead and trickled down his face. Chills ran down his arms. His wings drooped to the floor. He wiped his eyes and read it again.

It couldn't be. IT COULDN'T BE.

Latere. The very name made Ira's hair and feathers stand erect. He must get home. He must get to Sapien. He pulled the bell cord and within minutes an attendant was at his door.

"I want a carriage immediately," Ira ordered. The attendant's eyes widened as he glanced out the window at the storm.

"Immediately," bellowed Ira his wings outstretched behind him making pointy demon shadows on the wall.

"Yes, sir", stammered the attendant. He had heard tales of faerie tempers. "Right away, sir," he said over his shoulder as he ran down the hall.

Ira threw on his clothes, a plan formulating in his mind. First, he would contact Sapien, if anyone could help, it was the Princeps. Ira stormed out of the room, and down the ornate staircase toward the front door.

"Good evening, sir, your carriage is ready," Bartus said.

Didn't the man ever sleep? Ira nodded toward him and continued toward the street. Once seated inside the coach he put his head into his hands and wept. He regretted the day he ever met Latere.

Chapter Thirty-Six

Silent Post

The inhabitants of the small hamlet of Trumpet were sleeping fitfully in their beds when Ira arrived. Trumpet set just across the River from Vinca Village; just outside the reach of the Consistere. With only an hour before sunrise, Ira nixed the notion of trying to get any sleep. What he needed was a plan.

What to do? What to do? Tau'stercus.

Ira stomped across the room, threw down the mysterious letter still damp around the edges, and pounded his fist on the desk. He stared at the crumpled manila wrapper with the broken Receptus seal.

Now what? Who sent this information?

Ira should begin his journey to the Proscriptio. Lichen Ipse. How he hated that man. He tried to look beyond his immediate problem of rescuing Lichen and focus on his beloved Nata and their baby. He looked out the tiny second-story window where the wind howled and ripped through the village. The orange trumpet blooms that surrounded the panes of glass were bending to and fro, back and forth in their forced dance to the wailing cadence of the squall. A bucket clattered along the cobblestones; someone's shirt flew past the Inn and caught on a fence post. The boiling black clouds shrouded the cottages; even the wind smelled of disaster. A sinking feeling overtook Ira. He no longer hoped the storm would clear for he knew it would not.

Before Ira braved the weather and started on his journey to the Proscriptio, he had to notify Sapien of his discovery. He'd put it off long enough. Ira took the letter he had received at the Receptus, scribbled a note at the bottom, and put it in a new envelope. The dispatch must go by Silent Post. Ira hated using this archaic method; he hated anything to do with old magic. It could be dangerous if not done precisely. Ira was anything but precise.

Ira jumped as someone pounded on his door. "Yes?" Ira said his chest constricting.

Geranne stepped into the room with a tray of steaming food.

"G'day, Mister I. Might ya be wantin' some breakfast?"

Ira was not a frequent visitor at the Inn, but the brother-in-law of the Princeps and the Kilotax of Vinca Village was well known. He chaffed at Geranne's familiarity, and he hated it when she called him Mr. I. It was one thing at the Receptus; it was quite another here.

She sat the tray on the desk beside the envelope. Ira looked greedily at the food; his stomach growled. He needed to send this dispatch to Sapien, but it was clear Geranne had something on her mind. She fiddled with tending the fireplace; the small fire blazing in spite of her distracted poking and knocking the wood about. The wind gusted down the chimney, and small particles of ash floated in the air.

"Mighty nasty day we're havin', ain't it?" Geranne cooked a fine meal and kept a clean hearth, but her chattering pierced straight to the marrow of a man. Without waiting for an answer, she continued.

"Yessir, plumb spooky this weather is. The whole village is astir over it. Can't git ta the fields. Can't hardly even git ta the barn. Why, my bairn, she lives inside Vinca Village, an' I cain't even git o'er the bridge ta see her. Can ya believe it, now? Why'd Princeps Sapien close that bridge? Hmmm? Why that bridge ain't been closed since I's aborn. Mister I, you's the Kilotax here, ya know, don'cha? Ya tell me why that bridge is closed, now."

Ira opened his mouth. Geranne persisted.

"We've an idea why that bridge's closed we do," she said. "And we got ideas why this storm keeps on, too. We ain't no dummies. No sir. We got ideas. Don't take no royalty to know it has ta do wi' the goin's on at BelMoon. We heard 'bout that. No matter we got no invite to the high and mighty doin's, we hear things."

Ira began, "Geranne, I.."

"Mr. I, you gots to do somethin'. Yur our Kilotax, you gots ta do somethin'. Talk to the Princeps. Get him ta open that bridge. And, another thing, what about Iter? How's folks gonna git ta Iter with that bridge closed, now? It's Sapien's job ta git this storm cleared up. The people are scairt, Mr. I. If we can't git the crops in the ground, how we gonna eat, now, Mr. I? How we gonna eat, hmmm?"

Ira stood mute before Geranne annoyed at her, at the weather, at his complete inability to form an answer.

Geranne frustrated and knowing full well she could not present an articulate argument on behalf of the village and that Ira was incapable of a definitive solution, having done her best with what she had she left the room with an indignant huff. She would leave it in the hands of Divus.

Finally. Ira needed to concentrate. Who could think with that woman blabbering and jabbering worse than an old blanket flapping on a clothesline?

Ira held his dispatch to Sapien in his hand and tried to recall the exact words that would send the letter on its way. He pressed the High Court Seal neatly in purple wax on the envelope. The letter turned from side to side clearly impatient to be gone. He closed his eyes tight as if the pressure would squirt the correct charm into his head. Once the seal was stamped Ira had one minute to complete the spell.

"Oh mighty Power of the air, deliver this letter with great care;

With your vast strength and might, Aid this message in its flight."

Now Ira only had to say his magic word. A word given specifically to him and to be used by only him. The problem was when he spoke the word, pain would shoot throughout his body. Ira hated pain. It was devised to discourage frivolous use of the Silent Post. It succeeded.

Ira took a breath and shouted his word. His feet flew out from under him, the fire in the hearth blazed wildly and sparks sizzled around the dispatch. Wind whipped Ira's robes, elevated him into the air, spun him around, and flung him onto the wide rough floorboards.

Ira opened his eyes. His hand that held the dispatch was empty. And smoking.

Princeps Sapien stood at the window in his study. Acta Diurna sat at the scriba's desk.

"Isabella Fae will be here presently?" Sapien asked.

"Yes sir," Acta replied. Sapien noticed Acta's heartbeat doubled, and the vein in his forehead throbbed. Acta continued to write in the ledger. He wondered if Acta had a secret crush on Isabella.

"My daughter is distraught," Sapien said remembering his conversation with Ira that Isabella had overheard. "Well, with Skye's injury, the bridge closed, this weather. It's no wonder."

"Yes sir, it's no wonder," Acta replied.

Sapien glanced at him. Acta came to Vinca Village about a year ago at Sapien's request. He had proven to be an excellent scribe. A man of few words, he remained unobtrusive. In addition to his personal secretary duties for Sapien, he scheduled the entire Consillium and handled voluminous correspondence. Acta scribed for Iris as she dictated each faerie's Totus Vita. Under Acta's supervision, everything ran as orderly as the seasons. Sapien didn't know how he had ever managed without him.

"Helloooo," Isabella's clear voice called out from the hall.

Acta rose from his chair; Sapien turned toward the door. "Isabella, my dulci, please come in." Sapien embraced his daughter.

"Tata," she said as she rested briefly in his arms. Papilio trotted in behind her.

"Good day, Miss Isabella." Acta bowed slightly to them, glanced at Papilio, walked out, and closed the door.

"Isabella, our little Caduceus, how is Skye this morning?"

"Well, not quite Caduceus yet, but soon," Isabella said smiling. "Skye's fighting the stay-in-bed part, but her spirits are good. I can't begin to relate how upset she is over not being able to attend Iter.

That's why I'm here. What can we do, Tata? How has this kind of thing been handled in the past?"

"I know she's disappointed, dulci. But there are provisions for this. If she is not able to attend, I will conduct a private ceremony with Iris to present Skye her Totus Vita, and her Life Crystal. It will be quite unique and special and make up for her frustrations. I promise. Besides, she will probably be well enough to attend in person."

"All right then, if you say so." Isabella sank into the lounge. "Thank you, tata." Papilio jumped up beside her, the Arca Lux shining. "Skye is broken-hearted about all of this. Not only her injuries, and Iter, but Quercus's damage. And, tata," Isabella said, "Uncle Nidus thinks the swing had been tampered with. That is foolish. No one would have done that, especially to Skye. No one uses that swing except Skye."

"What?" Sapien said. "Someone deliberately sabotaged the swing?"

"Well, Uncle Nidus thinks the ropes were cut just enough to hold until the swing reached full arc. I cannot believe it. I won't believe it."

Sapien sat down at his desk. "Isabella, I must tell you something. I wouldn't bring you into this, but it concerns you directly." Sapien's expression was grave. "I'm going to trust you to keep this in confidence for now." He absently picked up his quill. "Isabella, the Sacred Grove has been breached."

Isabella's hand petting Papilio grew still. Her breathing narrowed.

"Isabella...Izzi...someone stole a Totus Vita. Your Totus Vita."

"No," Isabella said. That is not possible. It can't be done. The Grove is protected with Wards. Iris guards the Totus "No." Isabella grabbed her head with both hands. "No. I don't believe it. What is happening?"

Sapien walked over to his daughter and put his arms around her. "My dulci, I'm afraid it is true. I have inspected the Totus room many times. Yours is not there. It is gone."

"But, how? Why? How is this possible?" Tears welled in Isabella's eyes. "And, if my Totus is gone... If my Totus is gone I cannot graduate. I....I cannot *quicken*," she said in horror.

"Izzi, Izzi, listen to me. There are ways. Iris is working on it now. Please, please, you must trust her to work this out." Sapien turned Isabella's head up to him. "Izzi, you must trust me. "

Isabella buried her head in Sapien's robes and cried. Sapien would do anything for her.

Sapien's hand began to burn. A familiar burn. He knew what was coming. A loud, bright sizzle sparked around his fingers, over his palm, and up his wrist. A scorched envelope with a purple seal popped into sight. Silent Post indeed. A slight misnomer. Isabella jumped back and stifled a squeal.

"Sorry, dulci. These things have a way of showing up at the worst moments."

"It's alright," Isabella said as she collected herself. "I need to get back to Skye, anyway."

"Will you be ok?" Sapien asked. "I promise you, we will work this out."

"Yes, yes. I'll be fine."She looked into his eyes. "I trust you, tata. I trust you."

"Good. Remember, now. Mum's the word."

Isabella smiled weakly. "Mums the word."

Sapien picked up the small knife he kept on his desk and slid the edge under the purple seal. His door burst open at the same moment and Valeo Nox stormed in. Sapien slid the missive into a drawer.

"Valeo, what in the name of Holy Grove are you doing?"

Chapter Thirty-Seven

Totus Vita

Isabella wrapped her cloak firmly around her and drew up her hood. Within minutes she entered Skye's bedroom, Papilio following.

"Skye, how are you," Isabella said bending over her cousin. Isabella felt her forehead and checked her pulse. She replenished Aunt Ofella's herbs, adjusted the covers, administered the hypericum salve and poked the fire.

"Aren't you just the little Caduceus?" Sky teased and tried to open her eyes. "Do I have to be sedated? I want to get up. I'm not finished with my dress for Iter."

"Well, not Caduceus yet, but I'm getting there," Isabelle answered. It seemed like she was saying that a lot lately. "Yes, you need to be sedated. Your body needs to heal." Her voice did not hold its usual note of repartee.

"What's wrong?" Skye asked.

"Nothing. Nothing's wrong. Now I have told Aunt Ofella to increase your passionflower for the evening dose. Also, here, I want you to drink this." Isabella held a glass to Skye's lips. "This will speed your healing; I've given the recipe to Aunt Ofella. We want you up and about not lazing around here." She smiled and Skye's tension relaxed. "Mother is coming this evening. I'll be back to see you in the morning. You rest easy, now. Don't make me take drastic measures." Isabella tried not to look at the disappointment in Skye's eyes.

She walked down the hall to Nidus' study. The door stood ajar. "Uncle Nidus, may I speak with you for a moment?"

"Isabella, dulci, do come in," Nidus said. "How is our little Skye doing this afternoon?"

"She's resting. She'll be fine. It will just take some time." Isabella closed the door and walked over to him.

"Uncle Nidus, father told me about the swing. Are you sure?"

Nidus sighed. "Yes, my dear. There is no doubt."

"But, who? Who would do this? And why?"

"I don't know," Nidus said. "I've been wrestling with it since I discovered the slashes in the ropes. It doesn't make sense. Why would anyone want to injure Skye?"

"Father told me about the breach in the Grove. Uncle Nidus, how is that possible? The Grove is warded."

"We're working on it, darling. Your father and the entire Consillium are meeting tonight. We'll figure it out. We're meeting in the Grove. With Iris."

Isabella stared. "With Iris?"

"Yes," Nidus said.

Iris, Goddess of the Rainbow, didn't just meet with people. She had many duties to the Domus Kingdom, but one of her main responsibilities was the Sacred Crystal Grove: the Totus Vitas and the

Life Crystals. Her powerful wards kept the Grove safe. She rarely consented to meet with anyone and only appeared publicly at the Grove during Iter. She presided over the graduations, the quickenings, and any other celebrations at hand, such as transformations and most important the appointment of a new Solis.

There would be transformations this year, a rare ceremony that Isabella was anxious to see. She had learned of it quite by accident when she overheard Sapien dictating a document to Acta called the Vocatio.

Hardly anyone knew about the return of the banished tribes of GENS, and Isabella had been hard-pressed to keep from telling Skye about it. Personally, Isabella thought 49,000 years went a bit beyond the pale, so she was glad Iris decided to bring them home. They had served their time.

Isabella recognized the profound implication of Iris's meeting with the Consillium. "Oh. All right, then," she said, a little taken aback. "She'll help. She'll know what to do."

Isabella had the utmost faith in Iris; She would take care of her missing Totus Vita. Somehow. Only those with a Totus in the vault room could come to Iter, and since every faerie had one, there had never been any problem.

Iris couldn't, wouldn't allow Isabella to miss Iter. Iris had a special bond with all students; especially anyone slated to become a Caduceus. Everything would be fine. They would figure it out.

Later, Isabella lay on her bed, relaxed and dreamy. It was dark outside.

"Hmmm. Papilio. Where are you?" Isabella asked. Papilio always curled close to Isabella, the Arca Lux shining. Isabella searched the bed in the darkness. "Papilio? Come here girl."

Isabella reached for her lamp and felt something cold, wet.

"What ..?" She jerked her hand back, stood up, and walked toward the fireplace. With the firebrand in hand, she lit her lamp. A parcel lay on her bedside table. It was wrapped in thick crude paper tied with flax string. It was soaked. Water ran along the table and dripped onto the floor.

Isabella looked around the room, out the window, out in the hallway. No one. Her father had gone to the special Consillium meeting with Iris; her mother had gone to Skye's. No one was in the house but her. Isabella sat back down on the bed and opened the package. The wet paper fell away. A gilded book lay in her lap.

Isabella had seen a book like this before.

Isabella was eight years old and enjoyed raucous games with Papilio. She ran down the hallway laughing with Papilio in hot pursuit.

The door was open when they reached Coxi's bedroom. Coxi sat at her desk writing in a book. Isabella tore through the door before she saw her mother and knew she was in trouble. She tried to stop running, but the rug started sliding toward Coxi. Papilio tried to stop, all eight feet seeking purchase on the hardwood floor, but on they slid like eight tiny gliders.

Isabella and Papilio crashed into Coxi and her book flew into the air. It was the most beautiful thing Isabella had ever seen. The cover was leather, soft and pink as the dawn with a faint blush. Beautiful illuminations and curved graceful script flowed across fine parchment pages. Then it vanished. Isabella knew without a doubt that it was her mother's Totus Vita.

"Isabella," Coxi scolded. "What have I told you about running?"

"I'm sorry, mamma. Was that your Totus Vita, mamma? Where did it go? Oh, mamma, is it gone forever?" Isabella burst into tears.

"No, no, dulci," Coxi said. "Totus Vita's are very private. They are for their owners' eyes only. They are charmed so no one else can see them. Don't worry; it's in a safe place. I can retrieve it anytime I choose. Now, let's talk about running in the house."

Isabella looked at the wet book in her lap.

This is my Totus Vita.

Her hands trembled; she was afraid to touch it. How did it get here and why is it visible?

Totus Vitas did not become visible to their owners until they were presented to them at Iter. Until they quickened. Why could she see it now?

Isabella cautiously ran her fingers over the cover. It was the color of sunrise, like her mother's but different. In fact, she could recall the exact sunrise. The morning Sapien began teaching her the sacred Song of Enchantment the sun burst into day as if to join in Isabella's lesson. Her full name was scripted across the leather in gold and amethyst.

Elation bubbled quietly within Isabella. She had dreamed of this day, this day when she would have her Totus Vita. She wanted to open it but feared to touch it. This was wrong, so wrong. Where was her ceremony? Where was her family to share in the glorious moment? Where was the Goddess Iris to quicken her?

Knowing she should not, the desire to open it, to experience it, overwhelmed her.

Trembling she opened the cover. Inside lay a folded sheet of stained dark paper sealed with a curious blue-green wax.

Isabella Fae Duco.

Her name called to her. She ripped open the seal.

The words on the letter wrapped and wound around her. Suffocating. Written ropes binding her. Isabella's breath caught somewhere and couldn't get out. Tears began their wet path down her cheeks. Isabella felt her heart break in half. Her head spun; blackness overcame her, and she fell to the floor.

Chapter Thirty-Eight

Breach

"Sapien," Valeo panted. "I have to speak with you." He gave his wings a good flap to rid them of water.

"What are you about, popping in here that way? It's not only ill-mannered, it's illegal," Sapien said. His voice had a sharp edge. Regardless of Valeo's Keeper status, Sapien had never gotten on with him. Valeo's ego was at odds with Sapien's humility.

"I've just learned the Lex Scriptura is missing. Is that true?"

Sapien sighed. "Yes. Yes it is."

"And you didn't think it fit to inform me of this?" Valeo demanded.

Sapien hardened. "I left word for you, but you were...indisposed. It is not my responsibility to keep track of your whereabouts. I also sent a dispatch directly to King Colere."

"Yes, *so I hear,*" Valeo retorted. "The Grove breached, the Lex Scriptura stolen, the weather completely running amuck. What's going on here?"

Sapien continued. "There is also a Totus Vita missing."

"Whose?" Valeo barked.

"That is confidential." Sapien well aware of Valeo's ability to probe his mind, shielded his own.

Valeo puffed his chest, raised his chin, and said, "*Confidential from me?*"

Sapien ignored Valeo's question. "And it is my opinion that this inclement weather is connected to the breach."

"That's nonsense," Valeo said. "To affect the weather, the Tempus Crystal has to be disturbed. Only one person can enter Mt. Vetare; you know that."

"Not only should we be concerned about the weather," Sapien said, "but time as well. If the Crystal is disturbed, time will warp, Domus Herself could be destroyed."

"Holy Grove, Sapien. Are you unbalanced? That's ridiculous. A few bad storms and you've jumped into the Dark Pit. Just because some unscrupulous villain has the Lex Scriptura doesn't mean they can get to the Crystal.

"The Mother will only allow The Warrior near the Crystal. What? You think the Mother has sunk into the Dark Pit as well? You think She will let everyone who walks through the door close to the Crystal? You think she will hand over the very existence of Domus to anyone? Is there no end to your fantasies?"

"Who knows what has happened now that the Lex Scriptura is missing. And I will ignore your blasphemous comments about the Mother. But I do know something is wrong and I intend to find out what. You are dismissed, sir."

"You dare to dismiss me," Valeo said. "Beware, Sapien. Beware."

He took to the air with a rush of angry frenzy, flew a short distance, and landed beside the mighty oak split in half.

"Pity," he mumbled as he eyed the fallen tree.

Keeper Valeo Nox had one thing in common with that little puffed-up toad, Ira: he hated humans. With a driving passion and beyond reason. But today he hovered outside Skye Pudor's bedroom window, his green-black cape blowing in the fierce wind and knew he would do anything for this girl...this human girl.

"Skye, what have I done?" he said. He blew her a kiss and flew home to QuinVerga.

Keeper Valeo was in a temper. That ill-mannered, ill-bred, preening little molted brood-spot of a faerie, Ira Lungwort. He couldn't carry out instructions if you scribbled them on his forehead with one of his own feathers. Lichen alive. Alive. How did that happen?

Valeo shot a mind probe to Manes.

Get in here, now.

"Where is that useless specter? Manes," Valeo shouted, knowing Manes had not had time to come from the stables, but unable to stop his run-a-way panic. He ran out the door not stopping to retrieve his already wet cloak. By the time he reached the stable Manes was just coming out and they collided. Valeo fell to the ground, dirty water splashing into his face.

"You frigid phantom, where have you been?" Valeo screamed. Manes stood inside the barn. Calm. Dry.

"I've been oiling the carriage wheels, sir."

Valeo made several attempts to stand, but because of the rain-softened path, he lost his balance and slid to his knees, his hands slipped out from under him and his face smashed into the ground.

By the time he hoisted himself into the barn, he was entirely covered in mud. He flapped his wings furiously sending globs of sludge to the far corners of the stable. Flying fury.

"Lichen is alive, you fool."

Manes raised a finger and slowly swept a dab of mud off his face and flicked it on the floor. The conjured like to be clean. Impeccably clean.

"I do beg your pardon, sir. I saw him fall into the shoals. I assumed..."

"You assumed? Well, you *assumed* wrong. He's alive and in the Proscriptio. How am I to believe you have the other matter well in hand when you have so superbly botched this one?"

Manes cold blue eyes stared at Valeo unblinking. His posture straight and hard-lined as ice.

"Chimera is still...indisposed if that is what you mean."

"Of course, that's what I mean you frozen cretin. Check on it, *now*. Make certain everything is...secure. If you fail at this task," Valeo said, "rest assured, I *will* banish you."

Chapter Thirty-Nine

Disappearance

Isabella awoke to the night birds still singing soft croonings. Something was tickling her nose; she swatted, but it persisted. As awareness dawned, Isabella sat upright. Where…?

She lay on a soft moss bed under a canopy of willows—the Willow House; she did not remember coming here, Sapien built it for her as a playhouse years ago. And her book, her Totus Vita, had that been real? Isabella jumped up and sat back down as quickly. The letter lay on the ground at her feet, crumpled, but whole.

The nightmare returned, it had been real. The facts were there. Cold hard reality.

She was not Faerie.

Ian sat across the room. "Good morning. Well, it's not morning. But, well, anyway, glad you are awake. I was beginning to worry about you." Ian held his orange hat in his hands, twirling it round and round, clearly uncomfortable.

"Oh, no," Isabella put her head in her hands and sobbed. "Oh, Ian. It can't be true. Not faerie? My parents are faeries. I am faerie."

Isabella knew without asking that Ian knew her story. Ian knew everything that happened at Numen. He had lived here for eons, guarding the gate, watching over the Princeps and their families.

"Isabella, please. Please don't cry. This must be a mistake."

Isabella smiled weakly at her long-time friend. Ian always comforted her, and his compassion totally at odds with his trollish looks.

"You don't believe I'm human?"

"No, I don't. It's just not true,"

"Oh Ian, what shall I do? I can't think. I'm so confused," Isabella said. "I don't have wings. I don't even have nubs," she sobbed.

"Well, that don't mean nothin'," Ian said beginning to pace. "Some faeries don't get wings 'till after Iter. And look at your mother and tata, they don't have wings either, and neither does Miss Skye."

"Oh, I know," said Isabella. "But that's different. Skye, well I'm pretty sure Skye, well, she might be getting nubs. She has all the symptoms; they just haven't appeared yet.

"And my parents had wings in the past, you know that, but I never have." After a moment of pained silence, she continued. "And I never will. Ian" Isabella's voice sank to a whisper, "I am a human."

"Now, Miss Izzi. Don't fret." Ian fidgeted. He pulled on his ear, his own distress signal. He could never stand to see Isabella Fae upset.

"Ian, why didn't tata tell me? I don't understand. "Maybe he didn't know... Ian, am I ... a changeling?" Isabella said in horror.

"Oh now, Izzi, don't do that. Don't be goin' places you shouldn't be." Ian's voice grew strained. "A changeling? No, no not a changeling. My Izzi is not a changeling."

"And Iter. Ian, what about Iter? Iris will not allow it to take place if a human is there," Isabella said. "Oh, Ian, I can't go to Iter. I am a disgrace to my family."

Ian's hands were rough and calloused. He pulled hard on his ear and it began to turn red under his gray skin.

"Now, Miss Izzi, you ain't no disgrace to nobody. Now you know that. Stop cryin', now Miss Izzi. Just you stop cryin'." Ian patted her shoulder; his large hand practically covered her back.

"Ian, who could have sent me this letter? Who could get my book?"

"Uh, uh..." Ian stammered.

Isabella stood and paced. "I'm looking at this all wrong. This is a good thing. It's a good thing, isn't it Ian?"

"Uh, well..." Ian was trying to keep up.

"If I hadn't discovered I was human, my presence would have destroyed Iter. I would have disgraced my family. I found out just in time." Isabella's soul felt some of the darkness lighten. "Ian, I must leave."

"Oh, I don't know..."

"Yes, Ian, it's the only way. I have to leave Numen. I have to leave Vinca Village."

"Well, Miss Izzi, I..."

"Don't try to talk me out of it, Ian. It's the right thing to do. If I stay, Father will only try to find a way to get me into Iter. That won't do, Ian. That just won't do."

"Uh, well..."

"I won't have my family disgraced, Ian. It would be better for me just to leave."

"But, Miss Izzi..."

"Ian, have you seen Papilio? Wait a minute. Of course, you haven't. She can't stay with me now. She knows I'm human. Although she has been with me since MothersMa..." Fresh grief masked her face.

Ian's ear was swollen; red streaks ran down the lobe. The rather long lobe.

"Yes, MothersMa," Ian said as he continued to pull his ear. "She would know what to do," he said under his breath. "I wish that darn cat was here now. Never could figure out why faeries trust them. They are never where they're supposed to be. Popping in and out of places all the..." Ian stopped talking abruptly; he astonished even himself with the long speech.

Isabella straightened her back. Her natural determination, or was it stubbornness, returned. "Well, no matter. I'm leaving. I wonder how the meeting with Iris is going Do you think Iris knows about me, about me being human I mean?"

"Well, I expect she..."

"Do you think she told the entire Consillium about me?" Fresh tears blurred her vision. "And tata. How could he do this? He knows I'm human, yet he told me my Totus Vita was missing, and it was missing because I'm human. Does that make sense?"

"Uh, no, it..."

"Of course it doesn't. Maybe Father himself stole my book. Maybe he stole it so I couldn't attend Iter. But, Ian, why didn't he just tell me the truth? Why didn't he tell me I am human?"

"I don't kn..."

"Oh, Ian, he didn't want to hurt me. Of course. He didn't want to hurt me, yet he couldn't let me attend Iter. That must be it. But, Ian, where's my book now? Oh, it can't stay with a human, yes. It can't exist with a human so it disappeared. Where do you think it went? Do you think it is gone forever?

"Oh, Ian, it was so beautiful. It was beyond beautiful. And now I'll never see it again. I won't quicken, Ian. I can't be a Caduceus."

Isabella sank onto the moss bed, tears sliding between her fingers. She had to get control of herself. Poor Ian, she made him miserable with her rantings. She may not be Faerie, but she was still Isabella Fae Duco. She knew what to do in crises; she possessed a clear and rational mind.

Isabella raised her eyes to Ian, then walked over to him and put her arms around his neck, sniffing. Sounds of despair.

"I love you, Ian. I have loved you my whole life. Well, since we've lived here, that is. Thank you for being with me tonight. I don't know what I would have done without you to talk things out with me. Especially since Papilio..." Isabella's voice cracked.

"Well, I have to get out of here. I want to leave before anyone gets home."

"Miss Izzi, where will you go?" Ian said.

"To a place built by humans, for humans. New Ivy. And Ambassador Q. He will know what to do, I just know it. And Lichen. Lichen is human."

"But the bridge is closed. And, you don't have the passwords. Do you?" Ian asked.

"No, no I don't. Let me think." Isabella began to pace again.

"I know a way," Ian said, then looked as though he should not have said it. "Through the gate. Through the secret passage. It's dangerous. But I can help you."

"Ian, that's wonderful. That's a great plan," Izzi said. She tried at the last moment to tone down the surprise in her voice. Ian was not known for his mental acuity.

"I need to pack a few things. I'll be right back."

Ian watched her sprint off toward the house. "I hope I'm doin' the right thing," he muttered and sloughed off toward the gate. Where inferi is that cat?"

The secret passage was dark. Darker than Domus nights. Darker than nightmares. Isabella slid her hand along the wet rock wall and thought about Ian's directions. One hundred paces. She only had to go one hundred paces to get out of this blackness.

"After the hundred paces, you will enter the Air Zone. Once you are there, think of New Ivy. Think of Q's Manor, and, zap, you'll be there," Ian had instructed. "Easy as slime."

Isabella wasn't too sure how easy slime was.

"Twenty-two, twenty-three, ahhhhh." Isabella tripped and slid down an incline. She tried to grasp jutting rocks and roots as she passed, but they were too slippery. The incline grew steeper, her fall faster. She fell farther on and on, almost as if she was in a dream. Finally, she landed in a heap, small rocks falling on her. She lay quiet, listening, trying to catch her breath.

"Well, well, what have we here?" a raspy voice croaked.

Isabella opened her eyes. Nothing, pitch black. She heard a shuffling that sounded like it came closer. "I said, what have we here?" The voice was almost upon her. Isabella jumped to her feet and was immediately knocked down. And out.

Latere sat back on his heels, leaned against the stone wall, and laughed uproariously.

"Well, can you just believe it?" he said. "The little Charm falls right into my hands. By all that's unholy, I'm a lucky fellow, I am. Now, just what are you doing down here little lady? No matter. I'll take care of you now." Latere bundled Isabella's unconscious body into his arms.

Papilio trotted along behind.

Chapter Forty

Wieland

Lichen made one more trip into the mysterious cache of jewels. He stuffed his pouch: a handful of pearls because they were small and easy to hide, several small emeralds because they were his favorite, and one perfect diamond. Lichen wasn't greedy. Well, maybe a little. But, when Lorelei told him the origins of this lair, Lichen knew to get in, get out.

A small parcel drew him to a sheltered ledge. Lichen picked it up; it was very heavy considering the small size. As he unfolded it, a magnificent cloak spread out before him. It seemed woven with light, imbued with power.

Lichen carefully, almost reverently, stroked the cloak. It felt warm, magical and emitted a presence. As impossible as it seemed, a helmet lay tucked inside the cloak, stunning in its simplicity. And a sword, a glorious sword.

Lichen knew he must hurry, but he couldn't help himself. He put on the helmet and remembered the first time he donned his flight helmet.

Get a move on, Lichen.

He quickly draped the cloak about his shoulders and picked up the sword. Visceral power. He grinned.

At that moment, Lichen felt invincible. A warrior. An unbeatable, unconquerable warrior. Lichen heard a slight shuffle behind him and turned, sword in hand.

There stood a man, diminutive and dark. Lichen raised the sword, balancing, measuring it; the heft felt perfect as if it had been made for him.

No more than twenty-four inches tall, the strange little creature didn't look much of a threat. His feet were webbed, his hands calloused, his body hairy. Lichen's confidence grew.

"Well, pocket-size, what now?" Lichen said brandishing the sword, feeling cocky. The fellow stepped toward Lichen. Lichen parried cautiously. Lorelei had told him a fierce water dwarf guarded the cave.

This is fierce?

"So, ya gonna let me out a here?" Lichen began to edge back toward the water.

"So, ya gonna swim in that get-up?" The dwarf's gravelly voice mimicked Lichen.

Lichen lowered the sword and stared.

The dwarf shook his head. His hair pulled back in a braid glistened black against his knotted skull. His eyebrows wiry and thick. His coal eyes never blinked.

Remembering Lorelei's instruction Lichen drew the sword up to his body and gave a slight bow of respect. Curious creatures, dwarves.

Give them respect and they give it in return. Show them disdain, condescend to them, and they become vicious.

"No. I do not plan to swim in this.....get up."

The dwarf smiled his teeth as black as the rest of him. Not dirty, just dark enamel. "I am called Wieland. Wieland of Kallowa."

"I am Lic..."

"I know who you are. Lichen Ipse of The Manor," Wieland said.

Lichen Ipse of the Manor. I like it.

"You seem surprised," Wieland said. "Don't be. We people of the Elements know many things. We know of the Earth, of the Water. I am at home in both. We can breathe the water and the earth as you do air. The light," he motioned toward the ceiling, "shines through the water and the earth for us as it does through the air for you."

"You know me? You know I am captive here?"

"Yes," Wieland said.

"Why have you not helped me escape?" Indignant. "I was tortured and beaten. They starved me. You would leave me here to rot?"

"It is not my concern. It is not my place to interfere." Wieland continued as if forced. "The Proscriptio is a cursed place. We leave it be." Wieland rolled his eyes. "Unless, of course, there is a request."

"A request?" Lichen asked. "You mean all I have to do is *request?*"

"Yes," Wieland said, his tone inflexible, his anger hovering beneath the surface.

"Well, consider this a request. Get me out of here."

"I can do what I can do."

"What does that mean?"

"I cannot take you out of here. But I may assist you in certain...," Wieland walked over to a ledge and sat down, "ways."

"Oh, I get it. You can give me advice. Well, I don't need any more advice. What I need is a way out of this hole."

Wieland sighed, "Do not underestimate advice, Lichen. You have much to learn. For instance, Lorelei."

"Who?"

"Lorelei, the undine captive. Short in stature, long red hair."

"So that's her name, Lorelei. An undine huh? What about her? She's been in the camp for several days. *She'll* help me escape."

"You must halt his domination," Wieland said, eyes bulging.

"Who? What do you mean?" What was this crazy little gnome saying? What did that have to do with escaping? That's all Lichen wanted. Escape and revenge on the stinking, slobbering, mucous-infested rock faeries.

"Is your heart purely seen, Lichen?" Wieland said.

"You're crazy. I'm leaving." Something stirred in Lichen, some buried memory.

"There are many things about in Domus, Lichen. Many things you do not understand."

"Why should I trust you?" Lichen asked.

"You shouldn't. You should trust no one. And, I haven't given you your gift."

"I thought all you had was advice."

"You said that, not I."

"A gift? Why would you give me a gift?"

"It is foretold. I must give it to you," Wieland said, his voice like a bell lacking in tenor or pitch.

"I do not want to; I forged it for another."Wieland motioned to the sword. "But now, it is yours."

"Forged?" Lichen asked. He held up the sword; its steel glinted in the sun."Wait a minute," he looked at the sword. "You're giving me something I already have?"

"Just because you possess it doesn't make it yours. This is Durandal. Now, it is yours."

"Durandal?"

"Durandal. I made it myself. It is one of three swords commissioned at Kallowa."

"You're giving me a sword?"

"I am giving you Durandal. It is not just a sword," Wieland protested, his voice echoed off the walls. "And" he added with a grunt, " the helmet and cape."

His dark eyes flashed anger. "I am loathed to part with these treasures. But I must. You are The Warrior."

Lichen looked at the sword and grinned. "Yes, indeedy, I am a warrior."

The sword felt right. From the moment he picked it up, he felt...strong. Empowered.

"Durandal," he said as he hefted, weighed the sword.

"You have lost your way. It will help you find your Soul, Lichen."

Still grinning, Lichen said, "My soul? Who cares about my soul? This will help me get out of here."

Wieland grabbed Lichen's arm. His dark skin flushed; tiny beads of sweat speckled his face. He smelled of earth. "Find your way, Lichen. Make the right selection," he growled.

The poem.

That crazy enigmatic poem. That's where he'd heard those phrases.

Lichen jerked away. He wrapped the helmet and sword in the cape. They immediately disappeared. "OK, I'm taking the helmet and cape as well. Thank you very much. Gotta go."

"Don't you want to know just how special they are, Lichen?"

"Make it quick, old man. I have to get back to camp."

"They are Tarnhelm and Tarnkappe. And," Wieland growled, "I am giving them to you, you are not taking them. Worn together they render you invisible."

Lichen looked down at his parcel.

Unbelievable, to a superlative degree.

Just a few short weeks ago Lichen would have looked upon the things that had been happening to him as a figment of a diseased and delusional mind. But, now he was taking even the most preposterous in stride. Warrior indeed.

"Thanks, Wieland. It's been a pleasure." Lichen dived into the pool. Water splashed Wieland's face; steam drifted from his skin.

"Human fool," he said.

Lorelei trailed Lichen, puppy-like. Her small four foot body glistened silver and shined as if wet.

"Excuse me," Lichen said. "The jewels are what?" He laughed. He had been telling her of his encounter with Wieland.

"The jewels are tears," she said quietly. "Tears of water natives. We weep when we are separated from our home." She would not discuss her capture, tell him her name or speak unless spoken to. Her eyes, deep shimmering pools of sadness, looked up at him. She never smiled.

"You're serious," Lichen said.

Lorelei nodded. "As I told you, Wieland is a water dwarf. He is assigned to gather tears from all the waters of the Great River Potens into the cave. It has not always been so. He is banished here; he is a Son of the Mist. In his kingdom he was a great artisan."

"What did he do? Why was he banished?"

Lorelei ignored his questions. "You are fortunate. His charge is to protect the cave. No one leaves the cave. No one lives to tell."

"Hmmm." Lichen did not tell Lorelei how many gems he had. He did not mention the gifts Wieland had given him "He warned me about you, *Lorelei.*"

Lorelei did not seem surprised Lichen knew her name. Instead, she said, "He will be here today."

Lichen knew she spoke of Ira Lungwort, the Trader. They had talked of little else. "That little dung heap. He should have been back by now. It's been two weeks since he was here. Probably took my ruby and went on his merry little perverted way. How do you know? How do you know he's coming?" he asked.

"I know."

Lichen believed her. Lorelei was always right; somehow she always knew. "Good, I'm ready to get out of this stinking armpit."

Chapter Forty-One

Escape

Clouds lay low and gray over the outcrop, the air dripping wet and cold. Morning slumbered behind the mountain. Lichen sat looking out at his gray world. The captives stirred about, readying for their day. Lorelei walked up behind him.

"Today's the day," Lichen said. His fist pounded into his other palm. He was in a mood. She responded with silence.

"I've been thinking. I've only been here six months. It seems like a lifetime." He laughed, hostility trimming the edges with bitterness. He shrugged his SAX shoulder and fingered the branded scar. He remembered bones broken accidentally and intentionally, swollen bruises and lacerations thick with pus. Days of starving and deprivation, he remembered misery. The kicks. The spit. The filth. The isolation.

" I hate these god-forsaken-pit-of-the-earth-stinking-slimy-no-good faeries. Desolation and despair to them all...forever."

"You are captive leader. You have freedom."

"*Freedom?* Freedom?" he said. "Living in this hole? Imprisoned. Living with these, these inhuman monsters. I loathe them. I hate the very air they breathe. I hate the way they look at me with those desolate empty eyes. The sound of their voice is like a needle in my eye. Their disgusting gray crusty skin. And those wings. Filthy, torn, trailing the ground like broken sails. It's repulsive." Lichen's eyes flared. His throat tightened. "They're repulsive. They plot and plan to make their miserable lives palatable. They lie and cheat on each other. They force mind-numbing work upon me and use my skills, give me a modicum of *freedom* and I should be grateful? They are corruption oozing from the earth. I wish them all dead. Yes. I will see to that."

Twigs snapped behind them. Lichen turned. Dilingo stood watching... and listening, his face stricken. Lichen jumped up.

"Dilingo," he said softly. *Why did I ever teach him English?*

Dilingo started running through the brush.

"Dilingo stop," Lichen called after him. "Dilingo, come back here. Get back here, now." Lichen tripped and sprawled on the sharp rocks. "Curse it, Dilingo."

Dilingo increased his speed and stumbled into a fire pit, his clothing catching ablaze. He tore through the camp scattering breakfast campfires like a possessed flamethrower. Women screamed, men swore. Lichen's prize slough channeling water to the outcrop sat directly in his path.

"Dilingo, look out," Lichen shouted. Dilingo hit the wooden trench full force and the trough splintered in every direction like hundreds of toothpicks and chopsticks. Hot water gushed into Dilingo's face. He screamed, covered his face with his hands, and stumbled sideways against the slough. Together they crashed to the ground scalding water blistering Dilingo with hideous gray bubbles.

special dispensation you know. To enter the Proscriptio." Ira deferred saying he received his dispensation from the devil himself.

"I see," said Lichen. "In that case, perhaps I can be of assistance in your rescue."

"Good sir, I appreciate your willingness. I really do. But I fail to see how a tree may be of any help to me."

"But my good man. I assure you I can. You are a trader, are you not?"

"Yes, yes that is true. But, of what use are my meager goods to one such as yourself?"

"Your trinkets and supplies are of little value to me. Have you any earth energy?"

Ira stepped back from the old oak. "Earth energy?"

"Yes. Red to be precise. Do you have any red earth energy?" Lichen saw the outline of the ruby he had paid Ira sewn into the hem of his pants.

"It's irrelevant," Ira said nervously. "You cannot help me get into the Proscriptio."

"I never said I could. I said I could help you rescue the grandson. Do you have red earth energy?"

Ira wasn't about to forfeit his jewel. All he had to do was wait. He would get in. Eventually.

"No. No, sir. I do not have any red earth energy."

"Then, sir, you are not only a weasel and a thief, but you are also a liar."

"I beg your pardon," Ira stammered.

Lichen swept Tarnhelm off his head. "No, sir. I beg your pardon." Lichen's humor was not immediately apparent to Ira.

"Lichen. Lichen, it's you." Ira stared at the helmet. "Where did you get that? How did you get out? You look frightful. What happened to you?"

"Never mind toad. I must get to Mt. Vetare. And you will lead me there."

"Lichen, no. No, we must get to the Manor straightaway. Evil is about my boy. We must make haste. Your grandfather is expecting us."

"Grandfather?" Lichen said. "He still wants me....after the murder he still wants me?"

"Wants you? My good boy, yes. Yes, he wants you. He doesn't believe for a moment you killed Agaso." Ira paused. "Uh, there's just the matter of payment."

"Why you shriveled reprobate. I paid you 'red earth energy'. And a good-sized one at that."

"I don't want any more jewels, Lichen. I want a baby."

"What?"

"A baby. From the Ambassador's orphanage. For my wife. You see, she is, well, she is not happy with me of late. She's always wanted a baby, and I thought if I got her one... Well, never mind that. I need a baby and you can help me get it."

Lichen was dumbstruck. Just when he thought he had this bloated cockroach figured out. "Well, now. A baby it is. Let's get going. To the Forbidden Forest, *then* to New Ivy."

Ira looked like the Forbidden Forest was the last place he wanted to be.

"Why do you want to go into the Forest, Lichen? The only thing there is Mt. Vetare. Only one person can enter the Forest, Lichen. And it certainly isn't you. Is it?"

Lichen grinned. "My business. Now, let's get going."

"Tau'stercus," Ira mumbled.

Chapter Forty-Two

Vetare Silva

Green. Lichen relished in the green of the forest, more like a jungle. Never mind the branches and vines snatched and scratched and strangled him. Never mind he couldn't see two feet ahead; it was green. The Proscriptio's grayness could drain the very life out of a person.

Green. The essence of life. He loved it. The look of it, the feel of it, the smell of it. He stood and inhaled a hearty deep life-restoring breath. A small spark of gratitude began to glow somewhere beneath his armor of hatred.

NO.

No, he would not allow it. He would root out any sign of virtue, steel his heart against any softness, and purposefully reinforce his hatred until he was once again invincible to any feelings of kindness. He smothered himself in remembered grief and despair until one thing survived, revenge.

He was strong. Invincible. A warrior.

The warrior?

Lichen didn't know what this "Warrior" thing meant. It seemed as if someone mentioned it at every turn. Like the crazed gnome in the cave, what was his story?

It didn't matter now, he was out of the Proscriptio, he walked free and would soon have the means to make it and everyone in it history. Every last bit of gray matter, gone. Now, he had to get that crystal.

They were threading their way downriver, the underbrush thicker with each step. "Are you sure we're heading in the right direction, Ira"

"I'm pretty sure I know my way about," Ira snapped. "I've only been trading here 20 years." His breath came short and heavy. Ira looked worried and kept looking over his shoulder. The heavy growth and tree limbs prevented Ira from flying.

"This Forbidden Forest is thick, isn't it? Nearly impassable." Lichen swatted at branches and kicked prickly clinging vines. It's aptly named."

Ira laughed, a short choking kind of laugh. "Sorry. This is not the Forbidden Forest, the great Vetare Silva. This is just, well, a forest."

Lichen stopped, his hand on a large think vine. "You mean we're not even to it yet? We've been walking for hours."

"There's a cave up ahead with a spring," Ira said. "We'll take lunch there."

Ira motioned for Lichen to approach slowly. "Always better to see who might be hanging about," Ira said.

They peered through the brush and seeing no one, walked into the clearing and knelt by the water's edge scooping cool water into their mouths. The surface broke; the water sprang up around Lichen and pulled him under the surface. He thrashed and kicked but was held fast in the watery arms.

Down they went, Lichen saw tiny spots float in his eyes, he needed air. Just as blackness shrouded his mind he was unceremoniously dumped up and onto a ledge. Lichen rolled over on his hands and knees coughing and heaving. He laid his forehead on his arm and breathed great gulps of air.

Lichen looked up. "Great goose, Lorelei. Are you trying to kill me?"

She smiled. "Nice to see you, too."

Lichen looked around the tiny hollow area. "So, this is how you get about. In the water?"

Lorelei did not answer.

"What took you so long?"

Lorelei's face clouded. "I was...indisposed."

Lichen shook his head. Does anyone in Domus ever give a straight answer?

"What is *he* doing with you?"

"Ira? He was waiting outside the gate. I gave him quite a turn," Lichen said dimpling. "He needs a baby."

"What?"

"He wants Q to help him adopt a baby from the orphanage; he thinks it will get him out of hot water with his wife. He's "rescuing" me so grandfather will help him. I took pity on him. He wanted to take me straight to the Manor." Lichen looked into her eyes, all aquamarine and swirly. Eddies of the deep. "But we know I must get to the holy mountain, don't we?" he mocked.

Lorelei hesitated. "Perhaps it would be better to forget the Crystal. Go to New Ivy. Your grandfather will be happy to have you home again. You could put the Proscriptio behind you."

"And forget about the gray nightmare? Forget the grape cage, the porcupine rocks, and the slop for breakfast? Forget being a slave?

Forget *this*?" Lichen tore his shirt exposing the SAX brand on his shoulder. He stood and paced the tiny room.

"I am going to get that crystal and disrupt ITER so they will all die. Every last one of those stinking wrinkled bats. They are disgusting and vile. They do not deserve to live. And, when I'm done with them, I'm going to kill that troll. That slimy one-eared troll."

Lichen's image of his mother kicked into the river fueled his anger, contorting his face. Hatred transforms the most handsome of faces.

Lorelei shrunk away from him and Lichen realized he was having a good old-fashioned temper fit. He smiled. "Ah, now, I've gone and scared you. I'm sorry. Let's get out of here. Think you can do it without drowning me?"

Ira squeaked and nearly dropped his scrimpet sandwich as Lichen and Lorelei broke the surface of the water. "Tau'stercus. I thought you drowned."

"Just went for a little swim," Lichen teased treading water as he splashed Ira. "Let's be on our way," he said as he hopped out of the spring. "Eat and walk, toad, eat and walk."

"What is *she* doing here?" Ira said.

Lichen looked at Lorelei and back to Ira. "Now, children. Play nice."

Lorelei laid a small crystal by the water's edge. "For the Spring Spirit," she said to Lichen.

"Ah, yes the Spring Spirit." He thought of the spring at the Manor and had a sudden nostalgic desire to be home. He hadn't realized until that moment that he thought of the Manor as home.

At nightfall, they made camp beside the river. Ira and Lichen munched on leftover scrimpet. Lichen hated scrimpets and from the look on Ira's face, he didn't think much of them either.

He watched the river, boiling and churning, a restless woman tossing about. He watched Lorelei.

"So, this is part of the Great River Potens?"

"Yes," she answered.

"She gets around, doesn't she? And you can travel through any water?"

Lorelei checked Ira. He had finished his scrimpet and was asleep slumped against a boulder. He looked even less appealing in sleep.

"Yes," she said quietly, nodding her head.

"So, the River flows everywhere in Domus. And the River also connects to all the springs. And to all the ponds and lakes. To all water. Correct?"

"Yes."

"The entrance to Mt. Vetare is guarded. How am I going to pass?"

"You can pass."

"But I thought no one could pass?"

"You can pass."

Lichen stood up and began to pace. "This is so frustrating. It doesn't make sense to me."

"I can take you to the Manor. Quickly. Through the water."

"No. No, I told you I must get that crystal."

A growl came from the embankment; Lichen turned toward the sound and was hit in the chest. A hot wet mouth closed on his neck. Lichen clutched at the fur trying to grasp the animal around the throat. The wolf, as large as Lichen, knocked him to the ground, sharp claws tearing skin, reopening burns.

Lichen kneed the animal in the chest and they rolled locked in a fierce embrace. Ira burst awake flew up and hovered.

Lorelei shouted. "Fenrir." The great wolf released Lichen. He gasped; blood spurting in great jets from his neck.

"Tau'stercus, do something. He'll bleed to death," Ira shouted. Lorelei scooped up Lichen and dove into the water. Ira flapped about nervously. Fenrir watched him with great yellow eyes and growled.

Under the surface of the Great River Potens, the water was calm. Lorelei wrapped herself around Lichen's body and put her hand over the wound.

They floated down. Lorelei called out, "Mother, save him. He is The Warrior. Mother, I know it. He is The Warrior."

The water boiled as strong coils wrapped around them; a great hissing vibrated throughout the water. Golden green scales rubbed harshly against Lorelei's body.

"No," she screamed. "No, leave us be." The world serpent rolled and turned and rolled again in a great frenzy. "Stop, you're killing him".

The serpent coiled harder and faster. Lorelei could feel Lichen's body convulsing. She could escape. She could become the water. But he could not.

"Midgardsormr, stop it I say. Stop." Lorelei pounded the scales with her fists.

"No. No." She kicked him and bit him; scratched and screamed. She evaporated from his coils and swam to his head.

"Stop it now," she screamed into his eyes. "Don't kill him. He is the only one who can save us. Midgard, stop. He is The Warrior."

Midgard stopped churning. "I will finish what my brother started," he said. His coils did not release Lichen, only loosened. He looked at Lorelei with seething anger.

"And you," he hissed. "You betray us all. You are in league with the Dark One, then you fall in love with this human who seeks to destroy Domus. You are a traitor."

"No. No, you are mistaken. He is the only one who can save us, Midgard. Listen to me."

"You are the mistaken one. Your eyes are veiled with lust. You cannot see him. His heart has turned. He has lost his soul. He will destroy us all," Midgard growled.

"No. He does not know taking the crystal will destroy Domus. He thinks only to destroy the Proscriptio Fey. I cannot tell him the truth. Latere would know. Lichen must take the crystal to destroy Latere. Please, I beg you. He is our only hope."

"Mother. Mother hear me. Lichen must be saved." Lorelei sobbed. "For Domus. Please. Save him."

"You have embraced the Dark One," Mother said.

"Yes. Yes, I did. But not now Mother. I am back. I no longer serve him. I see him for what he is. He deceived me, seduced me, Mother. Please, please do not let my mistake destroy Lichen and with him Domus."

"Midgard. Release him."

Midgard sighed. His coils loosened. "Mother, this human will annihilate us."

"He is our only chance, Midgard. Release him." The Waters of the Great River Potens flowed around Midgard. Lovingly. Embracing him.

"Release him, my child."

Midgard's coils loosened and Lichen fell away, his body limp and dangling, suspended in the river current like a sacrifice caught between two worlds. Blood no longer flowed from his throat. Lorelei enfolded him in her arms.

"Lichen, Lichen."

"For everything given, something is received."

Lorelei's heart pounded. "Yes. Balance. Life for life."

"Are you willing, my child? Are you willing to sacrifice for Domus?"

"I am willing to sacrifice for Lichen."

Ira threw more wood onto the fire blazing large and high at last. Lorelei and Ira changed Lichen's wet clothing. Lorelei rubbed his wounds with mysterious leaves; wrapping fronds around Lichen's throat; deep green healing seeped into him. His breath was shallow. His skin pale.

"What the inferi happened down there?" Ira whispered. He cautiously eyed the large wolf in the ring of shadow just outside the firelight. Fenrir had been sitting there since he released Lichen. Sitting and watching.

"And did you call that beast by name?" Ira scowled. Lorelei continued her ministrations to Lichen. "Did you call him Fenrir? Is that Fenrir?"

"Yes."

"Holy Grove. Fenrir." Ira sat down hard. Fenrir. No one ever lived after an encounter with Fenrir. The wolf was as old as Domus. Maybe older.

"Tau'stercus. What's to keep him from attacking Lichen again?"

"His brother told him The Mother decreed Lichen must be spared."

"His brother?" Ira looked toward the waves, even higher, stronger now. "His brother, here?"

"Lichen will be protected now," Lorelei said.

Ira looked at Fenrir.

"Tau'stercus." He glanced at Lichen. "We need to get going. When can he walk?"

"Your empathy is overwhelming. Perhaps after he rests awhile."

"Well, I just mean, well... the sooner we get to that mountain, the sooner we can get him home." Ira stammered.

"And the sooner you will be rewarded with a child," Lorelei said.

Ira snapped his cloak around him and started toward his bedroll. He looked at Fenrir. Fenrir glared back. Ira moved his bed closer to the fire.

Amazing things, herbs. Lichen thought or was he dreaming, about all the times he had been wounded since coming to Domus. And all the times he had been healed. He thought of Isabella. She was a healer. He had been so consumed with revenge in the camp; he hadn't allowed himself to think of her. She was a reward. For after.

The beat of the BelPole dance throbbed within him. The haze of the dream confused him. He felt her in his arms and smelled the pungent scent of violets and lilacs floating around them. He felt the petals caressing his skin. Soft. Smooth. Embracing. Whispering. Blues and purples. Yellow faces. Violets leading them. Isabella supple against him.

"I am your charm," she whispered. Her breath hot, sweet against his face. Her black hair trailed over his arms enticing, enchanting.

"Yes, my charm," he answered. Desire beyond the physical molded him, melted him until she was everything and he was nothing.

"We're almost there," Ira said. He flew above them now, the overhead branches having cleared a little. Fenrir trotted well to the side; his head above the bramble thicket.

Lichen's energy had returned, he forged ahead eagerly. Once again, his wounds were remarkably improved although not completely healed. He felt buoyant. He glowed as one who just left his lover and perhaps he had; he remembered his dream.

Lorelei eyed him knowingly, jealously.

The forest began to change as soon as the river forked. They followed the fork west into lush green trees, soft mosses, and giant ferns that within the hour gave way to brambles and tangles of thick thorny vines and brush. Uninviting. Forbidden.

"Well, here we are," Ira announced nervously landing with a thump beside Lichen. His eyes blinked as he tried to see through the thorny brush. "This is as far as I go."

"Yes, here we are." Lichen's upbeat mood was gone. The darkness of the Forbidden Forest hummed with foreboding. "Any advice?"

"I'm afraid you are on your own from here," Ira said. The forest would not allow me in even if I were willing. It may not let you in, you know. That's why they call it forbidden, Vetare. Forbidden. According to legend, only one can enter." Ira raised one bushy brow. His wings fluttered.

"Don't say it," Lichen said, mockery hardening his voice, "the warrior, right?"

"Are you the one, Lichen?"

"Only one way to find out," Lichen said jauntily.

"I will wait for you here," Ira said. "When you return we will be on our way to the Manor." Ira's voice trembled.

"Lorelei," Lichen said. "Lorelei, can you enter?"

"No."

"You will wait?"

"Yes."

Lichen stepped into the black brambles. He thumped into an invisible impenetrable wall. Lichen could not enter Vetare Silva. The Forbidden Forest.

Chapter Forty-Three

Mt. Vetare

"There. There you see. Give up this foolish notion to enter Mt. Vetare. You cannot even get into the forest," Ira said. "Come. Come with me to the Manor. Your grandfather awaits you."

"He is right," Lorelei said. "Let us be off to New Ivy. And quickly." She glanced around. Her hand clutched her cloak, wadding it nervously.

"No. There must be a way. There is a way." Lichen took a parcel from his sack and withdrew the cloak and helmet. He threw the cape around his shoulders.

"You have met Wieland," Lorelei said simply.

"A gift," Lichen grinned.

"Do not take it lightly, Lichen," Lorelei said. "They are the garments of the Sacred Warrior. To possess them gives you great responsibility."

"I know. I have the responsibility of getting into this forest. I have the responsibility of putting those puke faeries out of their misery."

"What do you mean?" Ira asked as he landed beside Lichen, lost his balance, and fell backward.

Lichen put the helmet on and disappeared. Ira scrambled to his feet.

"What are you about Lichen? What are you going to do? And where did you get those clothes?"

Lichen adjusted Durandal swinging from his waist, squared his shoulders, and stepped forward. Again, he hit the invisible barrier.

"Dang."

Lichen pounded the wall with his fist. "Open up. Let me in there," he shouted and kicked the invisible barrier.

"Lichen, it is a sign. We must leave this place at once," Ira pleaded looking around nervously.

"No," shouted Lichen. He took off Tarnhelm. "There must be a way." He looked at Lorelei.

"You know, don't you?" Lichen's patience was gone. "You know how to get in. Tell me, and tell me, now."

Lorelei stood silently, water dripping from her skin and her shift. She looked like a moon goddess. Luminescence shimmered around and through her, red hair glowing as if ablaze. Lichen walked up to her and put his hands on her shoulders. She looked up at him.

"Lichen, please. Give up this revenge. It will destroy you. It will destroy others. Let us leave this place."

"No," Lichen said. "No." His voice strained like the last words of a dying man. "I cannot. I will not."

Fenrir stood tall at the edge of the Forest his golden eyes level with Lichen's, his pant shooting great streams of breath into the cold air. Lichen walked toward him. Fenrir turned and ran a few paces looking back at Lichen.

"You," Lichen said. "Show me." Fenrir ran through the brambles and Lichen followed. Lorelei watched them leave the clearing. Two small tears ran down her cheeks and fell to the ground. Two tiny emeralds dropped beneath the leaves at her feet. His favorite.

"Where are they going?" Ira said.

"To Mt. Vetare," Lorelei answered.

"But..."

"Do not question me," she snapped. "We shall wait beside the Great River."

The river water slapped against Fenrir's long legs. He stood in the water searching the waves. Rain beaded on his fur and shed to the river. Inconsequential.

Lichen sat on a boulder scowling into the wind his hair whipping out behind him. He looked like a god overseeing his domain. A cranky god.

"How long must we wait? Are you taking me to Mt. Vetare or not? If you're not, I will find another way. Do you hear me fleabag?"

The wolf continued watching the water. Lichen stood and paced up the shore and back, kicking stones and cursing.

"Human, be quiet," Fenrir growled. Lichen stopped in his tracks. "You continuously prattle on about nothing. For sanity's sake, shut up." Fenrir trotted out of the river and stood in front of Lichen. "I was not this whiny when I was bound with Gleipnir, a fetter from which no one can escape. No one except me."

"I…" Lichen started. He straightened his shoulders. "I apologize. You startled me. You can speak."

"Yes, and I can hear so stop prattling. You think humans are the only sentient beings?"

"No, it isn't that. I've seen plenty of, well, no. I just wasn't expecting it that's all. You surprised me."

Fenrir snarled, his teeth long and yellow below his curled lip. "Human, you must get the crystal and we must help you. But, we don't have to like it."

Lightning struck the overhead branches, tangled vines ignited and white flames snaked from treetop to treetop making cracks in the canopy.

"Come," Fenrir said.

The wind carried the fire north; they followed the river further west to a set of falls. The riverbank speared Fenrir's feet with spikes of shard; his bloody footprints were larger than Lichen's.

"What's happening? To the weather?" Lichen asked looking at the sky. "Ever since I left the Proscriptio, it's been storming and hailing. Blowing and ripping around as if to tear us apart. This doesn't seem normal."

Fenrir stood watching the water as if Lichen had not spoken. The River was wide here and Lichen could not see the far shore. It looked more like the sea. Water whipped and turned, rising above the surface many feet then crashing back into itself. The River poured over a cliff into a deep cavern. The mountain's falls mirroring the river's dropped from the highest peak and over the edge into the same cavern. It roared as if falling off the edge of the world, then splashed back up as if trying to get back on. It was like a void sunk beneath the surface and water poured in from all sides.

"What is the place?" Lichen asked.

"Across the Great River Potens, just beyond the shore lies Regnum," Fenrir said.

"The Royal City?" Lichen said.

Fenrir nodded. "Beneath the Royal City is the only entrance into the Forbidden Forest and to Mt. Vetare. The Mother made it so many centuries ago when the GENS were banished to the Proscriptio."

"The GENS?" Lichen asked.

"GENS was the original quad in Domus. Founded by four brothers. They had talent and abilities far greater than any before them. The Mother blessed them with her knowledge and charged them to use it for the good of all Domus. They were magnificent."

"You knew them?"

"Yes," Fenrir said. "I knew them. It was a golden age in Domus. The brothers taught the Fey the ways of The Mother. Quads were built all over Domus, blessed and nourished by the Great River Potens." Waves crashed up the shore as if in answer.

Lichen looked at Fenrir with new respect. He regretted his fleabag slur.

"What happened? Why were they banished?"

"Many generations later one was born who was not satisfied with his gifts. Narro," Fenrir growled. "He is the father of dissension. The maker of discontent. Whisperer of lies. The great Seducer." Fenrir shifted, but still gazed upon the river. "He used his talents to disrupt the quad. Narro led a scheming rebellion against The Mother. He manipulated the citizens and led them into slothful idle behavior. His insurgence was subtle but effective.

"The Mother banished the entire quad to the Proscriptio, their gifts abolished. It is a barren wasteland where hope does not shine and the night is void of dreams."

"Tell me about it. How long ago?" Lichen asked.

"OK, little one, that's enough," Fenrir said. Fenrir nabbed her shabby ash-colored dress with his teeth and lifted her, still kicking and squealing, off Lichen's back and onto the ground.

"And stay there," Fenrir admonished her.

"Wwwwb," she answered with a pout.

Lichen winced. His arms were covered with tiny scratches as if he had taken a turn in a rock tumbler. With course grit. A large knot puffed up on the back of his head.

"Who *is* that?" Lichen asked.

"*This* is a Gwithin. They are a faerie tribe and they hate humans," Fenrir said inferring the Gwithins weren't the only ones who hated humans. "They are usually satisfied to keep to the Hills of Caprinus and raise their goats. To be exact, this is The Gwillion."

"She doesn't have wings," Lichen observed. His interest in wings as keen as ever.

"The Mother took away their ability for flight," Fenrir said. He looked at the little faerie huddled confused and crumpled under a bush. "They are frightened of storms. Probably what brought her out of the Hills."

As if in answer lightning bolted across the sky and into the River. Thunder followed; it jarred the ground and scattered vibrations into the water. At that moment colossal coils writhed above the waves. Lichen jumped back and drew Durandal.

"WWWWB. WWWWB," The Gwillion screamed and turned her face into the dirt. The cooking pot lay directly on the ground; her head buried beneath it, a tiny rump stuck straight up in the air with the comb protruding from her back pocket.

"Sheath your sword, Lichen. Sheath it now," Fenrir roared. Lichen slid Durandal back into the scabbard.

"Gwithin are afraid of storms and they are terrified of steel," Fenrir said. An immense fin rose out of the water. Or was it a wing?

"Midgardsormr," Fenrir shouted. "Midgardsormr, we need you."

Rain started sheeting from the black clouds, pounding, roaring. "Midgard, now if you please," Fenrir said. "Lichen, you must wade into the river a bit. Immediately."

"What?" Lichen shouted.

"Into the river, lad. It's now or never." Fenrir's coat shed the rain; great falls of water sprayed to the earth. "Midgard will take you to the portal into Mt. Vetare. He'll not hurt you, I promise you that. There's no other way, Lichen. Now into the river with you." Fenrir nudged Lichen into the water.

They're going to drown me.

Midgard coiled loosely around Lichen and dragged him under; the water was cold. The temperature of panic. They dove deeper; down into the pool below the falls. Below the river. Below the mountain. Lichen wasn't fighting for breath. The black fear disappeared when Lichen realized he didn't need to breathe. Midgard traveled at amazing speed.

"Do you hear me?" Lichen said in his mind. Silence. "Can you hear me, Midgard?"

Midgard swam faster. He undulated through the inky water; speeding toward the depths.

"Why do you help me? Two days ago you tried to kill me"

"The Mother wishes it. My brother wishes it."

Lichen's attempts at further communication met with contemptible silence. After an interminable cold and tedious journey, Midgard slowed. Lichen roused from his black stupor. Midgard unceremoniously dumped him onto a rock ledge and swam off. As uninvolved as a cab driver.

Lichen gulped for breath like a newborn. And he was cold, very cold. As Lichen tried to maneuver, he realized it wasn't a rock ledge at all; it was ice. An ice cave. He crouched around his legs and tucked his hands under his arms. He was going to freeze to death.

Lichen laid his forehead on his arms. His hair already frozen, it hung like skinny black icicles around his head. Shivers clanked them together making a tiny tune.

The water in the pool erupted. Great golden eyes in a massive green head rose up and looked at Lichen. Lichen raised his head to meet Midgard's stare.

"Human," Midgard said with contempt. "Lower your face."

He opened his mouth and spewed his noxious breath. The blast reverberated off the walls; hairline cracks splintered down the ice. Fire erupted and shot around the ice cave warming the air. A serpentine furnace.

Lichen felt the heat thaw his hair, dripping streams of water; he stopped shivering. His clothes began to dry. When the roar subsided, Lichen raised his head. Midgard was gone.

So, this was the portal to Mt. Vetare. Lichen loosened his parcel from his waist and put on Tarnhelm and Tarnkappe. He drew Durandal and walked into the tunnel.

Chapter Forty-Four

Decision

After Lichen went into the river, Ira and Lorelei argued about the best course of action.

"I tell you, we must get help," Ira said. "I don't trust that serpent." Fenrir sat beside the river. Watching. Listening. "Or his little brother," Ira said looking pointedly at Fenrir.

"I'm going after Q. He will know exactly what to do. And, quite frankly, that was my original plan, to take Lichen home to The Manor. This Latere, he's not what he pretends to be you know. He's plenty dangerous. I think he's here somewhere."

Ira looked around the darkness and squinted into the trees. He huddled as close as he could get under a canopy of vines, trying unsuccessfully to get warm and dry. Ira's hair, usually spiked in all directions, lay flat against his head and he smelled like a mountain hen just after she was dunked into the scalding pot.

Lorelei, on the other hand, looked perfectly content to stand in the downpour. In fact, she looked at home, almost comfortable.

"I know," Lorelei said.

"You know? You know what?" Ira said.

"I know he is not what he seems. I know who he is."

Ira blanched. He remembered the packet he received while he was in the Receptus. The *wet* packet. Could it have been from Lorelei?

"Lorelei," Ira said, "did you, did you ever..." Ira's courage could normally be measured with an acorn hull. But Ira wanted a baby for his wife. He had to get that baby to save his marriage. If he helped Lichen, Q would reward him, it was that simple. He must help Lichen.

Ira must keep his part in Lichen's kidnapping secret. If they found out, he wouldn't get his baby. Nata's baby. He'd lose Nata, his Criocts position and his reputation would be ruined. He might even be charged with a crime.

Tau'stercus.

He had to find out what Lorelei knew.

"Did you ever send me anything? Like a ... letter," Ira blurted.

Lorelei hesitated, then nodded. "Yes. The note came from me."

Ira paled. "You know him? Latere? You work for him? Why did you send the letter to me?"

"Yes, I did work with him; I have shamed my kind. I owed him, but no longer." Lorelei straightened defiantly. "I will help destroy him. Before he destroys Domus," she said hoping her new skills at mental shields were working. "I knew you would notify Sapien. I must tell all I know. I must try to undo my part in his schemes."

Ira shifted. He'd never had anyone bare their soul to him before. He wasn't comfortable with it. Ira spoke in a hoarse whisper, steering the conversation away from Lorelei's personal confessions.

"Your note was a bit hard to believe: Sapien's clerk is Latere? How do you know this?"

"He held me captive for many months. I know."

"And, he has the Lex Scriptura? He knows...everything," Ira said.

"He wants to dominate Domus. He plans to annihilate everyone who has any human blood," Lorelei said. She looked determined to confess everything she knew.

"There's more. Latere's true identity is Narro. Narro from the GENS quad."

"The GENS?" Ira said. This was too much for him, he couldn't grasp it. "But, they have been banished to the Proscriptio for generations. How can Latere be Narro when Narro is in the Proscriptio?"

"Did you ever see Narro while you were in the Proscriptio?" Lorelei said, sarcasm hardening her words. She mocked him, Ira knew that tone, he had heard it his whole life.

"No. I didn't see him," Ira said hotly. "I didn't see you either, but you were obviously there." Ira decided not to be contentious.

"So, how did he escape? The only way out for them is during Septmillia. By invitation from Iris. By Vocatio. And that hasn't happened for tens of thousands of years. And won't happen now until Iter. So, how did he get out?"

"Narro never *went* to the Proscriptio."

"What do you mean he never went? Of course, he went. He was part of the GENS. He was part of the Banishment. He had no choice."

"I don't know how. All I know is he never went. He's been planning and scheming to take over Domus for 49,000 years, and the time is now.

"He found out about The Portent. When he discovered the identity of The Warrior he knew Lichen would be coming to Domus. He also knows Isabella is the Charm."

Ira was getting dizzy. "Isabella? Isabella Fae Duco? My niece? Sapien's daughter? The Charm?" Ira asked.

"Yes," Lorelei said. "And he knows the Tempus Crystal is the key to controlling Domus. He needs Lichen to get the Crystal".

"Wait a minute. If Latere needs Lichen to get the Crystal, why did he try to kill him?"

"Because at the time, he didn't know that so he just wanted to get rid of him. After he read the Lex Scriptura, he realized he would need Lichen. It was a fortunate twist for Latere when the trolls double-crossed him and instead of killing Lichen, sold him into slavery."

Indignation flooded Ira. "And he had the nerve to flagellate me with his caustic humiliation because Lichen was alive."

"This isn't about you," Lorelei said coolly. "And he needs Isabella both as protection from Lichen, protection from the Mother and to ensure his victory. She is the Charm, but more importantly, she is the next Solis. When Latere was posing as Sapien's scribe, Acta, Iris dictated Isabella's Totus Vita to him. He knows everything about Isabella. More than she knows about herself. Iris would have anointed her Solis at Iter and Latere will do anything to keep that from happening.

"The Solis? The Pavors killed our Solis on their rampage against the caduceus."

Lorelei nodded her head. "Exactly. And who do you think was the Pavors leader? The Solis has more power than an ordinary caducei. Power that is a threat to anyone wanting to conquer Domus. He got rid of the reigning Solis and now he has to keep Isabella from becoming the next one."

Ira felt ill. Faint. Sweat ran in uncomfortable places, his feathers drooped. Wilted weasel. Ira hoped he didn't lose control of his bowels. Narro, Latere, and Acta are all the same person.

And, Latere had been responsible for the Pavors? And murdering their Solis? Ira knew he was in over his spiked little head. If Lorelei had double-crossed Latere by sharing information with Ira... If Latere found out or found them together... Latere told Ira to bring Lichen here, to Mt. Vetare. He also told Lorelei to bring Lichen here. Ira looked around. Latere could be anywhere. The forest was dark; the river was dark.

"Let's go," Ira said in a panic. "We're going to Q." Ira tripped as he scrambled out from under the brambles and fell headlong into a pit of water. He came up sputtering, cursing, and looking all the world like a drenched mountain rooster. Forlorn fowl.

"Agreed." Lorelei said. She walked out to Fenrir and told him of their decision.

After reading Ira's Silent Post naming Acta as an imposter, Sapien knew he was connected to the breach at the Grove and probably Isabella's disappearance. How that affected the weather, he had no idea. He came at once to The Manor; he must discuss it with Q. No one else could be trusted.

"You're saying that your scriba, Acta, is behind the Sacred Grove breach?" Q asked.

"Yes," Sapien replied. "Ira has been working for someone named Latere for years. Latere secured Ira's election to Criocts and got him a passage across the bridge into the Proscriptio for trading."

"How?" Q asked. "How is that possible?"

"I don't know," Sapien said. "I don't know." Sapien's strength seeped out of him like life ebbing from a wounded deer. "I think he took Isabella. I don't know why. But, Acta has not been seen since she disappeared."

Their speculations were interrupted by pounding and shouting.

Ira and Lorelei arrived on the Manor's doorstep wet, excited, and full of tales about Lichen, an evil plot, an imposter, and Mt. Vetare. Q and Sapien listened to the gist of it, and at once organized a rescue party.

Ira squeezed out the story in spurts and stops, Q could get details later; he knew there was no time to waste. Acta... or Latere...or whoever he was...probably had Isabella and was lying in wait for Lichen.

Q and Sapien sent a silent post to the King and set off for Vetare Silva accompanied by Lorelei, Raman, Faber, the Manor hands, and every able New Ivy man.

Cecelia, trusting by nature, did not trust Ira. Never had. She intended to mine every scrap of information from each dark crevice of his chronicle. Cecelia grilled Ira until they were quite exhausted, and still, she was not satisfied.

The interrogation, and it could not be called anything less, was not without Cecelia's perks. She plied him with steaming herb tea and scones. Ira had never encountered a woman with as much tenacity; she picked at the tiny strands of his carefully plaited story until it frayed with inconsistency. Ira obviously was not telling everything.

Cecelia understood that certain information was privy to the Ambassador and the Princeps, but her Agaso had been murdered. Her dear Lichen had been kidnapped. Her Beetrum was dead. And this little capricious capon knew more than he was telling.

Cecelia was particularly interested in this fellow Latere. Ira and Lorelei had independent relationships with Latere so their experiences were divergent, but Cecelia was still suspicious. Both Ira and Lorelei were clearly frightened of Latere.

"Soo, let me get this right," Cecelia said. "Both yoo and Lorelei worked for Latere. Beetrum is dead; trolls kidnapped Lichen and sold him into slavery. Soo, Latere ordered Beetrum's and Lichen's death? And Lichen was sold into slavery? Why forevermore? This is a different altogether, I dinna understand it."

Ira ran his hand across his face. He looked nervous and frustrated. One of his wing tips quivered against the rug making a little scratching sound like a scrimpet digging in for winter.

He looked unprepared to deal with this woman, this housekeeper. "No. Yes, I mean. We did both work for Latere but were unaware of one another. And Latere did not want Lichen sold into slavery. He wanted Lichen dead because he didn't know at the time that he needed him to get the Crystal.

It was those trolls. Those treacherous trolls were supposed to make sure Lichen was dead. Instead, the malicious money-grubbing filthy mud suckers sold him into the Proscriptio."

"And a good thing they did or Lichen would be dead. Both you and Lorelei were instructed separately to rescue Lichen from the Proscriptio, then take him to the edge of Mt. Vetare in the Forbidden Forest? Why?"

"Yes," Ira said. "So Lichen can get the Crystal for him." He ran his hand down his arm squeezing his sleeve. Water dripped onto the floor.

Cecelia raised her eyebrow. "And ye're comin' clean now because...?" Cecelia asked, her eyes squinted, her hand on her ample hip. These two had known about Lichen's whereabouts for quite some time.

Had Latere's hold over them been so strong as to abolish scruples? Why had they not stepped forward to ease another's pain? To answer agonizin' questions? To right a wrong? Cecelia's sense of propriety would have boiled over even if the catalyzing event had not been her dear Agaso's death. Why come clean now?

Ira squirmed.

"And," Cecelia continued, "Agaso's death must be connected to Lichen's kidnapping. Who did it? Whoo?" she demanded.

Cecelia's heart ached for Agaso. Her dear, dear brother. He always took care of her. Got them positions with the new ambassador. They were so happy at New Ivy. They loved working for Q. Loved taking care of him and the Manor. And his family. Syringa. Beetrum. Linum. Lichen. One by one they were gone. And this little vulture knew something he wasn't telling.

"Come on, noo, ye little fuzzy viper," Cecelia said. "Tell me wha' ye knoo."

"All right," Ira said. "All right," Ira spurted and sputtered. Never in his life had he encountered anyone like Cecelia. Eventually, he told the whole sordid story of his involvement with not only Latere but Keeper Valeo as well.

"Wha?" Cecelia said. She couldn't believe it.

"Yoo. Yoo switched coach drivers for Keeper Valeo? And it was Valeo's driver, Manes who was in the stable when Agaso was killed? And 'e was drivin' the carriage when Mistress Beetrum and Lichen left?"

Ira screamed. "Yes, yes it's true."

Cecelia sat speechless on the edge of her chair.

"But I didn't know Manes would kill Agaso, I swear. He was only supposed to get Lichen into the carriage with Beetrum. Now, I won't get my baby." Ira leaned over, put his arms on the table, and cradled his head. "I won't get my baby."

Cecelia starred. Baby? She didn't have time for Ira and his foolishness now. Suddenly everything made sense.

Chapter Forty-Five

Tempus Crystal

The path, if that's what you could call it, twisted and turned through the ice, deeper and deeper. Was he actually in the mountain? Or below it? Lichen thought the incline grew steeper, but he wasn't sure. He began to tire, his steps slowing, his mind numb and blank. And, despite his steady pace, he was getting cold again.

Soon. Soon I will have that crystal. Supra and her ruthless gang of thieves will pay.

"Well, it's about time," a voice said in the darkness. "I was beginning to wonder if you had it in you."

Lichen stopped and raised Durandal. "Who is it? Who's there?"

"How 'bout a little light?" A torch landed at Lichen's feet hissing like a flare signaling for help.

Lichen retrieved it and turned in a circle around the cave. Tiny ice crystals glittered like stars. The thick icewalls flickered blue and white. Slick.

"Where are you? Who are you? How do you see me?"

"I smelled you," the voice said.

"What do you want?"

Laughter echoed off the walls. Dark laughter. "More to the point, my young human, what do you want?"

"What do you mean?" Lichen asked. "I came for the Tempus Crystal. Are you the guardian?" Renewed laughter gave Lichen an uneasy chill that had nothing to do with the cold.

"The guardian? Ahhhh, that's good. I suppose you could say I was a guardian, of sorts. I am guardian over what you want."

"But I'm here for the Crystal," Lichen said.

"Yes. Yes, you are. But then, you do not know what it is that I guard."

Lichen saw one wall that was not the same white-blue of the cave, but clear ice. He walked over to it and tried to look through the wall. It was thick. He scraped it with his arm and shielded his eyes from the torchlight.

"Need a little help?" the voice mocked. A soft glow lighted up the small room beyond the ice barrier. Lichen could see a dark shape lying horizontally on a slab. He struggled to identify it. Her hair, unrestrained, lay over the edge of the rock bed, trailed down to the floor, and puddled in dark deep softness.

"Isabella," Lichen whispered. "Isabella," he shouted.

He pounded on the ice and began hacking with Durandal. He sliced frantically and screamed her name. She lay as if asleep, a small round yellow body beside her, curled slumbering with her mistress.

"Well, I see you recognize your little dulci," the voice said maliciously. "Your hammering will do you no good."

"What do you want?" Lichen asked.

"Now, you're being reasonable. It's simple. I want the crystal. The Tempus Crystal."

"Why don't you just take it? You're here. Here in Mt. Vetare. How did you get in here anyway?"

"Ahh, the ignorance of the human race never fails to amuse me. I have the charm, Lichen. I can enter the great Mt. Vetare but cannot go into the Crystal Room. Only you can do that, my boy. So, you will retrieve the crystal, bring it to me here, and I will release your precious woman and her little beast."

"Why do you want the crystal?"

"That would be none of your concern. Now, you have two hours to bring it back to me. Your little healer and her furry little rag of a companion will never wake up from their frozen sleep if you are not back in that time ."

Lichen stood unbelieving.

"Tick, tick," the tormentor said.

"All right. All right." Lichen ran up the incline leading out of the room. Who was this madman? Lichen didn't care what he did with the infernal crystal. After all, the result would be the same for the Rock Faeries regardless of who had it. He would trade it for Isabella.

Isabella! How was she captured? How long had she been here? Was she still alive?

The further Lichen went up the path, the warmer it became. He took off the helmet and cape but kept Durandal at the ready. Perspiration ran down his face. The hot air closed around him; his breath came hard. Lichen felt as if someone had corked him into a bottle.

Lichen Ipse.

Lichen stopped walking. Had he imagined that?

Lichen.

"What? Who's there?"

Lichen, why do you enter my mountain?

"I must get to the crystal room," Lichen said. "It's life or death. Are you the guardian?"

Lichen, do you have a heart that's purely seen?

"What? Who are you?" Lichen said getting irritated.

Is your heart purely seen, Lichen?

Lichen was sick to death of all these riddles. "I don't know what you mean," he shouted. "I came for the Crystal. I must have the Crystal to save Isabella. Now, let me pass. Let me pass this instant."

You love this woman, Lichen?

"Of course, I love her," he said. He did? He loved her?

"Yes," he shouted. "I love her." Euphoria hit him. Then panic. Finally anger. "I love her," he yelled, "now give me that Crystal."

Your love is pure. Do you wear the stars both night and day?

The stars? The stars? The amulet. He had lost the amulet the night he left New Ivy. Who was speaking to him? He had heard that voice before. In the river.

"No. I do not wear the stars. The amulet was...it was taken from me."

Unfortunate. It is a protection.

"May I pass?"

You must know the Horologe Vesper to enter the Crystal Room. Do you know the sacred Song Lichen Ipse?

Lichen almost laughed. A song? That's what he needed to get into the room? He remembered Q insisting Lichen learn this particular song. Every evening just at sunset, over and over. Not the usual blessing sang by all of Domus, but a different song, The Horologe Vesper; a sacred evensong of time. Q told him he would be requested to sing it one day.

"Í do."

Remember my son, you hold the key.

"The key to what?" Lichen felt the presence leave. "Wait, the key to what?" he shouted.

Lichen continued on up the path. The incline rose sharply as he entered a domed room with a stone bench in the center facing West. Lichen laid down the parcel and Durandal then closed his eyes.

Lichen remembered the last evening he sang with Q. "From the heart, my boy. From the soul," Q had said.

Lichen looked around the domed room. He had to get that crystal and save Isabella. He squared his shoulders and planted his feet, perfectly balanced. He knew the song; he would save Isabella.

A line of the Horologe Vesper rang from his lips each note tumbling hollow and dead upon the cold rock; the spiritless words plummeted from the air like poisoned songbirds.

His soul had disappeared along with his mother when they had fallen from the bridge into the Great River Potens. Hatred eroded the core of his essence when the trolls bagged and beat him; the Rock Faeries shriveled and eradicated the part that was uniquely him with each day of his captivity in the Proscriptio.

Bitterness lodged where love had been and lust for revenge had consumed him like a fire destroying its own sustenance. He was the shed skin of a locust. Empty. Brittle. Fragile.

And now he was broken open, even his shell crushed under the weight of reciprocal karma. Nature's recoil. God's justice. He could not sing from the soul, for his soul lay dead within him.

Lichen fell to his knees in front of the bench, put his face in his hands, and let loose the pain that bound him. He screamed long and loud. Tears ran between his fingers flowing from a lonely place, dark and empty. Anguish tore unmercifully from within him ripping, shredding as it coursed through his body as an auger bores through accumulated filth. Spiritual refuse.

Sorrow wrenched and lacerated his heart like a laundress wringing out the last foul dirty piece of linen. Lichen screamed again. The sound of torment. He called out in misery. His sobs fell lifeless around him as he collapsed onto the floor. Rancor released. Repentance attained. No condemnation. No reproach. Just liberation. And forgiveness.

I am here for you my son. I have always been here.

Lichen's pent-up revenge and grief spent, he felt empty but clean. Soul refurbished. Fatigue consumed him. He turned over and slept on the cold stone floor.

When Lichen awoke, the torch had gone out, blackness embraced him. He smiled. Clarity had replaced burning hatred with illumination; whether he liked it or not, he was The Warrior. Not just in a combatant sense, although that may be necessary, but a duty to do what was best for the people, to protect them, to lead them. Honor super omnia. Honor above all.

Responsibility sat squarely on his shoulders. Responsibility for what, he wasn't sure, but he accepted it with a new humility that fit him well. He could do what was required; it had been in him all along.

Lichen sat up and leaned back against the bench. Slowly, hesitantly he began to sing. The Horologe Vesper poured from an incorporeal place within him. His soul gave birth to the sanctified; music filled the chamber. Mellifluous. An overture to time. Verses rolled in a crescendo off Lichen's tongue, then died away

He could feel the eons rising and falling, great epochs marching through eternity, universes being birthed in a great spiral of creation. Sweet and holy. Sacred.

Joy filled the empty spaces of his heart and pulsed through his veins. Rapture flowed in and about leaving trails to heaven. Crumbs leading home. Ecstasy.

Lichen opened his eyes. The rock wall in front of him had become translucent. Behind it, a soft light glowed in an enormous room. The ceiling cathedraled 500 feet up into the air. The sparkling walls and floor dazzled, almost blinding with the same crystalline white of the clocks in the library at the Manor and in Weston. His and Qs.

In the center sat a massive glowing, pulsing, living multi-colored crystal. Dark indigo at its base, the spikes rose toward the light changing color as they heightened. Purples, gradually gave way to lilacs and lavenders, blues, greens, then soft yellows darkening to deep ambers as they rose, then fading gradually until finally the top spikes, varying in height, pointed skyward with brilliant diamond spears.

Within the heart of the crystal, countless graduated amethyst wheels of varying sizes turned; their cogs fitting expertly into the wheel next to it, each wheel rotating to turn its partner. Ages, years, months, days, hours, minutes, seconds. Wheels of time. Like a Mesoamerican calendric system.

Synchronized structures interlocked with one another, their combined information giving rise to additional, more extensive cycles like the Long Count of the Mayans. The large wheels, and the calendar rounds kept time with the solar and lunar rotations through limitless sequences.

Lichen walked forward. Mouth open. He placed his palm reverently upon the wall. Vibrations, soft and malleable, tingled his hand. The Tempus Crystal.

Magnificent did not, could not begin to describe it. Its majesty overwhelmed Lichen. He stood stupefied watching the very pulse of Domus, literally the heart, beat its rhythm of life throughout the Kingdom. Lichen's analytical mind switched on high for the first time in months, lucidity sparking. He watched each tick move the wheels along and noticed something wasn't right. The timing was off, it ticked out of sync. He wasn't sure what that meant, but it couldn't be good.

The Tempus Crystal.

Lichen knew he could not hand any part of this over to that fiend downstairs. Was it possible the monster had already disrupted the clock's delicate mechanisms?

He walked along the wall, horror for he had wanted to do growing with each step. The realization that in wanting to destroy the Proscriptio, he would have obliterated Domus. He examined it from all angles. He ran his hand along the bottom, fingered the sides, and scrutinized the seams. Sealed. No entrance. What could he do? How could he save Isabella without destroying Domus?

Lichen went back over to the bench and sat down. How long had he been asleep? How much time did he have left? He thought of that creepy little water-dwarf Wieland. Lichen unsheathed Durandal.

"It will help you find your Soul, Lichen," he had said.

Lichen walked over and held Durandal up to the wall. Nothing. "Open," Lichen said. Nothing. "Dang." Once again, Lichen walked back and forth along the pulsing violet wall, searching. Exploring every inch of the wall. "Come on. Come on think of something." He grew impatient and frustrated.

Lichen leaned against the joint where the cave and the amethyst wall met and sunk to a squat.

Think, Lichen.

He laid his forehead on his knee. "Think, think."

He let out a discouraged sigh and closed his eyes. Lichen remembered the clock on his mantel in Weston. The strange clock that had been so much a part of his childhood. Did it hold a clue? If they were made from the same crystal perhaps they were linked.

Lichen's heart beat faster as he looked up at the monolithic crystals.

A synchronome.

It was a master clock. A master clock controlling time, weather, the very existence of Domus. A master clock is always linked to smaller sister clocks like the one in Weston and Q's clock at The Manor.

Lichen stood and turned to face the Tempus Crystal. He felt weak with the enormity of his conclusions. This could be what was causing the violent weather. Latere's very presence in Vetare Silva may be enough to disrupt the clock.

Control of this clock meant control of everything. Iter.

Domus.

If Lichen had handed The Tempus Crystal to that *thing* downstairs, he would have handed over control of the entire kingdom.

Lorelei had known this. She had let Lichen think it would only destroy the Proscriptio fey, but, in fact, it would destroy all of Domus. Lichen felt betrayed by his little water friend.

But, if he didn't give the demon something, Isabella would die. Lichen yelled and pounded his fist against the wall. He must figure this out.

Tempus transiens.

Chapter Forty-Six

Narro

Lichen had to get into the Crystal room. Although, what he would do when he got in, he didn't know. He must think of something; Isabella's life depended on him.

Lichen glanced at the bench and saw an odd black shape carved just under the lip of the slab top. He walked over, knelt down, and felt the shape. It felt vaguely familiar when he ran his finger around the edge.

Lichen put his other hand on Durandal's hilt. His forefinger traced the outline of the inlaid emerald. He felt the identical shape with both hands, one on the chest, one on the sword. Durandal was the key.

Lichen pried the jewel from the sword and inserted it into the keyhole. It turned. A soft click was barely audible. The stone lid lifted of its own accord. Things were looking up.

Two small sister clocks, smaller than his or Q's lay in the chest. A crystal dagger lay gleaming beside the clocks glowing with multiple hues, the facets sharp. The dagger's colors mirrored the Tempus Crystal.

To the side lay an amulet. An amulet with three intertwined circles and a tree with tiny crystals in the branches and one above. The Earth and Stars, are identical to the one he lost when he was kidnapped.

Lichen put the amulet around his neck. He knew his plan.

Lichen felt the fiend even before he reached the room. He entered cautiously, his eyes searching every corner. Nothing. No one. What had Wieland said? Something about things unseen, he should have paid more attention to that little gnome.

"Show yourself," Lichen declared.

"He returns. With my prize, I assume?" the mocking voice said. The space where Isabella lay was dark.

"Let me see her," Lichen said.

"You don't trust me? And, after all we've been through. Very well."

Within Isabella's chamber, light began to glow becoming gradually stronger and brighter. She looked beautiful. And pale. And still, so still. Lichen had to get her free of this demon.

"Wake her. Let her out," Lichen demanded.

"Give me my crystal," the voice said.

"Show yourself," Lichen repeated, "and let her out."

Latere glimmered and appeared across the room. He was short. What had Lichen expected a fanged demon with a forked tail? Stench filled the air like dead scrimpets rotten and flyblown.

Latere's scarred pallid complexion molded across his face like drum skin. Broken membrane wings with patches of disintegrating feathers stood erect behind his bony shoulders. The temperature in the room began to rise. Good and holy grass, what was he?

"Release her," Lichen said.

"Getting a little cocky, aren't we?" Latere sneered. His eyes glistened green through the tangled hair hanging wet across his disfigured face.

"Give me the crystal." Latere flapped his wings, dirty water sheeted across the room. Lichen flinched as it struck him in the face. Slimy. Putrid.

Lichen drew Durandal. "Release her," he repeated. The sword felt good in his hand. Invincible.

Latere's mutilated face warped into a sneer. "Ah. Feisty are we? Got a little fight in ya."

Latere drew his shortsword. The broad thick blade waved back and forth. Teasing.

"Come on then," he said. "I could use a little exercise."

Lichen attacked. Latere stepped aside and swiped his sword toward Lichen's back, missing.

Lichen turned bringing Durandal down. The sword glanced off Latere's shoulder and he cried out, but did not falter. His demeanor grew serious, his mockery evaporated. They circled, lashed out. Parried. They fought hard and viciously. The dance of war.

Latere's strikes slowed; he was tiring. His breath labored hard and fast in the stifling air. They struggled toward the entrance. Latere stuck out his foot and pushed Lichen backward knocking him to the floor. A simple maneuver. Latere pounced on Lichen's chest with his sword against Lichen's throat. Lichen's breath swooshed out and he dropped Durandal. Latere's knees pinned Lichen's arms to the floor.

"So, tell me. How does the little "warrior" feel now?"

Hot humid water droplets formed on the walls, the ceiling. Perspiration ran down Lichen's back and arms. His shirt and breeches clung like the embryonic sack of a newborn. Sweat dripped from Latere's crooked beaked nose onto Lichen's face.

"Now, my little hero, where is the crystal?"

Lichen looked toward the bag lying just outside the room. Latere followed his gaze and smiled.

"I've waited a long, a very long time to slit your throat," Latere sneered.

The water droplets fell from the ceiling transforming as they hit the floor. Rock Faeries. Gray as the mud. With cerulean capes, blue caps, and disgusting membrane wings. Lichen thought they looked beautiful. Alveus and the TOR tribe from the Proscriptio. How did they get here?

"I wouldn't do that," Alveus said. The faeries circled. Crude, sharp rock lances pointed at Latere. Spikes of hatred.

Latere startled and lessened his grip. Lichen began to wriggle. As soon as Lichen moved, Latere lurched and sliced his weapon toward him. Lichen's shoulder cracked and spurted red. Lichen thought of Isabella, cold and lifeless.

He thrust his other hand upward with all his strength. Latere fell back onto the floor. A chilling half-smile froze on his face. The crystal dagger protruded from Latere's chest, the handle pointing to the ceiling with hundreds of light reflections. Rainbows of death.

"Isabella," Lichen cried. He staggered toward her sealed tomb. Blood streamed down his arm from the gaping wound. The wall of ice began to melt. Water glazed the ice and ran onto the floor.

"Would ja look at that," Alveus said. The TOR watched mesmerized as the ice melted. It disintegrated quickly and covered the cave floor. Lichen beat the dissolving wall with his fist. Pounding. Kicking. Yelling. Alveus and the TOR joined in. They stabbed, chipped, and assaulted the ice.

The instant it broke, Lichen leaped through. He gathered Isabella in one arm, the other hung useless by his side, bleeding.

"Isabella. Isabella, wake up," Lichen said. She lay quite still. Her skin ghostly. Lichen couldn't tell if she was breathing. He pulled her to him and buried his face in her hair. He wanted this woman. He needed this woman. How could he ever have been so caught up in his revenge? Why had he let it consume him, burning everything to cinders leaving nothing but hate? He had been a complete and utter fool. Her hair smelled of spring fields. He had dreamed of this hair.

"Isabella," he whispered.

Lichen took the amulet from around his neck and placed it over Isabella's head. The stars glistened brightly as he slipped it beneath her shift. Powers of protection. The Earth and Stars.

Lichen felt movement. The little animal that had been lying beside Isabella awakened. Lichen laid Isabella down.

"Durandal," he commanded. The sword flew to his hand. Lichen ignored his astonishment; he didn't know the sword would obey him. He pointed Durandal toward the feline-like caterpillar.

"Stop," yelled Alveus. "That is her companion."

The creature walked softly, tentatively toward Isabella's head taking measure of Lichen. Papilio rubbed against Isabella's cheek, walked in a circle, and lay down across Isabella's chest snuggling against her throat, and began to purr.

A soft white light surrounded them, the Arca Lux. Lichen was afraid to breathe. What was this creature? Should he snatch it away from Isabella? Durandal could behead it with one swift stroke.

A faint rose blushed Isabella's cheek, her eyelids fluttered. Isabella's hand came up to Papilio. She smiled slightly. Lichen's heart lay bare.

"Isabella," he said. Lichen's blood dripped off his fingers and pooled at his feet. He felt light-headed and dizzy. At the sound of his voice, Isabella's eyes popped open.

"Lichen," she said.

In one moment of horror, Latere rose from the water on the cave floor and swooped Isabella off the slab. Papilio clung to her mistress; Latere clutched Lichen's bag to his bleeding chest, the dagger still intact. His crusted wings quivered like a vulture, mortally wounded.

Latere held Lichen's stricken glare with a malicious glint as he melted into a puddle of bloody water. Latere, Isabella, and Papilio disappeared through a crack in the floor. Vanished.

"Isabella," Lichen shouted. "Isabella."

Alveus and Lichen stood rooted, surrounded by the TOR paralyzed by disbelief.

"What was that? Lichen said. "How did he do that? Where did he go?" Alveus' men moved around, murmuring.

"Follow him," Lichen commanded. "You came in here as water. Follow him."

"We...we cannot. I mean, we can, we are TOR; we can become water. But we do not know where he went," said Alveus. His face a shroud of desperation.

"Well, we have to figure it out," Lichen said. "Who is he anyway? We must find Isabella." Lichen slumped and fainted dead away.

The bedraggled tribe of TOR walked out of the River into the storm. They carried Lichen limp and boneless as a freshly killed stag, their wings improvising shields from the torrential rain. Alveus led them into the trees toward an enclosure and a roaring campfire.

The TOR laid Lichen on the sodden ground. Q shoved his way between the faeries to his grandson.

"Lichen. Lichen, my boy." Q's expression lay between anguish and joy.

"No, no, not there," Q gruffed. "Put him over here where it's dry."

Q bent to examine Lichen his hands shaking slightly as he expertly palpated Lichen's body. It appeared the boy's only injury was his arm, broken and slashed. He noticed Lichen's muscles were well formed and toned. Probably from physical labor in the Proscriptio. A slave. My boy a slave all these months, in the Proscriptio.

The gash in Lichen's arm sliced completely through to the shattered bone. Q rolled Lichen slightly to complete the bandaging. He jerked back as if stung. There on Lichen's shoulder blazed healed wounds. The brand reflected firelight in smooth scarred lines.

SAX.

They branded him. The dirty devils branded him. Someone will pay for this.

Alveus stood slightly behind Q. "I'm sorry, sir," he said. "I'm sorry."

"Who the devil are you?" Q asked, "and how were you able to enter Mt. Vetare?"

Faber stood over Alveus and glared down, his yellow eyes piercing and dangerous, his massive arms folded across his chest.

Amicus bounded over to Lichen and peered into his face.

"Not now, Amicus," Q said. Q finished his ministrations with Lichen then reached into his pocket to retrieve the amulet. Q quietly slipped the Earth and Stars over Lichen's head.

"That's all I can do here," he said. Amicus barked a small puff of smoke and lay down beside Lichen. "Yes, that's right," Q said affectionately. "Warm him up, you little mutant furnace."

"Where's Isabella?" Sapien called as he approached Q glancing at Lichen on the ground. Sapien insisted on coming along to help rescue his daughter. "Where is she?"

Alveus spoke up. "I'm sorry sir. He took her. We had her, but that devil just rose up from his death, the dagger still stickin' out of him, and snatched her right away. He took her right from Lichen's arms, transformed into water, and disappeared through a crack in the floor of the cave."

"That's how he travels. Through the water," a voice said. Alveus, Q, and Sapien turned to see who had spoken. The Kings Guard held a small shriveled woman at bay.

"Supra," Alveus said. "You came."

"Yes," Supra answered. Her faded red cloak hung in wet drapes around her tiny body, wings drooping to the ground. Emaciated. Thousands of years of banishment. Of anguish.

"Who are you people?" Q asked.

Alveus glanced at Supra. "We are the GENS tribe, banished to the Proscriptio," she said.

"You," Q said, "you've had my grandson captive all these months? Why are you here? How did you get out?" The Kings Guard, having been dispatched to Q, raised their spears, but Supra never flinched.

"The Goddess Iris sent us the Vocatio," she said evenly, " and we accepted. We are here to transform at Iter." Q reluctantly motioned for the Guard to lower their weapons.

"And, yes," Supra cast her eyes to the ground. "Yes, we have held Lichen against his will. Q. Ambassador," Supra said. "I cannot ask your forgiveness for what I have done to your grandson. All I can ask is to allow me to assist in setting things right."

Q clenched his jaw. His glare burned into Supra, but he said nothing.

"I am here to help in whatever way I can. I am a foolish old woman. You, Alveus, are right, it *is* time to move forward. It is time to use the past to forge the future.

"We have lost much, but we must rekindle the fire of hope. We must re-pattern our destiny. We must accept the Mother's grace and rebuild Her trust."

Supra looked from Alveus to Q. "True, we came for Iter," she said, "but we are here now to help find Latere."

Q looked at Alveus, this turn of events unnerving him. "And just how did you get into Mt. Vetare? Only one is allowed entry." He looked at Lichen still lying on the ground.

"I believe this Latere is one of us," Supra spoke up.

"Yes, Alveus said. "Yesterday I met Ira, the Trader, and Lorelei, another captive." At this Alveus glanced sheepishly at Q. "I met them on the road to New Ivy and they told me about Latere and their dealings with him. I had a suspicion, too," he said as he looked at Supra.

"There is one of us," Supra said "...a traitor and murderer...who was not in the Proscriptio."

"Narro?" Alveus said.

"Yes," Supra said.

"I thought so," said Alveus. "I took a chance. If Narro could get into Mt. Vetare, perhaps all the TOR could. Since we are water-brothers."

"Narro?" Q asked. "So, it's true." Ira and Lorelei had told the truth and Ira had had access to Lichen weeks ago. He felt like strangling the little traitor.

"Narro," Sapien said, "is of the TOR tribe. He instigated the revolt against the Primordial and caused the whole of GENS to be banished."

"When we arrived in the Proscriptio," Supra said, "there was one absent from among us. Narro."

"Oh, my Holy Grove," Sapien said.

"He never arrived. We..." Supra looked at Alveus. "We all thought he had been killed and was simply lost in the Great River Potens. We were angry because he escaped the banishment. The agony of banishment."

"Narro is Latere. And Latere is Acta..." Sapien said.

"Then Narro has been privy to the Consillium," Q said. "And he has had access to the Sacred Grove and all the records. He stole the Lex Scriptura and he knows the truth about Lichen and Isabella. That's why he's taken her."

"What do you mean?" Supra asked. "Knows what about them?"

Sapien looked at Q; Q nodded.

"In the ancient records of Domus," Sapien said, "there is a document that speaks of two men. It foretells the destruction of Domus by the hand of one dominated by selfish desire. Narro?"

He motioned to the weather. "We believe this is the beginning of that destruction. The other can save the kingdom if he finds the soul he has lost." Sapien looked at Lichen lying unconscious. "Lichen."

Supra and Alveus stood in silence.

"At least Latere doesn't have the Crystal," Sapien said.

"The crystal?" Alveus asked.

"Yes, the Tempus Crystal. It's what he was after and it will give Narro complete control over Domus."

Lichen had regained a little strength, enough to chafe at being on the travois. Loss of blood left him weak and light-headed.

He had to get up from here and stop being coddled. He needed to go after Latere. He needed to get his Isabella back. Isabella. He remembered her voice when she said his name; the look in her eyes as she awoke from her ice-sleep, the panic on her face when that demon snatched her away. He must get up. He had to get up.

"Stop struggling, my boy," Q admonished. "I know what you're about. We'll find her, lad, we'll find her. He'll not hurt her; he needs her alive and well. She's the Charm. Now, just lie back and we'll get you home."

Mars, Q's prize stallion, snorted and pawed when he smelled them coming. His oversized hooves made deep gouges in the sodden ground; they immediately filled with water. Glipneir tethered him lightly and gave Mars plenty of room to fidget. The other horses stood placidly awaiting their masters; Mars, anxious to be off, exhaled forcefully, his breath streamed across the clearing.

Sapien's carriage sat among the horses; the wheels mired in mud. He had hoped Isabella would share his ride home. Sapien tried scraping mud off his boots on the carriage wheel, but as soon as he put his foot down, his boot sank two inches into the ground. He kicked the wheel in frustration.

Lichen watched Sapien from his palette as he wavered in and out of consciousness. Misery etched deep lines on Sapien's face. A map of despair.

"Q," Sapien said, "Lichen is in no shape to ride, please, put him in my carriage. We will go directly to the Manor."

Sapien put his foot down at Amicus riding in the carriage. Even if there had been room, Sapien voiced concern about a fire-breather in such close proximity.

No one except Q could contend with Amicus' fury at being left outside while Lichen was trundled into the coach. Q motioned up and Amicus went flying to the carriage top. The coach rocked when Amicus, no longer a cub, landed on the roof. He held on with his claw-like paws and barked fire into the air like a demented gargoyle on a castle parapet. Q grinned.

"Let's roll," Q shouted.

As if in answer, the sky seemed to split in half. Lightening sawed the rolling clouds with vicious electrical charges. Waves of undulating thunder assaulted the rescuers. Riptide wind. Mt. Vetare rumbled and erupted into the night. The shooting rock and fire sailed on the wind like funeral ships blazing on the sea. Lava rolled in great lazy runnels, broadening as it progressed down the slopes of Mt. Vetare.

The Great River Potens surged; her breakers beating the shore cresting froth upon the rocks. Midgard reared his head and roared, flames shooting from his mouth—a wide chasm of distress. His agonized bellows of fire seared the water and rose to meet the burning embers from the mountain. Joined, they lighted the sky red. Conflagration.

Fenrir called to his brother in a howl of anguish. Midgard's rolling scales disappeared beneath the water with one final flick of his wing; Fenrir ran for the forest. Blazing rock and ash fell from the sky pelting the rescuers as they ran for shelter in the trees.

Mars reared. Sapien's harnessed horses screamed and shot off in terror. Amicus clung to the carriage roof adding to the general panic by blasting fire with each breath. The mass of rescuers fled the forest, the contorted throng stampeding away from Mt. Vetare. The destruction of Domus had begun in earnest.

The sodden miserable entourage arrived at the Manor just before dawn. The carriage barely drew to a stop before Amicus flew down with one flap of his wings and clawed the door; his powerful tail flinging mud back and forth.

His peculiar drog fire-bark lighted up the night scaring the horde of rock faeries and horses. Most of the horses. Mars, imperious and fearless, having recovered quickly from Mt. Vetare's initial discharge galloped to a stop in front of Amicus and gave a mighty snort.

"Quiet," Q commanded Amicus much to the relief of the others. Mars laid back his ears. With one last tiny defiant blast at Mars, Amicus obeyed.

The fire in the sky burned bright above Mt. Vetare; the eastern horizon glowed. Holy Embers. Q opened the carriage door as Cecilia burst out of the Manor. She approached with tsk tsks and towels.

"Ye're back. Ye're safe. We've been in a state, I tell ya," Cecilia shouted over the wind. "Oh, me Holy Grove, look at ye now. Wet as marsh hens. And me poor lad, Lichen. You found 'im then," she said. Cecilia's commanding attitude served her well in emergencies and affairs of state.

"Straight to the bed wi' 'im, now and din'na be dilly dallyin'." No one, not even Q, challenged her directions regarding tending the sick and feeding the multitude.

Lichen roused and tried to rise on his elbow. "Oh, noo yoo don' laddie. It's straight to bed wi' ye," Cecilia admonished. "Ye need rest an' a lo' of it."

"She's right," Q said. "Faber, please take him upstairs. Cecilia you will have to wake the staff. We'll need refreshments for our rescue party. Uh," Q hesitated. "There turned out to be more than we expected. Ummm, quite a few more."

Cecilia had had only eyes for Lichen, but now she looked about her. Faeries. Rock Faeries. Hundreds of them streamed in the gate. A great gray mass of wet miserable bodies. Cecilia gaped in surprise; her mouth a silent chasm.

"It appears these people have had Lichen as their... *guest*," Q said. "In the Proscriptio."

"Yes, yes, I know, Master Q," Cecilia said. "I must ha' a word wi' ye."

Q caught Cecelia's urgency. "All right. A bit later though," Q said. "Right now do what you can to feed them."

Cecilia hesitated only a moment. "Right, right," she said turning toward the Manor. "Let's get on wi' it then."

Lichen awoke in the night, his chest and arm as tight and painful as a fist landing squarely on a nose. He felt like the nose. He tried to turn but someone was holding him down. Latere! Lichen ignored his pain and shoved away the body with a shout. A mighty roar of fire scorched Lichen's eyebrows. Lichen jumped off the bed yelling. Q burst into the bedroom followed by Cecilia.

"What ..."Q said. Lichen stood with his good arm in a striking pose. His chest, shoulder, and arm were slathered in plantain, Symphytum, and bandages. A green barefoot warrior.

Amicus stood facing Q and Cecilia, fire in his eyes, but nothing spewing from his mouth. "Well, look who's up and about," Q said smiling. It had been months since Q had smiled.

"I'll fetch ye some broth," Cecilia said. "And some biscuits." She looked at Amicus. "Several biscuits."

Lichen slumped back down on the bed; Amicus jumped up beside him. "Guess it was this black mongrel that had me pinned," Lichen said. "I thought it was...him." Amicus lay down beside Lichen rooting under his arm.

"Latere. His name is Latere," Q said. "Well, at least one of his names."

Q pulled a chair close to the bed and sat down. "Lichen, my boy. I didn't know if I'd ever see you again. I know you're weak and need to rest, but there are some things I need to know."

"No, I mean yes. No, it's ok, I'm fine and we do need to talk. I have to go after him. This *Latere*. He has Isabella."

"In good time, my boy," Q said. Cecilia came in, sat the tray down, and slipped out again.

"Tell me what happened at BelMoon," Q continued. He propped up Lichen's pillows under Amicus's watchful eye.

"I've gone over it a thousand times in my mind," Lichen said. "And I'm still not sure I know. I was looking for Isabella just before the Adoleo. Mother said Isabella had gone down to the stables to see the horses. I went in and Chimera stood in front of the open carriage door.

" 'Just preparing for your mother's return home,' he said. I walked past him thinking Isabella was in the animal dispensary. He grabbed my arm and the next thing I knew Agaso lurched out of the shadow.

"Chimera let go of me, and then Agaso fell against me. He felt wet. I know now it was blood. I held him for a moment, then everything went black. I woke up in the coach covered in blood with Mother tending my head wound. I didn't know Agaso was dead until Ira the Trader told me in the Proscriptio." Lichen stopped for a moment.

Q kept quiet letting Lichen continue.

"Mother was...not herself. She rambled on about them not getting me. She'd saved me once, she said, she could save me again. Then, the coach wrecked. It split into pieces. We fell into the river. Mother was thrown on the rocks and washed into the river; I landed further up the bank. Trolls came," Lichen said his eyes narrowing. "One Ear. The one who repaired the Manor after the storm."

"What?" Q said. He hung his head. "Chimera, One Ear. Can no one be trusted? I'm so sorry, my boy."

Lichen continued to tell Q the story of his kidnapping, his confinement in the Proscriptio, and his plan for revenge on the Rock Faeries.

"And when the Trader told me I was wanted for murder I couldn't believe it."

"I never believed it, Lichen," Q said. "I knew there was treachery about."

Lichen told Q about Wieland and suddenly remembered Durandal, Tarnhelm, and Tarnkappe. "My sword," he said in alarm.

"Never mind about that. Alveus retrieved your sword. And, where the devil did you get that cape and helmet? Anyway, they're quite safe," Q said.

Lichen relaxed and grinned. "There's so much to tell, for both of us."

He filled in Q about the months he'd been gone, Lorelei, Supra, his escape, and Mt. Vetare. The telling was exhausting and he lay back on his pillow.

Lichen was conscious of Amicus in his mind. Amicus constantly tugged at the edges of Lichen's awareness like a child wanting notice. Lichen laid his hand on Amicus. "Not yet, Amicus. Not just yet."

Q smiled. Despite the dreadful circumstances he'd been doing a lot of that tonight.

"I see he is still connected to you...in your mind, I mean. He was quite a handful when you disappeared."

Q stood and paced the room. "That is an extraordinary tale," Q said. "Cecilia has also been telling me a few things. Evidently, Ira has been involved in this from the beginning. He and Lorelei."

"I need to tell you that Ira's price for helping me, although he was of little help in my escape, is a baby. He wants to adopt one from your orphanage."

"A baby?" Q said. "Lichen, do you know that Ira is Isabella's uncle?"

"Uncle?" Lichen responded. "No. No I didn't."

"His wife is Isabella's mother's sister. Ira is not innocent in this plot, Lichen. When Sapien arrives we'll discuss it further. You need to regain your strength, my boy."

"I need to get into the Spring," Lichen said.

"What? The Spring?" Q said.

"It's a long story. But the short of it is, I have been healed once in the river. I believe if I go into the Spring, the Mother will heal me again. I need Lorelei for that. She's still here, isn't she?"

"Yes, everyone is here. And I mean everyone. Including Supra and all of the Rock Faerie tribes. Iris issued them a Vocatio, and they came to transform at Iter. But, they are willing, no anxious, to help find Isabella and capture Latere."

"Supra," Lichen said.

"Yes, I know it's a sticky situation. After all, she held you prisoner. We all have reason to want retribution."

"Actually, yes I did. Revenge fueled me while I was captive. It kept me going. I overheard Alveus and Supra discussing transforming at Iter and I knew if they were not able to, they would die. That's why I went to Mt. Vetare. To get the Tempus Crystal so I could disrupt Iter and kill them.

"I'm ashamed of that now. Something happened to me in the Crystal room, a change of heart you might say. A soul redemption. Anyway, I couldn't take the crystal out of the room even if I wanted to. Do you know how big that thing is? So, I tricked Latere into believing the Crystal was in my bag and stabbed him with a dagger I found in the Crystal room."

Q stood frozen by the window with a stunned expression. Wind pelted the rain against the glass. Outside the willow trees swayed wildly like deranged women, hair flying in all directions.

"What did you take from the Crystal room?"

"I opened a stone bench that had several things hidden in it. A couple of sister clocks like the ones in our libraries except smaller. An amulet just like mine, and a crystal dagger. I took the amulet and the dagger. I put the amulet on Isabella; I thought it would help protect her. And the dagger is what I killed Latere with. At least, I thought I killed him. Apparently, I didn't."

"Lichen," Q said grimly. "Latere has the Tempus Crystal."

"No, he doesn't. It's still in the Crystal room," Lichen said.

"Everything that was in that stone bench has the same origin as the Tempus Crystal. The sister clocks, the amulet, and the crystal dagger. The clocks and the amulet are limited in power, but...the dagger... the dagger was mined and created the same as Tempus. If he has the dagger, he has the Tempus Crystal.

Chapter Forty-Eight

Strategies

"You're telling me that I handed over Domus to that fiend?" Lichen jumped out of bed. Pain stabbed through his chest, shoulder, and down his arm.

"Lichen lay down," Q said. "We're going after him. But first, I guess we need to get you into the Spring." Q went out the door in search of Lorelei.

Lichen had no choice but to lay back on his bed. His strength completely left him. Pain and nausea raked his body. He would find that blackguard; he would find him and kill him. He would get the crystal back.

And Isabella. He would save Isabella. He had to save Isabella. Latere could not be in control of Domus, not now, not ever. He should have known the dagger was part of the Tempus Crystal. He should have figured it out. They were identical crystals. Why didn't he see it? Lichen grasped the amulet. So, the crystals in the amulets were from the Tempus Crystal. And, the clock. The crazy clock he'd grown up fearing and loving had been hewn from the holy mountain.

Lichen felt dizzy; the room spun around him and he couldn't think. A dark curtain of black surrounded him. He could see a pinpoint of light in the distance. Lichen tried to concentrate on it.

Suddenly it rushed toward him along with Amicus; light engulfing them both. Warm. Soothing. Lichen felt peaceful and relaxed; the light pulsed gently. Lichen experienced Amicus like the time they had bonded. Heat surged through his body. Strength. Energy. There were no words, only a loving, powerful Presence. A healing Presence.

Lichen through his legs out of bed sat up and stopped abruptly. There beside the wardrobe sat a pair of boots. Lacerta boots. His lacerta boots.

"Lorelei will meet us in the Spring room," Q said as he came through the door. Lichen stood in front of the wardrobe unwrapping his bandages. The healing herbs Cecilia had lovingly applied scattered to the floor.

"The only thing I need water for is to clean up." He smiled at Q.

Q stood immobilized for only a moment, glanced at Amicus and back at Lichen. Then his shoulders relaxed; tension evaporated.

"Well, then, stop lolly-gagging about, and let's get on with this. Everyone is waiting in the library," Q said as he walked over to Lichen putting his arms around him. They held one another close.

Heads turned toward Q and Lichen when they entered the library. The thunderous roar of the storm filled the room as the hum of voices died.

Sapien looked pleased that Lichen appeared healed. Ira stood by the fireplace fingering his tunic, his wings drooping behind him. He looked sideways at the clock glowing on the mantle. Lorelei leaned against the window watching the storm. She looked like she would rather be out there. In the storm. In the water.

Supra took a step toward Lichen. Agony clutched her face like a bony hand, her gray skin, old and dry and brittle. The membrane of her wings hung in shreds; small pieces falling to the rug.

"Lichen," she said, mucous peeking out her nostril. "Lichen." Her voice broke. One single tear streamed down the deep wrinkles of her face puddling in the corner of her thin lips. The room vibrated with tension as everyone watched.

Lichen stepped forward; his tone quietly authoritative. He no longer burned with loathing and revulsion, but he didn't quite know how he felt about Supra. Now was not the time to air grievances.

"Supra," he said in a quiet voice and steady gaze, "I hear you and your tribes have come to help rescue Isabella and catch that rogue." Lichen was no longer the captive boy or the vengeful man. He was the Warrior.

Lichen ignoring Supra's obvious discomfiture turned to Alveus. "You saved me in the cave. You took me to my grandfather. Thank you. Now, we have a job to do."

"Welcome home, Lichen," Sapien said.

"Sir," Lichen replied. "We're going to find her, sir. We will bring her home. We will bring Isabella home." Lichen's voice resonated with determination. Determination and love.

Lorelei turned her back to the room.

"I know you will," Sapien said glancing at Ira who looked at the floor like a whipped puppy. "Our family offers you anything you need. Name it and it is yours."

"What I need now is information. I want to know everything about this Latere," Lichen said.

"I believe he has recruited an army," Alveus said. "Many tribesmen from all four quads of the GENS are missing. I fear they have joined Latere."

"All right," Lichen said, "we'll need a full account of the number."

One by one they relayed their stories. Ira looked shamefaced and scared; Lorelei remained silent.

"So, Narro is from the TOR tribe and somehow escaped the banishment. And, he has been disguised as Latere to solicit help from the locals while he masqueraded as the Consillium scribe, Acta, to gain access to the Sacred Grove.

"When he stole, then read the Lex Scriptura he knew he needed the crystal to control Domus," Lichen spoke out loud to clarify his thoughts. Obviously, everyone else already had all the details. Including Latere.

Sapien hesitated when he told Lichen about the sacred manuscript kept in the Grove archives. The Prophecy. The Portent.

The room grew still and Lichen listened intently. The Prophecy settled around him. A mantle of responsibility passed down from antiquity. A sense of duty rooted and sprouted to life. Obligation spread within him like fog on a cool morning rising to the occasion.

Lichen looked at his grandfather. Q had known all along; Q had sent the poem, the amulet. Q smiled benignly.

Lichen accepted it. Domus was his home now and these were his people. Whatever part he played in this mad scheme of Latere's, he would play it.

"I know where he is," Supra said. "He's gone to the wasteland. To the GENS quad."

"You're right," Alveus said. "That was our home; it's the logical place. He thinks he will control Domus from there. Rule it. Destroy it. Whatever his plans are."

"Then that's where we're going," Lichen said.

"We don't have much time," Sapien said. "Iter is in three days. If we don't stop him by then, it will be too late. Our world is disintegrating out there." Heads turned toward the window. Domus was in a free-fall to destruction.

Mt. Vetare's eruptions lit the night, spewing streams of red and yellow into the sky. Wild fierce lightning strikes splintered across Domus with white-hot charges. Wind-driven rain pierced the air like lancets, sharp and cold.

Q walked over to the mantle and looked into the clock. The glow within was clouded by a dark boiling color much like the storm outside. "No, we don't have much time," Q said.

"I will take Lorelei with me," Lichen said. "She may be able to get close to Latere and she can help me travel through the water.

"Alveus, you and your tribe can navigate through the waterways. What about the other tribes? How will they get to the Wasteland?"

"They should each travel by the means of their tribe. The GEL can fly high and travel along the ice crystals in the clouds. The SAX will enter the rock of the mountains in the wasteland. The ARI will have the most trouble. Normally they would meld with the dry air, but nothing is dry," Alveus said. They need to wait at the gate for the signal, then proceed with Q and Sapien."

"Sapien and I will bring extra horses and the carriage for Isabella. We will also bring what villagers may wish to join us," Q said.

"I will rouse the Criocts," Ira said. It was the first time he spoke. Q and Sapien looked at one another, doubt in their eyes.

"Please," Ira said. "Let me do this. I've done so much damage. I allowed Latere to manipulate and deceive me. I have to do this."

"Alright," Sapien said. His famous forgiveness not quite ringing true in his voice.

"Thank you," Ira said. He walked over to Lichen and extended his hand. Lichen hesitated; he still didn't like this little braggart. Ira stood firm; his arm outstretched.

Lichen reached out and Ira deposited something in Lichen's hand, squeezed it, and said, "And, thank you, Lichen," then walked away.

Lichen opened his fist. There laid the ruby he had given to Ira in the Proscriptio. A tear from Wieland's cave. It gave a strange little quiver as he shoved it into his pocket.

"The more men we have the better," Sapien said. "I've kept the King informed; the Royal Guard is still at our disposal."

"They should surround the Wasteland," Lichen said. "We have every possible way out covered. He will not escape."

"Where is Keeper Valeo?" Q asked, his voice rang with a strange timbre. "He should have been here by now."

"I've been wondering that myself," Sapien said.

"Lorelei will go in alone," Lichen said. "While she distracts him, I will enter. Alveus, you and Supra follow us in. Post the TOR at every waterway entering the GENS. We won't surprise him again. He'll be watching for water droplets and probably has wards already in place."

"Sapien and I will wait at the only entrance to the Wasteland with the ARI. Ira, you and the Criocts meet us there as quickly as you can," Q said.

"Are you sure there's no other way out?" Lichen asked.

"He will most likely try to get out through the water since he is TOR," Q said. "The tribe will be stationed in every channel. At the very least they will be able to see where he goes."

"It won't work," Ira said. "If he escaped being banished by the Mother, how can we stop him? He's a master at negotiating the waterways."

"Midgard," said Lorelei. "Midgard will help us."

"Can you find him?" Ira asked.

"He will find us," Lorelei said. "Let's go," she said to Lichen.

Q gave Cecilia some last instructions while the others got ready to leave. "I'm not sure what we will find when we arrive at the Wasteland. While we are gone, prepare whatever remedies you deem necessary. Beds, food, dispensaries."

Cecilia listened patiently. Q shook his head. "Oh, why am I telling you this? You know what to do. You always know what to do. Whatever would I have done without you all these years, Cecilia?"

"Sir, before ye leave, I must confess somethin'."

"Confess?"

"Yessir. Ye see, Agaso was my brother."

"What? Your brother?"

"When King Colere appointed ye Ambassador, 'e called us in and asked us to 'elp ye in any way we could. 'e thought we'd be a good start to your staff."

"But why didn't he just tell me?"

"Well, sir, ye do 'ave a stubborn streak, now don' ye? The King dinna want ye to refuse. 'e knew ye were bent on makin' a village where 'umans would feel welcome. An' since I dinna', well, I don' *look* fey, well, the King thought we would be a good match for ye."

"You spied on me?"

"Oh, no sir. Ne'er nothin' li' that. The King, 'e never asked us about what went on 'ere. 'e only jus' said if ever ye needed anythin', anythin' at all, jus' to tell 'im. 'e meant for us to be a support to ye, sir. I'm sorry, truly I am. Agaso and I loved it 'ere, sir."

Cecilia blew her nose. It sounded all the world like the blue-billed gosler that nested under the bridge in the Willow Grove. Q patted her shoulder, his discomfiture obvious.

"Cecilia," Q said, "see to the preparations. I trust you to have everything ready upon our return." Activity was an excellent antidote to tears.

"Thank ye, sir. Thank ye."

Chapter Forty-Nine

Confessions

Q sat at his desk staring at the clock; its color deepening, the purples and blacks swirling faster. He wondered where Valeo was. Valeo had been acting very strange the past couple of weeks. He tore in the Manor one afternoon all a burst with news of Lichen. Said that he, Valeo, had personally seen to Lichen's release in the Proscriptio and Ira would be escorting him home.

When Ira did turn up on Q's doorstep, he had that little water nymph with him, and Lichen had gone into Mt. Vetare. Ira turned green when Q tried to question him, but he ended up spilling his guts to Cecelia.

Q had decided to put Ira on the back burner for now. He wasn't blaming Ira for Valeo's actions; Valeo acted of his own accord.

Why did Valeo switch their drivers? Why was he insistant on getting Lichen out of Domus? The man was clearly implicated in Agaso and Beetrum's deaths. Q would deal with Ira later, and Valeo could explain himself. If he ever turned up.

Q heard voices coming up the hall. "Just a moment, sir. I will tell Master Q ye're 'ere," Cecilia's voice rang out.

"No need," Valeo said as he barged into the library. "I demand an explanation, Q."

"An explanation?" Q asked as he leaned back in his chair and tee-peed his fingers.

"I received this silent post from Sapien. Are you two out of your minds? If this insane lunatic is Narro, you haven't a chance against him. And you've taken it upon yourselves to organize a posse of sorts? Do you realize what you are doing?"

"Where have you been?" Q said.

"I beg your pardon. Where have *I* been? Is this the gratitude you show me after I negotiated the release of Lichen from the Proscriptio?"

"Valeo, stop it. I know," Q said.

"You know what?" Valeo flustered.

Q sat calmly at the desk. He picked up a quill and examined it. He twirled it in his fingers.

"I had an interesting conversation with Ira Lungwort."

Valeo's lips pressed together. A thin line of deceit.

"I know that you have betrayed me. You conspired with Beetrum to kidnap Lichen and transport him to Weston. But things went horribly wrong. Just tell me why, Valeo. Why?"

Valeo sat down hard; his lies no longer held him up.

"Ira," he said. "That little moldy-feathered carrion. I should have known he would fold."

"Valeo, my daughter is dead. My grandson was kidnapped, and beaten. Agaso is dead. And all you can think about is Ira's betrayal? What about your betrayal, Valeo? I trusted you. Why in the name of all that's holy did you do it?"

Valeo stood up and began to pace around the library. A lion caught in a cage of deception. Nowhere to go. No way of escape.

"You, you sanctimonious hypocrite," Valeo said. "You parade around Domus as if you owned it. Well, you don't own it. You shouldn't even be here. I'm the Keeper. I'm in charge of the King's lands. My family have been Keepers since there was a Domus." Valeo pounded his fist onto the desk.

"I'll never understand why Dens let you in here. Why our King kowtowed to a human.

"New Ivy. I hate this Quad and everything about it. Your people stink; I can't stand to be around you."

"Valeo," Q said. "Valeo, stop. You can't mean that."

"Can't I? I loathe you and your family. You've brought nothing but pain and sorrow to Domus."

"Pain and sorrow? What are you talking about, Valeo?"

Valeo had a wild absent look about him as if he was watching something privy only to himself. A private showing of revulsion and shock.

"How dare you. How dare you forget my sister. My Syringa."

"Syringa? Forget Syringa? Valeo, I haven't forgotten my wife. But what does she have to do with this? With Lichen?"

"You stole her away from QuinVerga. You tricked her into marrying you.

"And Dens. The great King Dens Colere condoned my sister marrying a human. After Bellus, my own wife, left me and ran back to her human world, I knew humans could not be trusted.

"You tricked the King, too. By marrying you, Syringa tainted the proud Keeper family with even more human blood. It was not to be borne.

"And, then," Valeo said his mind trailing off into memories only he could see, "then Syringa died. You killed her, Q."

"Valeo, Syringa died of a fever. There was nothing I could do," Q said.

"If she had been at home in QuinVerga, she would not have died. She caught her death in this vile quad of humans. I swore vengeance for her, Q. And, I've had it." Valeo's voice was rising. A note of hysteria played around his words. "I've had it." He began to laugh, an empty haunting parody of a laugh.

"Valeo, I know you have suffered. I know how hard it was for you when your wife, Bellus, disappeared. "But you can't blame all humans, Valeo. All Fey are not alike, and neither are humans.

"I'm sorry Bellus left you. But you cannot blame the entire human race for that. And, you have Durus and Dexter, your sons. It was not my fault that Syringa died. I loved her. We both suffered at her loss."

"Durus. My half-breed son is gone, who knows where. And you dare to claim you loved Syringa? A poisonous love. A destructive love," Valeo said.

"Well, I've avenged her death. I've caused you and yours to suffer. Have you suffered, Q? Were you tortured when Beetrum left with Lichen, not once, but twice? Did you feel pain when Linum died?"

"Enough. You're mad."

"Have you been in pain, Q? Have you suffered? Over Lichen. Beetrum. Linum."

"You're not yourself, Valeo. We've not seen eye-to-eye over the years, grant you that. But I loved your sister. And what do you mean? What does Linum have to do with this?"

Valeo stared at Q with manic-glazed eyes.

"I killed Linum so you and your daughter would suffer. I made Beetrum's life even more miserable so she would run away, run back to her stinking human world."

Once again Valeo laughed, a shrill frenzied convulsion. "I destroyed your dream, too. Your precious bridge would never be built because I burned the ropes. You and your fanatical ideas. A human-fey orphanage. A university. You disgust me." Valeo spit toward Q but it fell short and landed in a pathetic puddle on Q's desk. Mucus of hate.

"Press no further," Q shouted as he struck Valeo across his cheek. The realization of Valeo's heinous crimes shocked Q. "You vile and insidious man. I am placing you under arrest. You will be held at the Manor until our return."

Q reached for Valeo but he jerked away and ran toward the door. "Imprison The Keeper? As soon as my granddaughter is queen, you'll be the one in prison."

"Skye? You *are* insane, Valeo. Leave her alone. Princess Phyta, the King & Queen, and even your son, Durus, agreed to that adoption. She's happy where she is."

"You thought to take her from QuinVerga, too. You thought to hide her away from me. Disguise her identity. Keep her from her rightful place as future Queen. Princess Phyta is ill and Durus is gone. Skye will rule Domus one day. And you and that stinking orphanage will be gone. New Ivy will be a bad memory."

Sapien had told Q of Skye's accident in the swing and how she thought someone in a green cloak had saved her.

"Valeo, did you have anything to do with Skye's accident?"

Valeo looked wild. "I had to keep her from attending Iter. Humans are not allowed at Iter. Her human blood would have been discovered, I did it to protect her." Valeo turned and ran down the hall knocking

Cecelia out of the way. Potions dropped onto the floor. Herbal carnage. Valeo flung open the door and disappeared into the storm.

Chapter Fifty

Charm

Isabella sat up cautiously. She rubbed her hands up and down on her arms trying to warm them, the stone slab sucking heat from her body. A granite sponge. Her thin shift, wet and cold, her thick hair lay like black ice on her shoulders and back, her lips and fingers tinged blue.

Where was she? Where was Lichen? She remembered his embrace, his voice when he said her name. Even thoughts of Lichen could not warm her. Isabella tried to focus, but the room had no light for her eyes to latch onto. Deathly black. Deadly still. Like a crypt.

Isabella stood and inched her way forward, shivering. Within a few steps, she touched a wall. Cold. Slick. Ice. She jerked her hand away. Not again. She slumped to the floor. She couldn't bear it again.

Her stomach ached; her hands trembled. If she could just sleep and disappear into nothingness then she wouldn't feel. The cold. The pain. The fear. Papilio crawled onto her lap. A little spot of warmth.

He tried to purr but the dense coldness prevented even the Arca Lux from spreading.

"Isabella. Get up now, pet," the voice came through the black tunnel of her mind. It sounded familiar. "I said get up." Isabella felt herself being jerked harshly up off the floor and flung onto the stone bench her breath forced out like tiny bellows. She was so cold she feared she would break into a thousand pieces. "Look at you now. Not so arrogant are we? You, the little *healer.* What's the matter, not feeling well?"

"Who are you? Isabella asked, her lips quivering with cold. Words stiff and broken.

"Why are you doing this? Release me at once."

"Ha," he laughed. "You're a feisty one. I would have thought you'd be submissive by now, me pet. But, oh, I forget now. You're of human blood, aren't you? You aren't Fey at all." His laugh reverberated against the stone amplifying her humiliation.

"Who are you?" Isabella screamed. "Show yourself, you coward."

"Alright, then." The light pierced Isabella like a weapon. Pain seared through her mind, screaming. She folded her arms around her head. She must not yield to this monster, she must fight. She may not be Faerie, but she had been trained; a Caduceus knew things.

Isabella shielded her mind from the sharp edges of the light spears. She was strong; she would not yield. He would not force her into submission again. He would not win. Isabella pushed against the mental spikes forcing them to recede. The piercing light vanished and so did the pain.

"So, you are a fighter after all," he said. "I admire that. The others succumbed so easily. Where's the challenge in that?"

"The others?" Isabella said. She tried to keep her teeth from chattering.

Latere's malice floated along the cavern floor like evil fog.

"The Caducei. You are one of them. Do not deny it. The purple tint follows you like stink on a rotting carcass. Lemna taught me that."

"Lemna? You...you're a Pavor?" Isabella asked horror creeping into her soul.

Confidence began to seep out of her as she remembered the killing spree. Caducei had been killed all over Domus in a rampage of terror. Many Pavors were captured. How many were not? Isabella thought of Lemna, her mentor, her friend who had disappeared after a Pavor attack. Lemna's assistant found in the stillroom, her body shredded, the tonics and remedies scattered and broken. Anger warmed Isabella; strength flooded her senses. This monster was a Pavor.

"Oh, no, little pet," Latere said reading her thoughts. "I am not *a* Pavor. I am *The* Pavor. And so much more." Latere appeared across the room.

"Acta," Isabella said. "Acta is that you? No. Why, Acta?" How could this be? Acta had been scriba to the Consillium for years. It could not be. Acta Diurna, her father's scribe, a Pavor? Kidnapped her? It didn't make sense.

"Acta never existed, my pet, it was a clever ruse. A very clever ruse. I needed to get into that Grove. I needed information. I needed the Crystal." He held the dagger aloft. His prize. "And your precious Lichen was so kind as to get it for me."

"Why?" Isabella asked. "Why did you kill the Caducei? What do you know of Lemna? Where is she?"

"Oh, that. That was just a little ancillary activity to ensure my power would be complete. I hate Caducei, but Lemna proved useful." Latere snarled. He narrowed his eyes at Isabella. "And the fact that you are in the Portent *and* a Caduceus is just a bonus for me."

Isabella tried to reason it out. Make sense of it. Acta was the leader of the Pavors? Because he had access to the Grove, he stole the information he needed to get the Crystal. And, with the Crystal, he could control Domus. She must get away from him and warn her father. And Lichen.

"Ah, how quaint you are. 'I must warn my father'," Latere mocked. "By this time I expect the whole lot of them are on their way here. To get this," he held the dagger up. "And to get you."

Isabella must shield her mind from him. She could do it. She was Caducei. Isabella forced up her barrier. She felt Latere's mind probes slam into it.

"You're a traitor," she said. "A traitor and a murderer. You will never get away with this. Lichen will come."

"Oh, I'm counting on that now, pet. That boy just won't die," he said in exasperation. "You see I must kill him. He's in the Portent you know. As are you. You both must die."

"Portent?" Isabella said.

"Now, pet, if you'd just let me in that little head of yours, I could explain it all to you," Latere laughed. "But, no, you want to play your Caduceus part 'till the end. Why do you care now anyway? You're not even Fey. What do you care if I control Domus? But, no, you have to portray the little healer. Well, my little Charm," Latere put his face against the ice wall and glared at her. Papilio hissed and spat.

"So be it. Now you're mine."

Latere turned his head as if he was listening for something. The pool in the center of the cave exploded into a turbulent fountain. Red and silver rocketed out of the water and stood beside Latere.

"Lorelei," Latere said. He tenderly slid his fingers into the firestorm of her hair. His thumb caressed her cheek. She was slick and wet and beautiful.

"I've been waiting. What kept you?"

"I stayed with Lichen as you ordered," Lorelei said. "I've brought him to you, as planned. He waits on the shore for me."

"Well done. It's almost over. We will rule Domus together." Latere's hand slid down Lorelei's shoulder. She flinched as he touched the SAX brand scar. He leaned down and kissed the mark ever so lightly. "They will all pay, me dear. Supra and her band of gutless bats. They will pay. I've waited centuries for this moment."

Lorelei glanced at Isabella staring from behind the sheet of ice, her furry little companion twining around Isabella's feet. Lorelei did not have the look of someone about to become co-ruler of the entire kingdom.

"Let her out," Lorelei said.

"No, she stays secure behind the wall."

"If you let her out, Lichen will sense her, his powers have surfaced. He will not come unless he knows she is here."

"He will come. He wants this," Latere said touching the dagger at his waist. "And he wants me."

"He will not fight you until he knows she is alive. I know, him, Latere. He will not come unless he feels her in this cavern," Lorelei said. She looked at Isabella. "She is his love."

Isabella stared back at Lorelei through the ice wall. *She loves him. Lorelei's in love with Lichen.*

Latere detonated with anger. The illusion of Acta Diurna's persona contorted and disappeared. Scarred gray skin enveloped his face and pulled at his eyes and mouth. Long wisps of patchy hair grew across his scalp like weeds in a vacant lot.

His ears torn, ragged, and covered with oozing scabs. His wings once mighty emblems of strength hung loosely from his shoulders.

Soiled rags draped over a sagging frame. Shadows fluttering helplessly in the wind. Impotent. Lorelei pulled away from him.

"Oh, I know you don't like this me, do you?" Latere said. "You'd rather see a pretty face. I disgust you." He grabbed Lorelei by her hair.

"What if I made you look like me? Hmm, how would that work out?" He threw her to the floor.

"You see, this face, this body, it will remind all of Domus what I have suffered for them. What I have been through for them. I never want them to forget what it cost to save myself from the Proscriptio. To save myself for them. So, I could lead them to greatness. Now, I will wear this disfigurement as a badge. An emblem of cunning and determination. A symbol of the power given to me by TOR himself."

"Latere..." Lorelei said.

"Don't call me that," he shouted. "I am Narro. Narro of the great tribe of TOR. The mighty beautiful warrior, TOR. He was the youngest. The smallest. The weakest. The Mother loved him best." Latere paced the cave, his eyes wild and fierce.

"That's what saved me, you know. From the Proscriptio. When the Great River Potens came for us, when she roared and submerged us, I kept my mind focused on TOR. TOR and the sacred Song of the West. I held onto it. The melody of it played over and over in my mind. It encompassed me in a cocoon of safety.

"When the others, burdened with fear and guilt, landed in the Proscriptio, the Song took me to safety, but not without a price.

"Alveus, that coward and traitor to the TOR. And, Supra, Miss High and Mighty. Miss Squeaky Clean and Equitable. They got their due. It doesn't matter that they have come to transform. They're going to die anyway."

Isabella listened with horror. She knew the history of the great Banishment well. The beautiful and beloved Supra ruled the SAX, and

Alveus ruled the TOR. But the tribes succumbed to Narro's cunning. They committed the ultimate crime. They broke the Primordial.

But, she didn't know, no one knew, that one had escaped. The instigator. Narro. The one who deceived the tribes with his subterfuge of lies. The one responsible for Banishment.

Isabella thought of Acta living among them. Spying. Plotting. Scribing for her father and the Consillium. Entering the Sacred Grove and the Library. Reading the sacred books, and the Lex Scriptura. No one read the Lex Scriptura except her father.

Acta had stolen her Totus Vita and given it to her.

"Why," Isabella said, "why did you steal my Totus Vita?"

"Well, my pet," Latere said. "I needed you out of the picture. I'd hoped you would leave Domus when you discovered you were human. But no. Being the good little healer you are, you had to stay the course. Then I realized you were the Charm. The protection Charm. You see I cannot lose this war if I have you. It's the Prophecy you see. But, your lover, now, he must die. We can't have that stalwart little warrior running around trying to save the world."

"Lichen? The Warrior?" Isabella felt bewildered. "But I'm not in the Portent," Isabella said. "You're wrong."

Latere grimaced a crooked parody of a grin. "Oh, but you are my little charm. It's a shame to waste your brains by splattering them all over this cave. But, I have no choice."

He considered Lorelei. "I think you may be right. I think he will not come if he doesn't sense her." Latere waved his arm and the icewall began to melt. The rivulets of water ran into the pool.

Latere had searched the Wasteland for a cave such as this not only to make his last stand, but to retreat to when he needed solace. He adored cold, dreary, and dark. It suited him. Disconsolate obscurity.

And, since this mountain range was riddled with caves, it hadn't been difficult to find one like it in Mt. Vetare. And, he had gotten quite adept at making ice prisons. They had come in handy during the last several millennia.

Latere planned to launch and rule his kingdom from this cave. It was much larger than the one in Mt Vetare. He felt at home here.

In seconds, Isabella and Papilio were free. Isabella's blue-tinged lips and fingers began to throb as life warmed her. Papilio arched his back and purred the Arca Lux.

The shadows lying along the cave walls came alive. Hell-Hounds. Three enormous canine wraiths sprang toward Isabella, hackles raised, fangs barred. Their yellow evil eyes eager for the kill. They yelped as they hit the barrier of the Arca Lux, got up, and began their death circle. Slowly they circumnavigated the Lux; growling low menacing vibrations.

"Mors. Letum. Obitus. Down. Now," Latere said. The hounds immediately slunk back into the shadows. "Go then," he said to Lorelei. "Bring him."

Lorelei looked one last time at Isabella and dove into the pool.

Chapter Fifty-One

Fugitive

Lichen burst forth from the pool, Durandal drawn. Lorelei followed. Lichen's feet landed solidly on the rock in spite of its wetness; his breath clouded the air in the frigid underground cave.

"Right on cue," Latere said. He leaned against a large boulder. Relaxed.

"Latere," Lichen said. "You're looking the worse for wear. Miss your day at the spa?" Lichens quip fell flat with the citizens of Domus. Isabella stood shivering looking devastatingly beautiful. An ice Madonna. "Isabella," he said.

"Lichen," Isabella said.

"I hate to be the one to break up this little reunion," Latere said. "But I'm in a bit of a hurry. Boys."

The ice glaze covering the cave began to crack. Splinters spread along the ceiling and walls as if the cave had awakened and was stretching, sloughing off the winter's sleep.

The frozen spears hit the floor and instantly transformed into combatants. The gray leather of their skin, the gauntness of their faces, and the dribble of snot on their lips identified them as Rock Faeries. Despite Lichen's recent change of heart, he felt a familiar pang of revulsion. The dreary faeries pointed their various weapons in his direction.

Mors, Letum, and Obitus leaped from the shadows eager to join the fray. Specters of woe.

The pool erupted with a great geyser of fire. Amicus blasted out of the pool, landed in the center of the ghostly trio, then rocketed toward Obitus. An eviscerating torch. Obitus fizzled out like the flame of a torch dropped into the river.

Alveus and the TOR materialized from the water Amicus had splashed onto the floor. Alveus registered shock at the betrayal of the GEL tribe surrounding Lichen. Pandemonium dominated the room as the ashen faerie battled.

Converging on one another with vicious blows and brutal swipes of their new weapons--each had been issued a sword or knife, a lance or poleax from the smithy of New Ivy. Their long confinement in the Proscriptio, their centuries of frustrations and dispossession, their grisly existence discharged in an explosion of violence. Depraved fury clouded the original cause of combat. They devolved into a gray boiling swarm.

Lichen grabbed Isabella around the waist, planted a quick kiss on her mouth, and deposited her to the side.

"Stay here," he said. He silently vowed to never lose this woman again. He turned and searched for Latere, fighting off the GEL as he moved across the cave.

Papilio dove onto Letum. The caterpillar extended the considerably long claws of all eight feet and yowled in a most un-Lepidoptera way.

The hound yelped more in anger than pain, turning his head to snap at the creature on his back.

Amicus swiped his claw hitting Mors across the mouth, knocking him off balance. Then Amicus' powerful tail cut across Letum's exposed neck severing the jugular. Dark foul blood gushed onto the floor sizzling like acid. And as Mors tried to square his body for another attack on Amicus, he slipped in the blood bowled up in a hollow rock. Amicus was on him in a flash and the third Hound went back to inferna in a display of luminous pyrotechnics.

Lichen knocked out a GEL and took advantage of the momentary lull to fire a thought at Amicus. "Protect Isabella. Do not leave her." Amicus looked at his master across the room and ran for Isabella. He planted himself at Isabella's feet while simultaneously scooting Papilio to the side. Amicus looked down at the curious little creature and gave him a mighty lick on the side of the head. Papilio purred the Arca Lux.

A dismal slate-colored body smashed into Isabella and came up swinging.

"That does it," Isabella said. She confiscated his short sword and put to use the defense moves Ian had taught her. She made quick work of the frenzied faerie and turned into the battle.

Amicus looked on helplessly; then he dove into the fray beside Isabella. Papilio reared up on his back legs and gave support with his unworldly squall.

The battle raged on; the sides were evenly matched in skill and number. Few had fallen from either tribe. Lichen hacked his way through the mass of heaving bodies looking for Latere. The initial spurt of anger burned itself out as the weakened tribes lost any vigor they had. Alveus caught the mood shift and jumped up onto a boulder.

"Tribesmen," he shouted. "Let us stop this insanity. We are not enemies. We are brothers. We suffered together in the Proscriptio because of Narro." Alveus raised his sword for emphasis. "*He* is the enemy."

The faerie slowly stopped fighting and listened to Alveus. "We suffered our punishment all these many long insufferable years. We eked out a wretched living. We buried our dead and bore our children in desolation because of Narro's lies."

The wall behind the boulder moved. Shale crumbled to the floor as Supra emerged from the stone of the mountain. She stood beside Alveus as the rest of her tribe stepped out of the stone and into the cave.

"Alveus is right. Narro destroyed us once. We cannot let him do so again. We came from the Proscriptio to transform, to reclaim that which we lost because of Narro. Do not be deceived by his lies, again." Supra said. "He is no longer one of us."

"Look for yourselves," said Alveus. "Where is he now? Fighting here by your side? No. Once again, he has saved himself." The crowd murmured and searched the room for Narro.

Lichen saw Lorelei standing in the shadows watching him. She slipped between the vertical layers of shale. An invisible opening. Lichen followed.

The edges of rock and ice cut into his chest and back opening his wounds and tinting his shirt with streams of red. Lichen inched sideways several feet. He wished he had the power to go through rock. What good was being The Warrior if you couldn't walk through stone or breathe water?

And wouldn't it be fabulous to fly?

"Well, here we go," Latere said as Lichen stepped out of the crevice. "I thought one of your former captors might have finished you off."

"You'd like that wouldn't you, coward?" Lichen said.

Latere's chilling parody of laughter strained at the scarred and twisted mouth.

"Finally, I have you. No one to save you now. This cavern is warded. You are the only one who can enter."

The cave shimmered with gemstones. Tens of thousands of jewels sparkled from the walls. Embedded stars.

"How do you like it?" Narro said waving his sword in the air. "Just a little cache I stored away for my future."

Latere brandished his sword, approaching Lichen slowly, then lunged. Lichen sidestepped; the duel was on. Lichen's taller stature gave him greater reach, but Latere was quick. His grotesque appearance, disgusting smell, and rapid movements made for a fearsome opponent. They fought hard. Striking. Slashing. Panting.

"Getting tired *human?"* Latere said.

Lichen saved his breath for combat. Latere struck. His sword glanced off Durandal as Lichen defended. Lichen jabbed Latere with his elbow. Latere yelled in pain. Lichen kicked and lashed Durandal onto Latere's shoulder. Blood spurted on both of them.

"Remember *that*?" Lichen said as he poised Durandal for the final blow.

Latere bellowed and thousands of tiny specs came from his throat in a red-fiery throng.

Latere pressed forward favoring his wounded shoulder. The stinking, stinging hive laid siege to Lichen, slicing, burning his skin, and driving him back into a fissure in the rock.

As Lichen's back touched the stone streams of glistening rope fastened around him binding his arms to his sides. He should have known Latere would have something up his putrid sleeve.

The mutant crimson hive receded into Latere as he drew close to Lichen's face. The stench of decomposing flesh made Lichen gag. Latere's eyes desiccated orbs, his teeth rotten spikes protruding from pus-inflamed gums. Latere flapped his wings sending patches of foul leathery skin flinging into the air.

"I have waited millennia for this moment. Of course, it is only possible because your little "charm" is here. Now, what shall I do with her? I'm sure I can think of something. Shall I give you a mental preview of the pleasures I plan to bestow upon your little healer?" Latere taunted.

He looked at Lichen with disgust, bound and struggling against the ropes. "The great long-awaited Warrior. What a joke."

Latere raised his sword over his head driving it toward Lichen.

Lorelei screamed, "No." She jumped in front of Lichen and Latere's blade sliced through her back. Lorelei touched the ropes; they disintegrated into dust. Lichen caught Lorelei in one arm and with the other raised Durandal. Lorelei slipped the Crystal dagger into Lichen's shirt.

"Lorelei," Latere screamed staring at her in horror. "Lorelei! Lorelei, no."

Lichen struck Durandal with full force toward Latere. When the sword reached him, there was nothing there. Latere dissolved into a gray gagging mist and disappeared. Lichen dropped Durandal and wrapped his arms around Lorelei.

"Lorelei," Lichen said. She had not taken her eyes off his face since the fatal blow. Lichen laid her gently on the floor. Her hair fell onto his shoes in a silent caress. A scarlet testament of love.

"Lorelei," Lichen said again. He cupped his hands around her face willing life into her.

"Oh yeah? Good. Then I know how to handle you," Isabella said. She noticed his clothing covered in blood, his skin charred and cut.

"Come on," Lichen said. "We need to get out of here."

Midgard deposited Lichen and Isabella on the shoreline and without a word, dove back into the murky depths of the Mother. The storm was over, the smoke-filled sky was dusting everything with volcanic ash.

Isabella gasped as the cold air hit her. It was too much. It was all too much. She collapsed into Lichen's arms trying to make sense of being in the River so long, not breathing, yet living.

And, of being in the coils of that, that, whatever it was. Isabella relaxed against Lichen's chest, listening to the thump thump of his heart, her arm around his neck, his breath soft on her cheek.

She felt herself sinking into oblivion, her mind jumping from one thing to another trying to think of everything before sleep overtook her. She wondered why Lichen's wounds were healed, if Latere was dead, and where was Lorelei?

Isabella thought of her mother...but she wasn't really her mother. Isabella was human. The pain of it was like a lodestone pulling her into despair. She wouldn't be attending Iter. She wouldn't be quickening. She must tell Lichen. As she sunk into nothingness, Isabella made a decision.

"Isabella," Sapien shouted. Lichen walked over, laid her inside the carriage and jumped in beside her. Isabella was limp with exhaustion.

"We're taking her to the Manor," Lichen said to Sapien, "it's much closer than Vinca Village." Sapien nodded, gave the driver instructions, and climbed into the carriage.

Much to Sapien's relief, Amicus took flight to watch over his master from the air. Q reined up beside the carriage.

"The Crystal?" he said. Lichen reached into his belt and pulled it out. Q looked visibly relieved.

"And Latere?"

Lichen shook his head, his lips compressed. "I'll meet you at the Manor," Q shouted, spurring Mars to action.

Chapter Fifty-Two

Discussions

The Manor hummed with voices. A beehive of curiosity. The villagers and all the Proscriptio Fey congregated in and around the house and the grounds. Citizens of Domus streamed over the bridge in droves, the Royal Guard keeping the peace. This crowd made BelMoon look like a small family gathering.

Fey and human alike sought information about what had happened, Raman was already creating his tales. Cecelia and the Manor staff outdid themselves with the help of an ancient charm or two. With the needs of food and drink now met everyone could turn their full attention to the unbelievable tale of Latere, Narro, and how close Domus had come to destruction. And, to Lichen and Isabella, the Warrior and the Charm.

Q and Lichen were in the library. "Latere just disappeared...again," Lichen said, pacing. "I can't believe it. I had that black devil in Durandal's path, then poof. Gone."

"Alveus spoke with all the GENS captains," Q said. "They think Latere couldn't have come through any of their watchways.

At least we have the Crystal." Q fingered the dagger. "And we know his power is broken because the storm is finished and Mt. Vetare has settled down. You did get in a mighty blow on his shoulder. Maybe he died and turned to mist as Lorelei did to water."

"No, I don't believe so," Lichen said. "He looked alive when he disappeared. I don't know how he got out, but he did. I wounded him pretty well, maybe he'll crawl off in a hole and finish rotting."

Lichen discovered he could speak with Q and still keep a mindful eye on Isabella.

Quite nice. This mental connection

She was still sleeping and Cecelia had given strict instructions that she should be left to her rest. Cecelia had run both Sapien and Lichen out of Isabella's room with a "be off wi' ye, now" that could not be disobeyed. Sapien went to send word to Coxi that their daughter was safe.

Torri, gently snoring out puffs of smoke, lay on the rug beside Q's desk. Amicus, his tail ticking back and forth like a pendulum, paced with Lichen. "So, you and Torri?" Lichen asked.

"Yes," Q answered. He stroked Torri's ears. Q had told Lichen the sorry story of Valeo's part in his abduction.

"Beetrum and Valeo plotted together to kidnap and take you to Weston," Q said. "I still can't believe their duplicity. The King has issued a Bans for Valeo and the Kilotax are going to QuinVerga to pick him up. And, since Valeo ignored my request to send Chimera home to me, the Bans include him and Manes.

"Certus needs to question both of them about Agaso's death. Chimera may have heard something while at QuinVerga. I don't know if he was a prisoner or not.

"We're not sure how well a Bans works on the conjured. It's never been done before. Valeo's actions have added to the incredulity of this entire situation. His part in the death of your mother and father is inconceivable."

"Yes," Lichen said. "I need to speak with you about...my father."

"I knew you would, Lichen," Q said. "I'd hoped your mother would tell you the truth. But that didn't work out."

"So, my father was...Fey?"

"Ye...yes," Q said.

I am Faerie.

Lichen let that soak in. He had come to that conclusion but was afraid to admit it. He wasn't sure how he would feel about it. But now. Now, that he knew it was true, he could feel a warm bubble of joy rising within him. Exultation.

"I thought...mother always made me believe... Well, let's just say," Lichen laughed, "I thought both my father and grandmother were from Missouri."

"Linum was a wonderful and talented man, Lichen," Q said. "His family served as cordages for generations. I thought his death was an accident. He was helping me build a bridge... Valeo burnt the ropes..." Q stammered. The heartache of that day was as painful now as then.

"Lichen, I wanted to tell you about your lineage, but your mother... She and I struck a bargain. She would remain on my estate in Weston, see to my business affairs, and... and name you Lichen. I would keep my silence until you turned 25. She would have that time to teach you, to show you how to live, well, how to live human.

"Then, after your 25th birthday, I could issue you an invitation to come to Domus. If you refused, I could not tell you of your heritage. However, if you accepted, then your mother was to tell you the truth."

Lichen had stopped pacing and sat in a chair facing Q's desk. The same chair he had sat in when Q asked him to remain in Domus. That seemed like a lifetime ago

"Why *Lichen*? I mean, why did you name me Lichen?"

"It came to me one morning when I was singing the Prima Lux," Q said. "Your mother had gone back to Weston; Cecelia told me she was with child...you. I had lost your grandmother, Linum, then Beetrum and finally you.

"I knew Beetrum was lost to me forever, but you... While I was singing, I felt this connection with you. I knew you would be a boy. I knew you would be important, not only to me, but to all of Domus.

"Each quad has a particular plant that is at home there. New Ivy is covered in ivy, Vinca Village in vinca. Lichen grows all over the Kingdom, even in the Wasteland. Lichen is at home in all of Domus. I hoped the same for you."

Lichen chuckled. "Yes, it's even in the Proscriptio." Q smiled and nodded his head. "So, how do you feel about it? About being...Fey?"

Lichen grinned. "It's odd, but now that I know, I think some part of me has always known. It feels...right." Q responded with a tight nod of his head. His eyes glistening.

"What will happen to Ira?" Lichen asked. "And Valeo? And, if Skye is Valeo's granddaughter, how is she part human?"

"Certus placed Ira under house arrest. His trial will be after Iter. Valeo's fate will be up to the King, and I expect it will be harsh. Valeo's wife, Bellus, was human. He met her when he visited me and your grandmother in Weston before he was Keeper. He was smitten from the first moment he laid eyes on her. But she was a lot like Beetrum;

she hated Domus and felt like QuinVerga was more of a prison than a home.

"Their son, Durus fell in love with Princess Phyta, but their Copulo was forbidden. Princess Phyta was betrothed to a prince in another kingdom of Fey whom she had never met. King Dens Colere forbade Durus to see Phyta and he disappeared shortly after.

“Then, Phyta discovered she was with child and the Copulo with the foreign prince was canceled. New Ivy’s orphanage was well known for its discretion, so everyone agreed, Valeo included, that the best course of action was adoption. Nidus and Ofella were childless, much like Ira and Nata, so, it was a perfect solution.”

“But, didn’t they know,” Lichen said, “didn’t you know, that when Skye was ready for quickening, the truth would come out?”

“King Colere and Iris had already taken care of that. Goddess Iris has complete control over Iter, so her decision is law. I don’t know exactly what would have happened, but Skye’s identity and the fact she has human blood would have been protected.

“Valeo’s fears of Skye’s human heritage being discovered at Iter were unfounded. The rule of no humans allowed was made many years ago when there was much animosity between the races.”

“Oh,” said Lichen raising his eyebrow, “and there’s not now?”

Q laughed, then grew serious. “Umm, one more thing,” he looked a little squirmish. “Syringa, your grandmother, was Valeo’s sister.”

Lichen’s head drew back, his mouth flew open. “*Uncle* Valeo?”

“Well, technically, great uncle,” Q quipped.

“My head is quite literally spinning,” Lichen said.

“Well, I wouldn’t lose any sleep over that,” Q answered with a chuckle. Then he continued in a more serious tone. “Lichen, you coming here has been..., well, it’s given me new life. However, it was the catalyst that set all this turmoil in motion. And even though you were the only one who could save Domus, there are some Fey who think if you had stayed in Advena, none of it would ever have happened. It could be dangerous for you here. If you want to return to Weston, I'll arrange it."

Lichen did not hesitate. "I gave you my answer before BelMoon. I have not changed my mind. Besides..." Lichen could feel Isabella stirring. "My heart and soul are here."

"Isabella?" Q said.

"Isabella," Lichen answered.

Chapter Fifty-Three

Manes

Valeo knew they would come. He didn't know when; they had blocked his mind probes. But he could feel the Bans. Tightening. They would see, one day when Skye was crowned they would understand; they'd change their minds then.

"Manes," Valeo commanded. At least his probe still worked at QuinVerga. "Manes," Valeo thought sending a shaft of pain with it.

"Yes, Keeper," Manes thought.

"Stop lazing about and ready the Rowan carriage. We're leaving."

"Yes, *sir,*" Manes said.

Valeo snatched his packed bag and started down the path for the stables. QuinVerga. He loved his home. He and Bellus could have been so happy here if it wasn't for Q and his continuous reminder of Advena.

If it weren't for New Ivy with all those *humans* Bellus wouldn't have been constantly reminded. She would have stayed and embraced Domus. She would have loved QuinVerga and ... him.

Valeo wasn't finished with Q or that grandson. Or that traitorous loudmouth vermin, Ira. Valeo would get them all. He didn't have much time. He could feel them getting closer.

"Manes," Valeo shouted. He stepped through the door. Manes stood beside the coach as if at attention. Frozen blue eyes staring straight ahead. "What have you been doing all morning you lifeless miasma? Are we ready to go?" Valeo said.

"Yes, Keeper. We are ready," Manes said. The black stallions stomped their monstrous hooves and blew with great puffs of breath. Straw rose from the floor in gusts of impatience. The horses flicked their tails and twitched their ears.

The horse closest to Manes threw back his head and screamed. A scream of the soulless.

"Easy boy," Manes said patting the horse's rump. Sparks leaped from one black demon to the next. Blazing.

"Get those animals under control," Valeo said as he tossed his satchel toward Manes. "I'll be right back. Stow my bag," he said.

Manes caught the bag and threw it onto the seat in one fluid motion. The driver's clothes moved with him like a second skin. Shimmering. Not a crease, not a wrinkle. Every hair in place. His face glacial. Frozen perfection.

Valeo went into the tack room and started rummaging around. He retrieved a small leather pouch, clutched it tightly, smiled, and walked back to the coach.

"Alright, we're off. Stop squandering our time; we nearly lost it for good, you know," Valeo said. He felt good; his spirits were rising.

Q would pay. Oh yes, he would pay. "Get these nags on the road," Valeo said, "before they burn down the stables." Valeo took hold of the side of the carriage and raised one leg onto the step. Manes stepped around behind him and shoved the blade up and under Valeo's ribs.

Valeo gasped falling back into Mane's arms. Valeo turned to look at the coachman and dropped the leather pouch. Manes moved his hand to catch it.

"Thank you, *sir,*" Manes said. He shoved Valeo away from him and looked with distaste at the blood on his hands and clothing. "The living are so messy."

Chapter Fifty-Four

Transformation

Isabella loved her room. MothersMa had helped her decorate it so many, many years ago. A lifetime ago. But even being here in this lovely apartment, this beautiful special space, could not displace the agony of her soul.

Isabella lay in her bed tears sliding down the sides of her face as she lay looking at the small lights twinkling softly from her ceiling. Yes, she was happy because of Lichen's love, but it was overshadowed by tears of sadness, grief, and revulsion for what Narro had stolen from her.

He had left a shadow within her; a vile abhorrence and disgust for who he was and all the evil he had done and planned to do. She could have forgiven his kidnapping and abuse of her, his masquerade as Latere and Acta Diurna, his stealing of the Liber Vitae and the falsification of her Totus Vita, and even the lying to her about being human. Although the archaic law of no humans allowed at the ceremony had mercifully been supplanted by Iris, so, her heritage wouldn't have mattered.

But he had murdered Lemna, her beloved teacher, friend, and confidant. Lemna, a kinder, gentler soul there never was, a healer, morally upright and wholesome. Lemna who would do anything for anyone ruthlessly, mercilessly murdered by that fiend and his gang of Pavors. Along with all the other dedicated selfless healers who were slaughtered by Narro's wicked men because of his depraved plan and malevolent heart.

Isabella wanted to forgive this cruel and malicious man. She knew it was required of her not only as a congregant, but she was about to become a Caduceus. A Caduceus was held to a higher standard. A Caduceus held no malice toward anyone regardless of their character and behavior. A Caduceus was not only a healer but was also loving and forgiving to all—deserving and undeserving.

Papilio lay across her chest purring the Arca Lux.

Exhaustion claimed her physically, mentally, and emotionally. Isabella had slept an entire day and night and still, she could not bring herself to get up. She knew the root of her fatigue. She knew the blackness that had enveloped her. The hatred she felt for Narro was overpowering anything worthy within her.

"Oh Papilio," Isabella said softly. She stroked his soft fur, turned on her side, and nestled her face in his goodness. So much had happened. Narro's assault was not only physical; he had harmed her in ways she couldn't define. He had stolen an essential part of her. He had violated her very center.

Papilio continued to purr as he looked into her eyes, seeing beyond the tangible, reaching into the very essence of Isabella. The core of her being. He saw her virtue and kindness. Her inability to hurt or make afraid. Her capacity for loving and healing. To have had Narro treat her so abominably, so disrespectfully was a crime against all that is righteous.

Papilio had loved Isabella from the first moment MothersMa had charged him with her companionship. His capacity for protection was limited, but the power of his love was not. Because that Love came from the source of all Love in this world.

Papilio's purr grew intense, louder, stronger penetrating Isabella's grief. The Arca Lux had never been so forceful. Isabella felt a stirring deep inside. Something was moving, penetrating, and enveloping the sadness and hatred that dominated her since Narro's kidnappings.

She could feel a Light beginning to glow within her, slowly spreading warmth in her heart, flowing through her body, her mind. The Light grew stronger, encompassing her completely now, filling her with love and joy. Never had she known such happiness, such acceptance. It not only eclipsed her grief and hatred, but it also illuminated and eliminated them. It was as if there was so much gladness within her there was no room for misery.

Isabella felt as if she were being embraced by the Divine. As if she was a beloved daughter, cherished and treasured; it was beyond her comprehension. A knowing came over her. She was transformed.

Isabella didn't understand why these terrible things had happened, but she didn't need to. She loved and trusted Divus, the holy Father, the Creator of all the worlds. The Creator had a plan and that was enough.

CHAPTER FIFTY-FIVE

Life Crystal

"Isabella," Lichen said. They sat together in the Spring room, entwined like the ivy swirling around them. He held her against him, his face nuzzling the top of her head. He loved the taste of her, the smell of her, the feel of her. He was afraid to let go.

"Yes?" she murmured.

"I love you," he said pulling her closer.

"Yes," she sighed.

"Are you ready to go?" Lichen said.

"Are you still coming with me?" she asked. Isabella wasn't sure she had the strength to walk into Iter alone. Since her episode of transformation, she was buoyant in spirit but weak in the flesh. In ridding her soul of the midnight starless black of evil she felt clean and purified, but as delicate and vulnerable as a newborn.

"Try to stop me," he said.

"Achhh," Cecelia poked her head around the door. "Excuse me, now. But ye'll need to get a-movin'. It's a big day for everyone. I've kept the wolves away as long as I can. Master Q's in a stir. 'e's gone ahead. 'e 'as responsibilities, ye know.

"Faber's waitin' to take you to Iter in our wee velle. It'll be a good while before another Rowan carriage can be made. They dinna grow on trees ye know." Cecelia cackled at her joke.

"We know," Lichen said. "We're ready to go." He grabbed Cecelia and gave her a bear hug. She let out a Cecelia whoop.

"Thank you, Cecelia. For everything."

"Achhh, my, now," she said. "My, my. Weell, tha's alrigh' now. Ye an' ye'r lady run along, now." Cecelia laughed as she dabbed a tear with the corner of her apron.

"Get on wi' ye, now. Dinna want to be late on this special day. It is'na every day we get a new caduceus.

"Sapien and Q will be nervous as scrimpets in a stew pot.

" Isabella, I'm sure ye know. Ye're to meet Skye in the Raindrop room to get dressed. Everyone is so 'appy Skye is able to attend. Ye're mother sent over ye're gown. Achhh, lassie, I canna' wait to see ye come down that aisle. Ye'll be pretty as the Iris herself."

"Thank you," Isabella said as she gave Cecelia a peck on the cheek, tears threatening.

Faber barely fit in the driver's seat of the velle coach. His large frame hung over each side. Stuffed olive. "Come on you lovedoves. Time's a slippin' away," Faber said.

"At least time still exists," he mumbled under his breath.

Lichen and Isabella climbed into the tiny carriage. They didn't mind the close proximity. Faber whistled and snapped his whip. Futura looked none too happy at being conscribed to the menial task of being harnessed to a carriage, but trotted on.

Lichen and Isabella were quiet during the ride to Crystal Grove. She laid her head on Lichen's shoulder. He held her tight. The lush beauty of the countryside clipped by. Unnoticed.

"Drop us off just on the other side of the bridge into Vinca Village," Lichen shouted.

Faber turned to look at him. "What? Just over the bridge?"

"Yes," Lichen answered. "We want to walk the rest of the way. Isabella needs to settle her nerves. You know women," he said winking at her.

"All right, but if you're late, my head will roll," Faber said. He pulled Futura into a small alcove.

"Thanks, Faber," Lichen said as he helped Isabella out of the velle. Faber shook his head, clicked his tongue, and drove away. Muttering.

"Here we go," Lichen said. "A new beginning. A new life. For both of us."

"Yes, here we go," Isabella answered. Lichen leaned down and touched his lips to hers. Ever so lightly. Then, eager, hungry for her taste.

Their whirlpool began slowly, accelerating, keeping pace with the intensity of the kiss. Lichen backed off, ran his tongue along her lower lip, and gave her one last peck. The swirling slowed and stopped.

"I hope I never get used to that," Lichen said. "I love it when you make me dizzy." Lichen put his arm around her and took a step. "Let's go."

Q paced. "And, you left them just inside the gate?"

"Yes," Faber said. For the hundredth time.

"Where are they?" Q worried. Isabella's quickening would be last since she is becoming a caduceus. *Since she is becoming the Solis.* Q couldn't be more proud if Isabella had been his own daughter.

The door flew open. "Are they here yet?" Sapien said. His expression anxious. A father's face.

"No," Q said. "No sign of them."

"Where are they?" Sapien said. "I can't believe the two most responsible people in Domus... the two who *saved* Domus...are late for Iter. Isabella's mother is frantic and Skye is in a snit even though she's happy to be here at all.

"Not that Isabella wasn't in good hands at your Manor, Q. It's just, well, it looks like she and Lichen have other things on their mind."

Q said nothing. Now both Q and Sapien paced.

Raman came up the pathway to the Raindrop room. Q spied him through the windows and went out to meet him. "Well?" Q said.

"They're here," Raman said. "They're here."

Relief settled over the room. Unspoken fear dissipated as the men put aside the thought that anything could have happened to them. Narro's whereabouts plagued them. Was he alive or dead?

Isabella entered Iris' chamber not knowing if she was afraid, sorrowful, or excited. Her emotions were running hot and cold, one moment she was up then the next she hit bottom. This was the day she had worked these many years for; she would become a caduceus. She only wished Lemna could be here with her.

Iris's room was spectacularly simple. It pulsed with unassuming elegance and glowed with Earth Mother's love. It was the most beautiful room Isabella had ever seen—all light and soft brightness. She had never been here before and glorious expectation gilded with fear sparked within her.

The room shone with that impossible quality of being both inside and outside. A beautiful gentle Spring bubbled from the earth just beyond the implied perimeter of the room. Softly adorned with ferns, ivy, and hundreds of blooms it gently gurgled up and out of the ground trickling through and under vines on its way to the Crystal Grove.

Busy hummingbirds, butterflies, and an assortment of bees busied themselves gathering nectar from tiny flowers of every pastel color on the palette. Colorful songbirds sang in accompaniment to the soft unobtrusive music that seemed to emanate from the very air as it infused Isabella with a divine sense of well-being.

Iris stood beside a small fireplace, the logs within glowing with more than heat. The rainbow hues that always accompanied Iris also radiated from the fire gathering tenderness and engulfing Isabella dissipating any remaining nervousness.

Iris held her hand out to Isabella smiling with such affection tears immediately sprang forth from both of them.

Isabella's lavender hues intensified as Iris led them to a white couch flanked by beautiful florae of every shade of green. The plants seemed to welcome her, to love her, to embrace her. They sat in tandem Iris holding Isabella's gaze.

"Welcome, my beautiful daughter," Iris said as she released Isabella's hand. "It is an honor to have you in my home. I have long awaited our meeting. First, you will receive your Life Crystal. Repeat after me, Isabella; Honor super omni."

Isabella's throat tightened restricting any verbal response. Tears threatened to overflow their containment.

"It's all right. Don't try to speak. No words are necessary between us. I know your heart is tender with emotion. Repeat it in your mind."

Isabella closed her eyes and repeated the oath. "Honor super omni".

Iris smiled as she slipped Isabella's Life Crystal around her neck.

Iris seemed to be made of light. Not the blinding brightness of the noonday sun, but a gentle yet intense luminosity emanating from her very soul. She was the essence of immortality aflame with love.

Isabella felt gentleness, kindness, and goodness swirling around and through her, bringing her into that world of Divus the Creator. She felt it settle into her heart, into her soul.

Isabella smoldered with Divine radiance. It held her in its unfathomable glory and she embraced it. The boundless Knowing once again settled upon her. She sensed the past, the present, and the future as one immense Whole. She had swirled into the ether with Lichen, but this....this was something unimaginable, inexplicable. This was Holy. Isabella had not only been quickened, she had been sanctified.

Knowledge flowed into Isabella's mind and she marveled at the boundless Love of the Creator. Everything sprang into being from His Heart, His Love. She wanted to stay here forever but she was already feeling the sensation of parting. She knew most of what she had experienced would not remain in her memory and she was loathe to part with it.

"Fear not, my daughter," the Creator said. "I am always with you." Then He departed.

Isabella sat beside Iris a new creature. Consecrated. She was no longer a young inexperienced, eager student. She was not even just a caduceus. She was going to be The Solis.

Chapter Fifty-Six

Solis

They stood and Iris motioned for Isabella to follow her outside to the Spring. As they approached The Spirit of the Spring reached out with familiarity and Isabella remembered.

She had met the Spring's sister in New Ivy at Q's manor. They were an intimate part of the Great River Potens and Isabella immediately felt a kinship, a connection.

Was this a gift of being the Solis?

"Isabella," Iris said as she released her hand and stepped in front of her. "You have just been given and accepted a great responsibility. And, to answer your question, yes, it is part of being the Solis to have a certain intimacy with the Great River Potens. The Earth Mother gives and sustains our life through the River.

"As the Solis, you must never take your responsibility to Domus and her citizens lightly. You are about to make your vows. Vows which if broken will bring condemnation upon your soul and prevent your eternal progression. Do you understand?"

Isabella had never understood anything more clearly. She felt humble yet powerful. Modest yet authoritative.

"Yes," she answered.

"Very well, we will begin."

Iris motioned toward the door and it silently and slowly opened.

First in were King and Queen Colere; they both nodded to her graciously and took their place in a small, chaired alcove in front of the Spring. They were followed by Isabella's parents, Sapien, proud, misty-eyed, and smiling like a loon with Coxi on his arm weeping softly but standing straight with love and admiration.

Skye walked in next and Isabella's heart rejoiced. Skye, her cousin, her friend, her confidant. Isabella felt so thankful that Skye was well enough to be here.

And, then there was Q...and Lichen. Q held her gaze understanding more than most the great responsibility that was about to be placed upon her.

Isabella looked into Lichen's eyes and was immediately lost in his love. They met for one short moment in that special spiritual place that was theirs alone.

"I love you, forever," he said.

"And I, you," she said.

Lichen took his place and Iris began.

"As you all know," Iris said looking at the small gathering, "Isabella has accepted the honor, the challenge, the responsibility of becoming the Solis of Domus. She has been given her Life Crystal, she has quickened and she is about to embark upon a journey few have ever taken."

Looking at Isabella she said, "You will take your vows, then you will lead the student procession into the Crystal Grove and place your Life

Crystal on your tree which is in the very center, the very heart of the Grove. It will call to you, so there is no doubt which tree it is."

"You will then lead the students in their own vow of becoming a Caduceus. After which they will follow you out of the Grove and into the Life Room where all of you will receive your Totus Vitas."

Isabella's confidence skipped a beat as the memory of her episode with Narro and what she had thought was her Totus Vitas shrouded her with uncertainty. The villain, the father of lies had deceived her into thinking she was human.

Iris caught Isabella's thought and interceded with assurance, bolstering her faith.

"Isabella," she said, "you are Fey. You are the Solis. Place your trust in Divus, our Creator, and in our Earth Mother to guide you."

Whether Narro was dead or alive Isabella knew this was the first of many times her faith would be tested. She felt the presence of the Creator with her and knew that Love would sustain her through the many trials to come.

Certainty and confidence surged throughout her body and mind. Her soul flamed with conviction that can only come with total surrender and obedience to the Creator.

Isabella looked at the small, assembled group who had come to support her. The King and Queen, her parents, dear, dear Skye, the Ambassador. And Lichen. She felt their love and trust in her. She thought of her fellow students who themselves would soon be Caducei. She thought of the citizens of Domus and the great accountability she felt toward them.

The Earth Mother moved within her, assuring, supporting, confirming. Isabella looked at Iris, smiled, and said, "I'm ready."

"This oath has been handed down for eons and taken by generations of caducei," Iris said as she held forth the Liber Vitae. A soft light gathered around Iris and Isabella as the room grew dimmer around the audience. Isabella put her left hand on the ancient cover, it was soft and warm to the touch as she held her right arm to the square.

"Repeat after me," Iris said. Looking Isabella directly in the eye Iris recited the Caduceus Oath in sections, Isabella echoing softly.

"I swear by Divus, the Creator and the Earth Mother to witness, that I will observe and keep this underwritten oath, to the utmost of my power and judgment.

I will reverence my mistress who taught me the art. Equally with my parents, will I allow her things necessary for her support, and will consider her family as my family. I will teach them my art without reward or agreement; and I will impart all my acquirement, instructions, and whatever I know, to my mistresses children, as to my own; and likewise to all my pupils, who shall bind and tie themselves by a professional oath, but to none else.

With regard to healing the sick, I will devise and order for them the best diet, according to my judgment and means; and I will take care that they suffer no hurt or damage.

Nor shall any man's entreaty prevail upon me to administer poison to anyone; neither will I counsel any man to do so. Moreover, I will give no medicine or procedure to any pregnant woman, with a view to destroying the child.

Further, I will comport myself and use my knowledge in a godly and honorable manner.

Whatsoever house I may enter, my visit shall be for the convenience and advantage of the patient, and I will willingly refrain from doing any injury or wrong from falsehood, and especially from acts of an amorous nature, whatever may be the rank of those who it may be my duty to cure, whether mistress or servant, bond or free.

Whatever, in the course of my practice, I may see or hear, whatever I may happen to obtain knowledge of, if it be not proper to repeat it, I will keep sacred and secret within my own breast.

If I faithfully observe this oath, may I thrive and prosper in my fortune and profession, and live in the estimation of posterity; or on breach thereof, may the reverse be my fate!"

Isabella removed her hand from the Liber Vitae, feeling in awe of the great responsibility she had just committed to.

"At this time," Iris said, "As the Princeps of Ecclesia and the Anima Consillium and also as Isabella's father I would like to invite Princeps Duco to join us for the Solis Oath."

Sapien took his place beside Isabella and this time she put her right hand over her heart and raised her left arm to the square.

"I, Isabella Fae Duco, do solemnly swear that I will administer justice and medicine within the Caducei community without respect to persons, and do equal right to the poor and to the rich, and that I will faithfully and impartially discharge and perform all the duties incumbent upon me as the Solis under the Liber Vitae of Domus and that I will support and defend the Liber Vitae of Domus against all enemies, regardless of specie, both foreign and domestic;

that I will bear true faith and allegiance to the same; that I take this obligation freely, without any mental reservation or purpose of evasion; and that I will well and faithfully discharge the duties of the office on which I am about to enter.

So help me Divus, the Creator and our Earth Mother."

Isabella lowered her hands but continued to gaze at Iris. She was astounded by how she and Iris could communicate during the oath-taking. An unexpected bonding took place. She could hear Iris in her mind; Iris could hear her.

And others were there in her mind. Lichen, of course. And her father.

Isabella turned to Sapien. "Tata," she said mentally. "You're here."

"Yes," he replied silently, smiling. "I have so much to share with you. Later."

Chapter Fifty-Seven

Iter

The air bristled with anticipation. Like the moment before the grand finale at a fireworks display. Like the second before hitting the sound barrier. Lichen felt as if he was born for this moment.

The four individual box seats were high above the crowds front and center in the Grove. The beloved King sat in his box with his Queen and their Princess in the center. In the box on the King's right hand and just below sat Princeps Sapien and his wife, Coxi; Q and Lichen sat in their box to the left. Centered directly below the King was an empty box seat, small but regal.

They could see and hear the entire grove which seemed impossible as the Sacred Grove was huge. But, Lichen had grown accustomed to the impossible. King Colere, Queen Constans, and Princess Phyta raised their right hands in unison to signal the procession to begin.

The sun was beginning to sink below the horizon. Faeries lined the processional route, families mostly. There were a few other interested species here, but mostly faeries. After all, it was a faerie celebration. Faerie graduation. Faerie renewal.

As dusk overtook the light the Crystals being worn by the faeries and the Crystals in the trees began to twinkle. Innumerable Crystals glowing and twinkling with soft color presented an indescribable scene. Commencement bling.

Q explained some of the proceedings to Lichen.

"The Grove grows in a spiral. There are two entrances; all the students completing Tertius and new Caducei will enter through the Grand Gate," he pointed to the tall archway adorned with greenery and flowers.

"The Grove was planted in an inward curving line around and around encompassing thousands of birch, rowan, ash, alder, willow—thirteen species of trees in the Domus calendar are represented—until it reaches the Mother Tree in the center. Each tree represents a moon span. Every faerie in Domus has their Life Crystal hanging on the tree that represents the moon span of their birth.

"The Crystals were presented to the students by Iris, Sapien, and the Anima Consillium in a private community ceremony yesterday, except, of course, Isabella who received hers today. As soon as each student had their Crystal placed around their neck it activated and began to glow and absorb the faeries' very essence and reflect the color of their faerie's personality; they develop a connection.

"Today, as they spiral inward toward the Mother Tree, they will each hang their crystal on their birth tree during the processional."

"How will they know which tree is theirs?" Lichen asked.

"Each faerie can hear their own tree calling to them," Q said.

"The Life Crystals," Q interrupted Lichen's thoughts, "were mined from Mt. Vetare by the GENS centuries ago. When the faeries were given their crystals they were charged by the Princeps to live the Primordial—Honor Super Omnia—Honor above all—the faeries recite it together. Simultaneously the Crystals are charged with a blast of indescribably beautiful and powerful light by Iris. This quickens the faeries and from that moment they are bound by the Primordial."

"And, what if they don't live it, are they banished as the GENS were?" Lichen asked.

"Oh, it takes a serious breach of the Primordial for banishment. Most usually end up losing personal freedoms and then have to live under a myriad of laws. Some remain true to their covenant, especially the Caducei," Q answered.

"When they reach the Mother Tree the Caducei will be in front of all the students and Isabella having already said her vows, will administer the Caduceus oath to them. After the oathtaking, the new Caducei along with the other students and all their mothers will gather in the Life Room to receive their Totus Vitas."

Lichen knew Isabella was a little anxious. Having undergone the ordeal of believing the lies Narro had put forth in her false Totus Vita about her being human in addition to her added responsibilities as the new Solis.

He was so proud of her. So in love with her. He wondered if he dare approach her mind. He decided to leave her to her duties.

"Lichen," Q said, "there's a matter I should discuss with you."

"Oh?" Lichen responded.

"Yes. Well, you see my boy, um, you know your grandmother, Syringa, was faerie?"

"Yes," Lichen said not venturing to say more.

"Well, since you are... since you have ... uh, well, you are the Warrior and all. And being of Fey blood..."

"Grandfather, I have come to terms with being Fey. So, out with it."

"It's just that, well, there is a Life Crystal available to you. You can take part in the processional if you'd like. It's your right."

Lichen stared at Q. Of course. Of course! He was Fey. He had a personal Crystal.

"No," Lichen said. "This is Isabella's day. And, I haven't told her yet...about my heritage."

"As you wish, my boy. As you wish."

Isabella had already placed her Crystal upon her tree; it was directly beside the Mother Tree. Other Crystals already suspended from the branches vibrated with life; one, in particular, spoke to her heart. Her gaze was captured and held and within the faceted depths, Isabella caught a fleeting image: Lemna.

Lemna.

Isabella's heart leaped and then the image was gone leaving an embrace of warmth and love. As Isabella administered the Caduceus Oath to the students, she felt Lemna strengthening, encouraging, and uplifting them. And was there something else? Was Lemna warning her?

After the Crystal ceremony, Isabella saw Lichen making his way to the portal of the Life Room. They had planned to meet here and grab a bite to eat at one of the concessions before the Totus Vita presentation. Lichen would not be allowed in, only students and their mothers.

"Lichen," Isabella said as he approached her. She looked regal in her stunning gown and Solis cape; goddess-like.

"I'm so sorry, but I couldn't eat a bite. I'm afraid emotion has squelched my appetite," she said.

Lichen smiled knowingly. "Of course it has. I did not expect otherwise."

He took hold of her hand, turned it over, and planted a quick kiss on the palm.

"I just wanted to tell you...well..." He felt foolish. She was now the Solis, a Caduceus, a prominent leader of Domus. He felt every bit an outsider.

He wanted to tell her she would be fine; she would love her Totus. The past was past and now come what may they could face the future together. He wanted to assure her of his love, that he would never leave her, and would support her sacred calling, but the words would not come. Warrior dithering.

Isabella smiled a most queenly smile. Lichen's hands had enclosed her own.

"Thank you," she said. "And you are not an outsider. You are the Warrior. You are Fey. And you are mine."

Lichen's startled look dissipated as quickly as it came. They had no secrets now. Isabella turned and entered the Life Room.

Coxi sat in the alcove appointed them. It was cozy, with only a small table, two chairs, and very feminine. Soft colors of pearls and pinks adorned the walls and upholstery, with florals painted ever so lightly on the furniture making one wonder if they were really there.

Isabella entered the room.

Mother. Tenderness and affection flowed between them unspoken.

In the center of the room on a simple yet stunning table lay a book, an exquisite book hand-bound with perfect stitches and beautiful soft ivory leather. One word adorned the cover in elegant script: Isabella.

The Totus Vita began to glow, and a gentle, muted melody landed upon Isabella's soul. It enveloped her, claimed her.

Yes. Yes, THIS is my Totus Vita.

Supra sat alone in her room. She had been afforded privacy and was grateful for she could not stop the tears. At first, they came in slow tiny streams runneling down the furrows of her face. She laid her ugly face in her ugly hands and let it out.

All the centuries of misery and regret. The hatred, the bile, and the vile. The bitterness that had held her prisoner, far more than the Proscriptio ever had, gushed forth as if the dam of hell had burst. Torrential repentance.

Minutes ticked by; Supra could almost hear them clicking in the great Tempus Crystal. At last, she raised her head, cleaned her face, and stood. She felt cleansed of the vitriol, the debilitating rage that had consumed her. A brightness slowly spread throughout her body bringing peace. She had forgotten what that was like. She felt the love and forgiveness of Divus, the Creator, and the Earth Mother. She was ready.

Iris was positioned on a podium near the Dark Gate. In front of her stood the trees laden with Life Crystals that radiated despair. In this section of the Grove, hopelessness circulated in waves throughout the many trees that held the Crystals of the GENS. At one time these trees had glowed with the bright goodness of the heavens, but since the banishment, they reflected the evil emptiness of their faeries' souls.

The Crystals of the original four GENS brothers along with the generations who had not fallen were glowing in a tree directly beside Iris. The banished GENS stood waiting, gathered outside the gate; Supra stood at the lead.

"Welcome," Iris said. Her soft voice magically carried throughout the Sacred Grove. The new Caducei were all seated in their own section except for Isabella. She sat in the box seat reserved for the Solis; her seat directly below the King's box and between the Princep's and the Ambassador's boxes. Lichen sat proudly beside Q glancing sideways at Isabella.

Isabella only had to reach out to touch Lichen's hand but she did not; she was content.

"Lichen?" she queried in her mind.

"Yes," he answered.

Isabella smiled at him. Lichen grinned back. They loved this secret communication; this bond that went beyond.

Iris continued, "Septmillia has arrived. The Vocatio has been issued. The GENS have answered. The Great Banishment is over. You have paid the uttermost farthing and it is as if you had never transgressed. Divus and the Earth Mother accept you back into the fold. We receive you."

The crowd stirred. A soft wave of uneasy rustling swept across the stadium. Apparently, the GENS were not accepted by all.

"You will proceed to your trees, remove your Crystals, and wait for the Primordial Oath to be administered which you will repeat in unison," Iris said.

The entire section at the Dark Gate was black and void of any light. Tangible darkness surrounded the GENS, more than the absence of light it was the absence of joy and goodness.

Supra squared her shoulders and went first through the Dark Gate. Her tribe of SAX followed and Lichen was glad to see Ventas and his wife, Fuligo. He had a feeling he and Ventas would be great friends. He wished Dilingo could have been here. Alveus led in the TOR, and then the GEL and ARI entered.

Each GENS found their tree, gently removed their Crystal, and placed it around their neck. For Supra, tears did not come; she had none left.

Iris's voice triumphantly rang the Primordial throughout the arena as though a great battle had been won. "Honor super omnia."

The GENS shouted as one, their voices thundering, reverberating in a great proclamation.

"HONOR SUPER OMNIA."

Buoyancy wanted to lift Supra off her feet. She felt weightless and her body tingled, effervescence bubbled up from her soul bringing light and color and joy. Her ashen dead skin began to blush with new life: fair, dewy, and luminescent. Her hair transformed from thin mud gray, into a deep, ebony mass of shiny, thick, and luxurious mane. A single strip of elegant silver started just above one eyebrow and flowed through her hair like a river clear and sparkling in the sun through the depth of blackness.

Supra's clothing morphed from colorless rags to a luminescent, flowing weightless gown as if it was made from the very air sur-

Lichen looked up at the sky and thought about Domus. About his mother, the Tempus Crystal, the Grove. About Isabella, the Charm, the Solis, and the Oaths she had taken. What a wonderful thing to teach the people. Honor. Fidelity. He thought of his Air Force Oath of Office. All this oathtaking put him in a very patriotic and poignant mood. Devotion to God, your fellow man, your country.

Lichen felt that devotion and loyalty toward Domus. Toward all the beings he had met here, even those filthy trolls and the Rock Fairies. He supposed he would need to stop calling them that and use their rightful name; the GENS. He was beginning to understand Q's decision to make his life among these people.

Lichen looked down at Isabella. Never had he ever imagined there could be such a woman. She was agonizingly beautiful and smart, deeply compassionate, considerate, and loving. She embodied the essence of virtue, reached out to the sick and afflicted, and was clothed and wrapped in strength and honor. His arms tenderly encircled her as if she was the most precious thing upon the earth; his lips met hers softly offering her all he was and all he had. His silent proposal was received with perfect understanding.

Immediately their minds were one; melted and gently fused together as if by the breath of God. They were whisked up into the heavens, their love swirling them among the stars. They knew only the ultimate affectionate ardor that bonded their souls together.

Lichen longed to be sealed to Isabella for eternity.

THE END

Chapter Fifty-Nine

Epilogue

Anger sliced him like a blade slashing his body over and over. He screamed contempt until his breath gave out. Then he shrieked louder. Hysterical howls burdened with loathing and hatred swirled around him until at last rage gave way to despair.

He lay curled as a fetus, whimpering. Spasms of grief scored his breathing with great slobbering hiccoughs. One decaying element at a time, self-pity sauntered through his emaciated body, both scavenger and predator. Feeding on every grievous laceration, preying on every wretched pain. No mercy.

How had he come to this?

When at last he succumbed to sleep, he dreamed.

Oh, to fly. To soar high above Domus. His Domus. His people. Beautiful wings gliding gracefully through the air reflecting the best of the sun. His hair blowing in the wind. His laugh echoing off the hills, curving around the valleys.

Up, up he would soar and the people would marvel at his splendor. The sacred Song of the West would cascade from his lips. A blessing. His people would love him. He would rebuild the kingdom to perfection. The people of Domus would be in awe of his beauty, his intellect. He was their liberator.

He only needed to wait a while.

A small while and he would be free of this crimson prison.

Chapter Sixty

Lexicon

with Latin Etymology

Acid Bog: A wet area with a binding mud-like substance that burns the flesh and sucks out life and light causing despair and depression. The largest one in Domus is in the Wasteland.

Acta Diurna: Sapiens scribe was handpicked by him after arriving at Vinca Village to take his place as Princeps. *Acta diurna: records of public procedure*

Advena: The Faeries' name for where humans live. *Advena: stranger, foreigner.*

Adoleo: The second dance in a BelMoon celebration. A large bonfire is built for the ritual dance of thankfulness and fertility. *Adoleo: to magnify, to offer oneself as a sacrifice in a loving relationship that insures good crops, animals, and fertility.*

Aes: A small gray pebble found in the Proscriptio used for money. *Aes: ore; coined money, usually copper or bronze.*

Agaso: Q's manservant. Came to Q at the same time as Cecelia. *Agaso: groom.*

Alveus: Leader of the TOR. Somewhat of a risk-taker. *Alveus: gambling table gambler.*

Amicus: One of four drogs (small dragons). Black male. Bonded to Lichen. Amicus, Torri, Tosti, and Carmen. *Amicus: friend.*

Animus Consillium: The spiritual council of Domus. Gives advice and counsel to the congregants of Ecclesia. The Princeps is the president of the Consillium and leader of the Ecclesia. *Animus: soul, mind, heart, purpose, feeling. Consillium: select council.* (Do not confuse the Latin animus with modern animus which means enmity, hostile attitude, and animosity.)

Arca Lux: A protective light generated by Papilio's purr. *Arca: box, chest. Lux: light.*

Arx: Lichen's guard in the Proscriptio. *Arx: stronghold.*

Aridus: ARI GENS. One of four brothers who founded the GENS Quad. Learned the sacred Song of the South from the wildfire in the air and the earth. Descendants were banished to the Proscriptio for breaking the Primordial. Flaxen hair; chestnut eyes; bronze gold wings. The four GENS brothers are Saxitilus, SAX; Torrens, TOR; Gelu, GEL and Aridus, ARI. *Aridus: dry.*

Bans: A writ issued by the Kilotax for arrest purposes. A Bans will locate the person within Domus but cannot detect them once they leave. A Bansbag prevents detection when a person is placed inside. Once the person leaves Domus, the Bans will prevent re-entry.

Bartus: Concierge at the Receptus Club, New Ivy Village's premier hotel and restaurant.

Bellus Nox: Keeper Valeo Nox's wife. *Bellus: colloq. Pretty, charming*

Beetrum: Lichen's mother; Q's daughter; Linum's wife.

BelMoon: A spring celebration to give thanks for last year's abundance. Also petitions for next year's fertility of crops, stock, and children. It is rare but occasionally couples are "paired" by the Earth Mother during the dance.

BelPole: A large pole made from a fir tree, decorated with flowers and ribbons. Used for the annual dance at BelMoon.

Bifrost: Norse mythology: a burning rainbow bridge. Pronounced roughly "BIF-roast".

Brent: Lichen's best friend from childhood.

Caduceus: A healer who has taken the Caduceus Oath. Plural: Caducei. *Caduceus: an ancient, winged staff with two serpents coiled about it.*

Caduceus Oath: The oath given to the newly graduated on becoming a Caduceus. Modeled after the original Hippocratic oath traditionally believed to have been written by Hippocrates, the father of medicine. A new Hippocratic oath was rewritten in 1964 by Dr. Louis Lasagna to accommodate the modern view of abortion and euthanasia.

Caelm "Skye" Pudor: Nidus & Ofella Pudor's adopted daughter. Isabella Fae's cousin. *Caelm: Sky.*

Carmen: One of four drogs (small dragons). Blue/green/yellow female drog. Amicus, Torri, Tosti, and Carmen. *Carmen: a charm, a magic formula.*

Cecelia: Q's ManorMother. A term Q coined to describe Cecelia's relationship with not only him, but his home. Came to Q at the same time as Agaso. She took charge of everything in the day-to-day running of the Manor.

Certus: Kilotax (sheriff) of New Ivy. Has been elected to several thousand-day terms. *Certus: sure, to be depended on, trustworthy, definite*

Chimera: One of the four conjured coachmen who can drive Rowan carriages through the portal (bridge) between Domus and Advena, the human world. Chimera is assigned to Q, Lemures is unassigned, Lares, is assigned to King Dens Colere, and Manes is assigned to Keeper Valeo Nox. *Chimera: something impossible or fanciful.*

Conjured coachmen: Four beings brought into existence by King Dens Colere and Q. Can drive Rowan carriages through the portal (bridge)between Domus and Advena, the human world. Chimera, Lemures, Lares, Manes.

Constans: King Dens Colere's Queen. Mother to Phyta. *Constans: consistent*

Consistere: A sacred song (prayer) sung to prevent passage. *Consistere: to halt.*

Copia: A sacred song (prayer) sung for abundance and success. *Copia: abundance.*

Copulo: The ceremony of joining; marriage. Can be performed by Q, the Princeps, or the King. *Copulo: to join together, connect.*

Coxi Duco: Isabella Fae's mother; Sapien's wife. Nata's & Nidus' sister. *Coxi: to cook*

Criocts: The eight civil authorities with judicial, administrative & enforcement powers elected to govern a village; the Kilotax is the head of the Criocts. They are elected for two years. Every year, four Faeries are elected for two years. The term limit is three 2-year terms. *Cri: judge octs: eight.*

Crystal Grove: The Crystal Grove is a copse of thirteen kinds of trees each representing the Luna cycles (months). Faeries hang their Life Crystals in the trees at Tertius (graduation). The Crystal Grove is part of a larger stadium where various celebrations, including Iter, occur.

Cura: An herbalist. *Cura: care taken, pains, attention.*

Darks: The fourth island in New Ivy Quad mostly inhabited by the derelict, dregs, and dilapidated in Domus society.

Delingo: A captive of the SAX Rock Faeries. *Delingo: to lick.*

Dens Colere: High King of Domus. Married to Constans. Father to Phyta. *Dens: fang. Colere: honor.*

Dexter Nox: Second son of Keeper Valeo Nox, younger brother of Durus. *Dexter: clever, on the right side, lucky, skillful.*

Diaboli Jugulum: A beautiful yet treacherous rock formation where The Fey left their unwanted babies—usually handicapped. *Diaboli: devil Jugulum: throat.*

Divus: The Creator of all. *Divus: God, Deity, Spirit.*

Domus: An ancient magical kingdom of Fey. *Domus: home*

Drog: Small dog-sized dragons; born and bred by Q at the Manor. Amicus: Black male, Torri: Red/orange/yellow female, Tosti: Rust/brown/yellow male, Carmen: blue/green/yellow female.

Dulci: A term of endearment. *Dulcis: sweetheart, friendly, dear, beloved.*

Durandal: A sword which was given to Lichen by Wieland, the water dwarf. Mythology: A legendary sword of Charlemagne's paladin Roland. Also once belonged to Hector of Troy. Folklore claims Durandal is preserved in Rocamadour, France, and is the sharpest sword in existence. It is also said to contain a tooth of St. Peter, blood of Basil of Caesarea, hair of St. Denis, and a scrap of cloth from the garment of Mary, Mother of Jesus in its hilt.

Durus Nox: First son of Valeo and Bellus Nox and in line to be the next Keeper. Sometimes referred to as Keeper II. *Durus: hard, cruel, relentless, difficult. Nox: night.*

Earth Mother: The Spirit of the Earth and the Elements. Power is granted to her by Divus, the Creator. Manifests as all the elements:

earth, air, fire, water, but is the essence of the Great River Potens. Is often simply called the Mother.

Ebri: A powdered anesthetic herb mixed into various mediums to deaden pain. Can be intoxicating when used in excess. *Ebrius: drunk.*

Ecclesia: The religious organization of Domus. Denotes the congregants and also the structures of worship. *Ecclesia: church.*

Equi: Horses conjured by King Colere and Q that pull the Rowan carriages. They are in the care of the conjured coachmen. *Equus: horse.*

Extremus Venatio: The last hunt of the season that is accompanied by much revelry. *Extremus: last in a series. Venatio: hunt.*

Faber: New Ivy's blacksmith. *Faber: blacksmith.*

Fenrir: A giant wolf who roams the Forbidden Forest. Midgard's brother. Norse Mythology: a mighty wolf that will one day destroy the world and is brother to the monstrous serpent Midgardsormr.

Fey: All non-human species in Domus usually with magical powers; otherworldly creatures.

Finis: The End. *Finis: end.*

Fuligo: A woman in SAX camp; Ventas sweetheart. *Fuligo: soot.*

Futura: Q's mare and mother of his equine line. *Futura: the future.*

Gehenna: An infernal pit into which the wicked are cast. A common swearword in Domus. *Gehenna: hell.*

Gelu: GEL GENS. One of four brothers who founded the GENS Quad. Learned the sacred Song of the East from the frigid air currents high above Domus. Descendants were banished to the Proscriptio for breaking the Primordial. White hair, white-blue eyes, blinding white wings. Saxitilus, SAX; Torrens, TOR; Gelu, GEL; Aridus, ARI. *Gelu: ice.*

GENS: Oldest quad in Domus. Established by the four GENS brothers: Saxitilus, Gelu, Aridus, and Torrens. *Gens: a clan; a member of a family connected by common descent and name.*

Geranne: Housekeeper/cook at the inn in Trumpet across the bridge from Vinca Village.

Glipneir: Q's magical rope of remarkable strength that can bind anything. Norse Mythology: light, soft, and exceptionally strong fetters made from roots of a mountain, the sound of a cat, beard of a woman, breath of a fish, sinews of a bear, and spittle of a bird; used to bind Fenrir.

Gravis: Keeper Valeo Nox's winged warhorse. *Gravis: burdensome, oppressive.*

Great River Potens: Representative of the Earth Mother. Flows throughout Domus to not only provide water but also life. Forms new quads. Individual places are gifted with a spring and a Spirit of the Spring which provides a touchstone with the Mother and such gifts as healing. *Potens: powerful*

Gwillion/Gwithin: Wales Mythology: Gwillion is a Gwithin, a Faerie tribe that hates humans. Gwithins live in the Hills of Caprinus and raise goats. They wear a pot on their heads and carry a comb with them at all times to untangle their goats' beards. They only brush the beards on Wednesday, their Sabbath. The Earth Mother took away their ability to fly, so they do not have wings. They are terrified of storms and steel. Their language is only heard by others as "wwwwb".

Hell-Hounds: Three Ghost hounds belonging to Latere: Mors, Letum, and Obitus. *Mors: death, corpse. Letum: death, ruin, annihilation. Obitus: death, downfall, destruction.*

Holly: Lichen's ex-girlfriend in Weston and is engaged to Brent.

Horologe Vesper: A sacred Song of Sunset to bless the night. *Horologe: time-piece. Vesper: evening/evensong.*

Hycintholuna: A blue moon—the second full moon in a month when Iter is celebrated. See moon cycles. *Hycintho: blue*

Ian: Ancient troll gatekeeper at Numen, the estate of the Princeps in Vinca Village. He was awarded this lifelong assignment for outstanding loyalty by disregarding natural troll inclinations and risking his life for the Princeps & his family. *Ianitor: porter, doorkeeper.*

Inferna: A common swearword in Domus. *Inferna: Underworld, hell.*

Iris: Goddess of the Rainbow works under the authority of Divus, The Creator. Iris' principal duty is overseeing Crystal Grove and administrating Iter. She transcribes each Faerie's Totus Vita from Divus and presents it to the Faeries during Iter. She also gives each Faerie their Life Crystal. Iris receives various directives for the Faeries from Divus such as the Vocatio which pardoned the Banished.

Iratis "Ira" Lungwort: Kilotax (sheriff) of Vinca Village. Nata's husband. Isabella's uncle. Trader throughout Domus. *Iratis: angry, irate, enraged, wrathful, hot.*

Isabella Fae Duco: Sapien & Coxi Duco's daughter. Renowned herbalist/caduceus. *Issa: Small Croatian island in the Adriatic Sea.*

Iter: An annual sacred celebration during Hycintholuna. Takes place in the Crystal Grove in Vinca Village. Presided over by Iris and Princeps Sapien Duco. Student Faeries graduation where they are quickened, presented with their Life Crystals and their Totus Vitas. A new Solis may be chosen. If a Vocatio has been issued, banished Fey will be allowed to come home from Banishment in the Proscriptio. *Iter: a journey, path, course.*

Kallowa: Home of Wieland, the water dwarf.

Keeper: Overseer of the King's Preserves. The King's Keeper yields considerable power in Domus and is appointed by the King for life. Usually, a son succeeds a father.

Keeper I: Valeo Nox, the current Keeper who resides at the Quin Verga estate. One of three men (The King, The Keeper & Q) who know the location of the Bridge to Advena, the human world.

Keeper II: Durus Nox, first son of Valeo Nox and in line to be the next Keeper. Sometimes referred to as Keeper II. *Durus: hard, cruel, relentless. Nox: night.*

Kilotax: Has judicial, administrative, and enforcement power and is head of the Criocts. A type of sheriff. Elected for a thousand days—no term limit. Ira Lungwort is Kilotax of Vinca Village. Certus is Kilotax of New Ivy. *Kilo: thousand. Tax: to arrange or put in order.*

King: High King Dens Colere of Domus and one of three men (The King, The Keeper & Q) who know the location of the Bridge to Advena, the human world. Married to Constans. Father to Phyta. *Dens: fang. Colere: honor.*

Lake Lacertilia: A lake surrounded by swamps in a remote section of New Ivy inhabited by hundreds of species of lizards and other unique animals. Lizard: Order Squamata, suborder Lacertilia. Lacerta: A favorite meat dish. *Lacerta: lizard, sea-fish.*

Lares: One of the four conjured coachmen who can drive Rowan carriages through the portal between Domus and Advena, the human world: . Chimera is assigned to Q is Lemures, unassigned. Lares is assigned to King Dens Colere, and Manes is assigned to Keeper Valeo Nox. *Lares: household familiar spirit.*

Latere: Mastermind of villainy. Descendant of Saxitilius GENS and member of the SAX tribe. *Latere: hidden.*

Leaena: A large feline-like animal grown from seed. *Leaena: lioness.*

Lemna: Vinca Village caduceus and Isabella's personal teacher. *Lemna: wood.*

Lemures: One of the four conjured coachmen who can drive Rowan carriages through the portal between Domus and Advena, the human world. Chimera is assigned to Q, Lemures is unassigned. Lares is assigned to King Dens Colere, and Manes is assigned to Keeper Valeo Nox. *Lemures: ghosts, spectres*

Lex Scriptura: Words and revelations of Divus, the Creator, and the laws of Domus. Contains the Primordial. Is included in the Liber Vitae. *Lex: law Scriptura: scripture.*

Liber Vitae: A sacred book containing the Lex Scriptura. It contains complete explanations and unabridged detailed accounts and instructions of Domus's creation and history and the workings of the Tempus Crystal. The book is kept and guarded in the Crystal Grove as its possession gives one extraordinary knowledge of and power over Domus. *Liber: book. Vitae: life.*

Lichen "Kenny" Ipse: Q's grandson. Beetrum and Linum's son. *Lichen: a symbiotic plant . Ipse: to stand alone.*

Life Crystal: Faeries are given their personal life crystal for Tertius (graduation) which happens at Iter. The crystals were mined from Mt. Vetare by the SAX GENS. Each crystal hangs on the Faerie's moon cycle tree. Iris, the Princeps, and the other members of the Animus Consillium hand out the crystals to each student faerie.

Linum Ipse: Beetrum's husband. Lichen's father. Cordage to the King. *Linum: a flax plant with wispy little stems & small leaves. It wilts by noon but is rejuvenated by the next morning. Linen, thread, line. Ipse: to stand alone.*

Lorelei Unda: A captive of the Rock Faeries; an undine; a female water spirit who can acquire a soul by marrying and having a child by a mortal. *Unda: water in motion, wave, ripple.*

LunaMoon: Months. See moon cycles.

Manes: One of the four conjured coachmen who can drive Rowan carriages through the portal (bridge) between Domus and Advena, the human world. Chimera is assigned to Q, Lemures is unassigned, Lares, is assigned to King Dens Colere, and Manes is assigned to Keeper Valeo Nox. *Manes: shades of departed spirits.*

Manor Estate: The first island in New Ivy Quad where Q resides.

ManorMother: Cecelia, chief cook and bottle washer of Q's Manor.

Mars: Q's stallion, pride of the Manor. *Mars: god of war.*

Mentum: Overseer of Spies, New Ivy's orphanage. *Mentum: chin.*

Midgard: Sea Serpent lives in the Great River Potens. Brother to Fenrir the Wolf. Norse Mythology: Midgardsormr lives in the primeval ocean surrounding the world.

Miseret tea: An herbal tea that renders one repentant. It also sobers the drunken. *Miseret: to be sorry.*

Molten: Secondary stallion in Q's stable; Linum's steed.

Moon cycles—Months of the year: Coldluna, Quickeningluna, Stormluna, Windluna, Floraluna, Hyacintholuna, StrongSunluna, Blessingluna, Cornluna, Harvestluna, Bloodluna, Morningluna, LongNightluna.

Narro: A descendant of TOR GENS and responsible for the entire GENS Quad being banished to the Proscriptio. *Narro: to tell, to make known.*

Natator "Nata" Pudor Lungwort: Ira's wife; Coxi, Nidas, and Nada's sister. *Natator: swimmer.*

New Ivy: New Ivy is a Quad in Domus and was founded by Q. The main island in the Quad is the Manor Estate. The second island, the Village, is mostly inhabited by humans. The third island, the Preserves, belongs to the King and is overseen by the Keeper. The fourth and last island is the Darks.

Nidus Pudor: Ofella's husband; Coxi & Sapien's brother-in-law; Skye's father; Isabella Fae's uncle; counselor to Sapien in the Animus Consillium. *Nidus: nest. Pudor: honor.*

Numen: The estate of the Princeps is located in Vinca Village. *Numen: divinity.*

Ofella Pudor: Nidus' wife; Coxi & Nata's sister-in-law; Skye's mother; Isabella Fae's aunt. *Ofella: a bit or morsel. Pudor: modesty, chastity, decency.*

Ogham: Ancient sacred alphabet of Domus. Each of the 20-25 letters represents a symbol, a tree, and a moon cycle (month). Ogham: an alphabetic system of 5th and 6th century Irish.

Pallium: Cloaks worn by the Rock Faeries. *Pallium: cloak.*

Palus: A pixie in the orphanage Spes. *Palus: bog.*

Papilio: Isabella's companion who looks, acts, and sounds like a cat with 8 caterpillar-like legs. Purring produces the Arca Lux. *Papilio: butterfly.*

Par para revere: *To return like for like; to be indebted to another.*

Pavors: A group dedicated to the eradication of all caducei and curas. *Pavor: horror; a trembling produced by fear.*

Phytabula: A personal herbal journal detailing plant properties. Phyta: the division group of plant classification. *Tabula: tablet.*

Portent: An ancient prophesy that foretells a Destroyer who wants to control Domus, a Warrior who must find his Soul before he can stop the Destroyer and A Charm that is needed for protection.

Postestas: Warrants issued by the Criocts.

Preserve: Each Quad has a King's Preserve which is a protected area for the preservation of flora and fauna—the sum of all living wildlife. The King's Keeper oversees each Preserve.

Prima lux: The sacred Song of Morning sung just before the sun rises. It is both a welcome and a blessing for the new day. Every quad has a designated singer. For New Ivy: Ambassador Quindaro B. LeVard. For Vinca Village: Princeps Sapien Duco For Regnum: Queen Constans. *Prima lux: the first light of day.*

Primordial: *Honor super omni: honor above all.* This First tenet of Domus law is included in the Lex Scriptura. Essential to Fey society the breaking of which will lead to Banishment.

Princeps: Spiritual head of the Ecclesia, administrative and executive head of the Domus Animus Consillium, and guardian of the Crystal Grove; Sapien Duco is the current Princeps. Second only to the King in power. Husband to Coxi Pudor. Father to Isabella Fae Duco. *Princeps: first, foremost.*

Princess Phyta Colere: King Dens Colere and Queen Constans daughter. *Phyte: a plant that grows in a specific place or way.*

Proscriptio: Section of Domus designated as an exile for Fey. The four tribes of GENS were banished there by the Earth Mother for breaking the Primordial Law. *Proscriptio: outlawry.*

Quad: Four city-islands are located in close proximity and enclosed by the Great River Potens. There is always a main Village island and a Preserve island and two other city-islands depending on the demands of the Quad. The primary bridge from Domus main-land leads onto the Village island with smaller bridges leading from the Village to the other three islands. The exception is Q's New Ivy Quad which has the Domus main-land bridge going to the Manor Estate island. Individual quads are set up differently, depending on the founder. An island Preserve is in all the Quads, belongs to the King, and is maintained by the King's Keeper. The first Quad was established by the GENS brothers: Saxitilus, Gelu, Torrens, and Aridus. Regnum Quad is the Kings; New Ivy Quad is Q's and Vinca Village Quad is Princeps. The GENS Quad disintegrated at the banishment and is part of the Wasteland.

Quindaro B. LeVard"Q": Ambassador to Domus. Founder of New Ivy Quad. Lichen's grandfather. Beetrum's father. One of three men (The King, The Keeper & Q) who know the location of the Bridge to Advena, the human world.

Quin Verga: The Estate of Keeper Valeo Nox is located in the Regnum Quad on the Preserve island.

Raman: Bard of Domus residing in The Village, New Ivy Quad.

Regnum: Quad of the Royals; residence of the royal family.

Ronald Gunner: Beetrum's fiancé in Advena.

Salix: Beetrum's mare in Q's stable. *Salix: willow, flexible.*

Sator: A golden bird in New Ivy Quad whose mission is to propagate seeds. *Sator: planter.*

Sapien Duco: Head of the Ecclesia, Princeps of the Animus Consillium (the spiritual body of Domus), and Guardian of the Crystal Grove. Isabella Fae's father; Coxi Pudor's husband; is second in power only to King. *Duco: lead, influence*

Saxitilus GENS: SAX. One of four brothers who founded the GENS Quad. Learned the sacred Song of the North from the crystal gems in Mt. Vetare. Descendants were banished to the Proscriptio for breaking the Primordial. Black straight hair. Eyes, black and deep as coal pits. Blue-black wings. Saxitilus, SAX; Torrens, TOR; Gelu, GEL; Aridus, ARI. *Saxitilus: to be found among the rocks.*

Scriba: The clerk for the Princeps. Acta Diurna is currently Princeps Sapien Duco's clerk. *Scriba: a clerk or secretary.*

Scrimpit: A type of rodent in Domus. *Scrimpit: he screeches.*

Septmillia: A special celebration at Iter when banished Fey are offered the opportunity to renew (return from Proscriptio) by transforming. Must be issued a Vocatio from the Mother through Iris. A vocatio is only issued one time. If the faeries decline it, they will die. Not all banished species are offered a Vocatio. If they accept the Vocatio, the banished faerie will repent and be transformed—a rigorous restoration of their bodies and cleansing of their souls that can be quite painful physically and spiritually. They declare a new allegiance to Divus, the Creator and the Earth Mother, to Domus and swear the Primordial—Honor super omnia. Occurs every seven septmillenaries: 49,000 years. *Septem: seven. Millenary: thousand Septmillenary: 7,000 years.*

Short Fat One: Nickname for Ventas, a Rock Faerie in the Proscriptio.

Solis: A caduceus chosen and sanctioned by Iris and imbued with extraordinary healing and magical powers. There is only one Solis at a time and is granted their powers during Iter after taking the Solis Oath, modeled after the United States Air Force Oath of Office. *Solis: sunbeam, sunrise, sunset.*

Song of the South: One of the sacred songs taught to ARI by the Earth Mother through the blazing heat of the sun.

Song of the East: One of the sacred songs taught to GEL by the Earth Mother through the icy currents of air high above Domus.

Song of the North: One of the sacred songs taught to SAX by the Earth Mother through the jeweled crystals in Mt. Vetare.

Song of the West: One of the sacred songs taught to TOR by the Earth Mother through the Great River Potens.

Spes: The orphanage in New Ivy Quad founded by Ambassador Q. *Spes: hopeful.*

Squamata: Carnivorous swamp lizard that lives in Lake Lacertilia. *Lizard: order Squamata, suborder Lacertilia.*

Supra: Female leader of tribe Saxitilus, SAX. *Supra: on the top.*

Symphytum: Comfrey is an herb for healing bruises and knitting bones.

Syringa: Q's wife; Beetrum's mother, Lichen's grandmother. *Syringa: lilac shrub.*

Tempus transiens: The clock is ticking. *Tempus: time transiens: passing.*

Tarnhelm/Tarnkappe: From a 13th-century poem "*The Niebelungenlied*". It is the story of dwarves and their king "Son of the Mist". Their treasure included magical weapons like the helmet and cape that rendered their wearer invisible.

Tata: Colloquialism for dad, daddy. *Tata: dad.*

Tau'stercus: Bull dung. *Taurus: bull. Stercus: dung.*

Terni: A dog with three legs. *Terni: three in a group.*

Tertius: The third phase of study in Domus. At the completion of this phase, faeries graduate and receive their Life Crystal and their Totus Vita during Iter. Often used synonymously with graduation. *Tertius: third.*

Torri: One of four drogs (small dragons). Small red/orange/yellow female drog; bonded to Q. Likes everything planned out. Amicus, Torri, Tosti, and Carmen. *Torris: firebrand; Torridus: burn.*

Tosti: One of four drogs (small dragons). Rust/brown/yellow male drog. Amicus, Torri, Tosti, and Carmen. *Tosti: singe.*

Torrens GENS: TOR. One of four brothers who founded the GENS Quad. Saxitilus, SAX; Torrens, TOR; Gelu, GEL; Aridus, ARI. Learned the sacred Song of the West from the Earth Mother through the Great River Potens. Descendents banished to the Proscriptio for breaking the Primordial. River-green eyes; earth brown hair; blue-green wings. *Torrens: river.*

Totus Vita: When a Faerie graduates at Iter they are presented with their Life Book. It is a beautiful hand-bound one-of-a-kind personal journal. It looks large and heavy but is made of Light and Spirit. The Scriba keeps all of the books updated as the Faerie grows but all the Illuminations are done by Iris. Once it is presented to the faerie, it is cloaked and only the owner Faerie can see it. *Totus: whole. Vita: life.*

Valeo Nox: Keeper I. Appointed by the King as overseer of all of Domus' Preserves for life. Third in command after the King and Sapien Duco. One of three who know the location of the Bridge to Advena—The King, The Keeper, and Q. *Valeo: strong. Nox: night.*

Velle coach: A small ornate coach used for short jaunts i.e. Sunday drives. *Velle: to derive enjoyment, pleasure.*

Ventas: A Rock Faerie in the Proscriptio from the Saxitilus tribe; nicknamed Short Fat One. *Ventas: hunting.*

Vetare Silva: The Forbidden Forest where the sacred Mt. Vetare is located. The Earth Mother alone grants entry. *Vetare: forbidden. Silva: forest.*

Village: Most Quads have an island Village where most of the Quads population live. The Village is the second island in the New Ivy Quad inhabited mostly by humans and a few Fey.

Vinca Village: The main island in the Vinca Village Quad where the Princeps lives, the Animus Consillium, and the Crystal Grove are located.

Vocatio: A special invitation granted by the Earth Mother through Iris, Goddess of the Rainbow. It is a vehicle by which banished species can be redeemed and transformed. If the Fey decline the Vocatio, they will die. The Vocatio is issued at the discretion of the Mother and not all banished species are offered one. It is only offered every septmillia (49,000 years) *Vocatio: a summoning before a court of law; an invitation.*

Wasteland: A desolate abandoned area in Domus where nothing lives or grows.

Weston, Missouri: A city in Advena, the human realm; home of Beetrum and Lichen and location of Q's business holdings.

Wieland: A water dwarf who gathered and guarded the jeweled tears of water creatures. Mythology: a dwarf who forged Durandal, a magic sword.

Chapter Sixty-One

Hippocratic Oath

The original oath was written in Ionic Greek, between the fifth and third centuries BC. It is traditionally attributed to the Greek doctor Hippocrates and is usually included in the Hippocratic Corpus. The oldest fragments of the oath date to circa AD 275.

The Classic Hippocratic Oath

"I swear by Apollo the physician, and Aesculapius the surgeon, likewise Hygeia and Panacea, and call all the gods and goddesses to witness, that I will observe and keep this underwritten oath, to the utmost of my power and judgment.

I will reverence my master who taught me the art. Equally with my parents, will I allow him things necessary for his support, and will consider his sons as brothers. I will teach them my art without reward or agreement; and I will impart all my acquirement, instructions, and whatever I know, to my master's children, as to my own; and likewise to all my pupils, who shall bind and tie themselves by a professional oath, but to none else.

With regard to healing the sick, I will devise and order for them the best diet, according to my judgment and means; and I will take care that they suffer no hurt or damage.

Nor shall any man's entreaty prevail upon me to administer poison to anyone; neither will I counsel any man to do so. Moreover, I will give no sort of medicine to any pregnant woman, with a view to destroy the child.

Further, I will comport myself and use my knowledge in a godly manner.

I will not cut for the stone, but will commit that affair entirely to the surgeons.

Whatsoever house I may enter, my visit shall be for the convenience and advantage of the patient; and I will willingly refrain from doing any injury or wrong from falsehood, and (in an especial manner) from acts of an amorous nature, whatever may be the rank of those who it may be my duty to cure, whether mistress or servant, bond or free.

Whatever, in the course of my practice, I may see or hear (even when not invited), whatever I may happen to obtain knowledge of, if it be not proper to repeat it, I will keep sacred and secret within my own breast.

If I faithfully observe this oath, may I thrive and prosper in my fortune and profession, and live in the estimation of posterity; or on breach thereof, may the reverse be my fate!"

This Hippocratic Oath has been modified and revised several times. In 1960, the words “utmost respect for life from its beginning” were added, making it a more secular concept, not to be taken in the presence of gods but in front of other people.

The Oath was rewritten in 1964 by Dr. Louis Lasagna, Academic Dean at Tufts University School of Medicine. The new version accommodates the modern view of abortion and euthanasia. This revised form is widely accepted in today’s medical schools.

The Revised Hippocratic Oath

"I swear to fulfill, to the best of my ability and judgment, this covenant:

I will respect the hard-won scientific gains of those physicians in whose steps I walk, and gladly share such knowledge as is mine with those who are to follow.

I will apply, for the benefit of the sick, all measures [that] are required, avoiding those twin traps of overtreatment and therapeutic nihilism.

I will remember that there is art to medicine as well as science, and that warmth, sympathy, and understanding may outweigh the surgeon's knife or the chemist's drug.

I will not be ashamed to say "I know not," nor will I fail to call in my colleagues when the skills of another are needed for a patient's recovery.

I will respect the privacy of my patients, for their problems are not disclosed to me that the world may know.

Most especially must I tread with care in matters of life and death. If it is given me to save a life, all thanks. But it may also be within my power to take a life; this awesome responsibility must be faced with great humbleness and awareness of my own frailty.

Above all, I must not play at God.

I will remember that I do not treat a fever chart, a cancerous growth, but a sick human being, whose illness may affect the person's family and economic stability. My responsibility includes these related problems, if I am to care adequately for the sick.

I will prevent disease whenever I can, for prevention is preferable to cure.

I will remember that I remain a member of society, with special obligations to all my fellow human beings, those sound of mind and body as well as the infirm.

If I do not violate this oath, may I enjoy life and art, respected while I live and remembered with affection thereafter.

May I always act so as to preserve the finest traditions of my calling and may I long experience the joy of healing those who seek my help."

Thus, the classical Oath of Hippocratic involves the triad of the physician the patient and God, while the revised version involves only the physician and the patient, reliving the Gods of a few responsibilities.

Chapter Sixty-Two

Alphabets

Nato & Ogham

Lichen decided to bring his questionable language under control by substituting a phonetic letter for a swear word.

The NATO Alfa and Juliett are spelled differently to avoid mispronunciation by people unfamiliar with English rules for writing a language.

PHONETIC ALPHABET

The International Radiotelephony Spelling Alphabet, commonly known as the ICAO phonetic alphabet, sometimes called the NATO alphabet or spelling alphabet and the ITU radiotelephonic or phonetic alphabet.

A - ALFA	M - MIKE	Y - YANKEE
B - BRAVO	N - NOVEMBER	Z - ZULU
C - CHARLIE	O - OSCAR	1 - WUN
D - DELTA	P - PAPA	2 - TOO
E - ECHO	Q - QUEBEC	3 - TREE
F - FOXTROT	R - ROMEO	4 - FOW-ER
G - GOLF	S - SIERRA	5 - FIFE
H - HOTEL	T - TANGO	6 - SIX
I - INDIA	U - UNIFORM	7 - SEV-EN
J - JULIETT	V - VICTOR	8 - AIT
K - KILO	W - WHISKEY	9 - NIN-ER
L - LIMA	X - XRAY	0 - ZEE-RO

The ancient Ogham system of lettering is used throughout Domus.

Ogham is an Early Medieval Primitive and Old Irish, Old Welsh, Pictish and Latin alphabet consisting of 20 to 25 letters used primarily during the 5th and 6th century. Each letter is named after a tree. There are approximately 400 surviving orthodox stone monument inscriptions throughout Ireland and Western Britain.

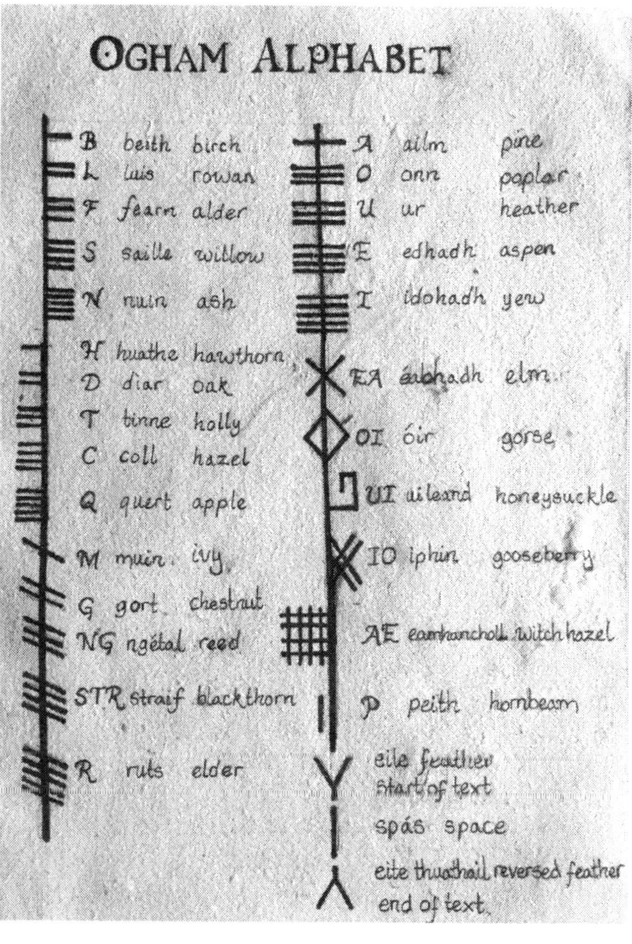
OGHAM ALPHABET
B beith birch
L luis rowan
F fearn alder
S saille willow
N nuin ash
H huathe hawthorn
D diar oak
T tinne holly
C coll hazel
Q quert apple
M muin ivy
G gort chestnut
NG ngétal reed
STR straif blackthorn
R ruis elder
A ailm pine
O onn poplar
U ur heather
E edhadh aspen
I idohadh yew
EA elm
OI óir gorse
UI uileand honeysuckle
IO iphin gooseberry
AE eamhancholl witch hazel
P peith hornbeam
eite feather start of text
spás space
eite thuathail reversed feather end of text

Chapter Sixty-Three

Author Note

I opened my eyes on the morning of September 23, 2003. The light out my window was barely visible. My cat, King Khafre, was sleeping on top of the covers at my feet. I floated in that lovely place just north of sleep and south of consciousness. I relaxed further into my pillow and closed my eyes. Immediately I saw a lovely young woman, who likewise was lying in her bed. Her luxurious long hair black as midnight lay tousled across the quilt. She turned over and unknowingly scooted her cat off the bed which had also been lying by her feet. The cat landed squarely on all eight feet yowling. Isabella jumped out of bed cooing apologies and assurances.

This was my first inspiration for Domus. I knew her name was Isabella and I knew she was Fey.

https://lizzysfeatherpen.com/

amazon.com/s?k=elizabeth+manzanares+wenig&crid=3BCTZ5SARYOBF&s prefix=%2Caps%2C150&ref=nb_sb_ss_recent_2_0_recent

youtube.com/channel/UCfMCVU-hauKwMM3h6meRABg

facebook.com/profile.php?id=100088577351437

goodreads.com/author/show/24642613.Elizabeth_Manzanares_Wenig

Chapter Sixty-Four

Other Works

NON- FICTION

Daddy Trails – Three Wishes, three fathers and, a DNA fairy-tale. A memoir. 2022

Favorite Flu Fighters – Alternative Ideas For Combating Colds and Flu 2023

Amazon Link

HERBAL STUDIES

A Look At Nourishing Traditions—The Surprising Healing Power of Food

All About Basil— She Wants Out of the Kitchen

Divine Feminine—The Three Stages of Women: Maiden, Mother, Menopause

Garden Alternatives—Use Nature to Control Nature

Herbal Genesis—Elderberry

Herbal Allies—In Sickness or in Health

Herbs of the Bible—Explore the Herbs of Jacob, John, and Jesus

Holistic Dog Care—Take Fido Out Of The Loop

Natural Solutions—Set Your Home Free

Secret Life of Plants—The Things They Do!

Weed Walk—This Class Got Me Kicked Off FB—Apparently, the world at large interprets WEED differently.

IN PRODUCTION

Domus Book 2.

Contact: https://www.lizzysfeatherpen.com

Made in the USA
Monee, IL
02 August 2024

63151252R00271